To Sonia,

Congratulations on winning the Goodreads Contest. I hope you'll love the playful venom and sardonic banter in these pages. Thanks for being part of this strange and wonderful journey—

Most Sincerely

THE
AMBER
MENHIR

THE
AMBER
MENHIR

Jonathan N. Pruitt

SPINNER
LOOM PRESS

Edited by Conor Welter with Robin Fuller & Eddie Nunez
Artistic Consulting by Amanda Banker
World Map Produced by Michael Carey
Interior Designs by Iram Allam

Spinner Loom Press
Tampa, FL 33544

To Loss, a stern but very gifted teacher.

"And on the precipice of Calamity, when humanity's twilight nears, the menhirs will be our beacons of hope for a withering world. In them we must trust, for imagination and discovery are our only hopes."

— An excerpt from the *Menhir Conclave Charter*

Prologue

CHESA CARESSED THE PUCKERED scar on her side and recoiled. Her mind wandered again. Though self-training like hers required one to maintain their focus, in that moment, she could not suppress a smile. It was a day to celebrate, after all, to let herself feel what happiness she could, so long as it didn't interfere with the task at hand. Her dark hair, cut short to accentuate her jawline, sat lacquered into wavelets pinned against her scalp and adorned with delta pearls. She clicked her nails against her marble tub perch. The window nearby provided few clues as to how long her mind had wandered. It remained dark out, chilly, and the sky was slathered with low-lying clouds that discouraged any hope of moonlight.

"A dark night for dark deeds." She chuckled.

Chesa stole a glance at herself in the standing mirror across the bathing chamber. Her slight frame and ageless features were displayed to full advantage in her robes. Though the fabric hung loose around her legs, arms, and neckline, a grey sash was cinched around her waist to accentuate her modest breasts. The important parts remained featured, despite the middling fabric. One often needed to dull the lily to execute one's plans.

In a life that was rarely her own, Chesa embraced herself in that moment. But her moment of quiet celebration was interrupted too soon by a soft spewing like a breaching whale, followed by a gurgle. She looked down into the steaming water at the naked man submerged there. Liam's nose pierced the water's surface and sucked in a breath before he slid back into his watery tomb. The generous veins upon his arms stood out, as though he were still struggling against an unseen force binding him. One side of Chesa's mouth quirked up. The many days he'd spent sculpting his virile physique would soon enough be wasted.

He arched his back with a gentle thud. The movement sent his body up to the water's surface like a sad, suffocating fish flopping through gelatin. Just before his nostrils breached the surface, Chesa pressed a finger to the tip of his nose with a throaty sigh, pushing him back to the bottom of the tub. Liam's leafy green eyes opened wide. Their gazes met, and the tension in his body relented. A trail of bubbles escaped his mouth in an aqueous sigh of defeat.

He'd been a brute in life, and a powerful adversary to many scholars. His perfect bone structure, imposing stature, and easy likability had made leadership an effortless inevitability. Staring down at him, Chesa wondered if Liam had ever worked hard for anything in his life. Men of privilege, like him, so rarely ever did. No doubt he had never suspected his end would come at the hands of a servant . . . but life in the Amber Menhir was full of surprises.

"Oh, don't look at me like that." Chesa clucked her tongue. "You've been riding this leopard for quite some time. Had it not been me, someone else would have come."

Liam's eyes drooped shut, and his body spasmed in a tedious attempt to steal more air. Chesa let out another little sigh. He acted like some brainless sea creature dragged onto a boat—one that failed to realize the inevitability of its situation. This time, his nose sucked in a bit of air.

Chesa rolled her eyes. "Can't you see?" she chided. "You have lost, dear scholar. Give up, my liege!"

Liam flexed his helpless form against Chesa's thaumaturgic binding. His strength of spirit was indeed undeniable. Most people so privileged broke under real adversity. At least, that had been Chesa's experience. But Liam's exception, however remarkable, remained irrelevant.

"Such a pity," Chesa purred, looking down at the scholar. "The one night you're actually imperiled, and your precious mau isn't here to protect you." Her tone turned flat, each word edged with ice. "What an unhappy coincidence for you."

Chesa sidled around the tub's perimeter, gliding her nails along its edge. She paused above a gilded table set to one side. Upon it sat an etched snifter containing a few drops of fortified wine.

"It is so convenient when one's prey thwarts itself with self-defeating vices. . . And what is this here?"

A glazed teacup sat a little away from the snifter. Chesa lifted it to her nose and inhaled. She dipped a fingertip into the tea and touched it to her tongue. Though sugar dominated the milieu, a metallic aftertaste betrayed the tea's true nature. Chesa wiped her tongue on her sleeve. Even a few drops of such concoctions could incapacitate.

"So, the rumors were true?" she admonished. "The golden spawn of Lord Kensington had a dreamflower addiction. . . Not that I can chastise anyone for an overabundance of vices." She winked at the submerged scholar, and her expression hardened. "But what was someone like you running away from?"

Liam did not answer.

"Well, in the end, not every mystery gets solved, I suppose." She gazed down at Liam and took in two slow breaths. Her fingers flicked through a series of gestures with practiced precision, each held for just the appropriate measure of time. To the untrained observer, the sequence appeared as little more than chaos.

Liam's body convulsed, but then his lulling mind betrayed him. His fists became placid open palms. The bulging veins in his arms, shoulders, and chest receded into his flesh. His face went slack, and his pupils grew wide. Only the tiniest coronas of his green eyes remained visible. Finally, Liam's shoulders sagged, and his body curled up like a giant man-fetus. His lips parted in unknowing relaxation. A faint burbling of air from Liam's stupefied features was all that breached their shared moment of silence.

Chesa continued her flurry of hand motions. "Anything worth doing is worth overdoing," she reminded herself aloud.

Liam drifted in reply.

With her tidy work complete, Chesa rose. She straightened her meager garments and flexed her aching hand. Taking stock of the bathing mirror, she examined herself one last time, then slapped the snifter off the table. It fell between the table and the tub and shattered, sending tiny shards spinning in every direction. She took the emptied wine bottle, turned it on its side, and rested it on the table. Finally, she lifted her grey servant's cowl and slithered into his bedchamber.

Chesa paused in the doorway, glancing back at the steaming soup that contained Liam's corpse. "A sad waste of well-cultivated man flesh," she admitted.

In the bedchamber, Chesa whipped the scholar's linens from his bed with a snap of fabric and assessed the scene's believability. In her mind's eye, she could see the spectre of Liam's drunken form stumbling from bedchamber to bath. His penchants for dreamflower and wine made her job almost too easy. Almost.

Chesa scanned his room and frowned at the gilded, swirling inlays that riddled Liam's furnishings. She approached the cherrywood door leading out and pressed her ear against it. Though she deemed it unlikely that anyone would be out this late, delicate work required every precaution, and some scholars kept odd hours.

The hallway beyond stood silent. She slipped from the room, carefully closing the door behind her. Glass oil lamps illuminated the pale grey walls of the towering hall beyond. A biting autumn draft sent her skin rippling with gooseflesh. Or perhaps it was the scholars who called these halls their home? The Delvers' quarters always made Chesa feel small, as though something watched her. She shuddered. Then she pulled herself upright and fled, keeping her eyes low as she did.

She took care not to seem rushed as she moved. It was imperative that no one discover Liam's fate for at least a few hours. With luck, someone would not discover him until morning. By then, Chesa hoped, his body would be a bloated, rotting wreck. The visage and smell might cause whoever discovered him to panic and compromise any lingering evidence. If the gods were good, they would make it so.

Chesa's trek back to her quarters passed without disturbance. She glided through the vacant halls to the servants' quarters adjacent to those of the Delvers of the Mind. Entering her bedroom, she sighed as she closed the door behind her. She took a seat on the room's only stool before a chipped washbasin and mirror. Undoing her oceanic finery took more time than she liked. She lifted a comb to her hair as a voice rose from behind her.

"Have you accomplished your task?" the voice growled and echoed.

She flinched, sending a pearl tumbling from her hair into the basin with a clink. As she glanced into her standing mirror, the room appeared empty. But when she turned, her gaze fell on an entity she had never imagined seeing. A tumbling pool of shadow where no such shadow should exist writhed, seeming to appraise her as it did.

Chesa gave a start. "I did. The Delvers will be staggering soon," she explained. "It will appear that he drowned. I don't know how he had managed to broker the relationships with the other noble factions, especially the Weavers, but that's all over now. A dead Primara cannot broker anything. The Delvers will be clamoring over one another for the chance to be his successor, as is their way."

"Well done. A fractious menhir is less dangerous for all," the shadow replied. The vaguest impression of a smile touched the undifferentiated swirling mists near the center of the nexus. "Your instincts continue to improve." As it spoke, the edges of the figure's form writhed, producing tiny streams of smoke.

"What's next?" asked Chesa.

"Though we may hope," the shadow intoned, "that the union between the Delvers and Weavers was the foretold unification, we cannot know. Watch the Primaras closely, Chesa, and ensure that they scramble over the Harvest. We must take care that another unification does not spawn in this one's wake, and we must remain ever vigilant for a Blurred Keystone. I feel the pulse of change before us. We will not be the only ones looking."

Chesa's eyes widened. "Watch the Primara? The Keystone? Does this mean I've made it?"

"You have done well," the shadow replied, its tone cautious. "Your work will help us forge the siege engine that demolishes the world before us and ushers in a new dawn. For now, though, sift through the wreckage of the crumbled alliance, and keep your ear to the ground."

"But I've made it?" Chesa insisted, surprised by her own insolence. Various pleasure centers in her brain ignited in a heady rush. Or maybe that was her envy of Liam's dreamflower?

"I predict that even your greatest detractors among the Disciples will now be mollified by your deeds."

A thousand questions blossomed all at once in Chesa's mind. But then, faster than it arrived, the figure vanished, sliding back into the corner of the room like black water through an unseen crack.

A moment later, Chesa found herself gazing into her standing mirror, frozen in the midst of combing her hair. The click of another pearl as it landed in her washbasin drew her attention. She reached in to pick it up, but it was gone. Startled, she counted her pearls once, and then again to be sure. Not one, but two were missing.

CHAPTER 1

Harvest

THE MOST TEDIOUS THING about near-immortality was the litany of people who believed their ideas, their schemes, their personalities, and so on to be original. They never were. In truth, there were only so many cards in the deck of life, and one saw them all within two generations. Only the most superficial of dressings distinguished one living platitude from the next. To see people as anything different was to romanticize them, which was never wise. And yet, it was a Langcraw's duty to serve, to guide the less fortunate, sullen and shortsighted as they were.

Or so said Eva Langcraw, Tara's mother.

Tara seated herself at the breakfast table and attempted to look serene yet contemplative. Her gaze traced and retraced the dark linework in the table as she wondered whether Larus or her mother would descend upon her first.

Portraits of the Langcraw matriarchs gone by levied their judgment down on her, their glares testy enough to chill glaciers. Another set of portraits hung beneath the matriarchs, smaller and less fine. The variability in the servant portraits always astounded Tara. Larus's portrait hung nearby. The artist had captured the square-faced ruggedness of Tara's nanny well. Larus appeared miserable to be in her own portrait, as was her way. Beside Larus was her mother. She possessed a more delicate mouth than Larus's, which resembled a toad's. Larus's maternal grandfather resembled Larus only a little. Some might have even ventured to call him handsome.

Tara found it odd how people of modest beauty could mix to produce plain offspring, just as the hideous sometimes spawned captivating features. Had Tara not been bound for menhir training, she might have enjoyed pairing servants. She certainly enjoyed their company more than her mother deemed pertinent.

The Lady Eva Langcraw's effigy stood over her usual seat at the head of the table. Like the genuine article, it bestowed onlookers with disdain. Tara's grandmother looked the same. Narrow eyes and delicate noses adorned the faces of both women. They might have been mistaken for twins, had not their hairstyles and attire distinguished them as intelligentsia separated by centuries. Familial resemblance smoothed successions. A less-than-observant servant mightn't notice Tara when she replaced her mother in another century or three. And all the better too.

Eva Langcraw strode into the dining room, sending Tara bristling with unexpressed anxieties. The Lady Langcraw donned a high-necked ivory gown. She tolerated no jewelry, which was her way, apart from a modest bracelet composed of garnets and silver, though that piece served a very special purpose. She seated herself beneath her own portrait, and her gaze turreted to Tara.

"You're awake. Good," her mother noted. "We've some last-minute matters to sort out before our friends from the menhir arrive."

"Of course," said Tara. She rose in her seat and met her mother's glare with a dispassionate version of her own. Tara reminded herself that today anything could be a test.

Something like a smile tugged around her mother's eyes, but it retreated.

"I hope I don't have to remind you not to speak about our financial affairs, nor our predilections or distastes while away," lectured her mother. "Most scholars will not take kindly to your ascendency, and there is far more at stake than just some person's life."

It seemed Tara's mother would not don mittens for her parting wisdom, though that surprised Tara little.

"Obtaining a working knowledge of thaumaturgy is a formality for leadership," her mother went on with a dismissive wave of her hand. "Learn what you must, and return to your duties. Nothing at the menhir has far-reaching consequences if you do your job. Be ignored and survive."

A servant moved into the dining room bearing boiled eggs atop silver stands. He placed one before each Langcraw and vanished. The stands bore the sinuous lines of the Langcraw crest—a reminder of one's allegiances, no doubt.

"The scholars will do much in three years to persuade you to see the world as they do," her mother chided as she cracked her egg. "Remember the usefulness of the menhirs, in principle, but recall that they are a different matter in practice. We serve them because it serves our purposes to do so."

"I shan't forget," Tara recited with a suppressed moan. Sometimes her mother treated her like some special breed of imbecile.

They ate their meal together for a time in awkward silence.

Her mother sighed as she finished her egg. The whites around her eyes appeared pinker than usual. She moved as if to scratch the wrist bearing the garnet bracelet, but halted herself.

"That looks like it hurts," Tara offered, indicating the bracelet.

"Our estates are considerable, and it is your ascendant year." Her mother let out a long breath. "The expectation on us is steep, but temporary. We should be back to the usual offering by the next Harvest cycle." She eyed the bracelet and frowned. "Whenever our friends at the menhir deem that should be." The Lady Langcraw squinted at the bracelet. "Sometimes I'd swear that these things get more parasitic with each Harvest."

Tara adjusted herself in her seat. What remained of her egg did not seem so appealing anymore.

"One small mercy in your departure is that this little parasite will depart with you," her mother said, jostling the dangling garnets on her wrist. Crimson welts spotted the flesh beneath. "The price we pay for order. . ."

"Have you seen Larus?" asked Tara.

The muscles around her mother's jaw clenched as her nostrils flared. Never a good sign. "She did not wake you?" her mother asked.

"She did," Tara lied, sensing the oncoming heat. Harming Larus the day she left for the Amber Menhir was the last of Tara's goals. "She wanted to confirm some of the Harvest's accounting." Tara rose from her seat, her egg unfinished. If her mother hadn't seen Larus either, then something was amiss. "With your leave, I'd like to visit with her again before the scholars arrive."

Her mother rolled her eyes. "Only because it's today. You concern yourself with servants too much. Especially Larus."

"I'll remember that," agreed Tara. She turned to leave, but her mother cleared her throat, and Tara halted. "Yes?" she asked.

"The Amber sent a missive requesting that I ready our lineage papers for them," said her mother.

"Oh. Very well," said Tara. She turned to go.

"Don't be a fool!" her mother's voice boomed. "The Amber asks for documentation for good reason, and does not send last-minute missives on a whim."

Tara paused. "What do you suppose is wrong?"

Her mother rose and brushed the front of her gown. "Someone's died, and not the typical plebian. The Primara, maybe even the chancellor, are frightened about something. They're searching for someone or something to blame."

"I see," Tara murmured. "Does that truly concern us?"

"A Tilter of the Hourglass ascends this year," her mother intoned, her eyes tracing Tara up and down. "And something at the menhir is awry. That is no coincidence. Remember that starting today and until you leave the Amber Menhir, each scholar and every ascendant is your adversary or rival. Now is no time to be sloppy, Tara. Say your goodbyes, and take care with your words while you're away. I'll see to our papers."

Tara's mother rose and left. Typical.

Larus's quarters sat a little away from the Langcraw Manor. Crisp morning fog clung to Tara's pale dress as she trudged her way there. She knocked at the rosewood door to the cottage.

"A moment!" Larus growled from somewhere inside.

Some believed Larus's father to be a badger.

The door swung open, and Larus fixed Tara with a leathery scowl, but it melted away. "What are you doing here?" she grumbled, though Larus's grumbles bore a thousand hues. "Get in before you catch cold!"

Larus stepped from the doorway, and Tara entered. A straw bed, a modest nightstand, a mirror, and a trunk harboring Larus's personal effects formed an odd rectangle of furnishings.

Larus closed the door and sat on the edge of her bed with a stifled grunt. Her grey hair appeared damp with sweat. A webwork of buttery gold strings with green gems sat upon Larus's nightstand. Larus was not the sort for finery. Tara averted her eyes.

"Spoiled the surprise, did you," Larus mumbled. She nodded toward her nightstand. "I wanted to give it to you when you woke, but I've not been feeling myself this Harvest."

"You're not the only one this Harvest," Tara assured her. She perched herself on Larus's trunk and faced the gnarled servant. "Here, let me."

Tara lunged at Larus before she could recoil. She unsnapped the silver band from Larus's calloused ankle and latched it to her own. The garnets surged with a hungry light as Tara covered the parasite with her dress.

"Ignorant girl!" Larus hissed, though already the flush of life surged up the woman's neck and into her face. Her eyes brightened, but her scowl deepened.

Tara held up a slender hand, and Larus fell silent. Nobility was not without its advantages.

"It is my ascendency," Tara noted. She mocked her mother's imperious tone. "I'd rather suffer a band for a few hours myself than see you ill the day I leave. You owe me that."

Larus went to rebuttal.

"It is a Langcraw's duty to serve," said Tara.

The wind in Larus's sails ceased at once.

Tara nodded. That phrase always worked. "Now, I'm off to the library to enjoy a bit of contraband before I go. I hope to see you again before I leave?"

"Spoiled child!" Larus chided, though hints of sweetness lurked beneath the woman's gravel as she groaned. "You know you will."

With Larus accounted for, Tara retreated to the front library to distract herself until the scholars came.

The muskiness of old volumes always put Tara at ease, and today she needed it more than usual. She took her customary position on the edge of an old pew that her mother had purchased from merchants a century earlier. There, only few inches from Tara's usual haunt, sat the tome: *The Mau that Run the Menhir.* Tara lifted the volume to study it. Perhaps Larus had placed it there for her. Tara flipped through a few pages of the novel. Though *The Mau that Run the Menhir* was not the contraband Tara had first held in mind, it sufficed. The satire retold bits of the Amber Menhir's history in colorful terms through the eyes of the predatory felids that inhabited the institution. In the end, one by one, a glinting black ball of yarn lured each of the mau into biting it. Thereafter, a gruesome fate befell them.

The author of the novel had fled the menhir under dubious circumstances centuries ago. It seemed silly to Tara that the scholars continued to ban a book so old—especially one that suffered such atrocious writing. But scholars were careful sorts.

As the morning pressed on, now and again a servant approached the main entryway and interrupted Tara's literary bemusement. Each sported a tender-looking ring of blisters around a wrist or ankle. Some servants bore two such rings. Their shoulders drooped, and their reddened eyes appeared to look everywhere and anywhere save for Tara's direction. They grumbled and cursed as they tossed their gorged bracelets in buckets beside the entry. Tara opened her mouth to apologize for the lengthy Harvest, but thought it better not to remind them of the source of their pain.

The midden of bracelets grew over the course of the morning. Those not there to deposit a saprolite band took care to avert their eyes from the tower of garnets as they passed. Tara couldn't bear to look at the bracelets long herself. Larus's niece had donned her bracelet for just a day this cycle before she started suffering fainting spells. Only the fact that Larus's bracelet rested on her own ankle prevented guilt from overwhelming Tara.

By noon, the book before Tara grew tedious. She continued to hold the novel, but her eyes peeked over its brim out the window to the drive. Fog banks in the surrounding hills continued their morning retreat. At last, from one of the shrinking pools, a pair of riders emerged. Tara's stomach whipped itself into a knot. She jumped back from the window and pivoted to find Larus behind her.

Larus glowered at her. "Oh, you'd better be nervous! Give me that!" She crouched down and unclasped the saprolite bracelet from Tara's ankle. Tara stifled a hiss, though relief washed over her to be rid of the thing.

"If your mother caught you wearing one of these out of cycle. . ." Larus went and tossed the garnets on a heap of their kin.

"If I know her. . ." Tara chuckled. "I think I've seen the last of her for today."

"If one of the scholars saw you wearing it!" Larus countered. "You'd have more to worry about than some blasted lineage papers!" She returned to the library alcove to scowl at Tara a bit more. Larus always relished a good scowl.

Tara straightened her dress. "Is this your way of saying you'll be worried about me when I'm gone?"

The scowl luxuriating on Larus's brow faltered. She stuffed a hand into her pocket and pulled out the golden lacework Tara had spotted earlier.

"Sometimes you make me regret whatever sentimentality remains in these bones," Larus groused, though she approached Tara with something like a smile. "This is for you."

Tara accepted the piece with a small genuflection. "You shouldn't have." The web of gold unfurled into a loose hairnet. A milky green stone adorned each junction. "What stone is this?"

"Amber," said Larus. "Green amber."

One pale eyebrow lifted as Tara clasped the gold netting around her tumble of blonde curls. "Green amber?" she repeated.

Larus's dark eyes met Tara's a moment before she turned away. "The merchant in Sandenvale said green amber isn't fossilized. Not completely, anyhow. There's something alive inside it still, eternal, but never quite ossified."

"Oh, Larus, that's sweet—" Tara started, when a knock came at the door.

Tara turned to see two riders just outside the windows flanking the entryway. A tall man with dark features dismounted and beheld the Langcraw Manor as he brushed off his maroon robes. He gave a nod of acknowledgment to the stable hands already busy loading Tara's trunks.

Tara leaned toward Larus. "Do you think that man's a scholar? He's got the robes for it."

"You're asking me?" Larus scoffed. She threw an arm up as she bustled away toward the kitchen. "You've got to worry about yourself, child. I've got to see to logistics."

Tara turned and studied the second rider. Her dark grey attire and raised cowl marked her as a servant. Puffy cheeks and deep-set eyes dominated her farmwife features. Her cowl concealed her hair, but age lines riddled every seam of her face. The riders exchanged words. Then the woman dismounted, and the pair approached the door.

Larus reappeared, bearing discolored papers beneath one arm. She opened the door and swept into her lowest genuflection. "This way, Masters. You must be exhausted. Can I offer you refreshments?" She gestured the visitors into the sitting room.

"Papers!" boomed the man's voice.

From the library, Tara heard the rustling of the paperwork.

"Everything's here, Masters," Larus assured them.

A Langcraw servant bearing a plate topped with tea and fruit made his way to the sitting room. Tara followed behind.

The plump woman in grey flicked her attention to Tara and looked at her with eyes a bit too clever. No one sat.

"You must be Tara!" chirped the woman. "I know a Langcraw's features when I see them, I do!"

Tara supposed most anyone at the menhir could say the same, though it was the mismatch between the old servant's eyes and her saccharine tone that captured Tara's attention most.

"May I introduce Tara Langcraw," Larus interjected with a sweeping gesture. "Lady Langcraw, this is Thaddeus Blanchet, of the Architects of Forces, and his companion, Lydia Ash."

Tara bowed, casting her gaze down. "A pleasure."

Architect Blanchet nodded, and Ms. Ash bowed deep for a woman of her age. Architect Blanchet approached Tara with a grin.

"We are so pleased to count you among our ascendants this year, Ms. Langcraw," he said. A pleasant series of lines embellished his eyes. "We have a sizable group from the Spiral joining the menhir this year. You're in good company."

"I'm looking forward to it," Tara lied. All her mother's warnings still echoed fresh in her mind.

"It's been too long since the menhir recruited a Tilter of the Hourglass," said Architect Blanchet. "You must study hard! The world needs more like you, my dear. Few noble bloodlines have produced that thaumaturgical aptitude so reliably as your own."

Tara feigned a smile. "I'm honored to train at the Amber Menhir."

"The honor is ours," replied Architect Blanchet, but his tone turned uneasy. "Have you got everything? I don't mean to rush you, but we do have a long ride. We've left the Ward boy back at the Spring Road, and we have to pick up someone at the Bianchi estates. There's been some unrest in the Independent Cities, owing to the smallest kerfuffle at the Amber. We just can't afford to be traveling with ascendants at night. I'll review your lineage papers on the way."

"Why the interest in papers this year?" Tara asked. She doubted he'd answer, even if he knew.

"Ah," replied Architect Blanchet, "an interim measure required by one of the Primaras. A few scholars have taken an interest in lineages with more protean aptitudes than your own. Seeing as the Langcraws have never displayed an aberrant expression of thaumaturgical aptitude, the measure needn't concern you much."

"I see," said Tara, studying the man up and down. She tried not to let her attention linger on her lineage papers tucked beneath his arm. Tara turned to Larus. "If I have forgotten anything, I could write?"

"Superb!" Architect Blanchet boomed. "I'll count the Harvest to ensure everything is in order, and we'll be off!"

"Thanks for your hospitality!" added Ms. Ash as she angled for an exit.

"Please do extend our best regards to the Lady Langcraw," Architect Blanchet went on.

Larus frowned at the uneaten refreshments. Her eyes flicked between Tara and the Architect.

"Lady Eva Langcraw, of course, extends her warmest wishes to the Amber Menhir," Larus replied. Her gaze paused on Tara, and her brows knitted.

Architect Blanchet and Ms. Ash departed with quick bows, collecting the Harvest on their way out. It struck Tara how neither of them had waited for her mother's arrival. Then again, residents of the menhir might know better than to expect unessential gestures from Eva Langcraw.

Tara and Larus stood together alone.

"I suppose. . ." Larus began, her voice breaking off as her gaze remained on Tara. "This is goodbye. Don't go forgetting everything I've taught you. And don't go embarrassing us all either!"

"What if they ask me to stay longer?" asked Tara as she studied Larus. "What if they ask me to become a scholar and stay there forever?"

Larus smiled, but the expression did not reach her eyes. "The Langcraw estates existed before you were born. They can manage without you. You'd be missed, but I won't let things fall into disarray."

Tara returned the gruff woman's smile. "I should think you wouldn't."

They stopped at that. Were Tara not a Langcraw, she imagined she might have leaned forward to hug her former nanny. Instead, she smoothed her features, adjusted her new green amber finery, and turned her back on the woman.

Outside, Tara could feel Larus's eyes on her, watching her through a window. She hoped her mother might be among the silent observers as well, though Tara deemed the odds scarce. What were three years to a Langcraw anyhow? Tara mounted her gelding.

Architect Blanchet breathed hard as he poured the Harvest garnets into the tumorous saddlebags flanking his mare. He worked with gloved hands and sharp eyes, taking care not to let a stray bit of the caustic metal touch his skin. His horse whickered and whinnied.

Tara eyed her lineage papers as Blanchet placed them in a leather pouch at his waist. The Architect looked up, catching Tara's eyes with his. Something stony and unyielding galvanized his expression.

"Ready?" called Ms. Ash. She took her mount up to Tara's.

Tara wrenched her eyes from the Architect's.

"You'll be back before you know it," Ms. Ash assured her.

Tara remained silent. The tedious and unhelpful pleasantries of a servant provided her little comfort. Instead, Tara focused on not looking back at the Architect, nor searching her manor windows for ghosts that might not come.

The riders all paused a moment, gazing back at Langcraw Manor. Frost still kissed the boxwood maze around Tara's home.

"I think we should be off," Tara asserted.

To her surprise, the others complied.

She spared her home no further attention. A task stood before Tara, and it was clear. She must survive the menhir and make her lineage proud. Everything else was not worthy of serious consideration.

CHAPTER 2
Fast Friends

COUNTLESS ROWS OF GNARLED grapevines, some laden with fruit, glistened in the midday sun. Seeing them sent a pang of pride through Tara. Riding apart from the others, she drank in the hues of gold, crimson, and chocolate speckling the leaves. She hadn't ridden this far out from her manor in some time. Apart from fields and a few small vassal villages, there wasn't much to see.

Tara studied her fellow riders. The Architect and the menhir servants babbled amongst themselves, paying the heritage vines around them little heed. It was clear to Tara they knew little about winemaking; otherwise they would have been impressed.

Ahead at the confluence of the Spring Road and the Langcraw estates, more menhir servants on horseback gathered, each of them clad in the customary grey robes. The servants adjusted their cowls as they spotted Tara and her escorts. Ms. Ash cued her horse to trot, passing by Tara to greet the other servants. Beside them rode a boy in plain trousers and a green shirt bearing scrollwork. He rode atop a workhorse; his considerable height and weight seemed to demand it. Tara took stock of the boy. Given his lack of scholar's robes, Tara concluded he must be the promised Ward ascendant.

The boy twisted in his saddle and beamed at the riders as they approached.

"Ms. Langcraw, this is your first ascendant colleague, Mr. Roland Ward," Architect Blanchet announced.

Roland Ward boasted a tanner complexion than any field-worker Tara knew. A dense constellation of freckles and moles dotted his two helpings of brow.

"It's good to meet you, T-Tara. I hope your ride was nice," Roland offered.

Tara wasn't confident in how to respond. His odd breathing before words caught her off guard, and her skin went hot as she searched for words of her own.

"I like your coat," he added.

Tara gave him a cool nod. "A pleasure."

She kept her features still as she examined him. Ms. Ash and the others glanced between the two soundless ascendants. Tara found herself wishing, not for the last time, that she were alone. She took in a breath and shot the Architect a pleading look.

"Well, there will be plenty of time for you to become acquainted later," called Architect Blanchet. "We should be going, or we'll miss dinner!"

Roland's face beamed again at the mention of food.

As the caravan headed east, Tara situated herself alone at its tail. She watched Roland Ward as he made small talk with each of the menhir servants and the Architect. After their second afternoon stop, it seemed it was her turn for Roland's attentions. Tara spotted his approach and spared him a feeble smile. A huge grin split his face. Tara looked away, suppressing a sigh.

"How's your ride going?" he called, drawing his mount beside hers.

"Fine," she replied. She studied the apple orchards lining the north side of the road. She wished to be alone, but she didn't want to appear heartless either. At least, not before she had a better measure of Roland.

Roland grinned at her. "You seem like you m-might be thinking about something important."

Tara did not answer. He hadn't really posed a question.

"Maybe you're worried about your aptitudes?" he asked. His face twisted up with concern, which only made Tara want to vanish even more. Was he pitying her? "I w-worry about mine too. My family says that's normal for ascendants."

Tara rolled a shoulder to relieve some tension from the long ride and insipid conversation.

"Do you think you'll be like the rest of your f-family?"

Tara sighed. "Whatever do you mean?"

The boy's eyebrows shot up. "I mean . . . you know," he stumbled. "With your aptitudes."

"You are not making sense," Tara replied, with a bit more iciness than she intended.

"I mean, the aptitudes we're supposed to learn at the menhir," he clarified. "The th-th-thaumaturgical kinds."

Tara turned away from him and suppressed another sigh. "My bloodline is strong. I will develop the same aptitudes as my mother, grandmother, and so on. It is why I am here."

Roland scrunched up his face. "You've never thought it might work out different?"

"No, Roland," she assured him. "My family has transmitted their aptitudes with absolute fidelity. Our records go back thousands of years. Ask Architect Blanchet to see them, if you're doubtful."

He blinked at that. Perhaps he was worried for himself? Perhaps he wanted to develop a sense of solidarity with her? Tara could not be sure.

"S-some ascendants show different aptitudes than their parents," said Roland. "I've heard some ascendants don't show any thaumaturgical aptitudes at all."

Tara had never heard of one of the Wards being denied full admission to the menhir for thaumaturgical barrenness, though the phenomenon was not unheard of. Still, Roland's concern suggested his lineage might not be as firm as his family projected.

"I suspect those kinds of ascendants stem from poor developmental environments. That is not the case with the Langcraw line," said Tara, letting an edge creep into her voice. "Do you have any other personal questions for me?"

He barreled on, "Will you really live forever?"

Tara groaned, then hated herself for doing so. "Nobody knows how long they will live, Roland. Not you, not me. I may be thrown from this horse and sever my spine. We could be killed by bandits from the Independent Cities. It's the same for all of us."

She gave him a stony look, hoping his curiosity might be stayed.

"Not like that." He chuckled. "I mean, you know, if nothing bad happens to you, won't you just go on living?"

No one had ever conveyed to Tara how the typical noble knew about the Tilters of the Hourglass. Larus seemed to understand the gist. Langcraw servants had to. Generations of servants grew and died, while Eva Langcraw remained unchanged. It was not the sort of thing people overlooked.

"You've g-got to tell me!" Roland pleaded. He sounded like a child.

"Not exactly," she said, rolling her eyes. "Assuming I manifest the aptitudes of the Tilters, I will age slower than most, but parts of me will age more than others."

Tara scowled at herself. She hadn't meant to reveal the last bit. How soon she forgot her mother's warnings.

"What about you?" she parried.

"Oh," he replied with a shrug, "my f-family are farmers. We're Weavers of the web through and through."

Seeming satisfied with the fruits of his interrogation, Roland took to ferreting out bits of lunch from his teeth with his tongue. When that failed, he made obnoxious sucking sounds to excavate the stubborn bits. After a long while at that, Roland turned his attention back to Tara.

"What happens when the parts of you that age faster get old?"

Tara flinched. He had to be playing a game.

Roland sucked a bit of apple from a gap at the front of his mouth.

"Not all aspects of the body are poised to be arrested through thaumaturgy," Tara explained. "In time, the parts that age the fastest decline, just like with anyone, and the Tilter dies."

"Oh," said Roland. "Maybe you'll be the one to figure out how to live f-forever!"

His vacuous optimism endeared him to her, in a small sort of way. Though Tara could not help but wonder whether someone like him could survive at the menhir—or in the life of politics afterward, for that matter. That thought pained her somehow.

They rode together in silence for a while longer.

"Have you ever been to Sandenvale?" Roland asked.

"I have not," Tara confessed, avoiding his searching eyes. Instead, she examined the fields of pink and purple flowers lining the road to the south. The plants bore long, slender leaves with clusters of flowers at the summit of each shoot. It surprised Tara that the crops had not yet given up their gems to autumn.

Tara turned to find Architect Blanchet riding back to her and Roland.

"What are those?" Tara called to him, indicating the flora to the south.

The Architect looked out at the sea of flowers. "Those are nicos. The kind people smoke," said the Architect. "You've never seen them in bloom before?"

Tara shook her head.

"Those and dreamflowers are the major products of the Bianchi estates." He gestured not far ahead. A huge gilded sign beside a fork in the road read 'Bianchi' in lacy scrawl.

"Ms. Ash and I will leave you here for a short while," the Architect said. "We'll be back in a few hours. Keep your wits about you while we're away."

Tara and Roland nodded. Then Architect Blanchet and Ms. Ash pressed their horses into a trot, heading south into the Bianchi estates. Tara dismounted and guided her horse away from the group. The others broke from their saddles. Roland took up his usual chatter with two of the remaining servants not far from the Bianchi sign. Tara did her best to ignore them.

"Oh, we've been at the Amber Menhir for years now, we have," the chubby servant woman gushed to Roland.

"That's where Lara and I met!" said the skinny man beside her. He reached out and grazed the woman's pudgy arm.

Lara laughed and fixed Roland with a serious look. "You wouldn't believe it, but we were raised in vassal villages on the same estate up north, we were."

"Do you l-like it at the menhir?" Roland asked.

Tara watched the servants smile at Roland as they conversed. He eased the servants somehow.

"Oh, good gracious, yes," Lara said in a hushed tone, still loud enough to be heard. "I'm so glad to be at the menhir, Master Ward. It suits me much better than being a vassal. It suits Clarence and me both."

Something uneasy passed in the woman's expression. Tara had never heard of a vassal abandoning a noble bloodline before.

"I shouldn't say, Master Ward," Clarence added, "but not every noble bloodline treats its vassals with respect. Truth be told, not every scholar does either."

"Hush, now," Lara scolded. "Most of the scholars work too hard to give us any notice at all. It's too much idle time that causes most evil, that's what I say. I try not to blame the Kensingtons for the things they did when we lived up there. Too much cold weather's to blame!"

Tara's jaw dropped. Her vassals would never have engaged in such appalling slander. She cleared her throat and approached. The two servants fell silent. Roland faced her.

"Excuse me," Tara interrupted. "Roland, may I speak with you?" She paused for emphasis. "In private, please."

Roland murmured something to the two servants, then walked over to Tara. Tara angled herself away from the slanderous lovers, but not before shooting them her most withering frown.

"Roland," she instructed, "those two are going to get themselves into trouble. Best not to consort with that kind."

Roland just stared at her. Tara let out a long breath, reminding herself to be patient.

"You mustn't let servants feel it is okay to express such views. They should speak of the menhirs with reverence," she said with incredulity in her voice. "They should not speak ill of their former lords either. I am not convinced that this woman's absconding to the menhir isn't a criminal act. You cannot afford to be associated with that. Not now, Roland."

Roland's face twisted up. "I d-don't know that she said anything so bad," Roland replied, giving Lara a doe-eyed glance. "I don't know many other noble bloodlines." He looked Tara up and down. "But I don't think most people would mind a vassal leaving if they really wanted to. I wouldn't."

Tara considered how best to convey the issue to him with tenderness while still penetrating his excessive optimism.

"Roland, a lord provides their vassals with employment, safety, shelter, prosperity, and a sense of belonging. Their relationship with their lords is sacred and time-honored," Tara explained in a tone reserved for children. "Lords do not abuse their vassals, because to do so is often considered criminal. But it is a serious act of treachery for a vassal to abandon their post and then slander a bloodline so. I am surprised the menhir would let such a person cross their threshold, let alone shelter them. I suspect that what that woman conveyed to you is a secret, and a secret she's foolish for conveying aloud."

Tara turned away from Roland and mounted her horse.

"Clarence! Lara!" Tara called from her mount. "I have conferenced with Roland, and we agree it is essential that you do not share so much of your histories. We will extend to you the favor of discretion, and we will overlook this disturbing mishap."

The lovers exchanged glances.

"Thank you, ma'am," replied Clarence.

"Yes, thank you, Master," added Lara.

Tara softened her features and nodded at each of them. When she glanced down, Roland fixed her with a stony expression.

"What?" Tara said.

"I didn't say anything like that," he replied.

Tara sighed. "I apologize," she murmured. "I did it to protect them. I do not want to see them dashed by the menhir or their former lords. Love has blinded them. They need to be protected by people like us."

Tara waited for Roland's side of the apology. But his hard expression did not subside. He stared at her for a long moment before he walked away in silence. Tara considered scolding him for sulking, but decided to hold back on another lesson.

Riders reappeared on the road to the Bianchi estates with the sun still high over the horizon. The lovers exchanged smiles and clambered aboard their horses. The other servants shot Tara quick glances and did the same.

What was wrong with these people? Tara could not say. After all, she had made it clear to everyone that she would not punish them for their crimes.

A newcomer trotted beside Ms. Ash on a pearl mare from the Bianchi estates. Skin as rich as topsoil enveloped the girl, all the more accentuated by her garish riding dress. Ms. Ash gesticulated with both hands as they went. The laugh that came in reply from the Bianchi ascendant rose over the din of riders. Their shared merriment did not subside until they drew close.

"Everyone," the Architect announced, "this is Peony Bianchi. Peony, I'd like you to meet your new colleagues, Roland Ward and Tara Langcraw."

"A pleasure," panted Peony. She dabbed at her brow with a canary-yellow sleeve. She tolerated slicks of makeup over the outer portion of her eyes and her lips. Dimples on her cheeks suggested imminent laughter, and the expression did not subside.

Tara gaped at the girl.

"The others have already had their break," replied the Architect. "So, if you're ready, Ms. Bianchi, we can be about it."

Peony laughed. "I'm happy to be out of here sooner rather than later."

"Then off we go!" called the Architect.

Tara resumed her customary position at the caravan's tail. Roland and Peony rode side by side ahead of her. Tara studied their backs. The glint of Peony's trunk caught Tara's eye as she watched. Paintings of flowering trees and the silhouettes of birds in flight covered her trunk. Beside it on the same cart rested two baskets of saprolite bands.

Tara found herself scratching her ankle as she eyed the leeching garnets.

"Roland, right?" Peony began. "Tell me about you."

Roland's mouth opened and closed. "W-what do you want to know?" he stammered.

"Everything!" she exclaimed. "Start with where you're from, what your family's like, and what about the menhir has you excited!"

"Uh. . ." He glanced back at Tara. The Bianchi girl asked a lot of questions. "I'm from the Central Spiral, just a little n-northwest of here. My family grows timber. We all go to the Amber Menhir. One of my brothers just came back. He'd hoped to stay longer. . ."

His voice trailed off at the last.

"That happens," Peony assured him. "Almost nobody stays at the menhir for life. There wouldn't be enough space. The continent couldn't afford it. Some ascendants don't even make it through their first year. It's a big deal that he finished his three years!"

Roland smiled at Peony, but his eyes bore concern.

"No one in my family has gone beyond the basics of thaumaturgical training," Peony added.

Roland's bushy brows shot up.

"Who knows, maybe they'll send me away in a month! It would be just my luck." She chuckled.

"You w-won't get away that easy," Roland added, gesturing to himself and then Tara. "None of us will."

Peony's smile weakened for a moment, and then it resumed its prior incandescence. She continued to barrage Roland with questions that grew ever more personal. From time to time, when Peony looked away, Roland glanced down at her riding dress, which was cut much too low for anyone sensible. Worse, Peony did much the same when Roland looked away.

Tara rolled her eyes at the girl's predatory behavior. After a few hours of watching, Tara needed relief from the pair. She guided her horse around her fellow ascendants to the front of the group.

Ms. Ash spoke in hushed tones with Architect Blanchet. They did not acknowledge Tara's approach.

"We're lucky the Bianchi girl was waiting for us on the road. You don't see that often. And with the Harvest ready too. She has a Tilter's intuition, it seems." Ms. Ash chortled.

"Yes," mused Architect Blanchet, stroking his chin. "The Langcraw girl might be given a run for her money. Hmm? Wouldn't that be interesting? So many of their ilk turn out to be barren upon finer assessment. Though some might say the entire Tilter faction is barren in a way. . ." The Architect chuckled. "The little Bianchi is an inquisitive little minx too. One wonders how she'll fare."

Tara felt the color drain from her face, and her cheeks went hot. She spoke before she could stop herself. "You don't actually think she'll become a Tilter of the Hourglass?!"

The two riders gave a start. Ms. Ash possessed the decency to give Tara a sheepish look, but Architect Blanchet's jaw clenched, and his eyes went stony.

"Ms. Langcraw," said Ms. Ash. "I didn't see you there. Well, as I'm sure you know, it isn't uncommon for there to be hints of an ascendant's aptitudes prior to training."

One of Architect Blanchet's dark eyebrows rose as he looked Tara up and down. "No doubt you've displayed premonitions of your own, right?" he added.

Tara stared with her mouth agape. She had not. Moreover, she'd never considered that there might be two Tilters of the Hourglass in her cohort. Her mouth went dry.

"You know as well as I do, Tilters don't grow on trees," Ms. Ash added, studying Tara with a frown. "None of the Bianchi family have shown any aptitude for manipulations of time. Architect Blanchet will check her papers to confirm, but it isn't the sort of thing the menhir would overlook." Ms. Ash's frown deepened. "Are you alright, Ms. Langcraw?"

Tara took in several deep breaths. "As you say," she murmured.

Tara wrapped herself in a blanket of silence thereafter, but it

brought her no peace. She could not help but perseverate on the painful notion of being side by side with Peony for the next three years.
What if Peony turned out to be a more talented Tilter of the Hourglass than her? With her vulgar face paints and disposition for exposing
her bust, Peony would not be a welcome nuisance. Tara prayed to the
gods that Ms. Ash's soothsaying would be proven false. If the gods were
good, it had to be so.

CHAPTER 3

Sandenvale

THE CARAVAN REACHED SANDENVALE just after dusk. In day-
light, Tara supposed the town might have been charming, but
the simplistic architecture shrouded in darkness left it feeling
bleak and desolate. Buildings bearing low profiles, most with pale stone
walls and shallow, dark roofs, lined each street. In Tara's examination,
the central arteries of the town lay dormant.

Bloodshot eyes and drooping expressions fixed themselves on
almost every servant in the caravan. Most rode in silence. Peony and
Roland, however, continued their merry chatter as though they'd only
just started.

"We made it!" cheered Peony. "That wasn't so bad!"

Why she deemed a day's ride worthy of celebration left Tara guessing.

"Our accommodations are just there," Ms. Ash cut in as they descended one of the city's main streets. "Left at the next junction with
the pond, The Silken Pillow. You can't miss it. Enjoy the quiet this
evening while you can. By sunrise, this street will be bustling with merchants."

"The menhir has imposed an early curfew on the locals so we could
arrive in peace," said the Architect. He eyed the shuttered windows to
either side of their path. Not even a stray dog scurried in evidence.

The Silken Pillow spanned the next city block on their left. Had it been a private residence, it could have rivaled the Langcraw manor in size. The building lay split into three subsections, with a gabled entrance separating each. Music and laughter poured out of open windows. A series of oil lamps encircled in colored glass dotted the building's front. Each cast a different hue of blue light. The rest of the town appeared devoid of streetlights.

"Ms. Bianchi, Mr. Ward, and Ms. Langcraw, we will have your belongings taken to your rooms. We've made excellent time, thanks to Ms. Bianchi," announced Architect Blanchet. "You're welcome to consort with your new peers, but don't stay up too late. We depart early tomorrow."

The ascendants gave confirmatory nods.

Ms. Ash eyed the other servants. "We'll be in soon. We need to attend to some particulars here."

The three ascendants and Architect Blanchet handed the reins of their horses to the menhir servants just as stable hands appeared from one of the gabled alleys. The Architect guided the ascendants beneath a gable and down an alleyway lined with checkered paving stones. Howls and melodies boomed from open doors to either side as they went. Architect Blanchet paused before a doorway where the conversations beyond were particularly boisterous.

"The main dining area is just here," said the Architect, flashing the three ascendants a smile.

Peony and Roland exchanged grins. They did not look back at Tara. She wasn't accustomed to being excluded. But she reasoned that the pair might not have been properly educated in the arts of conversation and diplomacy, as she herself had.

Dozens of sturdy wooden tables crowded the room beyond. Menhir servants, all in grey cowled robes, packed the space. Finely dressed young men and women peppered the room among the servants, looking about with uncertain expressions. A pair of harpers played dueling pieces from a raised platform near the room's center, though no one attended to them much.

Peony, Roland, and Tara stayed close to their chaperone. Architect Blanchet shot them a look over his shoulder. The smell of smoked meats wafted in the air.

"Not bad?" the Architect jested. "I need to confirm our arrangements, but help yourself to food and drink." He gestured to a lengthy serving table bearing sliced meats, roasted vegetables, and dried fruit.

"Are you hungry?" Roland asked Peony.

Tara noted Roland did not ask her the same.

"I can always eat," Peony replied with a fiendish smile. "Let's go." Peony gestured for Tara to follow. "Come on!"

They passed by a pair of young nobles focused on a gold coin on their table. An almost empty bottle of wine sat beside it. A young woman with dark, slicked-back hair in a part stared at the coin.

"What do you suppose—" Peony began as the coin flipped from one side to the other with a clap. No one touched it.

The dark-haired girl smiled and elbowed the man beside her. "What did I tell you?" she said with a smirk.

The man beside her gaped at the thaumaturgy. "Do it again!" he called, waving his hands about the coin.

The girl's smile faded. Beads of sweat dotted her greasy brow that hadn't been there a moment before. Peony, Roland, and Tara exchanged looks.

"Can she do it again?" whispered Peony.

"She p-probably can't," said Roland.

The girl looked up and fixed the three of them with a scowl.

Peony attended to Roland and Tara with a smile. "When will we be able to do things like that?"

Tara dropped her voice to a whisper. "Some noble factions develop their aptitudes before others."

"We've got p-plenty of time to worry about that later," Roland interjected. "Let's eat!"

Peony and Roland approached the food tables. Tara followed behind. She took care to take small portions of the leanest meats and vegetables, to lead her new peers by example. But when she joined Roland and Peony at their table, she was appalled to see that Roland, and worse, Peony had piled their plates nearly to the point of overflowing. They started eating without her too. She sniffed before taking a seat across from Peony. Tara watched with unease as Peony shoveled huge portions of slurried meats into her gullet like a farm animal. Roland did the same, but somehow managed to be louder about it. Tara could feel her face twisting with disgust. Relief fell over her as Architect Blanchet sat down beside her.

"Everything's settled now," the Architect relayed. "None of you needs to room with a stranger this evening. There will be plenty of that at the menhir."

Tara thanked the gods under her breath. She could use some solitude after the day's journey.

"Peony and Tara will room together," said the Architect. "Roland will be alone tonight."

Horror replaced Tara's relief as she realized that Architect Blanchet no longer considered her and Peony to be strangers.

"Roland gets a room to himself?" Peony joked. "That's fine. I'd rather room with Tara anyhow." She winked at Tara and shot Roland a grin.

Tara felt a pit in her stomach, but her sullen moment was interrupted by a man's voice from behind her.

"Thaddeus," the man sang. "Are these your ascendants? I'm here for their papers. My Primara will be organizing a report for the Amber Chancellor."

Tara turned to find a pale man with red hair standing over her.

A bit of spiced wine spilled from his brimming goblet as he commandeered a seat. The man's fluid motion and speech suggested this goblet was not his first.

"Good to see you, Viktor," said the Architect, noting the exaggerated movements of the red-haired man in pale grey robes. He fished out a stack of ledgers and handed them over. "Here you are. Everyone, this is Viktor MacClery."

Viktor MacClery flipped through the pages and sneered. "Another Ward. Didn't we just have one of you? The menhir has plenty of Weavers already. Your family seems to provide an almost endless supply all on its own."

The man's impertinence caught Tara off guard. Something around the Architect's eyes hardened.

"I g-guess we do have a big family. I never thought about it," replied Roland. He gave Peony and Tara an unknowing shrug.

Viktor made no reply. Instead, he turned his attention to Tara.

"A Langcraw too," the man drawled. His tone took on a mocking note. "Now that is something special. We haven't had a Tilter ascendant in quite some time. The last two anyone remembers turned out to be barren." The man's smile broadened. "The Tilters need a success more than most, Ms. Langcraw. Let us hope you're not just another high-flying disappointment, hmm?"

"I am sure the Tilters of the Hourglass are looking forward to Tara's arrival," Architect Blanchet agreed, reaching out and giving Tara's shoulder a reassuring squeeze.

Viktor scrutinized the Architect, then Tara, and rolled his eyes.

"Those two over there are Lavinia Thalsem and Derek Arachvelle," Viktor announced, gesturing to the girl who'd flipped the coin earlier and her companion. "Thalsems are superb Architect stock, as you'd know, Thaddeus. Derek's line is a bit iffy. He hopes he might be an Evader. His lineage papers are a mess, the poor scrub."

"Evader?" asked Peony in a hushed voice toward Roland.

"Why, an Evader of Death, my dear," mocked Viktor, clucking his tongue. "Are you so unaware of the basics of the menhir's structure?"

Peony shrunk beneath the question.

"What sect do you call home?" Peony blurted out into the silence.

Tara doubted whether such a direct question was seen as uncivilized in the menhir. She studied the man's face. He did not appear offended.

"Me?" Viktor replied with theatrical surprise. He pulled at his pale grey robes while staring at Peony. "I'm a Delver."

He added far more emphasis than necessary. Tara realized he was playing with Peony, whose expression remained blank. She appeared to have no comprehension of what the scholar had imparted.

"A Delver," he repeated with more force.

Peony flinched.

"A Delver of the Mind," Roland put in. He reached out a hand to touch Peony's. "He's saying he's a Delver of the Mind. 'Delvers' for short. They can touch the th-thaumaturgical threads surrounding people's brains."

Delver MacClery clucked his tongue at the ascendants. One of his eyebrows raised a little more each time Roland huffed in a breath. "Now, Mr. Ward, you don't intend to try and save this damsel every time she shows up unprepared? One worries you mightn't have time to do anything else." Delver MacClery cleared his throat and turned his attention to Peony. "Ms. Bianchi, may I suggest you take the next few weeks to bring yourself up to speed? It will save you from further embarrassment at the menhir. Count this incident as a kindness. You learned you were lacking among friends."

Peony adjusted herself in her chair.

The playfulness in his delivery had Tara's skin crawling. She frowned and looked at Peony. Mist had collected in her eyes. There was nothing of her former cheer about her.

"Architect Blanchet," announced Tara, "I regret that our long journey today has left me fatigued. Would it be acceptable to take this opportunity to retire?"

"It's no matter at all," said the Architect.

"Peony," called Tara. "Would you be so kind as to join me? I recall you being fond of cards, and I thought you might consider playing a game before bed."

Peony blinked. "Um, what?" she sputtered.

Tara locked eyes with Peony and then gave Delver MacClery a sidelong look.

"Oh! Yes," Peony replied louder. "That sounds nice. If it would help you relax."

"Wonderful!" replied Tara. "If you will excuse us, gentlemen."

Tara stood up and held herself as erect as she could manage. "Our rooms?" she asked with a glance toward Architect Blanchet.

"Upstairs. Room twenty-eight," he replied, passing Tara an iron key.

Tara and Peony gave the group pleasantries and departed. Delver MacClery scowled as they fled.

A knot of tension in Tara's shoulders dissipated as she passed through the doorway to the quarters. The room harbored two beds with woolen blankets and a pair of pillows each. Their travel chests rested at the foot of their beds. A single window offered a view of dark roofs as far as the eye could see.

Tara closed the door behind Peony and let out a sigh.

"I don't remember telling you anything about cards," said Peony.

"You didn't," Tara replied flatly. "I just couldn't bear to watch that man's rudeness any longer."

Peony looked at her feet and back at Tara. "Thank you."

"My pleasure," said Tara. "He should not have acted like that. Never mind your training before. You're an ascendant now, just like everyone else."

"Do you. . ." Peony began. "Do you think all the scholars will be like that? Will every word be a test? Some inside joke?"

Peony stared at Tara. Though she stood almost a head taller than Tara, something about her question made Peony seem so small.

"I daresay not," replied Tara with a stifled smile. "If they were all so cruel, I can't imagine that the bloodlines would send us to them for training. Some of us might even become scholars one day. One does not welcome new members to a family by brutalizing them first." Even Tara's mother exhibited more kindness than Delver MacClery.

Some of the fatigue around Peony's eyes departed.

"Anyhow," Tara added, "I know nothing about cards. My mother thinks them tawdry. I just couldn't think of a better lie in the moment."

Peony smiled and sagged onto her bed. "Well, that's one thing I can teach you. I'm good at cards. Veils and Poisons is my favorite game." She paused and laughed. "Maybe I'm tawdry."

Tara avoided Peony's gaze, though a smile touched her lips. She watched Peony from within her stoic silence for a moment and pondered the notion of playing a card game with a girl as brash as Peony. Larus would not approve.

"I'm not sure I'm fond of gambling," said Tara. "It always seemed to me that card games prey on hope, and a false impression of a player's odds."

"Gambling?" Peony sputtered. "Not every card game involves gambling. Normally you just play for fun, Tara."

Tara sat on the edge of her bed, facing away from Peony. "I'm tired," she said. "I wasn't lying about that. We should get to bed. We have a long day tomorrow. If Delver MacClery will be there, then we will need our wits."

Peony nodded, and the two ascendants readied for bed. Peony donned her nightrobe first, then removed her riding dress from beneath it. The sequencing seemed awkward to Tara, but Peony managed the matter with ease. Peony averted her gaze while Tara undressed. Tara wondered if Peony adopted the modesty for her comfort. Peony brushed off her riding dress and folded it, setting it on the end of her bed.

Tara cleaned her face and arms in the basin with a scratchy towel. She turned to Peony. "I'm done with the basin. You can use it now, if you like."

Peony looked at the basin and then at Tara. She shrugged. "I'm too tired. Removing this much face paint takes a lot of scrubbing." She chuckled. "By the way, I'm going to teach you some card games when we're finally at the menhir."

"It's a deal," said Tara.

Tara deposited the day's riding garment in one of her trunks and selected another dress for the morning. Peony pulled a jumble of bright fabric out of her trunk and started a bit of sewing. Tara almost gasped at the hasty jumble of items in Peony's trunk. The girl's dresses were mixed with face paints, bits of stray fabric, pairs of scissors, a vicious-looking razor blade, and an assortment of dyeing implements.

"You have vibrant tastes," Tara commented.

Peony chuckled. "Some say so."

Tara had scarcely blown out the last candle in their room before Peony's form went motionless and her breathing deepened. Tara closed her eyes and attempted to draw herself down into sleep, though, as was often the case, it did not come. Were she home, she might have paced about the halls. Here, she feared waking Peony, or stumbling into some lecherous ascendant.

An hour of waking stillness had passed when Tara heard a muffled clatter outside the window. She rolled over to face the direction of the noise. For a moment, she thought she'd imagined the sound, but then a figure passed by only a few paces from where she lay. Tara froze. Then a second form passed by.

Slowly, Tara rose from her bed, taking care to be light on her feet. She held herself low as she approached the window. Despite her caution, she fully expected to find an alley cat or some nocturnal trash-eating creature with tender eyes. She stifled a yelp as she spotted the forms of two people not four paces from her. One sat with their legs dangling off the edge of the roof, while the second sat cross-legged beside the first. They both stared down at the alleyway below.

"How did they get out there?" Tara whispered to herself.

For a moment, Tara could imagine Larus's chiding voice saying, "Send those fools away, and get some sleep!"

Whoever they were, Larus was right: Tara just needed to send them away. She checked the perimeter of the window and found a pair of latches at the bottom. Pressing with her palms, she pivoted the glass outward.

"You there," Tara called in a hushed tone. "Pardon me, but we're attempting to sleep in here. We would appreciate it if you went back to your rooms to congregate."

The pair jumped in surprise. The one with the folded legs unfurled herself and stood. The coin-flipping girl from earlier rolled her eyes at Tara. Lavinia something. The man beside her twisted around. Tara recalled his name better: Derek Arachvelle. Her mother often spoke ill of their family.

"Mind your own business," Lavinia spat, making no effort to quiet her voice.

Peony groaned behind Tara.

"I believe lurking outside my room and robbing me of sleep is my business. Whatever nefarious tendencies you are indulging in out there, please take them elsewhere," Tara whispered. She knew that response would put an end to the matter.

"Buzz off. I'm not one of your servants," said Lavinia, louder than before.

"What's going on?" asked Peony as she sat up, rubbing her eyes.

"There are hoodlums prowling around," replied Tara, gesturing out the window.

Peony moved beside Tara. The smell of rotting vegetables and over-ripened meats permeated the air from the alley below.

"Hoodlums?" Lavinia scoffed. "I'm not your vassal either, whoever you are. Now, you can either fuck off, close your window, and get back to however you two were wasting your time, or you can drag your asses out here to join us. It's not every day you get to explore an Independent City. I'd like to see what laypeople do when there's no noble bloodline around to organize them."

Tara seethed. She had never been thus spoken to in her life.

"We should join her!" Peony exclaimed.

"Join her?" Tara sputtered. "We're not joining this insane girl out on the ledge of a building the night before we go to the menhir! We must honor ourselves enough not to be led by idiots, Peony."

Tara had not finished her lecture before Peony crawled through the window with alarming familiarity. "Tara, grab my boots, would you?" she asked with a huge grin. "This is an adventure, Tara! When're you going to see Sandenvale again? It's not like we'll be enjoying a lot of free time at the menhir!"

Tara's jaw dropped open.

"Well?" snapped Lavinia. The dark-featured girl tapped her foot at Tara.

"Come on!" cheered Peony. "I'll make sure you're okay. I owe you."

Before Tara stood her soon-to-be peers. And Larus wasn't here to disapprove. Peony wasn't wrong about the menhir's iron grip either. Tara's skin tingled, and goose bumps spread across her arms and neck. She glanced at her bed. Sleep could not come now anyhow, knowing ascendants were wandering around outside her window. She grabbed

Peony's boots and tossed them through the window. Then she slipped on her sturdiest pair of slippers and stumbled out too.

"You made it after all," Lavina observed with a hint of surprise in her voice. "Who're you?"

Tara stood in haughty silence as her slippers struggled to find purchase on the roof's slick tiles. She spared the drop to the alley below a momentary glance before answering, "Tara Langcraw."

"Langcraw?" said Lavinia, looking Tara up and down. "The supposed Tilter of the Hourglass? My family mentioned you."

Tara stiffened.

"I'm Peony Bianchi," Peony interrupted. "What're you two out here for?"

The gods had spared Lavinia the gift of height, but she caried herself in such a way that it made her seem fearsome. Lavinia rolled a shoulder in a feline shrug. "I figured we'd go for a stroll," she said, gesturing to the streets below. "This is Derek Arachvelle, and I'm Lavinia Thalsem," she added. "I couldn't sleep, and I spotted Derek out here, so I joined him."

"Who could sleep when there's a whole Independent City to explore?" said Derek. "We've been around the perimeter. There's a spot not far from here that'll be an easy climb down."

"Sounds like a plan to me," said Peony, giving Tara an uncertain look. "Does that sound okay to you?"

Tara gave a stiff nod and eyed Lavinia.

"Good. It's done then," said Lavinia with a sly smile.

The roof of the inn bore a shallow slope, though dew slicked its glazed tiles and threatened to become frost in the night air. As promised, Derek led them to a portion of the roof where stacked crates provided tiered platforms down to the alleyway.

Derek leaped to the first crate with an easy grace. He moved in a feral manner, engaging his arms and legs as he descended. Lavinia went next. She descended with inexpert movements, though she exhibited more athleticism than Tara had first assigned her. Derek held one of the crates at the bottom steady as Lavinia moved. She landed beside him seconds later.

"Come on!" she called.

Peony climbed down with a precision that rivaled Derek's. Her long extremities and flat, hard muscle flashed as she climbed. She landed with a flourish.

Tara hesitated. She considered heading back to their room. Nothing was stopping her. It was what Larus would have suggested. There might even be a reward for turning in the three rogue ascendants. Escaping their accommodations via rooftop had to break some rule or another. But turning in her peers might not be a wise means of introducing herself. Moreover, the notion of resting in bed for hours only to be regaled with tales of adventure by Lavinia tomorrow seemed a repulsive thought.

"Are you coming?" cried Lavinia.

Tara sighed. Then she plopped down to the first crate with a piteous yelp. It quivered beneath her, and she fell to her hands and knees. She froze, abruptly stricken with all the poor decisions that had brought her there. Lavinia snorted.

"You alright?" called Derek.

"I'm fine," Tara lied. Her voice did not ring with confidence. She breathed in and out several times, then resumed her fumbling descent. She was shaking by the time she joined the others.

"Where are we going?" asked Peony, glancing around.

No one seemed concerned about Tara's shaking and sputtering.

"Just follow me," Lavinia replied.

They slipped from the alleyway into the street, then darted through the modest pools of light from the inn's streetlamps, aiming for the darker streets to either side of the inn. At first, the ascendants did not speak. But as the inn disappeared, their boldness bloomed.

"Have any of you been to an Independent City before?" Tara asked. The others shook their heads.

"I don't understand how places like this work," said Lavinia.

"Independent Cities used to be common," added Derek. "But their citizens began fleeing to the estates of noble bloodlines for safety."

Lavinia smirked. "Of course they did. Places like Sandenvale are only independent now because of petulance. Laypeople don't really want to live in places like this. These cities rely on votes of approval for their rulers, who can't do anything to jeopardize their own popularity. How can anyone have a campaign of leadership like that?"

"They can't," Tara agreed. "It's why the system died, mostly. Just look around."

Merchant carts picked clean of their goods lined each street. Windows bore heavy shutters. Here, they seemed to serve for more than mere privacy.

"Thieves must be lurking everywhere," Tara scoffed. "Why else would merchants strip their wares each night, only to replace them the next morning? So much wasted effort. Lay society functions best when personal property is expunged. We are lucky to live today at a pinnacle of order and peace."

"You said it," said Derek. He scratched as his neck, revealing an irregular blemish along his hairline. He caught Tara's gaze and covered it quickly with his hair. "Though it's still fun to see how things were."

"Like touring a living fossil," Tara suggested, looking away from the others.

"Puh!" laughed Lavinia.

The four splashed in gazing ponds and took turns posturing in the stocks outside Sandenvale's political buildings. But the ascendants' thrill soon acquiesced to boredom. Sandenvale, for all its otherworldliness, grew small. Soon the ascendants found themselves revisiting familiar landmarks, only from different angles. After a few hours of meandering, they started back to The Silken Pillow. They could just see the pale blue light of the inn's streetlamps when a leathery voice called out to them.

"Oy!" It came from an alleyway not far from them. "You!"

The ascendants gave a start and stepped back from the alley's opening. Derek moved between Lavinia and where the voice had come from. Peony stepped before Tara.

Refuse sat piled before the alleyway. A disheveled cart with a missing wheel leaned against a wall beside the refuse.

"What's that?" said the voice, muttering to itself. "Fuck off!"

A low shadow emerged from the darkness that resolved into a humpbacked man. One of his yellowed eyes gazed off into the air, while the other fixed itself on the ascendants. His stained shift was barely long enough to be decent, and a dried slick of vomit covered the front of it. Even from a distance, Tara smelled brandy and piss.

"Who're you?" he barked. He belched and sputtered. "What're you doin' here?"

Lavinia straightened her spine and raised her voice. "I am Lavinia Thalsem, menhir ascendant and incipient Architect. Who are you?"

The man flinched at the mention of the menhir, but otherwise appeared unmoved by her statement. "I don't give a fuck!" he yelled. He stumbled sideways and landed hard on a pile of rags and empty crates. He spat curses as he struggled to right himself. His arched spine made it difficult for him to look forward even while standing.

"Perhaps you should care," Lavinia declared. "We're leaving this place, and you will treat us with peace."

"And you are in breach of the menhir's curfew!" Tara added in her most imperious tone.

The man mumbled, picked up a broken bottle, and threw it at Lavinia with a grunt. Despite his frail form, the bottle pitched through the air with speed. Lavinia pivoted too late. The glass struck the side of her face. She cried out and stumbled.

"Menhir bastards!" the man murmured.

"Let's go," called Peony. She gestured to The Silken Pillow as Derek helped Lavinia up.

"I know who you are. I know all about you!" exclaimed the man. He attempted to stand again, but fell. "You do whatever you like to us, don't you?! You think you can get away with everything. Stealing from the likes of us! I guess it's true you little bastards start off as bad as them!"

The man picked up a stone and hurled it towards Peony, but she was prepared and glided to one side. Tara followed Peony's movement, and the stone clattered on the paving stones behind them.

"You don't know us," Peony retorted. "We have not stolen anything from you."

Lavinia's cut looked ugly. A dribble of dark blood ran down her pale cheek.

"We need to get out of here," Peony said. She received affirmative nods from the others.

The man got to his feet, clasping a large shard of glass in one outstretched arm. He held it toward them, his attentive eye fixed on Peony. His mouth worked in exaggerated twitches, revealing a few brown lumps for teeth. "You give us those bracelets and necklaces to wear, don't you?!" he spat, gurgling and spitting as he advanced. "You steal our lives and our minds! Then you take us away!"

The ascendants backed toward the inn. Tara prayed the lamplights might frighten the scoundrel away.

"Sir!" Derek shouted, his voice desperate. "I warn you. . ."

But their attacker did not falter. He slid forward, desperate and putrid. His outstretched shard glinted in the moonlight.

"You don't frighten me, you little shit!" he yelled. "I've got nothing left you can take! It's goin' to feel so good to kill one of you little bastards before you can become a real problem!"

A sharp thaumaturgical crack echoed through the street as the man's elbow bent up at an unnatural angle. Thick fragments of broken bone split through his pale skin as he cried out. Below the elbow, the man's arm dangled lifelessly. His shard of glass clattered to the ground. Gouts of dark, almost black blood surged out in pulses from his arm as he collapsed, sobbing. He panted, his mouth working to convey words that wouldn't or couldn't come.

The ascendants froze with horror.

"Help!" he finally cried out. "Help! These bastards attacked me!"

The piece of glass beside him seemed so much smaller now to Tara. He sobbed and pressed his spent arm into his tiny shift.

"You did this!" he cried out as he rocked. "You took my family, my home, and now—" But the man's voice cut out, and his frantic speech grew more disjointed and weaker with every word. He looked around, but no one answered. Not a shutter moved.

"Are you alright?" came a commanding voice from behind them.

The ascendants all jumped. Tara turned to find Architect Blanchet approaching. He held a hand up in a sustained thaumaturgical gesture.

"Are you alright?" he repeated.

"I think so," said Peony.

"Lavinia's hurt," answered Tara.

The Architect grasped Lavinia's head and tilted her face up to examine her wound. She hissed as he probed at it, though she did not whimper.

"She'll be fine," he concluded.

"What about him?" said Peony, pointing to the collapsed form of their assailant. He sat silent and motionless.

"He won't try to hurt you again. I can assure you of that," replied the Architect.

"Right," agreed Peony. "But will he be okay?"

"Oh," replied the Architect, seeming disoriented by the question. "No, I don't suppose he will. He attacked you. That's a serious crime, even in Independent Cities. I saw the whole thing."

Tara and Peony looked at each other. Peony's face contorted.

"Should we do anything about him?" asked Peony.

The Architect reached out, touched Peony's shoulder, and gave her a small smile. "Let's get you back. I'll make sure someone attends to that."

Blood pooled to one side of the lifeless form on the street.

"Tara, you're okay?" asked the Architect.

Tara nodded, though she shook.

"Alright, then. Back to the inn," the Architect instructed. "The four of you will need to explain why you're out wandering the streets of an Independent City, and how you let yourself be assaulted by one of its inhabitants. There was a curfew imposed for a good reason!"

As the group departed, Tara observed a low light behind one of the shuttered windows. Maybe, she thought, someone might come to aid the old man once they were gone.

When they returned to the inn, Architect Blanchet forced them to explain the evening's events. They left out nothing.

"And what have you concluded from your experiences this night?" he asked.

"I'm not sure," said Peony.

"Even lay citizens can be dangerous?" asked Lavinia.

Something like paternal disappointment crossed the Architect's face. When he spoke, he sounded exasperated. "One would hope you've learned why the menhirs exist, and why so few Independent Cities remain. They're just disorganized messes without us."

Without thinking, Tara heard herself say, "Yes." The word tasted bitter in her mouth, but the Architect fixed her with the warmest smile.

"Your lives are more valuable now that you're ascending to the menhir," said Architect Blanchet as he ushered them up the stairs to their rooms. "Your lives are not only your own anymore. One of you might one day help the world circumvent Calamity, or make some other great thaumaturgical discovery. We cannot know, and so you must be careful."

Staring at herself in her standing mirror later, Tara struggled to make sense of the evening. Something about it all pained her. Yet one thing remained clear to Tara: she was glad she wasn't alone anymore. Moreover, a part of her just seemed to know that Peony was meant to be beside her. She smiled as she wondered whether that might be her very first premonition.

CHAPTER 4

Pomp and Doubt

THE SCENT OF FRESH-BAKED bread laced the morning air, bearing a hint of a fried or perhaps smoked meat alongside it; Tara could not be sure which. She and Peony joined the other ascendants downstairs, where Ms. Ash handed each of them two pieces of fruit for breakfast. Tara eyed the bruised produce and grimaced. She considered asking for a different set, but a glance into Ms. Ash's baskets revealed little better alternatives.

Seeming to spot Tara's disappointment, Peony leaned in. "Seems the bread and bacon are reserved for the scholars, or maybe the lay citizens."

Tara let a little wickedness touch her voice. "Celebrating our departure, perhaps?"

The pair made their way out of The Silken Pillow to where the other ascendants readied their horses with bleary expressions. No one spoke, but the scent of bread and char grew stronger, causing more than one stomach to rumble. Architect Blanchet sat atop his horse wearing an expression of iron.

"Barring any surprises," the Architect called out over the sounds of the bustling ascendants, "we'll arrive at the Amber Menhir by late afternoon. There is a customary gathering of scholars to celebrate the arrival of the new ascendants. Representatives of each of the six noble factions will be present. Customary black robes will be compulsory."

Lavinia sighed.

Architect Blanchet paused to eye her. "Ascendant instructors will be in attendance, so take care not to embarrass yourselves. The Amber Chancellor will give a speech, though his appearance will be brief. He has other obligations."

"When will classes start?" called Lavinia. Her hair glistened bright in the morning light.

Tara pondered how early the girl must rise each morning to appear so freshly greased.

The ascendants around Lavinia shrank and stepped back from her as the Architect swiveled his gaze. "Thaumaturgical instruction commences tomorrow, Ms. Thalsem," he noted with a flare of nostrils. "The ascendant schedule is identical for all."

"But what if we already know our aptitudes? What's the point?" Lavinia put in.

Now only Derek stood anywhere near her. His face paled.

Architect Blanchet sighed. "Regardless of noble bloodline, every ascendent is required to obtain a rudimentary understanding of each noble faction's thaumaturgy. Even though, in most cases, the training is purely theoretical."

Lavinia scowled.

A servant emerged from the inn, wheezing and panting as he carried two baskets, one dangling from each hand. He opened the top of each basket and poured rivers of garnet bands into a chest.

Tara's horse whickered and rolled its eyes, taking several steps away from the saprolite bands. She patted the side of the animal's neck and whispered in its ear, "Easy, now."

"They don't like seeing so many of those things all at once, do they?" asked Peony. She struggled to settle her mount.

"I cannot say I blame them," Tara admitted. "I would not want to fall into a bin of those stones myself. I can't stand having them around my wrist for more than a few days."

"Viktor! Milyna!" Architect Blanchet called toward the inn. "We're ready!"

The red-haired Delver, Viktor MacClery, emerged from one of the alleyways, wearing his pale grey robes. A fair-skinned woman with a corset top and billowing pants strode beside him. Her short blonde curls bounced as she walked. A heavy green riding cloak was draped over her shoulders, barely keeping the woman decent. Tara's eyebrows scaled her forehead as she eyed the attire.

"We should be off," called the blonde woman, whom Tara assumed to be Milyna. The woman slipped atop a tall grey horse and flashed the Architect a smile.

As they rounded the corner of the avenue leading away from The Silken Pillow, the whispered conversations of the ascendants and servants vanished. Smoke drifted up from the burnt frame of what was once one of the squat, dark-roofed buildings lining the street. The remnants stood only paces from where Tara and the others had encountered the old man the night before. She looked for the place where he'd fallen. But there was nothing; not even a stain remained in evidence. Tara's stomach lurched.

"W-what do you suppose happened?" whispered Roland.

Architect Blanchet's booming voice sent Tara recoiling. "There was fire at the bakery this morning. As a result, the menhir has extended its curfew for Sandenvale until the Harvest and the ascendants have arrived safely this evening."

"They can't leave their homes the whole day?" asked Roland.

"Sadly not," said the Architect in a saccharine tone that caused Tara's stomach to pitch further. "But it's for their own safety."

"Was anyone hurt?" asked Peony.

Trails of smoke ascended from a few glowing embers. The door-frame was among the few somewhat intact components of the building's structure. As Tara examined it, she realized the metal doorhandle looked warped, as though it had been crushed or melted by an intense flame. The handle, lock, and socket were all swirled in a jumbled, fused mess.

"It's sweet of you to be concerned, ascendants," Milyna answered. She guided her mount to join Peony, Tara, and Roland. She paused almost exactly over the spot where the old man had fallen.

Lavinia and Derek held their mounts only a few paces farther down the street. Derek stared at the ground beneath the blonde scholar.

Milyna cleared her throat. "If there were any injuries, it's none of your concern. The menhir will send scholars to liaise and determine whether any laws were broken."

"Like the curfew?" asked Peony.

Architect Blanchet's face went flat. "Exactly, Ms. Bianchi," he announced. "Now, follow Primara Okondo and Delver MacClery, and don't dwell any further on the matter."

None of the ascendants so much as looked up from the ground until the caravan snaked well and out of Sandenvale.

It was Peony who broke the silence in their tiny silo of ascendants riding apart from the others. "What's a Primara?" she asked.

"Sh-she's in charge of one of the six noble factions," replied Roland. "She's the leader of the Weavers of the Web of Life."

"She does not much look like a leader to me," Tara quipped. "If she leads at all, then she must use an unorthodox toolkit, to be sure."

No one replied.

"Tara," Peony murmured, "you don't think that fire was on purpose, do you?"

The question made Tara's spine go rigid. She looked up at the three scholars leading the caravan. They seemed far enough away for her to venture a response. "I don't know," she whispered. "But I think it's bet-ter that you do not probe the matter. It suffices to say that we mightn't yet know all we thought we knew about Independent Cities."

Peony's lips compressed into a line. No one said another word about the issue.

At their first stop outside Sandenvale, Tara wandered away to find a bit of privacy so she could attempt to eat around the bruises dotting her apples. Ms. Ash and several other grey-clad servants were gathered not far away, eating their own breakfasts.

"Now, girl, listen to me!" Ms. Ash barked at one of the other ser-vants. "You are to watch those two ascendants, and you tell me if they step one hair out of line. I don't care if Chesa isn't here to help. She's attending to more important matters, believe you me. Have I made myself clear?"

It seemed Ms. Ash did not grace her fellow servants with the aunt-like familiarity she bestowed on the ascendants. Tara studied her. Something about her dour expression and efficient bullying reminded Tara of Larus. Ms. Ash looked up and jumped at Tara eyeing the gath-ering of servants. Ms. Ash's scowl melted into an inviting smile in an instant. Tara nodded, careful not to let surprise or amusement show on her face. Then she withdrew to where she'd tied her horse. There she found Lavinia whining to Peony.

"I don't understand why we need to have training in thaumaturgi-cal ethics and history too," Lavinia mewled. "Anyone of noble blood should already know such things."

Peony gave Lavinia an uncertain smile.

"I, for one, think it useful to be reminded of one's history," Tara interjected with her haughtiest air. "How can one see where they're going if they don't know from where they've come?" She sniffed and looked down her nose at Lavinia. "A good lesson is worth repeating."

Lavinia rolled her eyes and headed away in a huff. Tara turned to Peony.

"Thank you," Peony mouthed.

"Any time," said Tara. "So long as you'd do the same."

"You can count on it." Peony chuckled.

Cliques of two or three ascendants rode together for the rest of the morning. Peony, Roland, and Tara rode together, with Lavinia and Derek not far away. When any two groups neared each other, their members eyed one another and veered apart.

All morning, the ascendants squinted off into the east, hoping to make out the menhir's silhouette on the horizon. Each time someone thought they spotted it, the others would mock them as the mirage menhir turned out to be a farmhouse, mill, or granary.

When it came time to stop for lunch, the ascendants collected their bread and dried fruit from the servants. While wandering back to her horse, Peony paused. "How about we try and have lunch with one of the other groups?" she suggested.

Roland shrugged.

"I would rather not," replied Tara. She eyed the groups of ascendants situated in twos and threes on tufts of grass by the roadside. None of them gave inviting looks.

"How about just Lavinia and Derek?" Peony added. "We know them already, right?"

Tara opened her mouth, but Roland answered first, "W-why not?"

Tara sighed. She tried not to sulk as she followed her companions over to a tuft of grass where Lavinia and Derek sat taking their lunch. Peony plopped down and beamed at Derek. Roland sat beside her. Tara selected a perch atop a stone a bit farther away.

Lavinia peered at Peony. "What're you always smiling about?"

"I'm just excited to be going somewhere new," said Peony, her smile widening.

"The Amber Menhir isn't going to be a vacation," Lavinia sneered.

"There's still plenty to be excited about," Peony added, taking a bite of her bread. "Aren't you excited to learn thaumaturgy? I keep imagining what my aptitude will be."

Lavinia sneered at Peony, who appeared not to notice. Or perhaps Peony was playing with Lavinia.

"I already know I'm going to be an Architect of Forces. No mystery. What's there to be excited for?" Lavinia retorted.

"You still don't know how strong you'll be," Peony explained. "You might be a prodigy, or you might barely have any power at all."

Lavinia flinched. The others exchanged worried looks.

"Me t-too," Roland piped up. He'd finished his lunch in moments and now examined Tara's dried fruit. "I haven't shown signs of any aptitude. I'm worried I'll be the last to show them."

Derek wrung his hands. "Not everyone in my family who ascended manifested aptitudes," he confessed. "Some of them just . . . left."

"Really?" Peony asked. "What happened to the ones who left?"

Lavinia stood up and sniffed in Derek's direction. "I think I'll go for a walk before we start moving again."

"Are you okay?" whispered Derek. "You know, after last night. . ."

"I said I'm going for a walk," snapped Lavinia. Without so much as a glance toward another ascendant, she stormed away.

Peony and Roland stared at each other.

Derek watched Lavinia's back for a long moment. Then he turned to Tara and the others. "Maybe I'll go for a walk too," he said tonelessly. Then he stood and left.

Tara noted that he did not follow Lavinia.

"What happened?" asked Peony.

"People don't usually t-talk about the strength of their aptitudes.

Lots of people think it's a bad thing when a member of a noble blood-line can't use thaumaturgy," Roland explained.

"Some won't even consort with bloodlines they deem inferior to theirs," Tara added.

"It isn't anyone's fault," said Peony. "No one wants to fail or get thrown out of the menhir."

"It doesn't matter," Tara said. "If an ascendant cannot see and manipulate some kind of thaumaturgy by the end of their first year, they leave. I've heard that scholars study failed ascendants before they go. I'm afraid the Arachvelles have suffered more than a few such embarrassments."

"Study? Like with anomalies?" asked Peony.

Tara eyed the girl, wondering how she could have been raised by a noble bloodline and yet know so little. "Yes," said Tara. "Very much like what they do with anomalies."

Peony's face went blank. Roland placed a huge hand on her shoulder.

"Everyone up!" Delver MacClery called. "Your restful lunch together has ended."

"Not restful in the least," Tara quipped to herself.

Neither Peony nor Roland chose to comment.

Derek rode alone at the tail of the caravan after lunch. Tara wondered how many of the other ascendants knew the Arachvelles' reputation. She hoped, for his sake, it was not many.

Peony and Roland chattered like old friends again. Tara watched them from within her customary silence. She could not help but smile a little at the return of Peony's unquenchable spirit. Something about it put Tara in a brighter mood. She might have a garish sense of style, and she might be clueless about the workings of the world, but there was something intangible about the dark-skinned girl that rendered her enjoyable. As for Roland, he stared at Peony quite a lot. Perhaps he found the girl attractive, though Tara couldn't understand why. Peony smiled far too much to be respectable. If someone smiled at everything, then how did you know how they really felt?

"Peony's lucky a guy as big as Roland likes her," sniped Lavinia. She rode up from behind to canter beside Tara.

Tara prevented herself from grimacing.

"Peony's as tall as any woman I've ever seen. Not many men would be brave enough to go after someone like that. She'd better hold onto Roland, that's for sure." There was something fiendish to Lavinia's smile that seemed to search for comradery.

Tara rolled her eyes, replying, "I cannot see how it's any of our concern. Besides, I cannot say the difficulty of Peony's finding a dalliance should be anywhere near as challenging as it would be for you."

Lavinia's eyes widened. Tara braced herself to spar with the girl.

"There it is," said Lavinia in a small voice.

Tara blinked. "There's what?"

"The menhir. . ." Lavinia breathed.

Tara went rigid and faced the horizon. Bright light bore down overhead, and she had to shield her eyes. Then her breath caught. There upon a flat stretch of land stood a blemish too great to be just another farmhouse.

In moments, other ascendants identified the shape. Soon the low bustle of the caravan fell silent. Tara noted that no one laughed. No one smiled. She wanted to drink in the moment, but a pit in her stomach grew as the caravan ambled in reverential or perhaps fearful silence. Roland and Peony drew their mounts nearer to Tara's. Soon all the ascendants moved in bands of larger and larger numbers, the cliques dissolving within the Amber Menhir's shadow.

A ceaseless wind began pushing through the caravan. The air blew hot and tinged with sulfur. Tara peeled off her riding cape, and she was not alone. Despite the late season, all around her, the ascendants removed gloves, hats, and capes as the temperature approached that of a Spiral's summer.

Tara glanced back at Derek. He rode farther behind than she had realized. He still rode alone too. She considered approaching him, but feared the gesture might paint him even more piteous to the others. Ascendants did not seem the sort to respond well to signals of weakness. Tara had to be careful.

As they rode nearer, the blurred form of the menhir and its smaller buttress towers resolved into a convoluted webwork of odd spherical structures aloft in the air, held together by a network of connecting tubes. There were dozens of titanic earthen chambers extending many hundreds of feet into the sky. A few of them appeared to have glass ceilings. It all looked to Tara like a stonework cast of some monolithic ant colony in reverse.

"They s-say it was inspired by the tunnels of burrowing beetles," breathed Roland.

"Yes," Tara replied, eyeing the massive building. "But how do the chambers hover like that? Surely they are not held aloft by those meager channels between them."

"I don't know," Roland admitted with a shrug. "I guess it's some kind of force thaumaturgy. People say the Amber Menhir taps into the raw magic of earth. It's what makes their force thaumaturges so powerful."

The caravan compressed as the Spring Road arced to the south of the menhir. The main road did not intercept the menhir itself. There was no sign to announce the menhir. Its molten aura and the moat of bare earth around it were enough to proclaim it. The smaller road that led directly to the menhir was lined with orange paving stones, gleaming like crystalized water droplets compressed flat. The horses rolled their eyes and whickered as clouds of sulfurous heat passed over them. The mounts hesitated to place a hoof on the gleaming stones. It required Tara's every effort to keep her horse moving forward.

Only a few paces away, Peony's mount reared up, screamed, and bucked.

"A little help?" Peony cried as her reins slipped from her grasp.

Tara darted her horse toward Peony. She seized the swinging reins as Peony's mount tossed its head and whinnied.

"Easy," Tara soothed. Peony's horse quieted, and its eyes locked with Tara's. "I think it's best for you to ride with me, Peony."

Peony nodded, panting. "Is it meant to be so hot here? Is something wrong, do you think?"

"I'm not sure," Tara replied. She called out to the others, "Derek! Roland! I think it's best if we all ride together from here."

The other two ascendants nodded and guided their distressed mounts toward Tara.

A pale-haired ascendant Tara didn't recognize shouted just as his horse screamed and toppled to its side, falling from the paved path and rolling onto the boy's leg. A series of meaty cracks rang out, and the boy screamed. He thrashed away from the burning saddle as the horse tried to haul itself up, stumbling again and again. Each of the horse's attempts became more desperate and useless than the last. Charred blisters, many bursting open, covered one side of the animal's abdomen as it rolled its eyes and screamed. The boy scurried like a half-crushed spider back onto the paved stones, panting and whimpering as he stared wide-eyed at his blistered hands. Tara managed to steady the mounts around her with soothing words.

Delver MacClery, Architect Blanchet, and Primara Okondo rode back to the middle of the column of struggling ascendants.

"Nice work, Langcraw!" called Architect Blanchet. "As for the rest of you. . ." he said, eyeing the whimpering ascendant covered in blisters. The acrid smell of burnt hair and horseflesh curdled in Tara's nose. "Anyone too weak to even approach the Amber is not worthy of its teachings. If you can't ride, then dismount and guide your horses on foot. Make your way to the citrine stairway at the front entrance. Anyone who cannot make it there within the hour will be collected at the menhir's convenience."

"Whenever that might be. . ." Delver MacClery added with a smirk.

In reply, the ascendants circumvented their fallen peer, none daring to make eye contact with him. They worked in groups to guide their horses into the menhir's shadow, where a mass of servants, all clad in heavy cowls, secured their horses. They led the animals up a ramp to elevated stables, worked from the same glinting orange rock as the road's paving stones.

The students gathered in an entry chamber at the citrine stairs' summit. The chamber's ceiling vaulted dozens of feet into the air. The crown of the room boasted a fresco depicting the symbology of the six noble factions. At the center of the painting glimmered a disturbing image: the cosmic trajectory of a planet approaching a nebula of pale purple. Even a mere depiction of Calamity sent a chill through Tara. She looked around at the other ascendants. Most of them bore mussed hair, and sweat cascaded down their brows and necks. They all seemed too rattled to notice the menace looming above.

Before the hour was up, the full mass of ascendants gathered at the top of the stairs, less the man who'd fallen. Architect Blanchet positioned himself at the front of the group.

"Well, everyone," he boomed with pride, "you've made it. To approach the Amber Menhir is a challenge in itself. The landscape has fended off more than a handful of lay militias intent on harming the scholars or impeding their work. Lucky for those lay militias, they were turned away before they arrived."

Milyna Okondo climbed the stairs, whispering to Viktor MacClery. Whatever she said appeared to please him, as he grinned, exposing his canines. The expression made Tara bristle. But he only bowed to Primara Okondo and departed down a corridor extending from the entry chamber. Primara Okondo faced the ascendants and gave the Architect a wink.

"Servants will see to collecting you in a moment," Primara Okondo announced. "They will guide you to your chambers. Don your robes, and behave yourselves. Henceforth, you will have many eyes upon you. Here you will learn how to see and touch the threads that weave the fabric of reality. Today marks the end of your lives as you knew them. From here onward, your aptitudes will add to the river of discoveries produced by this institution." A knowing smile crossed Okondo's lips. "I know you will not let us down."

Tara and Peony exchanged furtive glances. Other ascendants did the same.

"So, sweetlings, let me be the first to say it," Primara Okondo intoned. "Welcome to the Amber Menhir."

CHAPTER 5

Primara Council

C HESA SKULKED AROUND THE room's perimeter between brass sculptures depicting the Amber Menhir's zeniths of discovery. After all, servant feet could never tread upon the mosaic of the continent at the chamber's center. Colored icons dotted the map, depicting currencies the Primaras considered when devising their plans.

She'd spent her tedious afternoon polishing the six Primara thrones. The task of tidying the Amber Cathedra at the room's helm fell to a scholar. Servant skin risked sullying that object too, evidently. Chesa wondered how Ursielle had remained in his post for so long without defiling something so absurd as the begemmed cathedra. She bit her lip as she studied it from a pool of shadow and curled a resentful lip at her interlopers.

Two early-arriving Primaras sat upon their respective thrones. Chesa took extra care to ensure that Amus Clutton-Brock's wine glass remained full. She had filled it only moments earlier, and already it sat empty. Ursielle had conveyed that Amneris Klepsydra, the Primara of the Tilters of the Hourglass in attendance, always refused a second glass.

Amus Clutton-Brock gave Chesa a cheery smile as she brimmed his glass once more. She gave her lips an anxious lick as she watched the ruby drink cascade into his glass.

"You're too kind," he laughed. A perennial rosiness touched the man's cheeks.

Chesa observed nothing of the ambitious politician that her informants conveyed he'd been in his youth. Clutton-Brock more resembled someone's grandfather.

She set the decanter down and started toward the Tilter Primara with a tray of food. Primara Klepsydra provided a dismissive flick of her hand at Chesa and went still. Klepsydra kept her imperious amber eyes focused on something distant. Billowing purple fabric cascaded over her throne. Chesa rolled her eyes at the garment's preposterousness. Tradition ensnared every scholar in one way or another. With luck, Chesa hoped it might strangle them all outright one day.

The Architect Primara studied a notebook in his hand and mouthed something incomprehensible. Every Primara needed to present arguments for an increase in their faction's share of the Harvest. But why Primara Clutton-Brock studied so hard perplexed Chesa. The Architects of Forces luxuriated as the darlings of the Amber Menhir. Everyone knew that. Then again, in a room full of adversaries with their own plots, a misstep endangered much.

The door groaned open. Tafos Anaktisi and Hanson Nash entered together. Nash, the interim Delver Primara, spoke in hushed tones with the Evader Primara. Both carried stacks of documents. Klepsydra did not so much as swivel her gaze; only her eyelashes fluttered. Clutton-Brock eyed the pair over a yellow smile.

"I do not have time to explain the basics of multilevel Harvest economics to you, Nash," chided Anaktisi. "I'm afraid your education will need to be a trial by fire. No better way to learn, really."

Tafos Anaktisi, clad in the trim-cut yellow robes of the Evaders of Death, parted from Delver Nash with a bow. Nash, in his pale grey

Delvers robes, looked about the chamber and swallowed. He looked like prey to Chesa.

"Delver Nash! Wait—pardon me, I suppose it is Primara Nash, for now." Clutton-Brock chortled, gesturing to a seat across the chamber from himself. "The Delver Primara sits just there." Clutton-Brock's smile broadened.

Nash did not return it before taking his seat.

Chesa approached Anaktisi's side. He thrust his empty glass at her with a sniff, keeping his attention on Clutton-Brock as she filled it. Anaktisi cracked his neck, revealing a flash of bruises hidden beneath the neck of his robes. "Everyone slips one day," Anaktisi breathed. He swirled his glass and smirked.

Chesa went to the Delver Primara next. "Wine, my liege?" she offered.

"Oh!" Nash sputtered with a start. "A bit of wine might help my nerves. Fill it and go."

Chesa did before slipping away to attend to the others.

Aurora Kakoff, the elected leader of the Sounders of Echoes, slipped into the chamber with little notice from her peers. She carried a tidy stack of tomes with organizing markers protruding from the edges in a neat line. She nodded toward Klepsydra, who continued to stare off into nothing. Kakoff took her seat beside Clutton-Brock and adjusted her brown robes.

Chesa made her way to the pair of them.

"So nice to see you, Amus," murmured Kakoff.

The old Architect Primara looked up at her and smiled. This version even touched his eyes.

"Have I missed anything, my dear?" asked Kakoff.

"Not yet," Clutton-Brock replied, scanning the room. "Though one wonders where our colleague Primara Okondo has run off to. She's been so needy about our meetings since ceasing her treatments with LaTorre. It's unlike her to be late."

"What a shame it would be if she were absent today. Though, she does have an annoying knack for showing up at moments crucial to her cause," replied Kakoff with a twinkle in her eye. Her gaze lingered on the interim Primara for the Delvers of the Mind.

Nash pulled at his hair as he pored over his notes again and again.

Kakoff cleared her throat. "Now he looks to be out of his element, doesn't he?"

Clutton-Brock winked. "I should say so. A missing Weaver Primara, and an interim Delver Primara amid a meltdown. The gods are generous to us this night."

Chesa emerged from a shadow behind the Architect Primara and filled his glass. Neither Kakoff nor Clutton-Brock appeared to notice her as she slipped to and fro, studying their machinations. If things went well, Chesa would have much to tell the Disciples.

"Is there a protocol for an absent Primara who hasn't organized a proxy?" asked Kakoff with a simper. She gestured towards Delver Nash. "Even Primara Kensington arranged for someone to advocate for the Delvers on his behalf."

"Well. . ." Clutton-Brock chortled. "If Primara Kensington could arrange affairs in overture to a demise he likely did not anticipate, then I cannot see why Primara Okondo should be excused."

Chesa left the pair to offer others food and drink. Each Primara wrote notes in foreign alphabets and in grammar only known by their factions. From her shadow of servitude, she watched their furtive glances and their knowing smiles. To them, she mattered less than an insect, but the smallest insects could still possess powerful stings.

"The chancellor is late—again," said Kakoff. "I cannot see why he gives a speech to the ascendants."

Clutton-Brock shook his head. "Their compliance eases the Harvest. Plus, we don't want any of the little dumplings whining in their letters home," he mused.

Kakoff's face turned flat. "I cannot see why we haven't made it compulsory to read and approve all their mail. The random inspections are insufficient."

"Wine!" called Primara Nash.

The door to the Primara Council Chamber swung open, and the Amber Chancellor strode in with brusk professionalism. He took to the Amber Cathedra at the far end of the room and arranged his amber robes to sit just so.

"Primaras, you honor me with your presence," he boomed. "Primara Nash, I am especially appreciative to see you here."

The interim leader for the Delvers of the Mind looked up from his notes with bloodshot eyes.

"I appreciate you bearing this duty in spite of the loss. We know your faction has suffered much with Liam's death," said the chancellor.

Nash stiffened before replying, "The Delvers have lost an important asset in his passing. I am proud to serve in his stead, if only for now."

Several in attendance adjusted themselves in their seats.

"We are so thankful to have you," the chancellor added. "We will start with cases for transformative research from each faction. Then we'll hear a report on the Harvest. We can conclude with core allocation requests for the next cycle." The chancellor paused as his attention settled on the Weaver Primara's vacant seat. "Has anyone heard from Primara Okondo?"

They all exchanged unreadable glances. It seemed no one welcomed an opportunity to confess their involvement.

"She should be here by now," mused Clutton-Brock. "She was riding with the ascendants, was she not? They arrived hours ago."

"Indeed," replied the chancellor. He slid back in his seat and studied the entryway.

"Send a servant for her," offered Anaktisi, nodding towards Chesa. She flinched away from the sudden onslaught of eyes.

Chesa genuflected. "I would be happy to inquire about Primara Okondo's whereabouts, Masters," she answered, keeping her voice miniscule.

A lie.

"See that someone checks the Weavers' quarters," said the chancellor. "If she doesn't appear, we might adjourn to private meetings to discuss core allocation requests. Organizing a time that suits the entire Primara Council once is onerous enough. We don't have endless time to dispose of Harvest business."

That garnered nods from all.

Chesa might have screamed if the situation had allowed it. She needed to find Okondo fast if she wanted to learn anything about the Harvest. That was, after all, her mission for the night. She held her expression still and departed.

The hall beyond contained a row of servants' desks this time of year. This hour, they sat unoccupied, save for one middle-aged man stooped over a pile of ledgers. Chesa decided a firm approach might serve her particular situation best.

"Pardon me!" she called. "Would you be so kind as to go the Weavers of the Web quarters? Inquire about Okondo's whereabouts, and inform them that her presence is needed here at once. If she is missing, then have the Weavers send someone in her stead."

The man gazed up through thick spectacles and blinked.

"Did you hear me?" said Chesa.

"I, uh. . ." he began, gesturing toward the documents before him like it was some great clerical wall of excuses.

So much for patience.

Chesa seized the man's wrist and dug her nails into his flesh. "I told you, the Amber Chancellor requests Okondo's presence, now!"

The man whimpered as Chesa jerked him from his seat.

"Whatever you say!" he pleaded. "I'm sorry!" He clambered back from Chesa, turned, and ran.

Chesa glanced over her shoulder to the Primara chamber. The door remained motionless. Had she been too loud? She thought not. She peered back at the bolting servant. He fled without further question, so she sidled back to her greater task.

The Amber Chancellor watched her enter, like a sparrow examining an insect. "You're back?" he noted. "Without Primara Okondo."

Chesa kept her eyes down. "I've sent for someone to inquire about her at the Weavers' quarters," she explained. "I didn't wish for you to want for anything while she's found." Chesa hunched her shoulders. Scholars loved meek servants.

"Very well," agreed the chancellor, though he kept his eyes on Chesa long enough to form a worm in her stomach.

"Primara Clutton-Brock, what transformative research do the Architects propose this cycle?" inquired the chancellor.

Clutton-Brock cleared his throat. "A proposed collaboration with the Onyx Menhir aims to convert heat into crystalline energy, to create stones that emit light, or more."

The other Primaras posed several of the politest questions before the Chancellor probed, "Is there any other news from our friends at the Onyx Menhir?"

"A vein of troth crystals was discovered during mining by our collaborators there," added Clutton-Brock.

The Primara Council went still.

"And?" demanded the chancellor.

Amus replied in a cool, reassuring tone, "The Onyx claims to have destroyed the vein. My informants corroborate this narrative, and convey that Silka Strauss, the Onyx Chancellor, holds no other plans for the crystals. As useful a weapon as a troth crystal might be, no one wants a resurgence of muted slavery among scholars."

"That is good to hear," called the chancellor. "Now, let us bring your proposal to a vote. Distribute the voting slips."

Chesa carried a bronze bowl to each Primara for them to deposit their vote. At last, she brought the bowl to the Amber Chancellor, who enumerated the votes without speaking. He burned each piece of parchment upon a candle beside him, which emitted a tendril of colored smoke corresponding to each faction.

"The study you've outlined strikes all as fascinating, Amus," said the chancellor, burning the last slip of parchment. It released purple smoke. "Yet I fear this proposal does not breach the threshold of a transformative study at this time."

Clutton-Brock nodded and took his seat. Chesa studied the expressions of the other Primaras. They all frowned their disapproval. Nash clucked his tongue, while Kakoff dabbed at dimmed eyes.

The next four presentations bore the same sequence. Primara Anaktisi of the Evaders of Death outlined studies to lure out the energies of bracket fungi to heal blood infections. Nash proposed studies aimed to enhance alertness in human subjects for days. Primara Kakoff introduced research to suppress thaumaturgies over designated spaces. Primara Klepsydra of the Tilters gave a dreamy lecture about harnessing the energy of almost worlds.

Some faction leaders argued their proposals with passion and zeal. Others described their proposals as though recalling a forgettable breakfast. Yet others spoke in incomprehensible, dreamy language. None of it mattered. Without exception, each proposal enjoyed a ceremonious rejection.

Chesa stole glimpses at a few slips of parchment as she ferried them. On every one was scrawled a denial of resources, even from the Primaras who spoke passionately for a proposal before the council knifed it in secret. Chesa pondered whether tonight deviated from standard practices, and doubted it.

After the final proposal met its end, the chancellor paused the proceedings to await the Harvest manager.

Nash wandered over to Primaras Clutton-Brock and Kakoff during the break. Chesa followed.

"A wonderful proposal, Amus! Simply amazing!" Nash oozed. "Just imagine the doors that could be opened if we could craft stone that provided illumination! I'm appalled that the proposal was not selected for special funding!"

"Not as appalled as I am about your wonderful research on alertness!" bemoaned Clutton-Block. "I cannot believe anyone would vote against you!"

Every conversation echoed the same. The Primaras caterwauled and lamented the failure of one interesting proposal after another. The obvious hypocrisy of it all left Chesa stunned. No one seemed outraged in the least about their own failed proposal; they saved their philanthropic tears for their colleagues. All the while, the Primaras slathered one another with genial smiles and emotionless doll eyes, save for Klepsydra, who remained physically and politically catatonic in her seat.

Architect Blanchet arrived at last, carrying a stack of parchment cards. He positioned himself at a modest podium near the entrance of the chamber. The Primaras took their seats, and with a small nod from the Amber Chancellor, the accounting began.

"The demographic returns of the Harvest were in line with our expectations. Vassal and Independent Cities alike remain prosperous. A new tuber vegetable developed by the Emerald Menhir has enabled households on poor soil to farm a complete diet. Pregnancies are up, infant mortality is down, and we anticipate increased Harvest collections for the decade to come," Architect Blanchet explained. "Harvest from the noble bloodlines remains within expectations, with some surges from those families sending their heirs, as is customary."

The counsel listened with cool expressions.

"Architect Blanchet," interjected Kakoff. She fidgeted with her brown robes as she spoke. "Do you have any sense of how the enhancements to the saprolite bands impacted the wearers this cycle?"

Now, that caught Chesa off guard.

"Thank you, Primara Kakoff," replied Blanchet. "A quantitative comparison of the new method against the former has not been conducted. Still, by my observations, none of the affected populations noticed an increase in the severity of their tax. Tissue scarring appeared consistent with previous cycles. We didn't ask questions of the wearers, fearing we might tip them off and cause more friction with the Independent Cities. We propose a switch to the new version of the bands for the next Harvest, without notice. That is, if the controlled studies in the anomaly pens corroborate our findings from the field."

Whatever that meant, it seemed important to Chesa. She studied the Primaras for further clues. They all leaned forward in their seats. Even Klepsydra latched her mantis-like stare upon Architect Blanchet.

"If the operation is successful, we expect a sizable increase in the efficiency of the Harvest from the Spiral," Architect Blanchet concluded. "Along with increased fertility, thanks to the Emerald's tuber. Soon the Amber Menhir will be the richest in the Menhir Conclave!"

"Interesting," said the Amber Chancellor. One side of his mouth slid up. "Then comes the question of whether to tilt this discovery to our advantage in silence, or to monetize it and make it available to the other menhirs."

Chesa observed glinting eyes upon several Primaras.

Aurora Kakoff cleared her throat. "Excuse me, Chancellor. You pose an important question. However, I am curious, does the solution need to be so dichotomized?" she probed. "Could we not split the difference? What if we were to produce a flawed variant that we monetize and share, whilst retaining a superior version. . ." Her voice trailed off for a moment as she studied her audience. ". . . for ourselves?"

"An interesting topic," the chancellor replied. "To be discussed in our private meetings together in the coming weeks."

Chesa needed to find a means to insinuate herself into those meetings too. With luck, Ursielle or another Disciple would know how.

Broad smiles bloomed on the face of every Primara, except for Nash. His gaze fixed upon Chesa. Her chest tightened. The last eyes she desired were his. She needed to keep her cool.

". . . and so, we anticipate a saprolite budget nearly fifteen percent greater than the prior cycle. We are distilling the Harvest now. Disbursements will arrive soon," Architect Blanchet concluded before stepping back from the podium.

"Thank you for that," said the chancellor. He exchanged knowing looks with several of the Primaras. "You may go."

Architect Blanchet bowed and departed without further ceremony.

"You there," the chancellor called to Chesa.

She lowered her eyes.

"You can leave too," he commanded. The chancellor turned his attention to the Primaras. "We will adjourn. I'll have someone investigate Okondo's whereabouts."

Chesa genuflected and made to depart. She had drawn within a pace of the exit when a quavering voice sounded from the far end of the room.

"You there!" it called.

Chesa twisted to find Primara Nash approaching.

He drew himself close and spoke in a hushed voice. "Report to the Delvers' quarters tomorrow morning. Be there by first light."

Her hand moved to the pocket where she often kept her bag of pearls, but she caught herself. "As you say," she murmured. Chesa turned, sparing one last glance over her shoulder before leaving.

The interim Delver Primara eyed her back and smiled as she went. If Nash knew something he should not of his predecessor's death, then Chesa needed to sort out a plan, fast.

Halfway back to her quarters, someone stormed down the corridor toward Chesa. It was Primara Okondo. Her crop of blonde curls hung loose. She wore emerald robes sopping with sweat. An ugly series of tears tattered the bottom of her robes, exposing deep scratches on her pale leg.

"Primara Okondo!" called Chesa in surprise. "The others are looking for you! Are you alright?"

Okondo drove past Chesa, fuming unintelligible words under her breath as she went.

Chesa wished she could have witnessed what unfurled in the adjourned meeting next. Whatever happened, she hoped it made them all miserable. They deserved it.

CHAPTER 6

Sensing the Threads

T HE STRAW MATTRESS AND isolated pillow left much to be desired. At least the pillow for each ascendant contained feathers, though resting one's head upon them rewarded the perpetrator with stabs of quills.

Tara sighed as her eyes came to rest on the second bed in her room, knowing its destined occupant for the coming year. Roommates had sat across from one another at the welcome celebration the night prior. Tara had plumbed new depths of self-pity as Lavinia Thalsem took the seat across from her. Lavinia's scowl conveyed that she too might find the assignment less than thrilling. Tara's mother always said to ignore adversity. Well, adversity hath laid her egg, and from it hatched Lavinia.

Seated on the edge of her bed, Tara shamed herself for having assumed Peony might be her roommate. The fact that Tara had deemed it a premonition bore a special sting. But she supposed it did not matter. Lavinia would have to do for now. Though the thought of watching her gloat over flipping coins for a year had Tara moaning.

"What did you think of the Amber Chancellor?" asked Lavinia. She combed her hair before their only mirror.

Tara awaited her turn . . . whenever that might come.

"What do you mean?" she replied.

Lavinia turned. "I expected something grander. Didn't you?"

Tara blinked. "Grander?"

Lavinia sneered with incredulity. "We're the menhir's newest ascendants. Our discoveries, words, and deeds create the future. The chancellor spoke for just a moment and then crept off. Our meal wasn't special either."

True, it all left one feeling like cog in an assembly line. Still, Tara attempted to sound dispassionate. "Formal events are often that way. Anticipation robs them of their glory."

Lavinia scoffed. "Don't go making excuses for them. I intend to alert my family to our treatment. We bleed dearly to support the menhirs. Ascendants are provided this one moment, and it was half-hearted. Shameful!"

Tara disagreed, at least in part. After all, instructors from each of the noble factions had attended. Esteemed residents and visiting scholars had participated too. Tara found the gold-brocaded robes of the Ruby Menhir scholars especially intriguing.

"What subjects do we have today?" demanded Lavinia.

Tara held up the parchment containing the week's schedule. "Thaumaturgical Ethics is first. Then we have the Architects of Forces and Tilters of the Hourglass this afternoon."

"Our classes are side by side," Lavinia noted with a smirk. "I imagine most roommates are wondering who will show aptitudes first, but that isn't a useful question for us. Perhaps the lesson with the Tilters will help foster your aptitudes—assuming you're meant to have them."

Tara cocooned herself in unreadable stillness. Lavinia's smile lessened. At last, she relinquished their mirror with a huff, and Tara took her place. Lavinia loomed nearby, not making any effort to hide her study of Tara.

"Who do you think will be next?" asked Lavinia, apparently not interested in hearing Tara's response as she barreled on. "I suppose it will be Architects and Weavers that show their aptitudes first. That's what they say. I think I was the first Architect in our class. Do you think that means I'll be the strongest? They say the first to express their aptitudes are often the strongest, which wouldn't surprise me."

"That might be." Tara winced. It seemed her bedchamber might need to be avoided henceforth.

After grooming, Lavinia and Tara went to the dining hall together. Tara spotted Peony with little trouble. Her brash makeup and mop of braids contrasted with the sea of black robes. Roland took a position across from Peony, and Derek Arachvelle perched beside them.

"I just don't like layers," Peony explained. "Newer ascendants are stuck beneath older ones. The scholars' chambers are above the ascendants, and the administration's above theirs. It all sends the wrong message."

The other ascendants gaped at Peony's naivete.

"How did you imagine it would be, Peony?" said Lavinia. "Did you think we would occupy the top of the menhir? Did you imagine the nicest housing would fall to you? Of course not. Scholars are here for life. Some of us won't make it through the year." She eyed Peony. "Why waste anything good on something destined for the trash?"

"Weren't you just lamenting the quality of the ascendants' feast?" Tara put in.

Lavinia took a seat near Peony, who, in turn, fixed Lavinia with a scowl.

"I didn't expect royal treatment," countered Peony. "I just don't like the way the menhir is organized. It feels. . ." She paused. "Psychological."

"Well, you'll just need to endure that feeling," Lavinia quipped. "The menhir does not bow to the likes of you. The Bianchis only make their way in society by hawking vices."

Tara flinched at Lavinia's truthful lance, but Peony only rolled her eyes. They ate what remained of their breakfast without speaking.

Their Thaumaturgical Ethics class resided in a complex adjacent to the ascendants' quarters. Black carpets ran down the center of the corridors through the complex, adorned with the symbology of the six noble factions at either hem.

Tara eyed the tapestries, sculptures, and paintings situated in the halls as they went to their first class. She paused before a tapestry of their world as it intercepted a cluster of planetary bodies. Wistful blues and deep purples governed the piece's composition. In the image, their world split apart as it passed through a foreboding constellation of ice and rock.

Someone joined Tara at her side. She turned to find Peony.

"It's beautiful," said Peony, indicating the tapestry. "And awful. I don't know why they'd put it here."

Tara imagined herself flickering in and out of existence as cosmic powers caused everything she knew to fracture and disarticulate. She wondered for a moment if experiencing Calamity would hurt.

"It's here to remind us," Tara replied. "They want you to remember why the menhirs are here. It may be thousands of years off, but our time to discover a solution to Calamity is not limitless. A work just like this one stood over the entryway too."

Roland and a handful of other ascendants paused behind her and Peony.

"Do you really think Calamity is beatable?" asked Peony.

A shiver went up Tara's spine. Few put it just so.

"I hope so," murmured Tara. "Though I suspect it will take a team of thaumaturges. Perhaps the tools for the solution have already been discovered."

"We'd better get going," Peony suggested.

Something in her hushed tone reminded Tara of the old man back in Sandenvale, and the litany of questions shielded from ever being put into words thereafter.

"Right," Tara replied as she pulled herself from the image. "How was your first night with your roommate?" she asked, anxious to distance herself from the topic of Calamity and her thoughts on Sandenvale.

The corner of Peony's mouth quirked up. "I don't have one."

"Don't have what?"

"A roommate."

Frothing envy swept over Tara. The gods had cursed her with Lavinia Thalsem for an entire year, while Peony enjoyed a quiet miracle.

"How did you manage that?" cried Tara.

Peony opened her mouth to speak, but paused and closed it. Tara considered prodding, when a wave of chatter spread over the ascendants ahead. A tangled mass gathered before a door thrice the size of any normal entryway. A daring ascendant at the front knocked.

There came a brief pause before a creaking voice replied, "Enter!"

The ascendants opened the door, revealing two sets of tiered seating opposite each other. A modest central floorspace stood between them. The stairways boasted a treacherous steepness. Nestled against the wall opposite the entry was a scholar. He stooped at a wooden desk flanked by bookshelves. Chalk dusted his emerald robes. The space's muskiness reminded Tara of the libraries back home.

"Be seated, be seated," croaked the man. He gestured to either side of the hall. "Pick a side, and hurry up about it!"

The ascendants did. Tara seated herself midway up a staircase. She watched Peony vault to the opposite side. Her needle heels seemed all the more precarious in her ascent. Peony's easy athleticism somehow annoyed Tara.

Once everyone was seated, the bent scholar stood up with a creak.

"I hope he doesn't die during class," sneered a familiar voice.

Tara turned. Lavinia sat just one row behind her.

"You stand on the shoulders of giants!" announced the old man. A thin sheet of flesh beneath his chin wobbled as he spoke. "You've already taken your first steps to becoming part of the Menhir Conclave and saving the world. You may only be ascendants now, but that is where every great mind started. For time immemorial, the menhirs have identified the greatest challenges in our world and slain them time and again."

A small mote of pride surged in Tara's chest.

The man gazed from student to student. "You are privileged to occupy the greatest menhir of them all. Members of the Amber have produced some of the most important thaumaturgical advancements ever made. And one day, a scholar will make such an important breakthrough as to vanquish Calamity itself, and that scholar will be forever immortalized."

Despite his stature, the man's voice bellowed, ebbed, and flowed. Tara found herself leaning toward him.

"I am Weaver Gregor Peebles," he noted with a small bow. "I am your Thaumaturgical Ethics instructor. I have served here for fifty years. In this course, we will review what the menhirs stand for, why you are here, and why the continent is organized the way it is."

Tara nodded rapturously in concert with her peers.

"I propose we start with a little game." He smiled, approaching his desk. "Who among you can list two of the noble factions within the menhir? Hmm? Raise your hand."

Dozens of hands shot up. The old scholar selected a lantern-jawed ascendant Tara did not recognize.

"Yes, Mr. . . ."

"Abeton."

"Yes. Mr. Abeton. Two factions, if you please."

"Architects of Forces and Weavers of the Web," called the ascendant.

Peebles nodded, and the ascendant grinned with smug satisfaction.

"Indeed, those are the menhir's two largest factions," explained

Weaver Peebles. "But can anyone name the two noble factions with the lowest memberships?"

Fewer hands raised this time, but Tara's rose among them. The man's eyes fell upon her.

"You there!" he called, pointing a knobby finger. "Langcraw, is it?"

Tara held her pride at bay. "Yes, sir. I believe they are the Sounders of Echoes and the Tilters of the Hourglass."

Weaver Peebles smiled before answering, "That is correct. The two least numerous factions are indeed the Sounders of Echoes, whose role it is to defuse troublesome thaumaturgical workings, and the time-wielding Tilters of the Hourglass." The instructor's voice turned severe. "But do not let their obscurity fool you. Sounders and Tilters address questions of cosmic implications. Small numbers do not equate to small importance. If our society exalted only the most abundant forms, we'd be worshiping laypeople!"

An inkpot fell from the scholar's desk with a bang, littering quills across the floor. An animal ambled out from under the desk to study the fallen implements.

Tara gasped, and she was not alone.

It exhibited proportions too large and feral for any ordinary cat. It stood two feet tall or more at its shoulders and possessed bulky limbs. The feline studied the room with bright green eyes split down the middle by slitted pupils. Thick grey fur covered its body. From the base of its back, not one, but two twitching tails emerged. It leaped upon the desktop and turned its eyes to Weaver Peebles.

The room stood still.

"Don't be alarmed," he reassured them.

The almost-cat growled and squinted at its onlookers.

"This is Grizelda, my mau."

The mau rotated its head like an owl to face him and repositioned its paws.

"Mau serve as scholars' defenders. Each faction has cultivated their own breed. This beautiful creature is a Weaver mau."

The mau nudged his hand, prompting the scholar to stroke behind its ears.

"They are not to be underestimated," he warned. "They are fearsome when provoked. You would do well to remember that their station here is above yours."

The mau twitched its ears.

"Enough on that," announced Peebles. He went to shoo the mau away, but the mass of fur narrowed its eyes, and the old man abandoned his plan. "Who can name the final two noble factions?"

He scanned the upper tiers of seating and selected a girl not far from Peony.

"The Evaders and the Delvers," she called.

The old man nodded his agreement. "Nicely done. The Evaders of Death, who work to unlock the keys of immortality, and the Delvers of the Mind, who decode the secrets of our minds." His voice grew dreamy at the last few words, and his expression froze. He blinked with a start. "Each faction takes a different path to defeating Calamity, but no faction resides above another."

Peony raised her hand.

"You there!" called Weaver Peebles. "You've a question?"

Peony's expression wavered. "How did the six factions come to be?"

Peebles smiled. "An excellent question. Thousands of years ago, the continent beseeched its leading intellectuals to address Calamity. The world responded by sending their brightest minds to conference and document the thaumaturgical gifts manifesting in bloodlines across the land. They outlined six core thaumaturgical approaches that could circumvent Calamity and save our world. Those approaches, in time, evolved into the six perfect factions we know today."

"So, there have always been six?" Peony pondered. "How did the scholars know they'd reached the right number?"

Peebles's opaline face hardened. "What do you mean?" His tone sharpened. "What's your name?"

Peony squirmed and looked to the ascendants around her. They avoided her gaze.

"Peony Bianchi," she stammered. "I'm sorry, Weaver Peebles, did I say something rude? I didn't mean to misspeak. I just don't know as much about these topics as the other ascendants. . ."

The old man approached her side of the auditorium, and his eyes softened. He appeared almost relieved. "You ask an interesting theoretical question, Ms. Peony," said Peebles. "However, the initiating scholars of the Menhir Conclave spent decades determining which thaumaturgies could circumvent Calamity. Even if there were a more efficient organization, the world had to begin making progress rather than merely pondering the issue of faction organization. Our system has served us ever since. It isn't a useful question to fret over now about opportunity costs gone by. Do you understand?"

Peony dabbed her brow. "Yes, Weaver Peebles."

The room held still while the old scholar studied Peony. Tara found herself holding her breath too, wishing Peony could just be silent.

"W-Weaver Peebles," came a boy's voice from below. "Do you think all of the six noble factions are equally likely to solve Calamity?"

The old man's gaze shot to Roland. If there existed a line between gallantry and idiocy, Tara thought it must be very gauzy indeed.

"Excuse me?" asked Weaver Peebles, his volume growing.

"I was just curious," Roland continued with a shrug. "P-Peony's question just got me thinking."

Tara felt the color drain from her face.

Veins rose on either side of the old man's temples as he interjected, "No, no, no. We do not know where the next great discoveries will be made! The irrelevant study of one era fosters life-changing advances in the next. History is replete with examples. The only solution. . ." The man turned his attention to the broader class. "The only solution is to study it all. We must make every advancement we can. We must share what we have learned with our brethren, acknowledge those who came before us, and honor them by continuing their legacies!"

Apart from Peony and Roland, every ascendant nodded. Some wept. Wept. Tara's chin nodded too, as if of its own accord. Weaver Peebles's words rang true. Though Tara pitied Peony and Roland for their wanton curiosity, she knew embarrassment to be a harsh but effective teacher.

"You're dismissed," said Weaver Peebles. He shuffled to his desk.

The ascendants filed out in a sea of swishing robes and wet eyes.

Weaver Peebles leaned back on his desk as they went, his breathing heavy, but his eyes remained fixed on Peony.

Their afternoon class with Sila Zaravic, the Architect of Forces instructor, resembled an unmitigated celebration of Lavinia Thalsem's potential. Barring hyperbole to the obscene, Tara feared her roommate stood destined to be the strongest thaumaturge in their cohort. As they walked together to the Tilters of the Hourglass course that afternoon, Tara found herself chewing her lip raw.

"I'm not convinced that Lavinia Thalsem will wear success with humility," mumbled Tara.

"Oh, you think so?" said Roland with a flash of his teeth.

"She's easy enough to ignore," said Peony.

Tara scoffed. "Easy for you to say. You don't have to room with her. All she talks about is her own thaumaturgical strength—except for when she takes time to question my own."

"True," Peony admitted with a frown.

"Tara!" Lavinia called from over their shoulders. "Did you enjoy Architect Zaravic's show?"

Tara, Peony, and Roland exchanged looks.

"Most people don't know how much skill it takes to be an Architect," Lavinia added as she drew up behind them. "I would say I'm excited to learn about the Tilters, but everyone knows they're irrelevant."

Tara pivoted to Lavinia, but Peony grabbed her shoulder. Lavinia stepped back before a lazy smile crossed her face.

"Let's get going," whispered Peony.

Tara followed her, but Lavinia dogged their steps.

"Tilter Avevaios has been boring ascendants for as long as my family can remember." Lavinia laughed. "My grandmother says nothing useful ever came from the mouth of a Tilter of the Hourglass."

Tara's cheeks went hot. Why was she letting this dreary girl bother her?

An ash door with a warped hourglass in stone above it appeared a little away from them.

"Ignore her," said Roland. "S-she just knows that Tilters are rare, and strong Architects are everywhere. She can't stand it. A Tilter shows up once in a century."

It warmed Tara to hear the words come from someone else. Why else would Lavinia, a grown young woman, relish molesting her so?

The ash door opened without a sound. No one stood on the other side. All the ascendants froze before the doorway. Small tables cluttered the windowless room beyond. Canopied stretches of fabric arched in hues of blue, silver, and purple overhead. Cards and dice sat atop the tables. Fewer than a handful of lamps shone, drenching the space in shadows.

"Come in, everyone," intoned a woman's dreamy voice.

Tara joined the surge of ascendants inward. Two seats sat beside each table. Peony and Roland paired off at once, leaving Tara alone. A second later, Lavinia ducked into the seat across from her with a grin.

"I've been looking forward to this," she said.

A scholar drenched in billowing purple robes emerged from a wall, where she had perched unnoticed a moment prior. The folds of her robes dragged behind her as she wove between tables, garnering snickers from several ascendants. A silver mop of braids like Peony's cascaded down the Tilter's back as she studied the ascendants with azure eyes.

"I am Leticia Avevaios," said the Tilter. Her eyes stayed fixed on something unseen before her, giving her a vacant, almost fearful countenance as she lectured.

Lavinia, naturally, rolled her eyes.

"It is the task of the Tilters of the Hourglass to prod the most delicate and elusive of reality's threads," Avevaios murmured. "We see reality on an axis of threads that ensnares all others."

Lavinia snorted.

Avevaios approached. "Tilters see objects not only as they are, but as they have been and could be. We see nigh-realities and almost-events everywhere. Though most are blind to this thaumaturgy, Lavinia Thalsem, it is no laughing matter, I assure you."

Lavinia went rigid.

Tara took her turn to beam at her adversary apparent.

"How'd you know my name?" sniped Lavinia. "Some kind of trick? You know my family?"

"You told me, my dear," said Avevaios. The Tilter fixed Tara with her watery eyes as she grazed tables and chairs with elongated fingers. "When attuned, our minds see the trails left by objects as they pass through time. An adept Tilter can seize those threads and braid them to suit her needs, and our abilities scale when we work together."

The snickers and smiles about the room extinguished.

Peony raised her hand and spoke. "So, the Tilters travel through time? Is that right?"

Gods be good, Peony had learned nothing from her encounter with Weaver Peebles.

"A common misconception, Ms. Bianchi," said the Tilter. "You have no reason to be afraid of such questions here. We have nothing to hide from you."

Tilter Avevaios studied Tara.

"You can't even time travel?" Lavinia chided. "Then why are you called Tilters of the Hourglass? Hourglasses tell time, don't they?"

Tilter Avevaios's attention swiveled to Lavinia.

"We draw upon the past we experienced and those nigh-pasts we almost experienced." Avevaios pinned Lavinia with her huge eyes. "We can learn from these almost-pasts, of what might have happened, but didn't quite. In some special cases, we can veto a first reality in favor of one of its almost-brethren. Though, such feats require great stores of saprolite wine and groups of Tilters in concert. But this is what the Harvest is for."

Lavinia opened her mouth as if to gripe.

As she did, the Tilter whipped a pair of dice from atop Tara's table. They clicked until they landed on a three and a five. Every eye there stared at them, save for Tilter Avevaios's. Her attention remained on Tara.

The ascendants around Tara gasped. Tara broke herself from the Tilter's gaze to find the dice depicting a pair of sixes.

"So what?" said Lavinia.

"Imagine it had been an arrow that struck your diminutive heart, Ms. Thalsem. But in an adjacent probability, the arrow only scraped a rib. Small differences in outcomes are not trivial," replied Avevaios. She nodded at Tara slowly, as if approving some train of thought in Tara's mind.

A pressure grew behind Tara's right eye as she met Avevaios's stare.

"Our aptitudes allow us to audit the webs of time, and on occasion, to spin the threads themselves. Though a Tilter is powerful on her own, her abilities are multiplied by her sisters," Avevaios explained. "Together, we see farther across the veil from our reality into adjacent worlds. And when it serves us, we can draw from those worlds and pull parts of them across the veil." Tilter Avevaios's voice grew hard as iron. "One need not accept the world before them as it is. Learn this from the Tilters if you can, ascendants. When Calamity is solved, it will not be from the workings of isolated scholars, jealously guarding their work. Collaboration is the strongest power any can possess."

Lavinia squirmed.

Tilter Avevaios's eyes flicked to her, and the pressure behind Tara's eye retreated. "Poisonous individualism is the rot of too many scholars. Learn now to see it in yourself, and expunge it."

In the gravid silence that followed, Tara promised herself she would do everything in her power to join the Tilters of the Hourglass.

CHAPTER 7

Predator and Prey

C HESA STARED AT THE ceiling over her bed, enumerating her observations from the Primara Council meeting. Most of all, she dwelled on Delver Nash's—or perhaps Primara Nash's—sudden interest in her. No wise servant desired the interest of a Primara. Not for long. Those sorts of attentions tended to bore holes in their victims.

Chesa needed to be at Nash's room by first light, which came early this time of year, sparing her from further hours of needless fretting. So, she rose, washed, and started on her way. She passed few scholars in the frosty corridors as she went. The runner beneath her feet changed from black to a pale grey as she neared her destination. No grand entryway announced the Delver common room; a nondescript hallway simply ended at it. Chesa searched the space for occupants. The grey-scale furnishings rendered it difficult to spot the mind thaumaturges in their grey robes. The gentle architectural curves and furnishings of the Delver Quarters lulled the senses, allowing the mind thaumaturges to focus their consciousness inward. None of the tubular fireplaces dotting the quarters housed active fires, only embers.

Chesa slipped down the hall to the Primara's chambers opposite the entryway. As she moved, a voice called from one of the side laboratories.

"I can hear you. I know you're there. Please?" the man sobbed.

Chesa winced and tried not to listen as she slipped by. The Delvers assigned a broader definition to the term volunteer.

"I didn't mean to!" the nameless man yelled.

Chesa quickened her step.

A tension wound about her neck as the Primara chambers' doors came into view. Chesa had never liked its ornate carvings and cherry hue. It bore nothing of the Delvers' standard aesthetic. She reached up to knock, when a shout came from within. Chesa leaned in to listen.

"Always a pleasure seeing you too, Weaver Peebles," soothed Primara Nash. "I hope you will feel reassured by our chat. For now, I do not believe your observations are grounds for concern, though I will keep an eye on matters for you. Now, if you would be so kind, I have another matter to attend to."

A croaking voice screeched in answer, "I have lived and served here for as long as you've been alive! I know when there are grounds for concern. And I'm telling you, this is how small problems become great ones. It is unwise to let descension proliferate, no matter its origin. Informing you was charity on my part. That . . . that . . . thing is not something we should have tolerated to begin with. This will bring us trouble, Nash. Mark my words!"

An acidic brightness laced Nash's reply. "Your superstition is noted, and thank you."

The doorknob turned. Chesa whipped herself back and stood up straight. The next moment, Primara Nash stood holding the door for an arch-backed scholar in emerald robes. Purple beds of veins flanked Weaver Peebles's face while his mouth opened and closed with incredulity.

"The menhir is not impervious, Nash, and neither are you! We cannot afford to let saboteurs endure," Peebles huffed. He brushed past Chesa and marched down the hall, muttering to himself.

Chesa held her face still and gave the Primara a placid look.

"Come in," said Nash, gesturing her into the bedchamber.

Chesa took care not to look toward the bathing room where someone had discovered the remains of the previous Delver Primara. She kept her eyes down. Primara Nash touched her back and guided her to stand atop a crimson rug before the bed. A muscle in Chesa's face twitched at his touch. As he closed the door, something hissed like a serpent from behind Chesa. She turned and lifted her hands, ready to defend herself.

There, perched atop a dresser against the wall, curled an orange mau with a white breast. Its forward-folded ears twitched quizzically as it studied her through bisected yellow eyes. Chesa eyed it as it produced another pharyngeal growl. It flexed its claws and flicked its tail against an open box of gilded finery. Chesa's breath caught as she spotted a familiar token. There among the jewels fit for the most privileged scholars sulked her middling delta pearl. She stepped back—right into Primara Nash.

"Don't worry," cooed Nash. "My mau will not harm you. He merely isn't accustomed to so many visitors in the morning. He prefers to sleep in."

Nash approached the mau, which kept its gaze on Chesa. He scratched the animal's chin, and its growls subsided. Then the Primara kissed the mau atop its head and closed the jewelry box. The mau opened its eyes and hissed again, exposing two rows of recurved teeth. Something like saliva ran down its fangs, dripping to the floor. Like every Delver servant, Chesa knew the venom of the resident mau well.

The Primara clucked his tongue as he sat on the edge of the bed, facing Chesa. "They can be moody animals, capricious and flippant about their preferences," the Primara lectured. "It's part of what makes them such wonderful companions. What would the love of an animal mean if it loved everyone?"

Nash paused and stared at Chesa. She felt unsure as to whether he wanted an answer, so she remained silent. Perhaps he would think her stupid. That often served her well.

He gave Chesa a sad smile and answered his own question. "Its love wouldn't mean a thing, Chesa. It would mean it didn't form real bonds."

He clucked his tongue and gave Chesa's body an appraising look. "I'm a bit of the same, really," he drawled, leaning back on the crimson linens that Chesa had mussed only a few weeks earlier. "I form meaningful bonds. I have people whom I like, who do things for me, and those I don't." One side of his mouth quirked.

In reply, Chesa wrapped herself in what she hoped seemed a veil of pathetic, weepy-eyed silence.

"Do you know what I think, Chesa?" he asked. The Primara seemed content to hold a one-sided conversation for now. "I think you're smarter than you look."

Chesa fought not to react.

"You've a knack for those cow-eyed expressions, but I saw you studying me at the Primara meeting. I have learned a bit about you since," he prodded. "I think I could use someone like you. Scholars too often underestimate servants."

She refused to meet his eyes. What was he playing at?

"Most servants are stupid. In the absence of thaumaturgical aptitudes, any servant is weaker than any scholar. Still, servants can move about the menhir with a lower profile than a scholar. I'm being watched these days," he said, offering Chesa a smirk. "People reason that I killed Primara Kensington."

Nash paused and held up a hand. "I didn't. If I had, I would have distracted the cleaning servants the next morning. They discovered the body soon after his could-be suicide, which could have gotten Liam's killer caught. Still, my possible involvement in his death has garnered me respect and fear. Which means, I receive more attention as of late. That binds me. Do you understand what I'm saying?"

A longer silence passed between them.

Nash scoffed at Chesa. "Perhaps you are stupid. But I'm willing to gamble on you yet. I could use your eyes from time to time. In exchange, I'll grant you relief from your normal duties. You can have a bit of free time. Gods know what you would do with it. . ." He laughed. "Do you think such an arrangement could work? Nod your head if you understand."

Chesa nodded.

"Good," he replied. "First, I'd like you to move from the servants' quarters here down to the ascendants' complex. It's warm down there. You'll like it. Second, I'd like you to provide me with a list of any ascendants who manifest the thaumaturgical aptitudes of the Weavers. I'll give you an extra special reward if you can report on their habits and routines. See if any of them are loners. For that matter, provide me with a list of any students who seem like they might be cut off from the rest of the group. Dissenter types."

Nash paused, and Chesa indicated her agreement with a slow nod. Nash's interest in the Weaver ascendants presented an oddity. And loners? Perhaps he intended to impose some kind of compulsion on them. With a loner, there stood less chance that anyone would notice. A few tweaks to the mind, and any dissenter could be the most fanatic loyalist.

"Lastly, I'd like for you to keep an extra special eye on an ascendant who has piqued my interest. Peony Bianchi is a mahogany-skinned girl from a farming bloodline in the nearest portion of the Spiral. Weaver Peebles seems to think she could become a problem. Let me know if you see anything strange." He paused again and scanned Chesa up and down. "Do you think you can handle all that?"

"What should I look for with the Bianchi girl?" she asked.

Primara Nash waved his hand in a dismissive gesture. "I wish I could tell you. The fact of the matter is that some of Peebles's generation are superstitious about ascendants that ask too many questions," he explained, giving her a level look. "Some time ago, a ridiculous myth was spawned among the Independent villages near the Onyx Menhir, that the Menhir Conclave's undoing would come from a scholar of ambiguous identity. The laypeople sincerely believed that a scholar—the Blurred Keystone, they call him—would slay us all." The man laughed more than Chesa deemed warranted. "Silka Strauss at the Onyx Menhir addressed the problem head on, and there's been no rebellion since. Still, the tale rattles the cages of the older generations. Just alert me if you see young Ms. Bianchi drafting plans for an explosive of some kind."

"Very well," Chesa murmured.

"Good," he said, standing up and approaching Chesa. He drew near to her, his face only a few inches from hers. His breath tickled her brow.

She wished to pull back, but she kept her eyes down. A fury in the pit of her stomach blossomed with each of his breaths.

"Good," he whispered as he studied her. "That's all."

Chesa's shoulders sagged. She turned to go.

"Oh, before you go. . ." he purred, granting her a predatory smile. "I think you should thank me."

She froze.

"I think you should let me give you a kiss. What do you say?" Laziness luxuriated in his voice. "Don't be shy."

She went rigid as he bent down to meet her face. His lips just grazed her cheek before he pulled away. Chesa did not react. Her instincts shouted at her to lash out, but the numbers stood against her . . . for now.

"See there?" he said, pulling away. He spoke to her like a child.

"There's more where that came from too, if you do a good a job." He strode over to a table beside the bed. Atop it was another small chest. He unlatched and opened it, revealing a stack of vials, each harboring a small volume of clear liquid. "And Chesa, don't be so demure with me from now on. If I gather that you're frigid or uncompliant, remember that there are a great many other ways a clever scholar could lure you into cooperation." He rolled a few of the vials with a brush of his fingertips and closed the chest. "Now, run along."

Chesa enveloped herself in a guile of serenity and restraint, genuflected, and left. She sensed Nash's eyes on her back as she went. As she closed the door behind her, his mau produced a growl that pealed through the animal's upper register. The sound reminded Chesa of the modest pearl that sat discarded—or not so discarded—among the Primara's belongings.

She retreated down the hall and willed herself not to hear the quiet sobs of the nameless man in the Delvers' lab as she passed. She willed herself to extinguish the gouts of anger and outrage that churned in her too. When she arrived back at her room, she closed the door and spat.

"Try me, Nash, I dare you!" she hissed. "Underestimate me, and I will address you, like I did your predecessor, and leave you mewling for death!"

She stared at herself in her tarnished standing mirror. The practice always calmed her. She recalled her promises to herself. "In time. . ." she recited to her reflection. "In time, even titans will succumb to the great unseen. You plunder and crush your enemies and countless others. But you will not live forever. I will slit open your back and lay my eggs within you, and they will grow. Their poison you will not feel at first, but they will proliferate and mature and metastasize, even if I am slain. And one day, you will stumble, and your efforts to repair my work will be in vain. You may never know my name, but my ilk will form cities and societies most beautiful, fertilized by your remains."

Chesa stared at herself in silence for a time. Her breathing smoothed out. The pain behind her eyes drifted deeper until it vanished. Patience and suppression imbued her sting. The best revenge was an ambitious plan, and plans required quiet preparation. The assignments Primara Nash provided her had blessed her, in a way. If the Bianchi girl rattled Weaver Peebles so, after so little time, perhaps something useful hid therein.

Once quelled, Chesa packed her belongings, tidied her room, and made for her new home. Three hours later, her things stored, she departed on her first reconnaissance mission on the new ascendants.

She spotted a fellow servant in the hall outside her new quarters.

"Excuse me!" Chesa called.

He paused and turned.

"Do you know where I can find the ascendants this afternoon?" she asked.

The man indicated a corridor to the right of a junction ahead. "They're down that way, in class," he said.

"Thank you," replied Chesa. "One further query, if you'll permit it."

The man nodded.

"You wouldn't happen to know the ascendant Peony Bianchi, would you?"

The man shrugged. "Tall. Sweet girl. I doubt she'll make it here long."

"I see," said Chesa. "Do you know if she has any gentlemen she's close to, who would know her well?"

The man scratched his chin. "There's that big fellow she seems close to. By the look of him, he's another Ward boy, I'd say."

"Excellent," said Chesa with a bow. "I know just the sort."

Luddite farmers, all.

She found the ascendants in the Delver classroom. She avoided the doorway and took a position where she could see the lecture floor and the first few tiers of seating.

A fat little man in grey robes stood before the room, lecturing. Chesa knew him to be Pat Lester. He blew his nose into his sleeve. A woman with an oily tangle of dark hair sat strapped into a Delver demonstration chair beside him. She uttered soft, slurring vocalizations of displeasure and wiggled against her restraints.

The Delver paused his lecture and gestured to the woman. "Now, if a low-functioning subject exhibits displeasure from the thaumaturgy, I find it best to sooth them. It makes the business much easier." The man rifled through his robes and plucked out a white blob of sugary candy. "Observe," he continued, placing the candy into her mouth.

Her mewling vocalization subsided at once.

Chesa bared her teeth.

"The candy is sweet, which the subject likes," he explained with a nervous little giggle. "But it also contains a fast-acting sedative to reduce her anxiety. Her defenses too, should a subject retain those."

Fire surged behind Chesa's eyes, but she held still and made at dusting something stupid with a rag.

The woman's thrashing slowed. She wore the red robes of an anomaly.

Chesa caressed one of the puckered scars on her back before catching herself.

Delver Lester pushed a slick of dark hair from his subject's face. A thick ring of raised blisters lined the woman's neck from a Harvest collar. Her loose tongue lolled from her mouth, and she licked aimlessly at her chapped face. She looked toward Chesa with vacant, stupid eyes. Chesa knew the woman from somewhere.

"Scholar LaTorre was once the continent's foremost expert on empathic thaumaturgy," Delver Lester explained. An exaggerated frown spread across his puffy face. "She pioneered workings that now enable the Delvers to sense the emotional states of others, and to help remedy impulsive disorders. The working involves extending the Delver's coconsciousness and integrating it into that of the subject's. Scholar LaTorre reached levels of cerebral intimacy that were unfathomable to the generation before her. Her works might have one day led to direct behavioral remediation in willing subjects, the complete elimination of misdeeds and crimes in lay society. Imagine it!"

Chesa doubted that had served as the research's real purpose.

Lester's voice turned quiet. "But one day, LaTorre slipped as she detangled her consciousness from a subject. LaTorre was, in time, able to exit the maze of the subject's consciousness, but she mangled sensitive regions of her brain during her escape. She has recovered much since then, but she will be forever unable to access her thaumaturgical capabilities. LaTorre's sacrifice teaches us a valuable lesson, ascendants. It is important work we do, but it involves sacrifice."

The ascendants looked on with stunned horror.

LaTorre appeared nothing like the powerful thaumaturge she'd been in life. Had Chesa not known the woman before, she might have thought this husk just another anomaly. Chesa shuddered at the dark metamorphosis.

"It is imperative that we honor the scholars of our past," Delver Lester continued. "Delver LaTorre served as a vanguard of her generation—but she was once in your seat too. And she knew then, like all of you do now, that if something unforeseen ever happened to her, her life would continue on with real meaning. She may not be able to produce thaumaturgical discoveries any longer, but her former works and now her mind serve as a fertile hunting ground for new advancements. She will continue to be a link in the chain of progress!" His voice rang with allegiance. "Each of us must do our part!"

Chesa stiffened and readied herself to depart. Even the trained mind could endure only so much before faltering.

"What happened to LaTorre's subject?" called the voice of a girl Chesa could not see.

Delver Lester's voice took on a theatrical tone of mysticism. "The subject was almost completely unaffected. They resumed their life with only the faintest impacts on their short-term memory. And even that side effect may have come from the mau venom consumed for treatment." Delver Lester seemed to ponder the thought for a moment. "Anywho, the mind is a labyrinth, where some paths lead to danger. Wandering farther than one is ready to can bring disaster. Those of you who develop the gift to traverse the tendrils of the mind, you must take care. Even the most gifted of us can suffer grave errors if we let our guards down. Now, off with you."

Delver Lester turned back to study LaTorre. She stared back at him and opened and closed her mouth with pleasant groans and wet, sugary smacks.

Chesa hurried away. She could not bear to see any more. She could corner the Ward boy for questioning another day.

Lying on her bed that evening, Chesa took stock of the pieces before her. Primara Nash's actions were infuriating, but something she could use, if she could control herself. She could play the role of Nash's prey, for now—a miserable strategy to endure, true, but such situations often bore the sweetest fruit. Nash's smugness would make it all the richer when he realized that the roles he dictated between him and Chesa, of predator and prey, stood switched in truth at the last. Chesa allowed the joy of that future moment to fill her up and sustain her.

CHAPTER 8

Ascending the Ladder

"**T**HIS IS POINTLESS," ANNOUNCED Lavinia. "I don't see why we have to sit here and watch them all fail."

She had a point.

Tara, Lavinia, and Derek stooped together over a dented iron table. The deepest of indentations could have housed a cup of tea. Budding Architects could be dangerous things, which explained why Architect Zaravic's classroom resembled a molten metal shop.

Despite much private pleading with the gods to the contrary, cold sobriety finally compelled Tara to accept Lavinia's thaumaturgical talents. No longer content to flip coins for audiences—which seemed almost quaint, in hindsight—now Lavinia could coerce flames to dance about her hands. More worrisome yet, she hurled stones as large as Roland with breakneck velocity. All the while, as Lavinia's talents blossomed, so too did her air of superiority.

Derek gave Tara a smile, which garnered a scowl from Lavinia. His smile promptly vanished. Despite Lavinia's abuse, Derek maintained an allegiance toward his once-friend, no matter her penchant for abuse. Tara tried not to grace Lavinia's chiding with responses, hoping a lack of fuel might lessen her acrimony. So far, it had not.

Tara resumed gazing at the marble nestled in one of the table's craters. She focused on the space between marble and iron. She tried to push her attention inside that crevice, hoping she might see a flash of thaumaturgical energy. At times, something seemed to flash in that infinitesimal space, but it always turned out to be just another sad mirage.

"Next!" cheered Lavinia. "I'm getting depressed just watching her."

"It's fine," said Tara. She gestured to Derek. "How about you try?"

He fussed with his robes and studied Lavinia before murmuring, "Why not?"

Derek leaned forward and placed his face close to the marble. The sad truth was that most ascendants failed at most thaumaturgical challenges placed before them. He gazed and gazed at the marble for several minutes while Tara and Lavinia watched. His neutral expression eroded into a frown, which deepened by the minute.

"Enough already!" Lavinia laughed. "You're going to hurt yourself."

At least Lavinia waited longer to chastise Derek than anyone else. Could not her delay be deemed a kind of friendship? Derek released a defeated sigh. Tara vowed to herself that if she ever became as talented a Tilter as Lavinia was an Architect, she would be magnanimous toward the less fortunate.

"Some of my family can use force thaumaturgy. I guess it just isn't for me," Derek confessed with a shrug. He avoided Lavinia's gaze and scratched the back of his neck at a series of dark blemishes that he usually favored hiding.

"Some lineages have diverse aptitudes," offered Tara. She avoided staring at his marks. "Perhaps you'll be a Weaver of the Web, or a Sounder of Echoes? There's still plenty of time."

"Stop trying to prop him up," chided Lavinia. "He's never going to succeed if you treat him like a child."

An image of scholars running tests on Derek flashed through Tara's mind, and she flinched. Her thoughts drifted to Delver LaTorre. She'd been a full Delver of the Mind, and look how they treated her. Her vacant expressions and chapped face insinuated themselves into Tara's dreams and each time she closed her eyes. Could the Amber Menhir do something like that to Derek? Maybe so.

"What are you flinching for?" Lavinia snapped at Tara. "He isn't going to nudge that marble, let alone sling it across the room. Save your cowering for when a real Architect is working."

Tara fixed Lavinia with a blank stare and prayed that a variety of ailments might befall her.

Derek turned his attention back to the marble.

"Derek, stop. It's not going to happen," Lavinia sighed.

"It's not as though many ascendants have shown an aptitude until now," Tara countered. "There aren't even a dozen Architects in our cohort yet, and they'll constitute a third of us by the end. And let me remind you, Lavinia, being talented does not entitle you to—"

Lavinia cut Tara off with a peal of laughter. "And maybe the rest of you are only here to help the scholars learn how to weed out failed ascendants? We don't need mediocre thaumaturges to defeat Calamity anyhow."

Derek looked away. Tara opened her mouth to convey a few Larus-unapproved insights about Lavinia, when something struck the ground near her foot with a click. She looked down to find a marble rolling beneath their table.

"I did it?" Peony called from across the room. She turned her beaming smile on Tara. "Sorry, Tara! It had a mind of its own!"

"A fluke," Lavinia groaned with a pang of hot air.

"Can you believe it?!" Peony sang. She faced Roland, who stood beside her at their table. "I'm going to be an Architect! I thought I had to be a Weaver! Everyone in my family is a Weaver. I guess I'm meant to be the black sheep after all!" She laced her arms around him and squeezed.

Lavinia's pale neck flashed red.

Despite her efforts to the contrary, a smile spread across Tara's face too. She lifted a hand to hide it. Peony's glee possessed a genuine infectiousness. The fact that her success upset Lavinia only made it sweeter.

"You've moved a marble," Lavinia grumbled. "I could do that before I arrived."

Peony turned toward Lavinia, and her expression froze. Then she burst out with another squeal of laugher.

Architect Zaravic, their instructor, strode over to them. "Ms. Bianchi!" she noted with icy contempt. "Full of surprises, aren't we? The Architects will be lucky to have you."

Lavinia's brows furrowed into canyons. Almost the entire room examined Peony's success with curses and frowns. Why so many ascendants responded to their classmates' success with bitterness puzzled Tara. Peony's success said nothing about them.

"Well, Lavinia," cooed Tara with no little venom, "it seems you'll be enjoying a great deal more of Peony in your future. Believe me, I know how happy that will make you."

Lavinia stared daggers at Tara.

Something about that filled Tara with warmth. Though, perhaps more so than even that, a sense of relief passed over her that Peony would not become their cohort's second Tilter of the Hourglass. Maybe the gods were not so bad after all.

Peony's jubilance sucked the energy out of the other ascendants for the rest of that day and into the next morning. As they went to their Weaver class the following afternoon, Tara noted that Roland seemed quiet and thoughtful, which wasn't like him. So, she joined him while Peony recounted her recent thaumaturgical surprise to another group of miserable peers.

"Everything alright?" Tara whispered.

"I'm fine," he replied with a shrug. "I was just hoping I'd be able to spend more time with her, ya know? If she became a Weaver, I c-could help her more."

"I see," Tara replied.

Roland's command over life thaumaturgy had revealed itself in their second week, and his progress since had kept pace with Lavinia's.

Peony made her way into the Weaver class, struggling to keep up with her flock of fleeing peers. Tara stole the moment to touch Roland's arm. He paused.

"I know you're disappointed, Roland, but it's important that we be happy for Peony. She's stuck with Lavinia as a colleague," Tara scoffed. "Peony's going to need our support. If you two are meant to be friends, or more, then occupying different noble factions will not stand in your way."

Roland nodded as they entered the greenhouse together. The glass ceiling and exterior walls of the Weaver classroom cast the space in dappled light. Tara took her seat beside Roland and Peony and avoided grazing the vine beside her. One of its huge, foul-smelling flowers loomed just overhead. Tara eyed the sunken troughs of carnivorous plants a few paces away. Weaver Ankathi, their instructor, meandered by to toss a rodent into one of their traps. The plant snapped its green sarcophagus closed, stifling a mousy shriek. Some of her plants could eat a whole mau, Weaver Ankathi said, were one dim enough to venture close.

Cages of birds flaunting iridescent feathers went wild at the sound of the snapping flower. Lavinia looked up from just beneath them and scowled. Their plumage mocked animals who resigned themselves to any one color, though their metabolisms rendered the seats beneath the birds dangerous selections.

A huge grey Weaver mau sat on a table before Lavinia, staring up at the flock. It bore an enterprising expression. Derek sat nearby, watching rat pups covered in protective scales in a tank. Their little eyes conveyed a menacing cunning. Tara preferred to sit by the plants. More peaceful company, for the most part.

Most of the Weaver's menagerie appeared to live on borrowed time. In a glass enclosure across the room luxuriated a predatory lizard, larger than half a dozen men, eyeing its gaudy neighbors. Tara hated passing the bog lizard's enclosure. Though callouses adorned its every appendage, Tara swore that one of its narcoleptic eyes had followed an ascendant once. Even the mau avoided the thing.

Weaver Ankathi touched Tara's shoulder as she slid by, lecturing, "So many beautiful creatures have disappeared from our continent! Without the Weavers' collections, such creatures mightn't have any hope of reestablishment. Worse, once they're gone, their secrets will die with them. Each such event extinguishes solutions to Calamity. Remember, ascendants, there are few challenges for which life has not finessed a solution. We must therefore take care to preserve our living libraries."

Roland just stared at their table, apparently ignoring the lecture.

"It's hard to imagine that, at one point, scholars destroyed imperiled populations of animals and plants just to prevent other scholars from studying them!" Ankathi mused with a frown. She rewarded the mau atop Lavinia's table a pet as she continued. "Now we must struggle to keep enough of each species to prevent the ill effects of inbreeding in our collections."

Several of the ascendants shifted in their seats. Many bloodlines mated cousins in the name of lineage purity.

"Let's see. . ." Weaver Ankathi's voice trailed off. She looked like someone's forgetful aunt. "Yes, that's right. Today we'll be attempting to witness and access the thaumaturgical strands of life where they are most concentrated! You'll be working in pairs."

Tara looked at Roland and Peony. "Don't worry," she sighed. "I'll find someone else." She joined a sharp-jawed ascendant not far from the bog lizard. Alister Coldewine's lineage produced renowned Evaders of Death, whose medical discoveries saved countless lives, as they were fond of reminding others.

"Of course, the threads of life are densest in their early stages," Ankathi explained. "You know, some scholars suggest that the entire aging process comes from the fatigue of unwinding thaumaturgical threads. Sound reasonable to you? The truth is, no one really knows if that's true—but debate is what makes the Weavers the Weavers!" Ankathi simpered at a joke no one else seemed to hear. Then she blinked around at the room and scratched her head.

"Get on with it," carped Alister.

"What was I saying?" Weaver Ankathi fussed with her spectacles. "Seeds!" she yelled. "Seeds are a fine example. All the properties need-ed to create any plant, whether a weed or a towering tree, are thau-maturgically encoded inside a seed. Within these tight encasings are all the instructions necessary to tell the plant where to settle, how to grow, how to protect itself, and when and with whom to mate. It is a wondrous thing!"

Ankathi deposited a seed atop each table.

"The intensity of those young threads," she continued, her tone sly, "is what makes them so easy to witness. To see the threads of life, you must penetrate the innermost sanctum of the organism. Try to bore a hole into its thaumaturgical medulla."

Tara spent a long time staring at her seed and nothing more.

"You take a turn," she said, passing the seed to Alister.

"I know my family's aptitudes, as do you. What's the point in us throwing ourselves against a wall?" Alister sneered. "To show grit? Fine, I'm gritless."

He had a point. Still, Tara decided not to give up.

"Perhaps the exercises prepare us in ways we don't yet realize for our own thaumaturgy? Besides, odd aptitudes do emerge sometimes in otherwise unadulterated families," Tara offered. "Wouldn't you rather be a surprise Weaver than a barren progeny?"

"I won't be barren." He laughed, putting his feet up on the table beside the seed.

Tara did her best to focus on the task, but Peony's laughter from across the room caught her off guard. Roland was coaxing energies into a ball of grass nestled in fertilized broth, causing it to grow before their eyes. Peony marveled as the grass grew inches in seconds. Its growth caused the broth to turn lighter, until it became clear as water.

"Even with thaumaturgy," Ankathi explained, gesturing to Roland's display, "you can't get something from nothing. Altering the strands of life requires drawing upon an existing resource, like fertilizer and water. Though saprolite wine can be used as a proxy for almost any thaumaturgical resource—"

Peony's shriek broke off Ankathi's lecture. Ankathi glared back at Peony and Roland.

"No, don't tell me. I want to see if I can see it on my own." Peony giggled. "I'll tell you when I see them."

Roland's jaw clenched. He took in several breaths and grunted. The original ball of grass in the broth had grown two smaller offshoots, each connected to their progenitor through a gnarled umbilical cord. Peony kneeled and peered through the broth. Her lips compressed, and her eyes narrowed.

"There!" she gasped, pointing at one of the offshoots. "You just touched the threads around that one!"

Roland shot Tara a look. A cluster of ascendants approached the display. Tara hurried to join them.

"Now you touched that one!" Peony shouted.

Ankathi pushed forward, but the cluster of ascendants did not part with ease.

"That one. Now that one! Now you've just touched the same one." Peony pointed at each tiny stalk in turn. The confidence in her voice grew stronger with each declaration.

Roland gave no indication of whether she was correct. Tara could see nothing special in evidence at all.

"What's all the fuss about?" Ankathi interjected. An edge tinged her voice, and the ascendants before her receded.

Heavy rivulets of sweat sloshed down Roland's sloping brow. "She can see where I touch the thaumaturgical threads," he panted. "Even when I hardly touch them. How?"

Ankathi's vacant features went stony. "Let me see," she commanded.

Peony shot Tara an uncertain look. Then she turned her attention back to the grass. "There," she whispered. "Now that one. Now you're touching the big one again."

The lines about Ankathi's eyes deepened. "You are correct, Peony Bianchi. It appears you can see life thaumaturgy in action. That's a wonderful gift. Mr. Ward. . ." Ankathi gave him a serious look. "As for you, it is more traditional to manipulate the thaumaturgies of the plants, not the surrounding unseen organisms. Thank you."

No one spoke for a long moment.

"Weaver Ankathi," Lavinia piped up. Her voice did not possess its usual snide assurance. "Peony can't be doing what she claims. She's an Architect. We all saw her move a marble just yesterday. Her aptitude has already been determined. There's no way she could see threads of life thaumaturgy. They're lying."

"W-we're not tricking anyone," Roland stammered.

"An interesting assertion, Lavinia. But a topic for another day," declared Ankathi. Her tone turned soothing, though Tara noticed sweat accumulating on her brow before she dabbed it away. Ankathi studied the faces of the ascendants. "Enough spectacle for today. I'll clean up here. You're all dismissed. Now."

The ascendants gazed back in shocked silence.

"You heard me. Go. And be quick and quiet about it!" Ankathi shouted.

The ascendants rushed to organize their things and leave. Whispered fragments of scandalized conversation peppered their groups as they went. As Tara exited, the hair on the back of her neck stood up. There, only a few paces away, skulked a slight-framed servant woman, watching the ascendants from the hall. She made a show of dusting a bronze statue of a mau, but her eyes smacked of calculation. Tara shivered.

An ascendant bumped into Tara hard, almost sending her to the floor with a yelp. When she looked up again, the servant had vanished.

Peony and Roland were last to leave. Over their shoulders, Tara spotted Weaver Ankathi. She stared at the exotic grasses, still as any statue. One of her many mau rubbed against her hand, and she pet the animal. It turned its gaze toward Peony and Roland and issued a whining growl.

"Did she say anything to you?" asked Tara in a hushed tone. "I've never heard of anyone wielding two thaumaturgies. Have you, Roland?"

Roland shrugged his giant shoulders. "I haven't," he admitted. "But I don't know much about the menhir, to be honest. It makes better sense to me that Peony would be like her family. Maybe the marble fell on its own?"

"I'm right here. And I didn't imagine anything," Peony interjected. "I didn't trick anyone either. The threads I saw yesterday were almost identical to the ones I saw today."

"I'm not convinced that's possible," said Tara.

Peony glowered. "Both times, the threads shimmered, like starlight, and whipped around so fast that I could barely make them out," she explained.

Tara looked to Roland.

"That's what I see too," Roland confirmed.

Another growl echoed from the Weaver classroom, this one loud enough to make Tara and Roland wince. Two shaggy Weaver mau now sat atop a demonstration table near the entrance to their classroom. They squinted their green eyes toward the ascendants.

"I'm not sure I like those things," Peony breathed.

"I don't blame you," Tara agreed. "Perhaps we can chat more about this another time. I do not like being surveyed by mau, and there is an odd servant around here somewhere that gave me a fright. I'd favor some privacy."

"After the class with the Evaders?" asked Peony.

Tara and Roland offered no objections.

Peony's quarters sans roommate served as the obvious rendezvous point. Her quarters featured the same furnishings as any other, save for having only one bed. But as she often did, Peony could not help but imbue the space with her exuberance. The multicolored pillows, rugs, and wall hangings strewn across the space singed Tara's sensibilities.

"How did you fit all of this prismatic nonsense into one travel chest?" Tara asked. She perched with crossed ankles atop the room's only stool.

"Oh." Peony laughed. "I made all those."

"Made them?!" Tara yowled. "When?"

Roland gave his muted version of amazement, his eyebrows lifting a fragment of an inch. He and Peony sat atop her bed.

A hint of pride touched Peony's voice. "I work on something every night." She stood up and opened her travel chest. "I just stash my supplies in here."

True to her word, multihued fabrics, scissors, and sewing implements crowded the chest's innards.

Tara surveyed the room with renewed appreciation. "But where did you get all of the fabric for these pillows and rugs, and those hangings on the wall?" She gestured to the clusters of flowers sculpted from fabric hanging here and there all around. Some of them resembled roses, others flowering nicos, and others mimicked flowers Tara had only ever seen in their Weaver classroom.

"Well," Peony explained, "I asked one of the servants, Chesa, for an extra pair of sheets or two. She seemed keen to help. I brought scissors and other supplies. Do you think I'll get in trouble for making them?"

"I don't think so," Tara replied. "But I don't know."

Peony looked to Roland, who shrugged.

"I guess it isn't really important," Peony assured herself. "So long as I don't get Chesa in trouble."

Tara stifled an eye roll. She had to remind herself that Peony sincerely meant what she said. Caring for servants Tara could understand, but placing their safety above that of noble bloodlines registered as absurd. But Peony Bianchi stood as no stranger to absurdity. Everyone knew that.

"Weaver Ankathi d-didn't look happy when we left," warned Roland. "She seemed like she had more to say."

"You need to tread carefully, Peony," Tara added. "My mother warned me that not every ascendant leaves here in better shape than they arrived. Some scholars don't like jilting the status quo."

Peony grimaced. "I don't want to upset the scholars. I try not to." She looked down.

Roland inched a bit closer to her. Tara thought he too looked like someone who had a great deal more to say.

112

"Weaver Peebles just doesn't like to be challenged is all." Tara sniffed. "Which is an odd preference for a teacher. Anyhow, avoid him."

"He always calls on me with the most difficult questions. When I get them wrong, I look like an idiot. When I get them right, he only gets more upset with me," Peony murmured.

Anyone with eyes could confirm the same.

"But now that you're a Weaver, Peebles has to treat you better. You'll be a member of his faction," Roland assured her. He placed a hand on her shoulder.

"Maybe," Peony replied. She toyed with the scarlet fringe of a pillow.

Tara examined the pair of them. They seemed like they could use some time alone for a moment.

"I've got some tea in my room," said Tara. "Would either of you care for any?"

They blinked back at her.

"I'll be back," Tara added.

She moved to the door and opened it with a start. There, only a few paces away, loomed Ms. Ash. They met each other's eyes.

"Ms. Ash!" Tara cried. "What're you—"

"Ms. Langcraw, a pleasure," Ms. Ash interjected. "I am afraid I don't have time to catch up. I'm here to fetch Ms. Bianchi."

Her gruff tone caught Tara off guard. "Peony? Now, wait a minute—" she began.

"Ms. Langcraw," the plump servant interrupted, "out of the way, please. I am afraid Primara Okondo will not appreciate delays of any kind."

"Primara Okondo?" Tara sputtered. She stepped aside on instinct without another word.

"Ms. Ash! It's nice to see you," Peony called, though her tone did not sound pleased.

"I'm not here to visit," barked Ms. Ash. "I've been tasked with bringing you to Primara Okondo. The matter is serious. I recommend that you select your most conservative footwear, girl. It's a long way there."

"I see," said Peony. "Can I have a moment?"

"Just a moment," said Ms. Ash. "Ms. Langcraw, Mr. Ward," she growled. "I'm sure you both have studying to do. I know you, Ms. Langcraw, must be anxious to get a head start on your lessons with the Tilters of the Hourglass. One hears things have not been going so well."

Tara gulped. "Not going well? But we've only just arrived!"

Ms. Ash stepped back into the corridor and replied, "I've heard that defense before from people sent away soon after. I do not want that for you."

Roland reached out to Peony and touched her shoulder.

"I'll be fine," whispered Peony.

"I'll be here when you get b-back," Roland replied.

The pair stared at one another long enough for Tara to turn away. Then, without another word, he rose and left. Tara gave Peony a small nod and followed behind him. Whatever the gods had planned for Peony, Tara prayed for their mercy.

CHAPTER 9
A Could-Be Home

S OME CLAIMED TO FIND much fulfillment in servitude. That
always perplexed Lydia Ash. She instead only endured a litany
of orders from pompous incompetents. That time when a long-
demented Weaver of the Web had sentenced her to obtain nineteen
mau molars for "research purposes" stood emblematic in Ms. Ash's
thoughts. Why nineteen? No one could say. Yet like it or not, menhir
protocol required all servants to be obedient, even for imbecilic orders,
and that sculpted ironclad patience in those who survived.

Any fool could see that the Ward boy suffered a fondness for the
Bianchi girl. So, Ms. Ash drew upon her well of patience and quelled
the urge to bark for them to hurry with their departing sentiments. Ms.
Ash liked the Bianchi girl. Though, something about her unsettled the
scholars. In Ms. Ash's decades of service and survival, few ascendants
ever breached the notice of a Primara. Fewer yet survived the affair.

Ms. Ash adjusted her sweaty robes and avoided tapping her foot.
The jaunt down from the Weavers' quarters provided her with more
exercise than her body appreciated. Though agitating at times, her
elderly plumpness paid its own version of dividends. For instance,
attractive young folks, whether servants or scholars, seemed to think
the plump somehow desperate for friendship or less capable of navigat-
ing the intricacies of life. The resulting damage to one's vanity aside,

one could leverage being mentally conflated with someone's beloved aunt to wounding effect.

Still, Ms. Ash tried to be understanding toward the youth. After all, in every novel she knew, the importance of a female character stood precisely proportional to her beauty. Raven-haired buxom beauties with drowning eyes enjoyed inevitable influence and intelligence in every tale. Should she instead bear a keg shape, then either sex work or bar-wenching resided in her very modest future. With models like that, how could anyone suppose anything different?

Ms. Ash pursed her lips as Roland Ward disappeared down the corridor to his room. The Langcraw heiress followed close. She appeared to study Ms. Ash in turn, with a piteous frown. Perhaps she reminded the Langcraw girl of a fat, demented relative cloistered away in some basement or tower . . . again.

Just as Ms. Ash opened her mouth to order the last ascendant to hurry, the girl emerged from her room. Peony Bianchi had donned her black ascendant's robes and pinned her mop of braids into a bun. Her boots boasted a dangerous heel.

Ms. Ash gave them a sympathetic wince. "It's a long way. Are you sure you can manage?"

"I'll be fine," chirped Peony, with just a touch too much shrill.

"So be it," said Ms. Ash. "Follow me, and keep up."

Ms. Ash navigated the halls with swift precision. Apart from the swishing of robes and the rhythmic clicks of the Bianchi girl's heels, they moved together in solemn silence. The faint smell of sulfur that permeated the ascendants' complex dissipated as they climbed. Peony fussed with her robes, but grinned whenever she caught Ms. Ash studying her. The girl had much to learn about donning masks.

They passed by dozens of servants and scholars as they went. All of them deferred the right of way to Ms. Ash. Being the assistant to the Weaver Primara provided an aura of respect. Ms. Ash avoided the eyes of the imperious Delvers of the Mind and did her best to ignore the Evaders of Death as they discussed the thaumaturgical threads of the pancreas. A rigid Sounder of Echoes passed by them, carrying several thought paddocks to the Central Archive.

"I hadn't realized so many scholars lived here," Peony breathed. She made no attempt to suppress her gaping.

Ms. Ash shot her a sideways glance. "Training ascendents is not the primary mission of the menhir."

Two clusters of scholars appeared at a junction ahead. Ms. Ash threw out her arm in front of the girl before she could prevent herself.

"What is it?" said Peony.

"Wait," whispered Ms. Ash.

The two factions positioned themselves on opposite sides of the corridor as they passed. A round-faced Delver mau hissed at the great, shaggy Architect mau when they drew close. Ms. Ash waited for several long moments, even after both groups vanished.

"Best not to get near scholars of different noble factions when they interact, especially these days," Ms. Ash explained. "I've seen a mau disembowel a servant with lightning speed when agitated. I'm not convinced one would spare an ascendant in a moment of heat."

The girl gulped. "As you say," Peony whispered from a parched throat.

They rounded a sharp turn, and the runner beneath them shifted to emerald.

"We're close?" Peony asked, eyeing the runner.

"Not far," confirmed Ms. Ash.

They took one more turn at a smaller junction and entered a corridor with a glass ceiling and walls. An orange waning sun shone through the glass. A few stars fought their way to prominence in the darkening sky. Even in the dimming light, the tenebrous canopy of the Weaver

Forest and its monolithic trees loomed in the distance through a huge crystalline dome.

Even after years of service, Ms. Ash still marveled at the Weavers' quarters. The girl eyed the planetary bodies speckling the sky above and slowed.

"Eyes forward," snapped Ms. Ash. "You're not here to marvel at stars."

She shook her head. "We're going in there?" Peony gestured to the dark forest before them.

"Indeed. Stay close, girl. The Weaver Forest can be unkind to the uninitiated or incompetent," cautioned Ms. Ash.

The carpet runner beneath them gave way to a well-trodden path as they advanced.

The Weaver Forest bore an indefinable climate. Faint breezes moved in currents like rivers through the towering trees. One second, an icy breeze had Ms. Ash's face and hands burning. Paces later, a channel of sultry earthen air choked her with its humidity.

"Where are all these trees from?" asked Peony.

"Everywhere," replied Ms. Ash. "The Weavers have acquired plants and animals from across the continent, and woven thaumaturgies to keep them healthy under glass."

Birds and mammals in wooden cages suspended from branches called down as they passed. Other creatures that slithered, crawled, or leaped unseen in the tangles overhead joined their evening chorus. At the next junction of footpaths, Ms. Ash guided them down a trek illuminated by glass spheres hanging from branches. Peony paused to study one.

"They're insects?" she asked, indicating the sphere.

"Indeed," said Ms. Ash.

The insects inside shot off a wave of pale blue light as Peony brushed their prison.

Ms. Ash subdued a smile. "They're tiny little thaumaturges themselves, in a way."

"I think it would be frightening to see the threads here," Peony said. "So much life all in one area."

"I'm told it can be jarring," warned Ms. Ash. "Some ascendants have harmed themselves irreparably by witnessing them without adequate experience. I've seen what happens to thaumaturges who suffer debilitating injuries. Best not to tempt fate, girl."

Peony promptly stepped back from the sphere of insects and snapped a stick under her heel. A Weaver mau issued a guttural growl in reply from somewhere nearby.

"Best hurry up," hissed Ms. Ash.

The pair doubled their pace.

Ms. Ash took them to the end of insect-lit path and paused at the entrance to the bog. The trees flanking the swamp boasted pale barks and exaggerated buttresses. Trilling choruses of insects produced green light that danced across the ghostly landscape. Their refrains swelled and skittered as Ms. Ash led them. The pair reached a landmass that sloped upward to a dense ring of trees. The Primara and her retinue resided therein.

Ms. Ash steadied her voice, in hopes of giving the girl a sense of stability, however cosmetic. "I'll announce you. You speak when spoken to, and answer their questions. No lies." She paused. "I'll be nearby, but I cannot intercede on your behalf." A pang of concern for the girl lanced through her, but there was little she could do under the circumstances. "Do you understand?" she asked.

Peony swallowed hard, but nodded.

With that, Ms. Ash guided them into the sloping glade.

Four scholars sat in seats sunken into the buttresses of trees. Their smooth bark made it seem like each tree simply acquiesced the space necessary to produce a throne. Peony shot Ms. Ash a searching look. Ms. Ash gestured to the center of the circle of thrones. Peony went.

A man's voice Ms. Ash failed to recognize grumbled in muffled tones, "Why someone like you is so preoccupied with this ridiculous map mystifies me, Okondo. I'll have you know that half of the Onyx still searches—"

"Quiet," Primara Okondo interrupted. "It is time to address more critical matters."

Primara Milyna Okondo luxuriated with her legs cast over an armrest of her throne. She shunned the customary emerald robes of the Weavers in favor of britches cut from a thin fabric and tucked into boots. Only a bejeweled, cinched corset covered her top. She studied the Bianchi girl without blinking. Several Weaver mau perched about her throne, staring at their could-be prey with glowing eyes.

The Primara held a wineglass in her fingertips. She swirled the red liquid inside, producing a soft glow. She turned to Weaver Ankathi, who squatted in a sunken throne nearby. Ankathi too held a glass of wine that produced red light as she sipped from it. Her pupils dilated, and she sighed. Several more mau rubbed against her legs. The layer of fur atop her garment danced in the insectile light. A grey-haired man with a wedge-shaped face sat in the throne to Ankathi's right. Delmar Cutner staired at the Bianchi girl with a grim expression and his jaw clenched. He wore the pale yellow robes of the Evaders of Death. At Evader Cutner's feet lurked a breed of mau that caught the Bianchi girl's eye. She stepped back from it. The creature's hairlessness accentuated its wolfish features. Folds of skin bunched around its mouth, giving it a wizened expression, while bits of sharpened bone pierced out from its spine and rear limbs.

Lysander Sze beamed at the Bianchi girl with a genial smile from his throne. He wore the square-cut pale grey robes of the Delvers of the Mind. He swirled a glass of his own, producing a faint red glow. A pair of impish dimples emerged on his face as he did. Lysander's orange mau purred and rubbed its deformed ears against the man's free hand.

"This is it?" Sze sneered at Ankathi.

Ms. Ash could not suppress a scowl. Sze's presence and that of his Evader counterpart smacked of questioning. But an effective interrogation required that the interrogator discern fact from fiction. Such a task required both a Delver and an Evader to be on hand.

Ms. Ash stepped up beside Peony and spoke in a low voice. "Primara Okondo, I apologize for our long delay. This is Ms. Bia—"

"Peony," Primara Okondo interrupted in a smoldering purr. She drew each word out like it was a luxury. "Of course! It's such a pleasure to make your acquaintance. Ms. Ash, top off my glass."

Ms. Ash darted to the pitcher of saprolite wine behind the Primara.

"Ms. Bianchi, a little birdie informed me that you may be an especially talented ascendant," Primara Okondo cooed as Ms. Ash refilled her glass. "Though I suppose you'll be recruited to a noble faction soon," she corrected. "But I wonder who will induct you." The Primara locked her eyes on the girl. "Of course, I would like to have you here with me and mine among the Weavers of the Web," the Primara said, pursing her rosebud lips. "Yet I fear your heart may be elsewhere. That would be a pity too. I do not know much of you yet, but I can tell we have much in common already."

The Primara cast her eyes down to the girl's flamboyant boots and arched an eyebrow. The corner of her mouth turned up in a sly smirk. Then she spun about in her throne and crossed her legs. The disturbance caused the saprolite wine in her glass to swirl and glow, though not a drop spilled. She sipped from it again, and her pupils flared further.

Peony fretted with the edge of her robe. "An honor to meet you, Primara Okondo."

"The Weavers draw upon the thaumaturgical energies of all life,

Ms. Bianchi," the Primara interrupted. "We understand that hidden in the thaumaturgical secrets of these beings are the solutions to Calamity and all of our world's problems. Did you know that life is found almost everywhere?" The Primara's voice took on an almost erotic tone.

"I suppose so. . ." replied Peony.

"There's nothing to suppose, sweetling," purred Primara Okondo. "Why, hundreds of feet beneath us, the primal forces of our world churn and boil. Architects reason that those mindless, chaotic churnings hold the secret to stabilizing our world in the face of Calamity. But the truth is that the Architects' proposed solutions are as likely to kill us all as they are to save us. A miscalculation on their part could cause our world to veer away from Calamity's orbit and into something even more cosmically murderous." She peered over her glass and flashed a smile. "The Architects are frankly too dim to notice, but just next to those primal forces they study is something else. Do you know what it is?"

Peony hesitated.

"Life," Okondo oozed. "Life clings to those fiery rocks and floats upward on plumes of gas from the earth's depths. Life flourishes in the deepest pits of the ocean, bearing pressures that would collapse any structure the Architects have fashioned. From the world's most arid regions to lands of ceaseless rain, life not only survives, my dear. It prospers."

Ms. Ash moved up behind the girl. She hoped her presence might bring her comfort. Peony's eyes flicked to her for a moment, and her breathing steadied.

Okondo cleared her throat, and some of the playfulness left her voice. "No, Peony, it cannot be denied: the Weavers are without a doubt the greatest of the noble factions. One day, we will discover a thaumaturgy that will allow any organism to pass through the forces of Calamity, and to come out the other side unharmed. We will save our world, which is why we do what we do, and why we know your home will be here with us. Does that sound good, Peony?"

The Bianchi girl glanced at Ms. Ash before she spoke. "I think so."

"That's wonderful to hear. Now, I've asked you here today to see if we are meant to be your forever home," the Primara went on. Her voice turned to a whisper. "Peony, can you provide me with a small assurance, please?"

Ms. Ash's throat went tight.

"Yes?" said Peony. She sounded confused.

"Can you please agree to tell me no lies today?" the Primara asked. The question sounded harmless enough, but Ms. Ash knew harmless questions from scholars were so often the most lethal.

"Yes, Primara Okondo, I can do that," Peony replied. She took another step back, and the heel of her boot sank into the mossy substrate.

"Would you mind if I took some measures to ensure that this is the case? Just as a precaution, of course. I trust you completely, but it is my job to both trust and verify," the Primara purred.

Peony dipped her head in confirmation. "That seems fine."

"Perfect," the Primara cooed, nodding to each of the men flanking her.

The Evader's brow furrowed in thaumaturgical concentration. The girl's body jerked to one side. Her arms and legs strained, and she lurched to her toes. Her mouth opened and closed, though no sounds came. Then the Delver of the Mind closed his eyes. When he opened them again, the Bianchi girl's expression went slack.

Ms. Ash wanted to act. She wanted to do something, but there was nothing she could do but watch . . . for now.

"Ready?" The Primara's voice bore its seductiveness no longer. "Ms. Bianchi, can you truly detect thaumaturgical threads of both force and life?" Okondo commanded.

The girl gave a weak indication with her head. Drool slipped from her mouth. "Yes—"

"Did you have any indication that you could perform these feats prior to your arrival at the menhir?" barked Okondo.

"No?" A note of confusion touched the girl's reply.

"You have never received thaumaturgical training before your arrival at the menhir? Is that true?!" the Primara insisted. She rose from her throne and took several steps toward the incapacitated ascendant.

"No," the girl whimpered.

"Delve her further, please" snapped the Primara, shooting Delver Sze an agitated look.

His reply came, airy and distant. "There's no cerebral indication of deceit."

Okondo turned to the Evader, who nodded without taking his eyes off Peony.

"Ms. Bianchi, have you ever had private contact with any Delver of the Mind, either at the Amber Menhir or prior to your arrival? Have you ever consumed Delver mau venom, or slept with a Delver?"

The Bianchi girl shook her head.

"What about. . ." the Primara thought aloud. "Have you ever had any indication that you might be able to sense the threads of the mind?"

The girl shook her head.

"How long have you been conscious?" Okondo probed.

"Twenty years," Peony breathed. "I'm twenty."

Primara Okondo studied the immobilized ascendant through squinted eyes. "Delver Sze, confirm for me that there is no evidence of thaumaturgical grooming by some meddling Delver. Scan her as hard as you need. I need to be sure that she's untainted."

Delver Sze went quiet for a time. Only the trilling insect choruses and the occasional airy squeak from the Bianchi girl punctuated the silence. Finally, he spoke. "Her brain has not been touched by any

Delver of the Mind." He paused and smirked. "Well, before my tender little visit today."

The Primara sighed and rolled her eyes. Then she looked at each scholar and spoke in a calm, measured voice. "I think we're done here." She turned her attention to Weaver Ankathi. "Are you satisfied now? No more hysteria henceforth?"

The old scholar shrugged. "Only one possibility has been removed. I did not recognize her by her speech, anyhow. Perhaps we can question her family. Bifurcated talents may be something in their blood?" The scholar's tone sounded curious. "If so, we should obtain them all."

The Primara licked her lips. "That would be a wonderful boon," agreed Okondo. "But that is an alluring opportunity for another time. Ms. Bianchi, a final question," she demanded. "Have you any indication that anyone from your family has exhibited talents in more than one thaumaturgical discipline?"

"No," she moaned.

"Release her. I've heard enough," Okondo declared.

As she did, Peony collapsed to the ground. The Evader's and Delver's faces relaxed. Peony released incoherent whimpers.

"Nice work, gentlemen," sighed Okondo. "I think we've ruled out one possible crisis. Unfortunately, there are still too many unknowns to let her go unwatched." The scholars around the Primara nodded their agreement. "If she is merely an ascendent with bifurcated talents, the phenomenon is not unknown. If this is the case, we must do our best to cultivate her talents in both thaumaturgies, while drawing her allegiance to the Weavers. Watch her closely. That includes you, Ms. Ash."

Primara Okondo directed her attention to the Delver. "Ensure her memory of this evening is scrubbed. Assign her as a clerk in the anomaly pens for a time as well."

Okondo turned to the Evader. "Sedate her and provide her some measure of comfort, if you can. Make sure her rest is as painless as possible, without killing her."

The Primara gulped from her glass and waved a hand toward Ms. Ash. "Lydia, another pour. When these scholars are done, return Ms. Bianchi to her quarters, and make sure she remains undisturbed. When she wakes, see that she finds her way to the anomaly pens. Mopping up their feces should keep her busy and remind her of just how bad things can get without powerful friends. . ."

Okondo swirled her wine and studied it for a time as her retinue basked in her contempt.

"One way or another," said Primara Okondo, "we must use this blurred little present to our advantage."

CHAPTER 10

Sedition

L IFE IN THE MENHIR had grown about as close to routine as Tara
imagined it ever could. Lectures, meals, and poring over tomes
on thaumaturgical theory occupied most of their time. More
and more ascendants discovered their aptitudes, and cold anxiety grew
among the others. Day in and day out, Tara witnessed Lavinia's aptitudes crescendo, while her own promise seemed ever more dubious.
Lavinia, of course, spared no opportunity to remind Tara of her inad-
equacy.

Tara and Roland sat across from each other at breakfast, both
wrapped in unaddressed anxiety. The Weaver Primara had summoned
Peony days prior, and only silence had followed since. They'd gone
to Peony's room together, but found it guarded by Weavers with ill-
tempered mau. Servants visited Peony's room from time to time. Ms.
Ash and a young woman with upturned almond eyes visited most
often. Tara caught Roland chatting with the younger one more than
once. But each time Tara or Roland attempted a visit, the guards sent
them away with assurances that Peony rested unharmed. The fact that
anyone would even consider deploying such a conspicuous lie shocked
Tara. Something was amiss. No, Tara realized, a great many things sat
amiss. The scholars simply prevented anyone from inquiring about it.

Tara read over her letter from Larus again and tried to suppress her annoyance that she'd received no such correspondence from her mother. Larus conveyed that the Langcraw estates and her mother remained well. The odd effects of the preceding Harvest appeared behind them. Paranoia prevented Tara from conveying just how bad things stood at the Amber Menhir thus far. Every leader knew that honest writing imperiled one's future, perhaps especially at the menhirs.

Tara frowned at her letter and sighed. Larus had spent her entire life subjugated in one way or another. Yet despite her harboring every reason to pity herself for her station, Larus remained iron-souled, yet innervated by veins of unexpected kindness. Something of Larus's grumpiness echoed in Ms. Ash too, though the latter woman concealed it better. Women like that could only be forged by adversity. Tara wondered if she could ever survive a week in their lives. She doubted it.

Tara glanced up from her letter to find Roland staring at his porridge. Ever muscle on his square face drooped with despondence.

"I can't do it," Tara blurted out. "I can't go watch that man give another insipid lecture about some hypocritical topic of thaumaturgical ethics again, Roland."

Roland's eyes widened.

Tara hushed her voice. "I don't accept that our ethics class is designed to have us debate the nebulous edges of what is and is not acceptable in research. That class is just a brainwashing procedure designed to tell us the way things are and to beat down anyone who doesn't accept it all with rapturous applause. It's the same way in every class. No question goes unpunished. Nothing turns the man purple faster than pressing against his propaganda."

Roland blinked. "We have to go to class," he whispered. "I know you're worried about Peony. But I don't think the scholars would ever really hurt her. She's from a noble bloodline, after all. We d-don't know what happened with the Primara. But when Peony recovers, she'll tell us." His tone bore no hint of irony or heat.

"You don't think Weaver Peebles had anything to do with Peony's sudden absence?" Tara scoffed. "Really?!"

"No," he assured her.

She sighed and examined her letter. Despite efforts to steady herself, the parchment trembled in her hand. She refused to look up at Roland, frightened that he might see her welling up with tears.

"You're okay," Roland soothed her. "P-Peony is going to be okay too. You'll feel better when she's back and your aptitudes start to show. Be patient."

Tara went rigid at the mention of her thaumaturgical aptitudes. Roland reached out to touch her hand, but she pulled it away.

"Don't encourage me," she whispered at last. "I do not often become weepy like this. We can't give it any energy." She took in a breath. "Perhaps I am being irrational, but I'm worried for Peony. I saw her naivete for what it was from the start. I should have done more to prepare her. Instead, I just let her teach me about . . . cards. . ." Tara shook her head. "I shouldn't let myself be seen like this. I apologize."

A minute passed before Roland replied. "You can say anything you want to me, Tara. You don't have to f-feel shame for feeling something. We're all worried about our fates. But things are the way they are here for good reasons. I know it. It'll just take us t-time to understand. We're all going to have growing pains, but we're not having them alone."

Roland's sudden eloquence startled Tara, jilting her back from her sulking pit. "Maybe," she mustered.

"Not maybe," Roland countered. His hand grasped hers. "Remember, I'm here for you."

Founded or not, the farm boy's optimism filled that moment. Tara realized then that she'd underestimated Roland from the start. He was not just some dimwitted bumpkin with a crush on Peony after all. Perhaps in time, Tara pondered, the three of them could become each other's keels . . . maybe.

Weaver Peebles smiled as he surveyed the room before lecture. His glee infected his mau too. The woolly grey beast thrust its body against Peebles's legs and nuzzled his emerald robes.

Tara looked down at the smug pair and seethed.

"Today we probe one of the central pillars of our ethical system: thought paddocks," Peebles began. He shooed the mau from his legs. "When a scholar dies, a living archive of thaumaturgical information vanishes with them. Apart from the Tilters, there are no data to suggest scholars are blessed with prolonged lives. Quite the contrary; accidents often extinguish the lives of the most ambitious and forward-thinking scholars all too soon."

Weaver Peebles's attention settled on where Peony often sat. A grin slicked his face. Tara's face went hot.

"This problem was identified early in the menhirs' establishment," noted Peebles. "The only way to avoid huge losses in knowledge was to create a system that could store, preserve, and protect the discoveries of one generation and transmit them to the next. So, early scholars developed thought paddocks."

Tara adjusted herself in her seat, trying to relieve her agitation.

"Can anyone tell me what language a thought paddock is written in?" asked Weaver Peebles with hint of mischief.

Lavinia raised her hand. Peebles selected her.

"It must be in High Common, right?" she announced.

"Not quite, Lavinia, but explain your rationale." Peebles encouraged Lavinia's incorrect answers more than anyone else's successes.

Lavinia hummed before replying. "High Common would allow members of the noble blood to access the information in thought paddocks, but protect lay society from doing so."

"You make a good point," Peebles cheered. "One of the primary drivers in the design of thought paddocks was to ensure that only trained scholars could access their contents. But your response is incomplete, my dear. Does anyone know what's missing?"

The old man scanned the room. No one offered a guess.

"Reliability in transmission," Weaver Peebles intoned. He clucked his tongue. "The difficulty with both Common and High Common is their rate of change. Vernacular evolution occurs in both languages, which means the discoveries of ages gone risk eventually being lost."

Tara at once appreciated the truth in his claim. Even in the Langcraw libraries, books written in Common a few hundred years prior often bore incomprehensible phrasing. The oldest volumes in High Common suffered the same.

Peebles studied his room. "So, what's the solution?"

No one replied.

Peebles's smile broadened as he basked in the ascendants' fear and ignorance. In his mind, he'd won.

"Linguistic evolution meant that scholars needed to devise a new medium for preserving their discoveries," Peebles explained. "They needed to create a code, sacrosanct from the decaying forces of normal language, and immutable for time immemorial. And the only way to ensure that this code remained untainted was to safeguard its use."

Nods speckled the room.

Peebles's voice crescendoed. "Thus, each noble faction created their own unassailable language to preserve their discoveries. Though learning these languages requires study, doing so connects a scholar to an intellectual network of contributors including all the greatest minds of a faction."

Of all the ascendants, to Tara's surprise, Derek Arachvelle raised his hand. Weaver Peebles paused and acknowledged him.

"Does that mean that different factions can't access each other's works?" asked Derek. Something like concern tinged his question.

Weaver Peebles nodded, causing his fleshy neck to quiver. "An excellent question, Mr. Arachvelle. Of course not. Permitting too many users to access a language risks garbling it. Members of one faction cannot access the threads used by another, anyhow," Peebles clarified. His eyes flicked to Peony's seat once more. "No scholar is permitted to bestow words of allegiance to more than one faction. Cultivating allegiance is one reason why the menhirs cease general instruction after the first year."

Derek's brow furrowed, but he did not question Weaver Peebles.

Whether or not they believed it, everyone knew of Peony's claim to see the threads of life and force. Everyone also appreciated her subsequent disappearance.

"No more questions?" Peebles pouted, with a sly smirk toward Peony's empty seat.

"No, Weaver Peebles," Derek muttered.

Peebles grinned at Derek. "I thought not."

Benches creaked as ascendants adjusted themselves in their seats.

"Actually," called Tara, "I have quite a lot of questions about this content."

Peebles's gaze snapped to her. "Oh?" he hissed.

"W-what are you doing?!" Roland murmured from behind Tara.

She took care not to let her mouth move as she replied, "Showing this wizened old man what it really feels like to be questioned."

"Excuse me, Ms. Langcraw, what's that?" called Peebles.

Tara prevented herself from flinching. "I apologize, Weaver Peebles," she lied. Her defiant heart pounded in her ears. "But how do you know that scholars can't develop aptitudes for more than one thaumaturgical discipline? Forgive me, but doesn't the use of different languages by different factions impede anyone from learning about each other's aptitudes? Or am I misapprehending something?"

132

Peebles's face went taut, though his voice remained saccharine. "We've spent thousands of years within this system, Ms. Langcraw, and we've never observed someone developing a true bifurcation in their talents."

Robes rustled from every corner. Peebles's eyes darted about as his face went scarlet.

"Don't do this, Tara." Roland warned. "It isn't worth it."

"No," Tara replied. "I actually think it is."

"Ms. Langcraw, is it me you're interrogating, or your neighbors?" called Peebles.

"I'm sorry, Weaver Peebles," Tara feigned, "but perhaps it takes more than a year. What if seeing the threads of a second faction takes two years of training, or five? Perhaps thaumaturges of one faction could, at the very least, know more about each other's works if they received more exposure. Why the rigidity? What're you afraid of?"

Stifled gasps came from across the crowd.

Peebles's voice retained its sugary coating, just as bulbous veins emerged on either side of his face. "What a lovely series of questions, Ms. Langcraw. I so appreciate your bravery in raising them. But it was identified many thousands of years ago that an ascendant's gifts emerge within their first year of training. Efforts beyond that are fruitless. Moreover, beginning to touch and manipulate one aspect of thaumaturgy causes the threads within a thaumaturge to undergo an irrevocable change, moving from a geometry of pluripotency to rigidity. This is not some esoteric policy plucked from thin air, Ms. Langcraw. This is thaumaturgical fact. You understand the word 'fact', don't you?"

The ascendants around Tara and Roland leaned away from them.

Weaver Peebles shuffled toward them. His mau sidled up to his side, giving Tara an avid glare. Her mouth dried beneath the mau's gaze. Then she became conscious of her knees for some reason. Bits of her peripheral vision faded as the sounds of the room shrank and the pounding of her heart doubled.

"But Peony can—" she slurred.

Peebles's glossy facade snapped. "That's enough, Ms. Langcraw! Ms. Bianchi displayed nothing more than a false start! Believe me, she does not enjoy the aptitudes of two factions. She is either mistaken, or more likely, she lies! She's been assessed by a Primara, and she'll receive the treatment she deserves for whatever condition she suffers!"

Peebles's mau flexed its claws and growled.

"Besides," Peebles sneered, "haven't you got enough to worry about already, Ms. Langcraw? How have your thaumaturgical aptitudes been developing, hmm?"

The room held its breath in stunned silence. No instructor spoke to an ascendent this way.

Somewhere at the periphery of Tara's senses, Roland murmured, "I'm n-not going to let you do this alone. They can't punish us all." He raised his hand and began speaking loud without acknowledgment. "How do you know that scholars aren't breaking the codes of other factions in secret? M-maybe thaumaturges like Peony are more common than you think?"

Tara's senses surged back into her.

The eyes of both scholar and mau flicked to Roland.

"Why, thank you, Mr. Ward. You raise yet another salient topic. Though, I will not be drawn into another debate with you or anyone regarding Ms. Bianchi!" declared Peebles. He pulled a white sphere a little smaller than a fist from his pocket. "Each thought paddock is impervious to physical forces. They're indestructible. One cannot simply break one open, nor memorize the language of another faction in secret to open one. Opening a thought paddock requires feeding it with thaumaturgical energy specific to the faction that generated it."

"But—" Roland started.

"That's enough! Not only that, boy!" snarled Peebles. He produced a vial of red liquid from his robes. It brightened as he jostled it. "Saprolite wine is the distillation of the energies the menhirs obtain from the Harvest. Without it, one cannot open a thought paddock. The process requires too much energy. It is forbidden to remove any quantity of saprolite wine from a menhir. This too ensures that thought paddocks are only accessible to scholars while at a menhir, and to members of the appropriate faction. No one can just open one up, Mr. Ward."

Benches creaked.

Peebles let out a long breath and waddled back to his desk. His mau followed.

"I'm feeling tired, ascendants," he muttered as he leaned against his desk. "Go."

"Run for it," whispered Roland.

As though in answer, every ascendant leaped to their feet in a stampede, fleeing the exchange.

Peebles's breathing steadied as the ascendants fell over one another, fleeing.

"Ms. Langcraw and Mr. Ward!" Peebles called before Tara could escape. "A word, please?"

It took every bit of Tara's strength to approach the scholar. She thanked the gods that Roland stood beside her as she did.

Weaver Peebles gave them a tight smile. "I would like to thank you both for taking such a keen interest in today's lecture. I so appreciate it when students engage with the material. As it happens, the Central Archive often needs volunteers to reshelve returning thought paddocks. It can be challenging work. I hope you both wouldn't mind if I volunteer you?"

Tara studied the man's expression. She liked libraries well enough, though she doubted any offer made by Weaver Peebles. Especially now.

"Maybe," answered Roland.

"I'm not sure I can," said Tara.

Peebles leaned forward and dropped his voice low. "Now, you listen here, you seditious little shits! I won't take no for an answer. There are always one or two of you dissenting little bastards in every cohort, but this year's festering with your ilk! So, whatever unfulfilled promises or authentic threats I need to make to force your acceptance, assume I said them. Trust that you both have everything to lose. Now, have I made myself clear?"

Roland and Tara answered in unison, "Yes, Weaver Peebles."

"Good!" he cheered. The purple in his face vanished at once. "Now, get!"

Tara followed Roland out. She spared a glance over her shoulder as they went. Both Peebles and his mau stared unblinking at their backs.

In that moment, Larus's chiding voice echoed in Tara's mind: "When one slaps the mau, child, they invite its bite. I hope for your sake you find it worth it."

CHAPTER 11

Caring for the Stock

S OMETIMES IT SEEMED SHE floated outside of her body, watching the comings and goings of caretakers, guards, and well-wishers like some spectral bystander. At other times, events about her moved like a disjointed fever dream, where outcomes preceded the events that caused them. When true consciousness returned to Peony, only one concrete presence pierced the sea of blurs, and that was Ms. Ash.

Peony woke wearing someone else's nightshift. Though sweat slicked her body, she smelled clean. A jolt of panic shot through her. She rose to cover herself, but realized she lay alone in her quarters. She knew she could not keep herself a secret for forever, but the menhir quickly taught one to convey themselves on their own terms, and only sparingly then. That opportunity might have passed her by.

Peony could not recall what had cast her into illness. She scanned her room for clues, but everything appeared as it had been. She went to rise, but only trembled and collapsed. So, she lay there, rested, and listened. More than once, the viperine hiss of mau registered from beyond her door.

After several hours, there came a knock. The door opened to reveal Ms. Ash carrying a tray with a tea kettle, cups, and a bowl of porridge.

She set the tray beside Peony's bed and sat on a tuffet of multicolored pillows.

"It's time you ate something, girl. It's been more than a week," said Ms. Ash. "Don't go saying you're too ill either."

Peony blinked at the food. She ran her tongue over her teeth and opened her mouth to speak, but only managed to cough. Her mouth tasted of rot. Despite her bleariness, she closed it at once.

"Ah, that. . ." noted Ms. Ash. "You've been sucking down sugar water and juice from rags for days. For a while, you couldn't even manage that. I've seen lots of people die who looked better than you before their exit. So, I mean business when I tell you to eat."

Peony reached for one of the cups, but it slipped from her grasp, clattering to its side. Before Peony could react, Ms. Ash rose and began pouring tea in the second cup. She offered it to Peony. She reached for it, but her arm gave way.

"Perhaps it's best I hold the cup and you drink, hmm? The last thing I need is for you to inhale some of this tea and develop an infection. The scholars are keen enough to run studies on you as it is. Let's not give them another reason, hmm?" Ms. Ash chuckled. "Not to mention, if you die now, after all of the work that I've put in, I'll be very cross."

Ms. Ash stuffed pillows behind Peony's back with unfeeling precision. Then she held the cup to Peony's mouth. The scent of peppermint wafted through Peony's sinuses as she sipped. Though the tea contained more sugar than Peony liked, it sent strength surging back into her. A minute later, she held the cup all on her own.

"Best eat something solid too," instructed Ms. Ash. "Trust me, you'll need it."

Peony complied.

They sat together for a time, nurse and patient, while Peony ate. Ms. Ash mixed admonishments and encouragement in equal measure as they did.

When the kettle was empty, Peony finally asked, "What happened? Was I sick? Am I in trouble?"

Ms. Ash's brow knitted. "Sick enough. You had a fever for a week." She let out a breath. "Better to focus on the future, I say. Primara Okondo has requested that you clerk for the Weavers. That's mixed news, if you ask me. I've never heard of someone clerking so soon after their arrival at the menhir. It's demanding work. I don't think your instructors will cut you any slack either." She flashed Peony a sly smile. "Especially Weaver Peebles."

Peony flinched at his name. "You know," she replied, "before I came to the menhir, I got along with most people. For whatever reason, since coming here, I can't seem to make anyone happy." She dabbed at her eyes before mist could gather in them.

"Don't worry about him," Ms. Ash assured her. "With luck, he won't be yours or anyone else's problem for much longer. I'd like to blame his disposition on his age, but he's been like this for as long as I've known him. He's just a bully, and threatened by progressive students. Though, the truth is that most scholars favor the status quo. They resent anything or anyone who jeopardizes it. Just being who you are will anger many."

Peony sighed. "I was so happy to become an Architect, because it meant I'd see less of Weaver Peebles. Now you're telling me all the scholars are the same?"

"Not all of them," countered Ms. Ash with a subdued smile. "Though you'd best learn not to speak ill of any scholar aloud."

"Why not?" asked Peony.

Ms. Ash scoffed. "The network of alliances and false alliances among scholars in the Amber is ever changing. It won't be long before half of the new ascendants are caught up in plots too. Schemes and machinations, girl—those are the real bones of the menhir. Best you realize it now, before you land yourself in even more trouble."

Peony's mind drifted to Lavinia. Ms. Ash's idea of the Amber Menhir seemed like just the sort of place where someone like Lavinia would thrive.

"Ms. Ash?" Peony began. She didn't want to seem vain by asking the question. "Did anyone come to visit me?"

"Indeed," said Ms. Ash with a wink. "The Ward boy, and that icy Langcraw gal. Seems they've become the new targets of Weaver Peebles's fury in your absence too. I'd say you three are peas in a pod now, if you weren't before!"

"Are they in trouble?" asked Peony.

"Not yet, but they've been sentenced to labor of their own," replied Ms. Ash. "Frankly, you might learn a thing or two from them. That Langcraw barely says anything. That gives scholars less to use against her. And that Ward boy, well, I think he's got a great many more thoughts drifting around in his skull than he ever expresses." She lifted three fingers at Peony. "Three years, girl. You can survive anything for three years. Trust me. Take your licks, learn what you can, and escape. You've got a life outside of this place that's worth preserving."

"As you say," whispered Peony, though she doubted her life following her time at the menhir would be as rosy as Ms. Ash assumed.

"I'll leave you to dress yourself," said Ms. Ash. She rose from her tuffet. "Now that you're awake, you're due for orientation for your new assignment. Primara Okondo intends to keep you busy, so that no Architects can meet with you outside of class. Seems she wants to keep you for herself. Between you and me, she'll be having you watched too, so tread lightly." She went to the door, but paused. "We've got to be heading down to the pens soon. I wish I could be more tender with you, girl, but the menhir has slim space for that." Her lips thinned to a line, and she left.

Several mau growled as the door closed behind her.

It surprised Peony to learn that the ascendants' quarters were not the lowest portion of the menhir after all. Ms. Ash explained that the catacombs beneath them contained numerous facilities for research requiring extreme heat or prolonged darkness. Most of the laboratories they passed together bore the symbol of the Architects of Forces. Peony guessed that their goal to create physical barriers to shield the world against Calamity might benefit from extreme testing facilities, like labs beside broiling earth.

"Are all these labs for Architects?" asked Peony.

Ms. Ash answered without looking back. "Not all. For example, these facilities are what attract most visiting scholars to the Amber. Visitors come from almost every faction. No other menhir has anything like these chambers. But the Amber bleeds its guests in exchange for access, though other menhirs do the same with their resources, of course. It's all part of their dance."

After almost an hour of walking, they entered a vast subterranean junction where the roiling earth quieted. One of the halls jutted off from the junction with no doors along its length, save for a pale metal entrance at the far end. No faction's symbol adorned its summit.

Ms. Ash guided them down the length of corridor and paused before the entry. She fixed Peony with a frown. "Beyond this door are the stock pens. Do you know what those are, girl?" she asked.

"I don't," said Peony.

Ms. Ash's jaw clenched. "Do you know what an anomaly is?"

Peony's breath caught. The Amber Menhir had once collected one of her vassals accused of being an anomaly. The Amber sentries had arrived within hours of the charge. Peony couldn't remember the man's face, but she recalled his screams for help. Everyone knew that the menhirs prized anomalies for the insights they provided into the hereditary nature of thaumaturgy. The way the menhirs saw it, their ilk were too dangerous to set free, too valuable to cull, and too interesting to lock up and ignore.

Something in Peony's face must have given her mindset away.

"You're right to be concerned," admitted Ms. Ash. "The stocks beyond this door house the anomalies and other cowed creatures for research. Only a subset of Weavers of the Web and Evaders of Death are permitted to interact with them directly. A few clerks, such as yourself, are trained as technicians."

Peony's mind treated her to flashes of her former vassal's pleas.

"Only a few servants have ever seen inside. From what I hear, it's not pleasant. A colleague of mine will keep an eye on you for me. Stay out of trouble, and tell no one what you see," ordered Ms. Ash. "Is that clear?"

Peony gulped. "I think so."

Ms. Ash inhaled sharply and reached for the knocker at the center of the door.

"Wait!" Peony interrupted.

Ms. Ash froze.

"Wait," Peony breathed. "I know I don't know anything about you. I honestly don't understand how I've gotten here. But my gut tells me that you're a friend, Ms. Ash. A real one. And I could use one of those right now. I owe you my thanks. And I hope I'll have the chance to return the kindness you've shown me."

Lines of concern gathered about Ms. Ash's eyes. "Where you're going, girl, you're going to need more powerful friends than me," she quipped. She grasped the knocker and paused. "But for the small amount it's worth, you've got my help when you need it. There are a few of us watching out for you these days. You're not alone." She rapped the knocker.

Loud thuds and the grinding of a millstone echoed down the hall as the door lurched outward. A low hum, like a colony of mammoth bees, issued from the room beyond. A handsome man of average height appeared in the doorway at once. He bore dark brown hair and darker eyes. The pale yellow robes of the Evaders draped his small frame, and he beamed at them both.

"Ms. Bianchi, I assume?" he asked.

Peony went to answer, but her voice cracked. "And this is Ms. Ash," she choked out.

The man arched an eyebrow at Ms. Ash. "Ah," he said. "You did well bringing her here, Ms. Ash, but you're dismissed. Ms. Bianchi, you follow me. No time to waste!"

"Thank you, my liege," replied Ms. Ash. She genuflected and retreated down the hall.

Peony felt a little smaller without Ms. Ash by her side, more exposed.

"Let me show you around your new home," cheered the Evader with a titter.

Peony entered, and the door closed behind her with a sonorous boom.

Giant glass tubes filled with yellow liquid glowed against the stone walls of the cavernous hall. Gas bubbles glided up the tubes, too slow for the medium to be water. A slumbering human rested within each.

"I am Lyle McCray, the attending scholar of this facility. My research examines how our brains manage and attend to pain. I attend to our anomaly assets to ensure their ethical treatment." McCray paused and gave Peony an appraising look. "It is our responsibility to preserve their useful life expectancy. You will assist."

"I understand," said Peony. "But I'm meant to be clerking for the Weavers. I'm supposed to be assisting with their studies."

"Oh!" McCray answered with a smile. "The Evaders and Weavers enjoy joint stewardship of the anomaly collection. Both provide clerks. You'll be assisting with the Weaver studies in this facility. Come."

McCray guided her through the room of mysterious tubes. The anomalies within them slept, unperturbed by their presence. None of them appeared to be in any pain, much to Peony's relief.

"Evader McCray," Peony began, "how do I tell if an anomaly is in pain when they're asleep?"

The Evader squinted at her with a sideways tilt of his head. "What do you mean?"

Peony gestured to one of the slumbering forms. "They don't appear to exhibit any pain or pleasure to me. Are they in a study now?"

His gaze followed her gesture to the tube nearest them. Then he burst into a wheezing laugh. "Oh, no, Ms. Bianchi. Those are not the subjects we attend to. Those are post-mortem specimen. We keep them in a broth pumped with a gas to prevent them from spoiling."

Peony blinked at the man, appalled, though she held her face still. "They're dead?" she clarified.

"Yes, Ms. Bianchi, those are indeed cadaverous specimen!" McCray snorted. "They're still valuable to us though. Their physiques were intact when they were ethically euthanized, so they're still sound for study. Examine them for yourself. They experienced countless procedures before their passing."

Peony approached the nearest tube. The specimen within hovered only a little above her. It had been female. Its body curled upon itself, naked and hairless, like some larva. Tiny incisions ran along its ribs and abdomen. Several of the wounds bore no signs of healing. Only thread sewn across them prevented the openings from puckering. Peony imagined herself in the anomaly's place, forever suspended in a tube for dispassionate scholars to gaze upon and probe. She winced.

"They're beautiful, aren't they?" McCray breathed. His words rang with reverence. "So peaceful, suspended there. Theirs was a life with real purpose. If you think about it, they each get to live a second life in service to the menhirs. They get to advance the discoveries of this institution for as long as any Tilter of the Hourglass. Some of these specimens will be more influential than many Primaras. One of them could even hold the secret to defeating Calamity." Evader McCray joined Peony before the tube. His lips almost brushed its surface. "I almost envy them."

His tone curdled in Peony's brain. She wondered how McCray had responded when he was first introduced to the cadaverous anomalies. The question disturbed her.

Evader McCray's lips parted as he stared at the suspended corpse.

"Evader McCray?" Peony whispered. "Are you okay?"

He shook his head. "If you think these are amazing, then wait until you see the living specimens! Have you eaten?" he asked.

"Not much," she replied.

"Good!" He chuckled. "Some find their early trips down here to be trying to their constitution. Only some though. I often take my meals here among the specimens. It relaxes me. It's where I get my best ideas." He met her eyes. "You'll check on the status of each anomaly each time you're here. You'll record any evidence of their discomfort, even if it's only suspected. You'll remove the remains of any perished specimen too. Anomalies in prolonged pain, and that aren't part of a study that requires it, must be euthanized." He cleared his throat. "Follow me."

Peony gulped, but followed.

McCray turned to her and chirped, "Don't worry, Ms. Bianchi. I'm the one tasked with administering retirements." He pantomimed chiseling a blade into the point between his eye and the bridge of his nose. "Our data convey that it's all painless for them."

At the far end of the entry hall resided a network of corridors lined with chambers containing small clusters of anomalies.

McCray's energy and zeal drew Peony's attention to him, despite her queasy stomach. "The lowest tier of anomalies is the Yellow Group. Yellow anomalies are used for studding and breeding." He winked at her. "An Evader transfers the ejaculate for the female's safety. Anomalies aren't so great at mounting each other on their own anymore. Weavers sometimes assist us, though that's always a pain!" He paused, as if anticipating a laugh. "Anyway, ejaculate is special, because it's responsive to both life and medicinal thaumaturgies. The fact that we can't sort out where it belongs is why we still know so little about it. Those things can be political."

Peony noted the yellow icon above several of the doors. Repetitive, rhythmic vocalizations reverberated from within.

A simper escaped Evader McCray. "You know, it's a well-kept secret, but some noble bloodlines require studding out to anomalies here. Tilters of the Hourglass, for example, often have fertility troubles. Their little temporal manipulations preserve most of their bodies, but their ovaries wither faster than the rest." A note of tenderness touched the man's voice before it returned to its usual brightness. "Anyway, we get requests for ejaculate from time to time. So, don't be surprised. Never a dull moment down here!"

Ledgers written out on parchment hung beside each door. A matrix of letters indicated the condition of each of anomaly during their previous checks.

"The Orange Group experiences momentary pain, for example, when we insert canula or take tissue samples or blood," McCray explained. "Yellow Anomalies transition to Orange Anomalies as needed. After Orange specimen have undergone several procedures, they can get fearful. When that happens, we transition them to Red. So, try and be gentle with the Orange; nobody wants to deal with a whiner that cowers too much." He paused and opened an observation slat in a door bearing an orange icon.

"I'm not sure I need to see inside just yet—" Peony began.

"Nonsense!" he cheered. "Observe! Most pens have observation windows." He indicated the grated hole in the door. "Make sure you look around for each specimen before entering. Sometimes they like to hide against the anterior wall and hug at you when you enter. They can be crafty!"

"Right," breathed Peony.

"Look!" he insisted.

Peony swallowed and peered through the slat. Three anomalies tottered inside in crimson robes, two men and a woman Peony recognized. A haphazard rosette, like a simple daisy, stood painted in rusty-hued slicks on the wall beside her. A small swarm of flies danced about it. She stood in a pool of desiccated blood. A rivulet ran down one of her legs as she swayed. Peony pulled back from the door.

"That woman's not an anomaly. That's Delver LaTorre!" Peony hissed. "She's in here like the rest?"

McCray clucked his tongue. "If a scholar experiences significant brain damage, then they transition to the anomaly pens. I admit, it's too bad about Savanna. I liked her. She seemed kind, you know, for a Delver. Anyway, Primara Anaktisi insisted that she be moved to the Maroon Group, so she'll probably not be around much longer. I don't know why he's taken an interest, but there it is!" McCray rolled his eyes.

"Has. . ." Peony breathed. "Has she been painting the wall with b-blood?"

"Again. . ." McCray sighed. "I've already had to move her several times to clean up her messes."

"What?!" cried Peony.

"Oh, don't worry!" he assured her. "There aren't too many artists around these parts. That annoying trait is rather unique to Ms. LaTorre. But don't be too impressed; she paints the same thing again and again. I wouldn't say she's getting any better either." He paused for another laugh.

"Whatever you say," replied Peony.

McCray sighed and opened the door. He gestured for Peony to enter.

None of the anomalies seemed to notice their could-be path to escape. One of the men faced away from the doorway, motionless. Another sat against the wall, staring at the open entry with a blank expression. Savanna rocked to and fro, making a forceful, phonetic "shh" over and over. Flies cavorted around her.

"We try to keep males and females separate to prevent unplanned couplings." McCray giggled. "Gravid females are kept on their own. But the males in here have been castrated, so they don't count."

Peony closed her gaping mouth.

"I know there's a lot to learn, but you'll get it all." McCray patronized her with an encouraging smile. "'Gravid' means 'pregnant,' but the term is typically reserved for animals, anomalies, and other specimens."

He guided them out and then down a hall where the doors stood farther apart. No observation slats resided in any of them.

"Are there no anomalies in these rooms?" asked Peony.

"These are the Red and Maroon Groups," said McCray. "Both are subject to prolonged pain during thaumaturgical procedures. But the Red Group are permitted relief to reduce their stress. The Maroon Group are not. Usually, that means pain is the focus of the project." The delighted scholar gestured at one of the doors with a maroon icon. "We're supposed to euthanize an anomaly after it's been used in three Maroon investigations, though sometimes we tickle that rule, if a scholar insists."

"Of course," said Peony. She wished she could be anywhere else.

"Do you have any questions?" chirped McCray.

Peony wracked her brain for something to say, but only achieved, "Why do some of the doors have no slats?"

"Ah, good eye!" McCray congratulated her. "Those are laboratories where active thaumaturgical studies with Red and Maroon Groups are ongoing. We can't have the clerks disturbing those, now, can we?"

Evidently not, and for that, Peony was thankful.

Hours later, as promised, McCray sat cross-legged at the foot of a yellow tube back in the main room. He watched bubbles creep up the massive cylinder while he ate his sandwich and hummed to himself. Peony wondered whether he hummed to help fill the awkward silence she found herself unable to fill.

Peony spent her afternoon cleaning up excrement and shuttling anomalies from one space to another. Later, McCray sentenced her to feeding the anomalies. Many of them suffered broken teeth and creamy lesions on their tongues and cheeks. McCray showed Peony how to examine them for decubitus ulcers, which could tunnel in sedentary specimen.

"You'll learn which of our little friends are the lazy ones!" McCray laughed as he patted her on the shoulder.

In the early evening, several Weavers arrived with chests of saprolite bracelets for Peony to administer.

"These saprolite bands go on the Red and Maroon Groups. Write down the number of each band on the anomaly's care sheet," instructed McCray. "The bands have been assigned at random, except for this one." He lifted one especially dark band of garnets from a chest. "This one's for Savanna."

As she placed the bands on the anomalies, Peony realized about half produced a faint glow as they contacted their host's skin. Though Peony pitied the anomalies, by the end of her day, their whines and unspoken requests to hug her shrank into the background. They smiled when her beaded braids clicked. So, she swayed her head often to pacify them as she worked.

When she finished with the bands, McCray dismissed Peony. She climbed back to her room with no little haste. At home again among the rainbow hues of her creations, she tried to distract herself from what she'd seen that day, though nothing worked. Again and again, her instincts treated her to the insight that someone like her did not belong in the menhir—and things that did not fit into the menhir's schemes died, or much worse.

CHAPTER 12
Procedural Safeguards

PERCHED ON HER BED alone, Tara reminded herself that the gods were not always evil. Lavinia remained away at her private lessons with the Architects, again, and for that, Tara gave thanks. Fueled by her private lessons and catapulting success, Lavinia had grown twice as insufferable, but then, Tara saw her half as much. Life, as always, displayed a mixture of give and take.

Tara practiced one-sided hands of Veils and Poisons on her bed, Peony's favorite card game, though Peony had refused to play even a single hand since her unceremonious return to classes. Tara's precision with deciphering a hand's rarity developed further each day, which helped her to deploy more competitive bids in her mock games. Peony had once said that the cards played in prior rounds were also important to consider, but Tara found that accounting too complicated . . . for now.

A soft knock came at the door. When Tara opened it, there stood the strange little servant woman Tara had seen lurking about the ascendants' quarters for weeks. Roland Ward towered beside her. The woman wore her robes cinched, but with her cowl pulled up over her hair. She greeted Tara with a customary genuflection.

"My liege, you are needed at the Central Archive," intoned the servant.

Tara studied her. The idea of enduring a nameless interloper amid all their other problems troubled Tara. So, she decided to address the matter.

"I've seen you often," Tara noted. She bowed her head and lowered her eyes, both rare honorifics for lay citizens. "I am Tara Langcraw."

The woman murmured, "An honor to serve, Master."

Tara added, "You already know Roland Ward. I've seen you two speaking in the halls."

Roland shrugged. The servant only genuflected again.

Tara cleared her throat. "Would you honor me with your name? I would like to know you better."

The servant recoiled at the question before answering, "Chesa, my liege. Forgive me, but please, we must be going."

Something about Chesa's dark eyes seemed at odds with her meek choreography to Tara. Tara wagered that Chesa hid things of far greater value than her mere name.

"As you say," replied Tara, though she eyed Chesa. "Lead the way."

Tara let Chesa guide them, but gestured for Roland to hold back. He did. When a sizable gap emerged between them and Chesa, Tara whispered, "I want to thank you, Roland, for sticking up for me with Weaver Peebles during lecture the other day. I don't know why I decided to act like that. I put us both in this mess. I owe you an apology."

Roland took in a deep breath and let it out. "It's okay."

"Forgive me for intruding," Tara went on, "but what do you and Chesa talk about when you're alone?"

"Oh, um, she asks about Peony," explained Roland. "And you. She asks how the other ascendants t-treat us, and which ascendants are friends with which."

"That kind of curiosity doesn't strike you as odd?" asked Tara. "A bit invasive?"

"No?" said Roland. "She's been nice to Peony, getting her those bedsheets for her art projects. And Chesa's helping me get gardening supplies for some seeds I brought from home too."

Tara eyed the servant's back before replying. "Careful what you say to her, Roland. Appearances can be deceiving. We cannot know to whom a servant reports. We've got to do our best to protect Peony, and ourselves, for that matter, thanks to me. Peony has only just re-appeared, and she's been quiet. We need to tread lightly."

Roland inhaled sharply, but nodded.

Mitzi Scrivener, the lead archivist and a Sounder of Echoes, awaited Roland and Tara by the entryway to the Central Archive. Its white metal doorway glowed as bright as any thought paddock. Tara recalled seeing Sounder Scrivener at the welcome ceremony months prior. Her pale brown eyes dissected the three of them as they approached. She spoke in a brisk contralto that matched her imposing height.

"Ms. Langcraw and Mr. Ward, I assume?" she said.

The pair bowed.

Scrivener gestured to the door behind her. "At the Central Archive, security and order are the keys to success. Remember that, and you will do well here."

"Security?" asked Tara. Order made good sense to her for a library, but security?

"From scholars," Scrivener clarified with a sniff.

"What do you mean?" asked Roland. "Which scholars?"

"Bah! Don't be so softheaded, Mr. Ward," Scrivener replied with a shake of her head. She adjusted her brown robes. "Not every scholar focuses on advancing their own studies. Some reason that it is not enough to succeed; others must fail. There is only so much

Harvest, after all, and ailing factions, whatever the reason, receive fewer resources."

"Scholars would steal thought paddocks just to h-hurt each other?" asked Roland.

Scrivener rolled her eyes, "They would, and have. Don't fool yourself, Mr. Ward. There have been more intellectual genocides here than any historian dares recount."

Tara kept her features devoid of emotion. She examined Chesa and caught the woman smiling.

"Thankfully, in the last few centuries, we've grown more effective at preventing such behavior," Scrivener reassured them. Her words turned clipped. "Scholars can engage in whatever political dances they like outside my archive. But in here, I'm in charge. You two will follow my instructions when inside my walls. The Central Archive is not of any noble faction. Its archivists give that up to serve. Yet to be an archivist also offers protection from the dance outside our walls. Neutrality is an outstanding defense, my dears."

Chesa choked.

"You!" snapped Scrivener, gesturing to Chesa. "You're free to leave."

Chesa withdrew with haste like some scuttling rat.

Scrivener eyed her back as she departed. Then she turned to Roland and Tara. "Now, to rid you two of thaumaturgies."

Roland and Tara exchanged blank expressions.

"Thaumaturgies?" asked Tara.

"Factions send clerks with all kinds of compulsions and observational working on them," Sounder Scrivener explained. "Usually, the ascendant has no idea that they've been manipulated. Moreover, it was a Delver servant who brought you here, which draws its own concerns. . ."

Roland grimaced at Tara. She returned his apologetic gesture with her haughtiest nod. It felt good to be right about someone's character.

"Now," announced Scrivener, "close your eyes and tilt your head back."

Tara followed the order, though the posture disoriented her.

Sounder Scrivener dropped a bead of water from a glass vial on the tip of Tara's nose. She flinched as the icy bead cascaded down her face. Scrivener repeated the process several more times. In each case, the droplet cascaded along a subtly different path. When she finished, she fixed Tara with a stony look.

"The Sounders' magic leverages entropy," she explained. "Most thaumaturgy creates order. One of the first lessons that a Sounder of Echoes learns is to jilt that delicate order with a little strategic chaos."

"It's that simple?" asked Tara.

"Simple?" Scrivener exclaimed. "You try it!" She arched a disapproving brown eyebrow before repeating the waterdrop procedure on Roland. When she concluded, she attended to the gleaming entryway behind her.

"Each of the three entry concentric portals requires that the entrant verify their noble faction," said Scrivener.

"How?" asked Roland.

"With a bit of blood. Like so." Sounder Scrivener produced a needle from her robes and jabbed one of her fingers. Then she pressed the blood droplet against a darker metal panel beside the entryway. The door jutted inward with a hiss. "Not so bad, really," said Scrivener. She handed the needle to Tara.

Tara studied the room beyond. At the far end of the white, glowing room stood another door, same as the first, save for a dark metal panel beside it. A moment later, the first door closed with a thwomp of suction.

"Ms. Langcraw, you first," ordered Scrivener. "You'll need to apply fresh blood at each door. Once the blood begins to clot, the system will no longer deem it viable. We've had an incident or two of someone attempting to use post-mortem blood."

Roland's face went pale.

"I've bestowed a thread of thaumaturgy that will allow you to enter, Ms. Langcraw, despite your having no thaumaturgical aptitudes as of yet," Scrivener explained.

Tara grimaced at the mention of her thaumaturgical shortcomings and stared at the needle. It appeared a small thing, really, jousting with one's finger. Still, something about it challenged Tara's self-preservation instincts.

Scrivener gave her a level look. "Go!"

Tara pressed the needle with reluctance into her finger until blood welled around the wound. Then she touched her finger to the panel, and the door hissed open. She paused and wondered what noble faction the system sensed her to be. A Tilter? A Sounder of Echoes? If the system identified her as a Tilter, then perhaps it meant she yet harbored a real aptitude. Right?

"Don't dawdle," chided Scrivener.

Tara advanced, repeating the same process as the second and then the third door. Two gleaming white chambers later, Tara emerged into a vast illuminated room. Roland lumbered up beside her seconds later. Endless rows of pale white stands stood before them. Upon the stands rested thousands or even hundreds of thousands of unassuming white orbs. The entire space glimmered a blemishless white, lit by the sea of thought paddocks. Tara knew in some abstract way that the Amber Menhir housed thousands of scholars and had existed for centuries. It followed that the number of discoveries archived would be vast. Yet the sight of it all humbled her still.

"Good!" cheered Scrivener as she joined the pair. The door sucked closed behind her. "I always like to see people's first impressions. Working in a place of grandeur can cause one to take it for granted."

"How many are there?" whispered Tara.

Even her whisper echoed in the stark vastness of the Central Archive. Tara noted that.

Scrivener smiled. "It's impossible to say for sure, Ms. Langcraw. New discoveries are logged almost daily. But I'm afraid you've got more processing matters to attend to." She gestured behind Tara and Roland.

They turned and gaped. Behind them sat dozens of wagon-sized metallic bins that overflowed with thought paddocks.

"These all need to be returned, and their corresponding sections need auditing," said Scrivener. "You two will see a lot of this place, and there is always much work to be done."

They spent their first few days in the archive returning thought paddocks to their proper places. Replacing a thought paddock only required setting the orb in its allocated groove. Removing a thought paddock, by contrast, required fueling the orb with a thread of thaumaturgical energy of the corresponding noble faction. Thus, Delvers of the Mind fueled their stands with threads of mind thaumaturgy, and so on.

"No amount of force, be it physical or thaumaturgical, can release a thought paddock from its binding," Scrivener explained. "Few veins of the ore necessary to create thought paddocks exist on the continent, and the Onyx Menhir is charged with their safekeeping."

Though Tara found replacing thought paddocks tedious to the utmost degree, it granted precious time away from the other ascendants—who, it seemed, relished reminding her of her lack of aptitudes more and more each day.

Tara blew out a breath as she surveyed the ransacked section on "Introductory Life Thaumaturgy and Plant Mobilization" before her. Well over half of the thought paddocks remained missing, despite her having searched high and low for them for days. As Tara fumbled to replace one of the few recovered thought paddocks, a throaty growl echoed from somewhere nearby. Tara glanced about, but saw nothing. She hated working in a section when one of the guardian mau took notice of her. She hated the Weaver mau most, perhaps because they reminded her of Weaver Peebles. She steeled herself and decided to work in another section, closer to Roland. Once a mau noticed you, they often became incessant. Another human's presence provided a primal comfort under those circumstances.

Tara ferried her tray of thought paddocks up to the Delver section. There, not one, but several round-faced Delver mau with their misshapen ears greeted her. She angled her path away from the animals, who rumbled at her as she passed. One of them let out a spittle-soaked hiss. She danced further away from the beasts, nearly dropping her tray of thought paddocks as she did. It appeared that all the guardian mau stood on edge today.

"Excuse me!" called a scholar's voice from behind her.

Tara turned to find Delver MacClery approaching her. The red-haired Delver who'd made a sport of harassing Peony back in Sandenvale glowered at her. Tara kept her face still.

"This befuddling place! Where is the section on perceptual biases?" snapped the Delver.

Tara waved for him to follow without speaking and guided him to the proper section.

He sniffed down his nose at her. "It's obviously all been moved since I was last here!"

Tara ignored the absurd accusation. "Please let me know if you need anything else at all," she murmured as she made for her escape.

Scholars seemed to know little of the Central Archive, and Delvers less than any other faction.

Tara returned to her task of replacing thought paddocks only a little away from Roland, though she had resumed work for only a few moments when a snide voice screeched from behind her.

"You're missing two of the thought paddocks I need from this section," whined MacClery. "This is outrageous!"

Tara ignored the familiar complaint. Roland did not so much as raise his head from the section on "Neural Empathy and Behavioral Remediation."

"He complains about two missing paddocks!" whispered Tara.

"W-we're missing a lot more than that in this section," Roland admitted.

Tara sighed. "Scrivener says the popularity of research topics changes all the time. Seems you've found a popular one."

"I guess," replied Roland. "B-but the same was true with the Architects' section on 'Extreme Planetary Bodies' yesterday, and the Evader section on 'Bowel Infections' earlier today."

"An odd combination, wouldn't you say?" remarked Tara. "Maybe someone's breeding virulent bowel infections to jettison into the heavens?"

Roland grinned.

"There just aren't enough archivists or clerks to keep up with demand," concluded Tara. "The section on 'Introductory Life Thaumaturgy' was picked clean. Though, I suppose that's to be expected for a faction as numerous as them."

"Maybe so," said Roland.

"I intend to log a complaint with my Primara!" MacClery called to no one in particular. "I will not stand for this!"

Tara looked down at her tray of thought paddocks and let out a pained breath.

"Why don't we cut out early today?" asked Roland. "If someone says something, you can b-blame me."

Tara opened her mouth to object, but Roland cut her off.

"Come on," he said. He rose and took Tara's tray of thought paddocks, setting it aside. "We've earned it."

"Fine," Tara sighed. "But just this once."

They descended to the lower level and took a path that navigated them away from the desks of several keen-eyed archivists.

"What do you mean, you don't have any of the thought paddocks on 'Deep Empathy and the Sedated Mind'?" screamed yet another Delver of the Mind. This one Tara knew well. Delver Nadmenny enjoyed the record of being the Central Archive's most persistent thorn under heel. "The section on 'Behavioral Remediation' is a wasteland too!"

Tara reasoned he could only be one or two rows over from them, by the sound of his voice. She raised a finger to her lips to remind Roland to remain silent as they crept. True to Tara's impression, just three rows over, Delver Nadmenny and Sounder Scrivener stood toe to toe. Both planted defiant hands on their hips.

"Thought paddocks are often checked out, Delver Nadmenny," countered Scrivener. "You must be patient. When a thought paddock is unavailable, a scholar often takes a few related works as an alternative. This means some sections can be sparse from time to time."

"Nonsense!" snarled Nadmenny. "None of these thought paddocks have been here for months! I've been here countless times, and received the same worthless excuses." His voice echoed through the facility. "If this issue isn't addressed somehow, and soon, I will take this matter to the Amber Chancellor himself!" He turned as if having delivered a lethal blow and strode away with the clicking of imperious boots.

Scrivener followed behind him, without the theatricality.

Tara touched Roland's shoulder. "Better to let them go before we exit ourselves, hmm?" she whispered.

Roland nodded.

Just then, the hair on Tara's arms rose, and she turned, expecting to find another guardian mau stalking them. Instead, a tall woman in billowing aubergine robes stared at them with huge eyes from the far end of the row. By her robes alone, Tara knew her as one of the Tilters of the Hourglass, though she traveled alone. Not a common sighting. She studied Tara with huge amber insectile eyes. Just as Tara's gaze met hers, the woman glided away without a sound.

Tara glanced at the nearest shelf of thought paddocks and sighed. "Of course we decide to hide in the Tilters' section." She covered her eyes and tried not to groan. "I must be such a disappointment to them."

"Who?" said Roland.

"Too many people to count," Tara remarked. "Let's get going."

They drew within paces of their exit when Scrivener boomed, "Roland! Tara!" She strode up to them. "I'm afraid Nadmenny has become more than a nuisance. Tomorrow, please audit the sections he's been complaining about. We need to see if the matter is as bad as he thinks."

So, the next day Tara and Roland spent their afternoon crouched and cross-legged as they scoured the Delver sections.

It took little time for Roland to spot the problem. Though slow of speech, he navigated the archive system as fast as any archivist. "Nadmenny's right," Roland admitted. "I can't find any of the w-works by Panirovo, LaTorre, or Otvlech. And they're the most prolific scholars in this section."

"Strange," said Tara as she scanned her notes. "What were those names again?"

Roland repeated them as she examined her list of missing thought paddocks.

"I can't find any by those authors either," noted Tara. "They're more than half of the missing studies from my section. Do you suppose someone's hoarding them?"

Roland studied his ledger before answering, "I d-don't know. We'll just have to tell Scrivener and see."

An hour later, they delivered their report.

"The Delver Primara will address the matter," replied Scrivener. She seemed reluctant to accept blame for the issue. "It's his faction that removed the items, and now it's his scholars that request them. Sometimes there are rifts within a noble faction, and those are to be handled internally. Not our problem."

Tara took care choosing her words. "Is it unusual to be missing so many thought paddocks from one noble faction?"

Scrivener pursed her lips. "Not especially. Though it definitely isn't common to have the entire life's work of several related authors go missing all at once."

"I see," said Tara. She exchanged looks with Roland.

"I'll handle the matter from here," Scrivener assured them. "I'll see that Chesa relays the issue to the Delver Primara for us. They know each other well. . ."

"Chesa?" Tara blurted out.

"Yes," said Scrivener. "The one who brought you here the first day."

Tara caught Roland's attention and mouthed the words, "We're in trouble!"

He grimaced.

"Well, thank you, Sounder Scrivener," Tara oozed with feigned positivity. "Time we should be going."

Tara waited until several corridors resided between them and the Central Archive before she whirled on Roland. "You cannot share any more information with Chesa."

"I c-can't just cut people off like that, Tara," said Roland. "I d-don't have it in me."

"Well, you'd better start!" countered Tara. "Chesa's been rather inquisitive, wouldn't you say? Now we've learned she has close ties with the Delvers—who, I must remind you, are not known for being especially . . . honest. . . And that's among scholars!"

Roland shrugged. "We c-can't blame a servant for the behavior of the scholars they serve."

Larus's face sprung into Tara's mind, and then, strangely, Ms. Ash's.

"There's some truth to that," Tara admitted. "But all the same, I'd ask you to guard what you say to Chesa until Peony's in better sorts, and we're all on better footing. Can you do that?"

Roland studied his feet. "Do you really think Chesa's some kind of spy?"

"Yes," answered Tara, without any hint of irony or restraint. "Didn't you hear Scrivener? That woman's a badger, and even she distrusts the Delvers. Not only that, but Chesa is close to the very pinnacle of their duplicitous faction: the Primara himself!"

"Maybe. . ." Roland drew out the word like some reluctant child.

"Bah!" scolded Tara. "Maybe nothing. We saw what happened with Peony when she just grazed the attention of the Weaver Primara. Peony's been almost catatonic since. And that's when Peony's not slaving away in the anomaly pens, which she says precious little about!"

"I get your point," Roland mumbled.

"It suffices to say, none of us stands to benefit from garnering the attention of another Primara," Tara concluded.

"Alright, alright," mumbled Roland. But then his face twisted up with something like pained thoughtfulness. "Assuming we haven't interested another Primara already." He shrugged.

Tara's mind raced as she traced the lines of possible cause and effect between the Delver Primara, Weaver Peebles, Primara Okondo, Chesa, Lavinia, and a dozen or more of their peers.

"Oh no, Roland. . ." she whispered. "I'm concerned you might be right."

CHAPTER 13

The Disciples of the Shadow

"**W**HERE IS CHESA? SHE'S late," cursed Ms. Ash.

Each Disciple sat upon a modest tri-legged stool, wrapped in robes with their cowls raised. Ms. Ash fussed with her sleeves and tried to calm herself.

"She was tasked by the archivists to deliver a letter to the Delver Primara," replied Ursielle. "She could be much delayed. We all know the unscrupulous nature of Primara Nash."

Next to Ursielle, a rail-thin man with sparrow eyes and a prominent nose leaned forward on his stool. "Each moment here is a risk I'm not sure we can afford," he spat. "Chesa is sloppy. With the new saprolite band study, there are Weavers and Evaders with requests at the anomaly pens at all hours. I cannot afford to be missing. I'd like to reiterate my view that it was unwise to recruit Chesa. Never mind her penchant for assassination."

"Patience, please, Mortimer," tempered Ms. Ash. "We can afford a moment longer. Chesa has earned her place among us."

Mortimer ran his fingers through his hair in flurried movements and huffed. Ms. Ash studied him. The man acted like a child sometimes. He cleared his throat several times, one of his favored nervous gestures.

"We cannot simply wait out the time that Primara Nash needs for another indiscretion," Mortimer snarled. "The mortality rates in the anomaly pens are astronomical, and the scholars are irritable. Moreover, there's a gut infection spreading through the stock, and I've got containment protocols to execute."

Ms. Ash opened her mouth to speak, when the door creaked. The entire room assumed complete stillness. Chesa slipped through the door and into the abandoned dining space.

Ursielle Hedrigal released his breath, causing bits of his girth to jiggle. "Chesa, so good you're here! We feared the worst!"

Chesa slid into an empty stool.

Urseille nodded to Ms. Ash and continued, "In the interest of time, let us proceed. I will begin with my report, if that will do?"

The Disciples issued confirmational gestures.

"Though the final decisions on resource allocation came late," Ursielle explained, "I can confirm that the Weavers of the Web have landed an upset. They will enjoy a thirty-percent increase over their last season's allocation. That, plus a ten-percent increase in the budget for the Evaders of Death, came at crippling costs to the Architects. The Delvers incurred a small decrease in their budget too, but one they view as tolerable, in light of the slashes to the Architects' schemes."

Mortimer leaned forward. "A thirty-percent increase? What happened?"

Ursielle sighed. "Amus Clutton-Brock confessed to the Amber Chancellor that he deliberately waylaid Primara Okondo before the last council meeting. It could not have been more effective for the Weavers. It seems the tug-of-war between the two has ended. The tides have turned for the first time in institutional memory."

"Confessed?" Chesa breathed, her tone incredulous. "Amus? He's gone senile at last!"

"What about the alliance between the Weavers and the Delvers of the Mind?" asked Ms. Ash. "Is there any hint that these events have changed that trajectory?"

Creaking stools adulterated the silence that followed.

"You are wise to raise the point," said Ursielle with a grimace. "It seems the Delvers have distanced themselves from the Weavers, for the time being. The demise of Primara Kensington—thank you, Chesa—linked with an herbal overdose piqued the interest of the more paranoid Delvers. The newest Disciple can speak more to that point." He gestured to Chesa.

A languid smile spread across her face. "There is a great deal of distrust in the Delver ranks towards the Weavers in the wake of Liam's death. They were hopeful that the Tilters' investigation would shed light on the event. . ."

There came a louder cacophony of unsettled stools.

Ursielle cleared his throat. "I am delighted to convey that the Tilters were brought to bear on that topic. The chronosequence audit was led by none other than Primara Klepsydra. All eleven Tilters were called in as soon as possible. Still, they proved incapable of extending their gaze far enough to observe the event itself."

Several attendees released their breath.

Ursielle turned to Ms. Ash. "Lydia."

Ms. Ash held her voice steady. "In other matters, the Bianchi girl does truly exhibit a bifurcation in thaumaturgical talents. I've heard senior Weavers refer to the mythology of the Blurred Keystone when speaking of her. Not good for the girl's longevity. Weaver Peebles has become quite the rabble-rouser about the matter. Scholars I thought ignorant of the tale speak of it openly. The girl has become an object of fascination for Primara Okondo in particular, who has taken to tutoring her personally. The issue is complex."

"Is there a record somewhere of the last bifurcation in an ascendant?" asked Ursielle.

Ms. Ash pursed her lips. "Primara Okondo met with several archivists about the matter. Seems the standard practice has been to neutralize such ascendants and transition them to the anomaly pens for captive study."

Gamaliel let out a gasp.

Ms. Ash prevented an eye roll before continuing, "It seems Primara Okondo is either playing with her food, or she plans to intercede on the girl's behalf. I cannot tell which. The swell in the power of the Weavers has caused the Primara's behavior to become less predictable. If Okondo intends to save the Bianchi girl, then her choice to have Ms. Bianchi toil in the anomaly pens is intriguing. Perhaps having her witness the fate the Primara might save her from is meant to inspire loyalty?"

"Perhaps," said Ursielle, sounding concerned. "A loyal Weaver who knows the workings of force thaumaturgy well enough to retrieve and read Architect thought paddocks would make an interesting pet for Okondo." He pursed his lips.

"Finally," Ms. Ash went on, "there is the issue of Saturnalia on the horizon. The passing of the baton from the Architects to the Weavers with lengthening days could cause even more mischief among the Weavers. I expect they'll soon be as bad as the Delvers."

"If you learn anything specific, Lydia, report it to me promptly for distribution," said Ursielle. He turned his gaze to Mortimer. "Mr. Palmer, how go the anomaly pens?"

Mortimer fidgeted with his robes as he spoke. "The saprolite band project has overtaken the facility. The adverse effects on the anomalies are. . ." He paused. ". . . most severe."

Chesa scoffed, "Architect Blanchet conveyed at the Primara Council meeting that the new bands had no detectable effects."

Mortimer laughed. "Someone has lied, or is simply ignorant. A Disciple of the Shadow must learn to detect both." He smirked at

Chesa. "I haven't finished organizing the data, but it appears the new bands milk far more energy from their bearers. The enhanced lethality is clear. Some scholars are arguing that mortality will be lower in lay society, where nutrition is better, but no one knows for sure. Evader McCray has petitioned the Amber Chancellor to administer the new saprolite bands in perpetuity on anomalies in the Maroon Group between their other studies. He's asked for those resources to be proprietary to the Evaders of Death, naturally."

The report made Ms. Ash's innards squirm.

"It is a dark thing McCray proposes," said Ursielle, brushing his chin with a hand. "I'll do my best to ensure the proposal is denied."

"Is the data safeguarded?" asked Gamaliel Stork. "Could you get access to it?"

Mortimer nodded.

Gamaliel held himself a little taller. "Then could you obscure the greater effects of the new bands? If they're no better than the former versions, perhaps we can dismantle any grounds for the switch? Why kill the dairy cow with a new technique that produces no more milk?"

Mortimer inclined his chin. "Not a bad idea. Not bad at all. . . And from the mouth of dear, sweet Gamaliel too. . . I'll see what I can do."

"Superb," said Ursielle. "Chesa?"

Chesa's eyes sparkled. "The Delvers infight more than ever. One subset is preoccupied with determining whether the Weavers murdered Liam. Everyone knew of his fondness for dreamflower, but the sudden accident smells fishy to some. Liam's plans to create a more lasting alliance with the Weavers are viewed by many Delvers as a ploy by the Weavers to murder him and destabilize the faction. They see the decrease in the Delvers' Harvest allocation as corroborative evidence. Naturally, the surge in allocation to the Weavers further drives this belief."

Ms. Ash leaned forward. "So, our plan with Liam Kensington

appears to have worked. A bridge within the Amber has been broken, some might say," she offered with a smirk. "A broken Amber means less suffering for all its subjects."

A smile touched the eyes of several Disciples.

"What does the new Primara, Nash, think about Liam's death?" asked Mortimer.

Chesa fixed Mortimer with a glare. "Nash's dispositions align with the other major faction within the Delvers. They're indifferent. Nash seems content to ignore or even cultivate rumors of his own involvement. The rumors garner him respect, and fear, and often both. Respect and fear are commodities that trade with excellent liquidity among the scholars, particularly the Delvers," Chesa crooned. "He is not much concerned with the Weavers. The tall poppy so often gets mowed. Conspicuous winning, Primara Okondo may soon find, is a fine way to lose."

The Disciples exchanged serious looks.

Ms. Ash took a small sense of pride in Chesa's insights. The other Disciples could view Chesa's penchant for violence however they would, but no one could contest her ability to intuit the plots of scholars. It took a predator to understand predators, or so Ms. Ash decided.

"Primara Nash is not wrong," said Ursielle. "An upset as large as the Weavers' will not go unanswered. Wise Primara do not discount the long-term effects of their machinations for immediate wins."

Chesa sneered.

"Is there anything else?" asked Ms. Ash.

"Yes," cooed Chesa. "Nash has taken an interest in ascendants that show talents in life thaumaturgy. He requested a list of them, along with reports of their activities. I've provided him with edited notes. Perhaps he fears the Weavers will become too numerous? He's also taken an interest in Peony Bianchi. That makes for two captivated Primaras. He too hinted at a myth of a messianic Blurred Keystone. Evidently,

Weaver Peebles, and perhaps others, believe the girl could become a rallying point for subversion."

Ursielle's jaw clenched. She already had.

"We must keep an extra special eye on Ms. Bianchi. It is worrisome that the scholars see the same potential in her as we do," said Ursielle. "Has someone seen to intercepting her mail?"

Ms. Ash interjected, "On that matter, I can confirm that the Bianchi girl has received no mail. At first, I supposed there might be troubles in the Independent Cities again, but my informants confirm that is not the case. Interestingly, both Primara Nash and Primara Okondo have placed similar requests to intercept Ms. Bianchi's correspondence."

"Interesting. . ." mused Ursielle.

"Primara Okondo has sent word to the Bianchi estates asking for more information about Peony's upbringing, but received no reply," said Ms. Ash.

"None?" Ursielle's brows scaled his forehead. "In response to a Primara?"

"Indeed," considered Ms. Ash. "Seems the Bianchi family is willing to risk much to remain tight-lipped about young Peony."

"On the topic of Primara Nash. . ." Chesa put in. "The newly appointed Primara has thrice now threatened me with vials of the Delver mau venom." She sniffed. "He's made it known that he has more direct means of obtaining my sexual compliance if I continue to resist. There were dozens of vials in a chest in his chambers. That's far too much for mere personal use, I'd say, and milking a mau is not a task I suspect one accomplishes on one's own. We should be on the lookout for poisonings."

The Disciples exchanged worried looks.

"These are disturbing things to hear," mused Ursielle. "I'm inclined to agree with your conclusions, Chesa." He looked at a short, pale-skinned man with light-colored eyes and bright red-orange hair. "Gamaliel, what of the Architects of Forces? How have they responded to these events?"

The little man took stock of the room. "Not well. I've never seen the Architects in such upheaval. No one anticipated Amus's confession. None of the other Architects have admitted to knowing of a plot against Primara Okondo. The decreased Harvest will be crippling. Many whisper their doubts of Amus Clutton-Brock's suitability as Primara. After two uncontested decades, even those close to him now say he's too old."

"Do you think he will step down willingly?" asked Ms. Ash.

Chesa sneered beneath serpentine eyes. "More likely he'll be escorted out by an enterprising ally."

Everyone paused. Gamaliel opened his mouth as though to challenge Chesa's claim, but closed it. Chesa's sinuous smile broadened, revealing a sliver of pearly teeth.

"It is unclear," said Gamaliel. "Two months ago, I would have predicted that Clutton-Brock would step down at a zenith of strength for the Architects, amiably. No Architects want a leadership change amid political weakness. Now. . ." Gamaliel's voice went thready. "It seems he's facing mutiny. He denies that his mind is slipping. He becomes combative whenever the topic is raised. He loses allies with each outburst." Gamaliel leaned back, looking pained.

"Do you have any idea of who might lead a coup within the Architects?" said Ms. Ash.

Gamaliel exhaled slowly. "Perhaps Chiaki Ono? She's met with all his vocal critics. She's organized meetings with officials from other noble factions too. Amus hates her with a passion. She paints him as a conservative anachronism. Meanwhile, Amus claims Chiaki is responsible for the disappearance of almost two dozen Architect servants for some secret project of hers. No one can say for sure."

Ursielle turned to Rachel Bourke. "How have the Evaders responded to these political waves?"

Rachel tucked a bit of her flaxen hair behind an ear and narrowed her eyes as she replied, "The Evaders bide their time, hedging their bets for now, but they see the tides turning against the Architects as a secular trend."

The Disciples turned to Ms. Ash, as though anticipating orders.

"First things first," barked Ms. Ash. "We must each see that our factions learn of the Evaders' plans to sap the anomalies perpetually. Scholars that rely on anomalies for their research will not be pleased, and no one will favor giving another faction a devoted perpetual Harvest! That should delay any progress on that front for a time! Chesa, see what you can find out about the mau venom, and the sudden interest of the Delvers in potential Weaver ascendants. We all need to keep an eye on Bianchi. Rachel, generate a list of the Evaders of Death meeting with the Weavers. Gamaliel!" She pointed a finger at the young man. "We need to know the likely replacements for Clutton-Brock, and any alliances they share with scholars from the other noble factions. Rifle all the way back through their days as ascendants. Old ties are often the strongest. We'll continue to monitor the Weaver plans. Mortimer!" She flashed the gaunt man a wicked smile. "What a shame it is that the new bands are twice as lethal, but produce no more energy for Harvest. Another false start. . ." Finally, she turned to Ursielle. "Do you think that'll suffice?"

He gave her a reluctant nod. "I can think of nothing to add," mused Ursielle. "I will convey our plans to our patron Shadow to see if he has uncovered anything helpful. I'll also try and scrounge up information on the Tilters of the Hourglass and Sounders of Echoes. Though I doubt they will concern themselves with these schemes, we must do our best not to be blindsided. Quiet scholars are still scholars, and that is more than ample grounds to distrust them."

Several Disciples scoffed their approval.

Then, quicker than it began, their meeting disbanded. The attend-ees gathered up their ciphered notes and returned to their lives as contemptable rats within the dismissible crawl spaces of the Amber. Each pulled their anonymizing grey cowls down over their faces and dissolved into the night.

CHAPTER 14

Inconsistencies

FRENZY GREW AMONG THE ascendants in the weeks leading up to Saturnalia. The scholars canceled general instruction for the week prior, a surprise which Roland enjoyed more than he thought he would. The Weavers still insisted on him attending private lessons, though his tutors canceled their sessions as often as not. But the work at the Central Archive showed no signs of ebbing, and Peony maintained her shifts in the anomaly pens too. The three outcasts took every opportunity to enjoy each other's company, even if Peony's spirits remained low. Her private room, with its cloth sculptures, colored pillows, and makeshift rugs, became their haunt.

"We've been searching for those missing thought paddocks for the Delvers for weeks! It's driving me crazy," Tara exclaimed. She sipped a mixture of white wine and elderberry liqueur from a fluted glass. Larus's care packages always reinvigorated Tara. "I do like the Central Archive. It's the one place in the menhir that acts like. . ." She struggled for the words.

Roland and Peony exchanged sly glances as a bit of kir sloshed from Tara's strange glass.

"Well," Tara concluded, "like the menhir should act. It has rules and ethics and procedures. And it abides by them. The archivists aren't glamourous, gods know, but they have dignity!"

Neither Roland nor Peony replied.

Tara shot them a look. Her eyes moved to their legs, which touched as they sprawled atop Peony's bed. Tara looked away, and Peony pulled her leg away from Roland's.

At first, Roland had thought Tara might become awkward or jealous about he and Peony's closeness. Closeness was all it was, at least for now. Roland suspected Tara knew that. Still, Tara had a ready way with the disapproving glares. In recent days, she'd taken to pretending their signs of affection weren't happening at all. The truth was that Roland did not much care who saw him display tenderness toward Peony. Everyone needed affection, and it pleased him to make Peony's world a little brighter. Her days were not easy ones.

Roland leaned over to Peony over and whispered, "Sh-she's been enamored with the menhir all over again since we started working in the archive."

"There are parts of the anomaly pens that are ordered," countered Peony. "There are rules. We just don't follow them all the time. There are always special considerations. The scholars call it 'professional discretion.'"

Tara took another long draw from her glass. "If your relationship with your stated ethics and procedures is flexible. . ." She hiccupped. ". . . then you don't really have either."

Peony's features flattened before she sighed. "I suppose you're right."

"Of course I am!" Tara asserted. "It's the basics of governance. There are rules, and they must apply to everyone. If there are to be exceptions, then those need to be detailed and abided by. The whole purpose of rules is to guide one through ambiguous situations. If a ruler cannot abide by the same laws as her subjects, then she reigns over a lawless land."

Her haughtiness aside, Tara's argument made good sense to Roland.

At least in Independent Cities, leaders who reinvented their laws in a self-serving manner didn't last long.

Peony nudged Roland and nodded towards Tara, who examined the back of her hand. They burst into a fit a laughter.

"It's a shame she's not drunk more often," Peony whispered.

Tara looked up from her hand. "You know I heard that!"

Peony shrugged. "I stand by it."

Tara barreled on unfazed. "Rulership is what we're made for, we Langcraws. We understand it."

"I guess my family's made for farming?" Roland suggested. "I know it's not as fancy as leadership, but I miss it."

"I don't care if I ever see my family again," scoffed Peony.

Tara sputtered and gaped at Peony. "Family is not a joke," she declared. "Within each of us is a seed of continuity that ensures our hereditary gifts never wink out. That continuity is vital to the maintenance of the Menhir Conclave, and to solve Calamity. The menhirs have their flaws, to be sure, but the noble bloodlines are sacred to a higher purpose!"

"You think your lineage is going to solve Calamity?" recited Peony.

It didn't sound like a question to Roland.

"I did not say that!" Tara retorted. "One does not know where the next great discovery will come from. The challenge of Calamity is multifaceted." She paused and let out a very thoracic belch. "It's like an investment portfolio, really. The menhirs maintain a diversity of thaumaturgical assets that increases the odds that, for any given challenge Calamity presents, a noble bloodline will possess the aptitudes to address it."

Peony appeared to ponder the matter. Then she replied in a quiet tone, "The menhir is in the business of maintaining diverse thaumaturgical talents. Is that right?"

Tara nodded with enthusiasm. "But of course."

"That's the secret to defeating Calamity?" Peony continued. "That's the whole reason the menhirs exist, and why diverse noble bloodlines are so important?"

Tara beamed at Peony. "I'm so glad my lessons are getting through. You're catching up, Peony!"

"Uh-huh," Peony went on with a sharp, flat affect. "Then why are there hundreds of brain-dead thaumaturges with unknown talents in the basement?"

A bit of sweetened wine dribbled from the corner of Tara's mouth. "What do you mean?" She coughed.

"Tara. . ." Peony began, adopting a voice Roland associated with his nanny. "If the Menhir Conclave wants to preserve thaumaturgical talent, if diverse talents are the key in the race against Calamity, then why are those anomalies drooling all over themselves and suffering from thrush?"

Tara stared at Peony, uncomprehending.

Peony pressed on with a bit more tenderness. "Those anomalies had talents that were not part of a noble bloodline. But they could have been the beginning of a new noble bloodline. Doesn't it make sense that an anomaly is how every new noble bloodline started? Aren't the menhirs squandering those opportunities by destroying them? Clearly, maintaining strategic diversity is not the primary motivation of the menhir. Or if it is, it's sharing equal footing with one or more other motives that we don't much hear about."

Roland wanted to look away. Tara's face twisted with strained confusion. She looked as though she might burst.

Finally, she ruptured. "I do not know why you have taken such umbrage with the noble bloodlines, nor how you've justified your subversive behavior toward your own family!" Heat flushed Tara's neck. "But it's clear you've been made to work in the anomaly pens as a warning, Peony—though it seems it is having the opposite of its intended effect. Your empathy for the stock is sweet, Peony, but misguided. If they weren't cowed, they could have hurt themselves and others. Yes, the medicine is harsh, but we cannot withhold it only because some are squeamish. I accept that the menhir has been harsh to you, but that does not mean our guiding principles are to be abandoned!"

"Tara," Peony said in a neutral tone, "I know it's tough to hear, but I think the anomalies are cowed so that they don't threaten noble bloodlines, like yours, that need ginger treatment in order to survive."

Roland wished in that moment that life thaumaturgy could help him disappear.

Tara and Peony stared at each other with defiant scowls. Tara's voice turned shrill, but Peony held herself still.

"I refuse to be caught in your net of self-pity, Peony," Tara spat. "I can assemble more of your story than you trust us with, your supposed friends. You were thrown out or something, weren't you?!"

The muscles in Peony's neck tensed.

"Struck a nerve, have I?" Tara chucked. "Now, hmm. . . What could it be?" She adopted an edge of malignant playfulness. "Your travel trunk was in complete disarray. You packed in a rush? You were just waiting for Ms. Ash and Architect Blanchet by the road, not at the house? You've received no mail from your family, nor anyone else. I wonder why. Roland, do you have any guesses?"

Roland opened his mouth and then closed it again.

"As opposed to all of the mail you've received from your mother?" Peony retorted.

Tara's cheeks turned violet. "You moved around like a ghost when you and I shared that room together in Sandenvale. The brash and playful Peony becomes demure and avoidant at bedtime? Then, you get your own room here at the Menhir?! No, little flower, there are precious few explanations for why you behave as you do, and why your own blood despises you. I won't be so cruel as to list them aloud. Just don't let your personal issues taint your vision of me, my family, or the menhirs' mission. As your friend, I must convey that your attitude has harmed you enough already. I pray you change it." Tara spun, wobbled a bit, and stormed toward the door.

When she opened the door to leave, Peony spoke in a low voice with her eyes cast down. "You do not act much like a friend."

Tara scoffed and slammed the door behind her.

Roland and Peony sat in silence. She avoided his gaze. When Roland reached out to touch her on the knee, she drew it away.

After a long while, Roland asked in a soft tone, "Sh-should I go?"

Peony took a moment to reply. When she did, she sounded congested. "I think that's best."

Roland wanted to stay. He wanted to comfort Peony, but she gazed away at nothing. So, Roland went to the door. He paused before opening it and turned back.

"Tara will come around," he murmured. "When she does, I hope you'll be forgiving."

Peony turned her head farther away.

"I need you to know she's my friend," said Roland. "So are you. Whatever reason you d-don't get mail from your family, whatever you think you need to hide from me, or Tara, or anyone, I want you to know that it won't send me away. You get to show each p-petal when you're ready."

He waited, hoping she might respond. When she remained still, he opened the door, spared her one last misty glance, and closed it behind him.

The next morning, Roland and Peony ate breakfast together in silence. Tara sat with Derek Arachvelle at another table. Derek stared slack-mouthed at his porridge. Weaver Ankathi had caught him attempting to free one of the rodents from her collection two days prior. As punishment, she sentenced him to feeding the bog lizard. The rodent he failed to save had acted as the first victim by his hand.

Fresh evergreen sprigs adorned every lamp in the dining hall and every corridor of the menhir to mark the impending Saturnalia celebration.

As for their triad, another day's labor resided between each of them and their three-day break. For Peony, that meant attending to her mystery studies in the anomaly pens. For Roland and Tara, it meant auditing a section of the Central Archive pertaining to rotting oceanic predator carcasses. Though few had ventured an interest in those particular thought paddocks for decades, Sounder Scrivener required their auditing just the same.

Tara remained draped in morbid silence as she and Roland made their way up to the Central Archive.

Roland worried that Tara might think he had taken Peony's side in their argument. He hadn't. Roland knew that everyone lost their temper sometimes. When they did, sometimes they hurt each other. Most often, they hurt their friends. Seeing as that was as it was, in Roland's view, the only way to hold onto friends was to learn to mend the damage dealt in anger.

"I'm s-sorry about last night," murmured Roland.

"I'm sorry too," piped Tara. "But Peony needed to hear the truth!"

Evidently, Tara was not yet prepared to consider all sides of the interaction. Roland decided to hear her out. "What do you mean?" he asked.

Tara took in a deep breath. "I realize you and Peony are close, Roland, but she has gotten herself into quite a lot of trouble because of her behavior. Good gracious, the girl is wiping up the excrement of drooling invalids! When will she begin to realize the error of her ways?"

A hulking Architect in deep maroon robes brushed by them. His wolfish, shaggy mau followed behind. It bellowed a hiss as it passed. Tara leaped aside, and Roland pivoted to let them by. Roland thought he recognized the Architect from somewhere.

"I don't think I'll ever acclimate to those creatures," mumbled Tara. She gestured at the mau as it vanished around the next junction.

Roland shrugged. "People c-can get used to anything. But that isn't always best. Was that Architect Blanchet?"

"I confess, I was too distracted by the mau to notice," breathed Tara. "But—"

Shouts rang out ahead.

"You will give me my due respect, or I will expunge that vulpine grin from your face!" boomed Architect Blanchet's harsh, paternal voice.

A second voice sneered in an arrogant whine, "I will not bow to the threats of an emotionally compromised inferior!"

Mau issued whining growls and throaty hisses.

Roland and Tara crept to the junction and peered around to glance at the exchange. Architect Blanchet's muscular frame stood out even beneath his maroon robes. Pale yellow Evader robes draped the other man's slight, willowy form. His bald mau paced behind him, panting, exposing a row of syringe-like teeth within its wrinkled maw. The Architect mau curled into a ball at its scholar's feet. Its long fur rose about its body, as though it were collecting static.

Architect Blanchet cleared his throat. "One bestows deference on scholars of the more affluent faction when right of way is contested, Evader!"

The Evader rolled his eyes and arpeggiated, "The days of my pausing to allow an Architect to pass merely for being an Architect are over. Everyone knows the Weavers have stolen your crown. It's best that you accept reality."

Without warning, the Architect's mau shot toward the Evader. The man flinched and stepped back, but his reflexes paled in comparison to the mau's feral athleticism. It closed the distance between the two scholars in the blink of an eye. It opened its maw and leaped, exposing teeth that more resembled canine than feline. The Evader released a shrill scream. His eyes darted around, desperate and wild. Roland caught his desperate gaze.

"Help!" the Evader screamed.

The giant, shaggy mau sank its claws into the man's robes. Its inertia sent him toppling. He threw up an arm in a piteous defensive gesture, but the mau bit and slashed at the man's midsection. The yellow robes were shredded into wet crimson ribbons in moments.

Architect Blanchet stumbled back in horror and called at his mau, "Dyla! No!"

The Evader pleaded as the mau atop him reared back and lunged toward his neck.

"No!" Tara screamed. She stumbled around the corner and toward the exchange as though she intended to intervene.

Just before the mau's teeth came into contact with the man's neck, the Evader mau blurred and connected with the Architect mau's midsection. The two beasts toppled across the corridor in a flurry of flittering claws.

Tara ran past the battling mau to the Evader. Roland gave a disbelieving start and lumbered behind her. Architect Blanchet turned and fled the exchange.

The Evader's voice trembled as he murmured to Tara with wide eyes, "Thank you, thank you! I need to get out of here. Get me away from here!"

Tara and Roland dragged the man to his feet and hauled him down a corridor. Roland did his best to ignore his blood-soaked hands.

The mau only continued their contest as though none of them existed. Though the Architect's mau bore a larger frame, the Evader mau sank its teeth into the larger animal's shoulder. The Architect mau writhed and rolled, trying to dislodge its rival, but failed. The Evader mau raised its hind limbs and issued fluttering kicks at the other's side. A snap of lighting filled the corridors, followed by the acrid smell of burning flesh. Welts and burns blossomed all over the Evader mau's skin as arcs of electricity shot out from the Architect mau's body. With a final flurry of kicks, the Evader mau spilled the burning innards of its rival.

Roland and Tara dragged the gibbering Evader toward the Central Archive.

The man pressed his hands to his stomach to stem the flow of blood. "It was his fault," the Evader slurred. "You saw. He demanded deference from me. Then his mau attacked. You saw!"

Halfway down the next corridor, a Weaver spotted them. The red-haired woman ran to them. She pulled a handkerchief from her emerald robes, wrapping it tight around the Evader's forearm.

"What happened here?!" she demanded.

Roland stumbled for words.

"This man was attacked by an Architect's mau," Tara explained. "The scholars had a verbal exchange, and then the Architect's mau launched itself at this man, without provocation."

Tara's lucidity impressed Roland.

"A mau attack!" the Weaver woman cried. "Follow me."

She led them to a nearby junction lined with various laboratories. They approached a door with the symbol of a winged serpent wound about a wand at its summit. She knocked. The door opened inward in a flash, revealing a pair of scowling Evaders in yellow robes. Both the men's faces bore sharp, prominent noses. Their expressions passed from agitation to horror as they took stock of the lacerated Evader, who seemed paler by the second.

"Come!" they hissed.

A labyrinth of glassware containing blood, bile, and other fluids crowded the laboratory beyond. Several metal tables like those Roland knew from abattoirs sat at the room's center. A rich and buttery miasma filled the air. The two Evaders placed the wounded man atop one of the empty tables. One of the Evaders positioned himself above the wounded man and began murmuring as he passed his hands over the wounded man's still form. The murmuring Evader smiled, but only just.

"I think he's going to be alright," he breathed.

Roland's shoulders relaxed a little.

The murmuring Evader turned to the Weaver and fixed her with a sober expression. "We will be sure to inform him of the identity of his rescuers, Miss. . . ?"

Tara stepped forward and opened her mouth to introduce herself, but the Weaver cut her off.

"I'm Erika Thornhause," she boasted. "It was but my duty to save him from the vicious mau attack!"

Tara gaped at Roland.

"A mau attack?" both Evaders cried out in unison.

"Indeed," said Thornhause. "It will be no surprise to you to learn that this man was attacked by an Architect's mau! The Architect fled the scene. The coward. Isn't that right?" Thornhause shot Tara a glance.

Tara looked as though someone had slapped her with an angry mau. She stood there, silent and appalled.

"Y-yes," offered Roland. "That's correct. He tried to call his mau back, but—"

"A ploy, no doubt!" Thornhause interjected. "He knew his efforts would be futile, after siccing his mau on this poor Evader! Unbelievable! The Architects are desperate and dangerous vermin! So close to Saturnalia too! Thankfully, the Weavers will be sedating the mau for the event with a new thaumaturgical working. We'll assure the safety of all scholars during the festival."

The Evaders exchanged unreadable looks. Weaver Thornhause's theatrics blended the truth with misrepresentation, facts with political inuendo. Roland doubted the Evaders accepted half of it.

"Well, Weaver Thornhause," cooed the taller of the Evaders, "we appreciate the Weavers' assistance in saving one of our own. We will be sure Evader Sandberg here learns the identity of his rescuer."

"Rescuer?" Tara breathed.

The second Evader added, "You can be about your dealings with these ascendants now. We will inform Primara Anaktisi of your efforts."

Thornhause stood up straighter at the mention of the Evader Primara. She bowed her head. "Inform Anaktisi that it was but the smallest matter for me. The Weavers of the Web of Life and the Evaders of Death hold many values in common. I am confident that our alliance against darker forces will only continue to grow."

The eyes of both Evaders sparked as they answered in unison, "But of course!"

Something about their resemblance and penchant for speaking together had Roland's skin crawling.

Weaver Thornhause guided Tara and Roland out of the laboratory. She bowed to the Evaders as she closed the door behind them.

Once outside, she turned to the two ascendants. "You did well alerting me to the attack. I will be sure to extend your names to the Weaver Primara. Perhaps she will thank you."

"R-Roland Ward," said Roland.

"I am Tara Langcraw," Tara announced in a regal tone.

"Ward. Your family are Weavers," sniffed Thornhause. "Langcraw, I do not know. . . Speak of this incident to no one. Is that clear?"

Agitation flashed across Tara's face, but then her features reorganized into placidity.

"We won't," said Roland, giving Tara a small look. "Tara and I n-need to get to the Central Archive. They're waiting for us."

Tara made to respond, but Roland grabbed her arm before she could interject. "Come on, Tara!"

Once several junctions lay between themselves and any hint of scholars, Roland turned to Tara. "We can't tell anyone what we saw," he asserted.

She studied him before replying. "I am not a fool, Roland Ward. Time is beginning to suggest you mightn't be either." She looked him up and down. "The Weavers are your future faction, and their favor is not one you can afford to lose."

Roland glowered. "That m-means Peony too."

Tara rolled her eyes. "I am not sure I'm likely to speak to Peony ever again."

Roland sighed. "She had a p-point about the anomalies. She didn't mean to hurt you. She's not like that."

"It's not my family I'm worried about," Tara replied imperiously. "I am just worried for Peony."

"Tara," Roland whispered, drawing close to her. "There are real dangers in this place. Peony is in trouble, b-but you could be in real trouble too, if you don't show your aptitudes soon. The point is, n-none of us needs to get caught up in some fight between factions. It won't end well. Remember what you said about avoiding Primaras."

Tara flinched at the reminder of her failed progress. Then she glared at him.

"I d-don't mean it as an attack," Roland pleaded. "But it's true. These scholars aren't kind to things different from themselves. They claim it's all for a higher purpose, and some of them might even believe it, but I'm not so sure. Now's not the time for loose lips."

Tara looked down. Roland gave her a moment to let it all sink in.

"I think everyone here is in d-danger," urged Roland. "It's too easy to make a misstep and end up on the wrong side of the scholars. It's true for Peony, it's true for me, and it's true for you t-too. I don't know much, but I know Peony is your friend, and sh-she's not going to betray you. Not ever."

Tara winced as she let out a long breath.

Roland stood there, studying her. He feared to apply any more pressure. Intelligent people with wills like Tara's could not be told what to think.

"Perhaps I made a mistake," muttered Tara. A mist dimmed her eye as she met Roland's gaze. "I should not have spoken about Peony's family. It was not my place."

That took Roland aback. Tara rarely recognized her own faults.

"Everyone has f-fights. Friends especially," said Roland. "We can't rely on much here, but I know I can rely on you and Peony. And I w-want you two to know that you can rely on each other."

Tara took a long moment to examine Roland. "Roland Ward," she replied with a smile, "you might be the most surprising person I have ever met."

Roland decided to take her words as a compliment, and he hoped time might heal the wounds between his two friends.

That afternoon, Roland and Tara were both hunched over the Weaver section of the Central Archive, looking for thought paddocks on beached carcasses.

"Scrivener says a group of scholars from the Pearl Menhir came here last year to look at one of these, but found the record missing," said Tara. She lifted a thought paddock from her tray and set it into its allocated groove. A pale blue light hummed to life as it fussed into its place among its brethren.

"M-maybe there is no such thing as useless thaumaturgical know-ledge," said Roland. He still vacillated on whether he deemed that true. He surveyed his ledger and sighed with satisfaction. "Seems we found all the missing ones here. Maybe that's a good sign?"

"What do you mean?" shouted Scrivener in a fluster. She was near-by. "This? This is Primara Nash's response?!"

A muffled, quieter voice mumbled something in answer.

Tara touched a finger to Roland's lips and gestured for him to fol-low. The pair tiptoed to the end of their aisle and navigated toward the exchange.

"Nash expects us to believe this?" huffed Scrivener. "None of the latter works of Panirovo nor any of the works of Delvers Otvlech or LaTorre are among the Delvers? What, does he think they all just van-ished? Ha! As sure as he's a Delver, he lies!"

A small voice mumbled in reply, "He proposes that the thought paddocks might have been misplaced . . . by the archivists."

"Misplaced?" Scrivener scoffed. "You can assure Nash that there have been no misplacements. The very idea that the works of all three would be misplaced in unison is impossible."

"I tried to tell him—" the quieter voice began.

Scrivener cut her off. "Three generations of scholars, mentor to protégé? No, this is deliberate manipulation by one of his Delvers!"

"Might LaTorre have misplaced the thought paddocks?" inquired the smaller voice.

"Impossible!" announced Scrivener. "LaTorre's room was searched following the incident. No thought paddocks were recovered."

"Ah," replied the other. "Can we determine when the thought pad-docks were removed? Was it one at a time, or all together?"

Sounder Scrivener's voice was low. "LaTorre's paddocks were

removed after her accident. I already checked. Few Delvers visited while the menhir investigated her death. I might have seen two of those greasy eels in as many months. Nadmenny started whining about missing Delver paddocks soon after."

"Perhaps there's something wrong with our security system," suggested the second voice. "Perhaps it's been tampered with?"

"Impossible!" Scrivener insisted. "It required a Delver to take those thought paddocks out of here. We'll remind Nash of that! Come!"

Footsteps crescendoed in their direction.

"Let's go!" whispered Roland.

Tara nodded, and they made their escape without even agitating one of the archive's guardian mau. They were back within the ascendants' quarters before either of them spoke.

"Either Nash is lying, or the archive's system is compromised," breathed Tara. "Either way, we need to help the archivists find out what happened. The menhir needs for the Central Archive to be functional and whole."

"I think this is another c-conflict we should stay away from," countered Roland. "Like the mau attack."

She blew out a breath. "But this issue is on our doorstep, and we're already working in the Central Archive. This is our chance to make a difference, Roland! To serve the menhirs! The Central Archives must be immutable for the menhirs to function."

"Maybe," offered Roland.

Tara scowled, but avoided pressing the issue.

They passed by the entryway to the dining hall and spotted Peony. She was shunting bits of root vegetables around with a spoon while she muttered to her meal. Roland touched Tara's shoulder. Tara pulled herself up a little taller and entered the dining hall.

"Peony, I need to speak with you," called Tara. She took a seat across from Peony.

"I've had a bad day," said Peony. "I'm not sure now's a good time. I honestly don't think it's safe to be near me anymore."

"I'll decide what's safe for me," replied Tara. She exhaled slowly and grazed Peony's hand with a finger. "I was unkind to you. It was not a fine showing on my part, and I regret it. Deeply. Your relationship with your family is not a subject I should critique. I failed to honor our friendship, and my. . ." Tara paused. ". . . error was grave and injurious. I hope you will forgive me."

Peony gave a start at the word "error." She beamed at Tara and stole a moment to give a side-eyed glance at Roland, who hovered nearby.

"That means a lot today, Tara. Thank you. I'm glad to have you as a friend, prickles and all!"

Peony stood and approached as if to hug Tara, but Tara rose and adjusted the front of her robes.

"Alright," said Peony, sitting back down. "Small steps."

They took their meal together that evening, almost like old times. There might have been one or two fewer smiles from Peony, but Roland could breathe again. After all, who else was he going to go to Saturnalia with, if not his two friends? Certainly not Lavinia. He'd sooner ask the bog lizard.

CHAPTER 15

An Overture to Celebration

E VERY COG OF THE menhir turned in preparation for Saturnalia, an event synonymous with celebration. Well, celebration for the scholars, anyhow. For her part in the affair, the scholars provided Chesa with a list of Delver mau and a schedule for their sedation and containment. The scholars, naturally, showed little interest in easing Chesa's task. They reacted as though Chesa had devised the policy herself. But the near-lethal mau attack only days prior necessitated stringent safety measures.

"You know, it isn't really your place to remind me of anything, is it?" Lysander Sze of the Delvers spat at Chesa. "I heard you the first time. If you don't like my pace, then I invite you to transport my mau down to the containment facility yourself. Hmm? How does that sound?"

His tiny orange-and-white mau, with its especially round face, looked at Lysander and mewled with pathetic eyes. It would have been cute, had Chesa not known its mouth was lined with recurved teeth that dripped with venom. The mau hissed at her back as she retreated from the scholar's chambers to attend to her other obstructionists.

Chesa examined her ledger and growled to herself, "Moyra Collins . . . Wonderful. . ." Moyra Collins had four mau, three of them female.

Chesa knocked and entered Delver Collins's rooms, and she was struck so hard by the pungent smell of mau urine that she stumbled back, gasping. A stratum of fur covered every surface, and bits of dander floated like rancid snowflakes through beams of morning sun. By the smell, Chesa suspected that at least one of the females was in heat.

"Delver Collins." Chesa coughed, dropping into her most obsequious genuflection. "Sorry to remind you, but you are due to take your mau to the containment facility."

The gaunt scholar looked at each of her mau and began to cry. Two of the animals slept atop elevated perches. The only male, which had belonged to the late Primara Kensington, stood statuesque by the scholar's side. Chesa gave the male a wary glance, but did not meet the beast's eyes, fearing that it might somehow decipher her role in its former scholar's demise. The last female rubbed its body against Delver Collins's leg, lifting its rear as though in estrus.

Delver Collins's tone was frantic. "Stop rushing me! I know what I need to do. I don't need some insolent whore of Nash's to lecture me about my duties. Get out!"

Chesa grimaced. It annoyed her that Primara Nash's lascivious stares and glancing touches breached the notice of other Delvers, though she was not sure why it had made her self-conscious. In the end, Chesa would much rather have been a whore than a smug, gaunt, virgin scholar sopping in the urine of a mau in heat. In any case, Chesa departed Delver Collins's rooms with the customary number of low genuflections and mousy thanks.

Two long and tense hours later, with every other Delver mau ferried down for containment, only Delver Collins remained obstinate. She lay collapsed on the floor outside her room, sobbing—again—with her four mau standing around her, studying her. It was all Chesa could do not to tap her foot. No one came to help Delver Collins. Perhaps she was too pathetic to acknowledge in her current state, but any other day, someone would have responded to her antics. That struck Chesa as odd. The ambient greys of the Delver common room had taken on muted hues of red all day too, which most times meant lust or agitation within the Delver ranks. Chesa imagined too much of either sentiment could overshadow Moyra's antics.

Glancing back toward the common room, Chesa noticed several groups of Delvers clustered into cliques, smaller groupings than usual, whispering among themselves. Was something amiss? She'd been away from the Delvers' quarters for months spying on the Bianchi girl and her friends at the behest of Primara Nash. Much could have changed in her absence. Whatever the case might have been, Chesa needed to be rid of Moyra to study the issue further.

"Delver Collins, Master, I must insist. . ." Chesa began.

"Why can't we just leave our mau in our private chambers like usual? Would that not suffice?" Delver Collins pleaded, as though Chesa had any power over the day's operations.

Chesa kept her eyes down and her voice small. "A wise thought, my liege. I do not know. But it is my understanding that Primara Clutton-Brock proposed the additional safeguard. Contingents of the Weavers and the Delvers were also supportive."

"Well, not me!" sniffed Delver Collins as she shambled to her feat. "That's all Nash's doing. He and his loyalists are happy to pander! Were it not for Lysander Sze, the Delvers would have gone the way of the Architects in this last Harvest cycle!" Complaining appeared to give the emotionally compromised Delver strength, and in fits and starts, Moyra started to follow Chesa at a glacial pace.

The mau containment facility resided deep within the guts of the Amber Menhir, beneath the ascendants' quarters and near to where Chesa knew the anomaly pens resided. The corridor before the containment facility was littered with scholars and their mewling mau. The operation was being manned by several dozen Weavers of the Web of Life, who worked to lure the mau with dried fish and minced organ meats into great metal cages upon wheels.

The mau were hardly cooperative. Any encouragement that was too forceful sent a mau peeling away in fear or anger. When it was Delver Collins's turn to cage her mau, she provided little assistance. She howled and threw herself onto the floor, then stood up, then threw herself to the floor again, wailing at the Weavers, "Heartless, that's what you are! How can you live with yourselves, caging up everyone's companions and guards? What about your mau?! Don't you have any remorse for caging them up as you do?!"

The Weaver attending to Delver Collins's mau gave her a level look. "The Weavers sedate each mau to ensure its comfort, and to make certain they cannot harm each other during containment. You may retrieve your mau tomorrow after the celebration has ended, or the day after, if you need time to recover." It sounded reasonable enough to Chesa.

"But why?!" Delver Collins screamed, just as another of her mau was snapped shut inside one of the steel cages.

"To ensure the safety of everyone at Saturnalia. Scholars know that the evening's events are in jest, but the mau do not. This is less stressful for everyone involved, and let us not forget the recent attack. . ." The Weaver sounded as though he'd recited the rationale ad nauseam.

Chesa examined the various trapped mau. Most of them cowered in corners or growled at anything that passed by. As Chesa watched the line of mau being ushered into the facility, a grey Weaver mau caught her eye. It slipped a paw through a pair of bars and purred as it studied her. That one, Chesa suspected, must have already been sedated. A moment later, Chesa spotted another Weaver mau with a similar countenance. Chesa sent out her thaumaturgical senses on reflex. There, nestled in a halo around the creature's brain, was a series of sedating threads of mind thaumaturgy worked into knots. Something about that bothered Chesa.

With another thud, Delver Collins screamed and fell to the floor, issuing heaving breaths between frantic sobs. The Weavers proceeded about their duties, stepping around her as though she were inanimate. Chesa just stared at the woman.

"Take me from this place!" commanded Delver Collins. "I can't bear to see them suffer any longer!"

The sedated Weaver maus looked happy enough to Chesa, though she wondered why the Weaver mau had experienced their sedation first. They did stand among the most powerful breeds. Chesa shrugged off her curiosity. After all, the maus were the Weavers' problem now.

Chesa put her arm beneath Delver Collins to give her support, though it caused Chesa to gag on the ammonia wafting from the woman's robes. Their return trip back to the Delvers' quarters was not going to be an easy one.

When at last Chesa deposited Moyra Collins in her chambers, emerald mists eclipsed the last vestiges of red along the corridor walls and ceilings. The scholars still lingered in cliques, but Saturnalia's customary lightness laced the room's disposition.

Robes that mimicked each noble faction's lay across sofas, ottomans, and chalkboards. Delvers everywhere stripped off their robes to drape themselves in hues of midnight purple, maroon, pale yellow, forest green, and chocolate. Saturnalia's frivolity blurred the lines of acceptable behavior at the menhir for almost all. Tonight, even an ascendant could don a scholar's robes in jest.

Chesa scanned the raucous room and frowned. True to Moyra Collin's caterwauling, Chesa observed that the room stood split into cliques orbiting Primara Nash, and those fewer in number orbiting Lysander Sze. The two groups respected an unseen border between their divisions. Chesa made careful note of who stood where.

"Chesa?" called Nash from his more populous nebula of sycophants. "Haven't you got a mission downstairs to attend to, hmm? Chop-chop!"

Chesa genuflected and went. She arrived at the venue halls to find her brethren amidst the preparations. Servants strung garlands over doorways and along corridors. Wreaths as large as Chesa dangled, suspended by painted cables that made the pine-and-holly clusters appear as though they floated. Gilded candelabras adorned serving tables that would soon host refreshments, including ample saprolite wine.

Saturnalia exalted excessiveness. Naturally, that meant that the Amber Chancellor had suspended the laws limiting physical relationships between scholars and ascendants for the evening. That meant Chesa would need to fend off far fewer advances. All the better. Let the ascendants enjoy it all and perhaps remember how it felt.

Sweating servants braided ribbons about greenery and candelabras. They huffed and stumbled to finish it all before the scholars arrived. Saturnalia emphasized the use of white fabrics in decorations, but multicolored lace adorned the odd wreath, with the six noble factions' hues depicted in equal measure.

Chesa found Ursielle Hedrigal in the main hall. He shouted orders at two dozen servants laboring to erect a stage in the room's middle. It would soon serve as a vantage point for the elected King of Mischief for the evening. Heavy scaffolding formed the stage's innards. The servants hoisted great metal plates over their heads to form the stage's checkered pattern of crimson and gold.

"May I be of service, Ursielle?" asked Chesa.

The man kept his eyes fixed on the stage's progress. One of the huge metal plates had slipped the year prior and destroyed an unsuspecting servant. The scholars tasked the survivors to clean up what remained of their colleague and finish erecting the stage. Not even a stain evidenced the man by the time the festivities started. The scholars had intended to publicly thank the slain servant for his service, but they forgot.

"Busy here, but perhaps Ms. Ash could use some assistance?" replied Ursielle before shouting, "No! We need two servants on each side of those plates. Four in total! Do not try with just two or three!"

Chesa grimaced as a plate wobbled over a triad of young men. The stupidity of it all still mystified her. A dozen Architects of Force could see to the decorations in a morning without risk of injury to anyone. Yet the scholars viewed superfluous use of thaumaturgical energies with extreme caution. They argued that they needed to reserve their energies for lessons or research.

Ms. Ash, as usual, barked orders to another ensemble of servants in the next hall. She instructed them on the construction of silver-worked fountains for saprolite wine. When filled, the wine would burble from their summits down a series of terraces in thin ruby sheets, as beautiful as they were needless.

"Just like that," lectured Ms. Ash. "Okay, now that you've mastered assembling this geometry. . ." She gestured to a three-tiered fountain atop the display table beside her. "We need four of them in each hall. Now hurry along! There are two other geometries you'll need to replicate, and one of them is quite challenging."

Teams of grey-robed servants scurried away, taking boxes of parts with them.

"Chesa!" shouted Ms. Ash. She smiled but dropped her voice low. "It's good you're here, girl. I could use a detail-oriented overseer. Would you confirm that they don't foul anything up? I've got to work on the next demonstration fountain, and I can't be in two places at once!"

"Of course," said Chesa. "Any news I should be aware of?"

Ms. Ash let out a thunderous peal of laughter at a joke Chesa had not told and then whispered, "Not much. The Bianchi girl has been wooed by the Weavers. The mortalities in the anomaly pens continue to rise. Ursielle was unsuccessful in blocking McCray's request to keep saprolite bands on anomalies ad libitum. Amus Clutton-Brock even endorsed the measure. Evidently, he's intent on spending his last capital as Primara to feather the Evaders' nest. Keep your eyes peeled, girl."

Chesa leaned toward her colleague. "There continues to be something amiss with the Delvers. I think Lysander Sze and Primara Nash are in open conflict. . ."

Ms. Ash raised herself up and thundered, "Enough depravity from you, girl, I've no need to hear the particulars of the private morphologies of one scholar or another, thank you!"

"Oh, thank you for that. . ." mumbled Chesa with a glower before she retreated to assist.

After erecting fountains, Ms. Ash tasked Chesa with setting out crystal goblets. After that, Chesa joined groups of other servants in ferrying large casks of saprolite wine, filling the fountains, and priming their ductwork to ensure their seals. At the last, a bit of saprolite wine sloshed from a misassembled joint. Chesa's breath caught. She studied the other servants. No one had seemed to notice the spill apart from her.

Seeing the pool of ruby had Chesa's eyes dilating.

"Pardon me, everyone," she mumbled, though she doubted anyone heard. "I. . ."

Long-subdued pleasure centers lit up across her brain, and the hair on the back of her head bristled with excitement. She snatched a rag from within her robes and sopped up the volume, taking care that no one observed.

"I need to step away to the privy for a moment," she murmured. "I hope you'll be able to complete the next fountain without me. . ."

No one cared. No one noticed. Chesa bathed in pleasure chemicals as she reminded herself that perfection always befell those who waited long enough.

She slipped toward the line of privies at the far end of the room, entered one, and closed the door behind her. Her head swam with euphoric anticipation. She leaned against the cool stone wall and reached into her robes for the moistened rag. Her chest heaved, and her breathing grew deep and labored. She let her hand graze the side of her robes and exposed neck. A diadem of elation wrapped around her brain. She placed the cloth into her mouth and drew upon it.

CHAPTER 16

Moderation

CHESA'S SENSES SURGED AS she sucked upon the rag. Distant conversations of servants drew near, sensual and melodic. The world's ordinary hues became enthralling chroma. The tendrils of thaumaturgy that surrounded the minds of those in the room beyond hypertrophied into thick ropes that begged to be manipulated.

Chesa lapped at the rag until no hint of saprolite remained, and a good deal longer still. It tasted of liquidized animal fat and organ meats. Its sybaritic richness risked stopping her heart, but in this state, restraint withered away. Her head swam as a sense of well-being and confidence overtook her. It took an effort of will for Chesa to slow her breathing and regain a semblance of external awareness. Cleaning up after drunken scholars had its perks.

Once her thoughts settled, Chesa exited the privy and made her way back to her private chambers. She avoided meeting the eyes of other servants, for fear they might recognize the wine's effects on her. She groomed her hair in her room, donned a few of her precious pearls, and steeled herself. She checked her eyes just before departing. They appeared like black saucers no longer, but only just. Chesa accepted that that would have to do.

When Chesa returned to the Saturnalia halls, scholars and ascendants stood among the servants. Most of them were strangers to Chesa, and a mixture of robes between factions anonymized them further. Chesa always took care when working mind thaumaturgy in the presence of others—unless she meant for them to perish soon thereafter. Tonight, with the presence of so many unknown eyes, she dared not consider even the smallest exhibition of power.

Chamber musicians arrived. The statuesque players wore sheer white livery trimmed with gold that exposed their athleticism in full. The sight sent Chesa's feral heart racing. It required no small amount of will to wrench herself away from them. A string quartet assembled in an ancillary hall. A cluster of harpists dueled arpeggiating glissandos in a second. A small chamber orchestra assembled behind the checkered stage in the main venue. Groups of scholars clustered about the players and gulped saprolite wine as they leered.

Gliding among the ascendants and scholars in her dark grey robes, Chesa maintained the most innocent and deferential expression. Prey is what I am to you. See me and forget. She watched an especially arrogant ascendant stare her up and down. He scoffed as his eyes met hers.

She genuflected.

The man sipped of his saprolite wine as he appraised her. His tender grasp on the crystal betrayed a lack of acquaintance with the drink. He smiled at Chesa and whispered something in the ear of a smaller man beside him. They laughed and rolled their eyes at her.

Without further provocation, the saprolite wine seized Chesa's forebrain and treated her to a vision of following the men into the privy, strangling them, and sucking power-imbuing wine from their entrails. She shook her head, and the vision receded. She provided the offending parties her deepest bow, if a bit delayed, and a flash of pouty eyes.

Chesa watched the scholars drink and congratulate each other over their self-celebratory studies. If lay society ever witnessed events like

Saturnalia, if they saw the world that their lives supported, she knew the continent would revolt on a scale never seen before.

A glut of scholars formed in the main hall, and Chesa went to inspect it. At the center of the swarm resided Milyna Okondo, the Weaver Primara, with Ms. Ash by her side. Her chosen attire consisted of a loose metalwork belt hung low over her hips, exposing generous pelvis, and pants composed of multicolored ribbons. A green bodice with brass studs in the form of creeping vines covered her top. Chesa tilted her head. In another life, she might have been this woman. Okondo whispered into Ms. Ash's ear between her inviting glances and dismissive laughs. If Ms. Ash was attending this show, that meant Chesa could be elsewhere.

In the other ancillary hall, Chesa located Peony Bianchi and her companions. Roland Ward grinned as usual. Chesa wavered on whether he stood among the dimmest members of his cohort, or the cleverest. It all depended on whether wisdom or luck spawned his infrequent insights. The cold-faced Tara Langcraw looked miserable and as out of place as usual. She had styled her hair in cascading blonde curls caught in a snood dotted with green stones. Tara fixed Chesa with a look and scowled. An annoyance Ms. Langcraw might be, but she boasted keen eyes. Chesa gave the ascendants a deferential bow and stalked farther from them into the crowd.

"I do not like that one," Tara called over the rabble.

Chesa slithered close, hidden behind curtains of scholars.

"Take it easy," answered Peony. "Chesa's a friend. We have no reason to distrust her."

Roland examined the nearest gurgling fountain. "Do you th-think we should try some of that saprolite wine?"

"What for?" snapped Tara. "It's good for fueling thaumaturgy. Otherwise, it's just a drug. It is not meant to be taken for fun. Besides, these are not circumstances in which I think it wise to explore new mind-altering substances."

All three halls grew denser with bodies. Servants turned the standing lamps down, bathing the hall in golden light. Grazes between scholars grew longer as they basked in the growing shadows.

"I don't think they're drinking the wine for their s-studies," noted Roland.

"Yeah? Me either," Peony agreed.

"Some are susceptible to overindulgence." Tara cleared her throat. "It seems scholars are no exception. That does not mean we should fall victim to the same." Her eyes settled on a sizable gap in the crowd near the food tables. "Perhaps I'll fetch something for us to eat?"

"I'm not—" started Roland, but Tara fled the rising tide of scholars before he finished. Her gemmed snood disappeared in the crowd. Roland reached up to move a bit of stray hair from Peony's face. He grazed Peony's skin as he did so, and they both smiled.

Chesa sighed, perhaps louder than was wise, and decided to follow Tara.

A tall, willowy woman with huge eyes served Tara. She wore black ascendant robes. A second graceful woman with silvery braids moved behind Tara, hemming her into an interaction.

"Langcraw, is it?" asked the woman serving. She carved roasted chicken into precise sheets and plated them. "How go your studies?"

Tara recoiled with a brief look of horror.

The woman serving clucked her tongue as she deposited roasted root vegetables onto Tara's plate. "Not well, then?"

Tara fussed with her robes. "I do not view that as an appropriate subject for discussion here," she replied. "Besides, I do not know you."

The serving woman fixed Tara with an unblinking stare. Her dark skin and eyes confirmed that she hailed from nowhere near the Amber.

She tilted her almost triangular head, like a robin studying a drowning worm after a storm.

"Maybe you could use a bit of tutoring," added the second woman behind Tara.

Tara twisted. "Tilter Avevaios?!" she gasped. "I did not mean to. . ."

Tilter Leticia Avevaios appeared forever caught in a languid dream. As with most Tilters of the Hourglass, only a paltry thread seemed to connect her to reality. Their faces, like praying mantises', sent Chesa's skin crawling. She took a step back from them on instinct.

"It is good you are here, Tara Langcraw," Avevaios said. "Do you know Primara Klepsydra?" She indicated the woman depositing carrots and turnips onto three plates.

"I. . ." Tara fumbled.

"The Primara and I agree it is time to intercede in your education," added Avevaios. "A possible Tilter ascendant is not a resource we can afford to let slip away. Worse, we fear your choice of peers has garnered the interest of some of the Amber's politically minded. We favor seeing you armed as soon as possible."

Primara Klepsydra inclined her chin, never blinking her eyes. "Tilter Avevaios and I have every confidence that your aptitudes will emerge in time. But we must take care to ensure your persistence until then."

Tara opened her mouth to speak.

"Private lessons are in order," said Avevaios.

"I'm already clerking at the Central Archive," warned Tara. "Between that and my classes, I am afraid my schedule—"

Klepsydra interrupted with quiet reassurance. "I will request for the chancellor to dispense with your other duties. They are needless."

Tara's mouth dropped open. "Actually, I quite enjoy my time in the Central Archive—"

"It is no more than a tomb for the Sounders of Echoes," said Klepsydra with a flick of her hand. "A tomb that has spent its long and painful life being robbed and manipulated by the other factions. If it possesses the illusion of safety now, believe me, it is only a mirage that conceals someone who has discovered a new means of manipulating it. The only true archives of any menhir are the Tilters. Our minds are the only vaults worth trusting."

Tara shook her head. "I thought no mind could be trusted with Delvers afoot? Pardon me, but should we even be speaking here?"

At the mention of the Delvers, the Tilters laughed. It sounded foreign, cold, and unpracticed from their long throats. The sound made Chesa take another step back.

"No, child." A hint of playfulness touched Klepsydra's voice. "We are not such easy quarry. First, we do not often allow ourselves to be alone with Delvers. We travel in groups. This enhances our ability to audit the history of an environment." She swiveled her head and flicked her eyes to study Tara from an alien angle. "Even in isolation, we devote a part of ourselves to auditing our recent past to ensure we have not been manipulated by a Delver. When such an event is discovered, we can search other nearby potentialities to avoid it."

"Pardon me, Primara Klepsydra, but I have a question," said Tara, "about the Central Archive and the Delvers. . ."

The dark woman's eyebrows raised. "Yes?"

"You suggested that someone might have found a means of manipulating the archive. Could someone of one noble faction pretend to be another? Say, a Delver of the Mind?" asked Tara. "Something strange has occurred, and I wonder if someone could masquerade as a faction other than their own. . . Perhaps have their blood read as a different aptitude?"

Chesa pressed closer.

"An interesting question," considered Klepsydra. "Perhaps even a dangerous one."

"Why?" said Tara.

"Because," murmured Avevaios, "many view evidence of blurred or pluripotent aptitudes with considerable suspicion."

"In the views of some," added Klepsydra. "Ambiguous aptitudes imperil the very heart of the menhirs."

A burst of laughter from nearby interrupted the Tilters. Chesa turned to find a fleshy woman in loose purple robes pouring a glass of saprolite wine over a man's bare chest from behind, whilst a third man lapped up the ruby cascade from the first man's chest. The eyes of all three bulged.

Klepsydra narrowed her eyes on the woman in the Tilter robes.

"Perhaps a being like your friend, Peony Bianchi, could trick the Central Archive's system," said Klepsydra. She leaned down to Tara's ear. "We have detected a ripple of potentialities on the near horizon, Tara Langcraw. We believe it might involve you or someone close. We do not often attend events like Saturnalia, but we needed to speak to you in a moment that would not draw unwanted attention."

Tara's mouth dropped open as her eyes fell upon Chesa. "Are you following me?" she cried.

Chesa dropped to one knee. "No, my liege. I'm only. . ." She noticed the pool of saprolite wine at the feet of the lusting scholars nearby. "Cleaning!" She almost fell over herself as she stumbled to sop up wine with the hem of her robes.

"Enough of this!" commanded Klepsydra.

Tara ignored Chesa to resume her enthrallment with her Primara.

"We will petition the chancellor tonight," insisted Klepsydra. "We will send a pair of Tilters to you each morning to collect you henceforth." Her words rang as cold as iron.

"If you insist," said Tara.

"Oh, and Tara Langcraw?" Klepsydra quipped. She examined Chesa as she stumbled about on the floor in search of any more saprolite. "Best not to consume any wine this evening. Let others frolic as they will. It is not worth a Tilter imperiling what is likely to be a very long life."

Klepsydra and Avevaios exchanged serious looks before gliding away without further exchange.

"Ow!" yowled the wine-drenched scholar beside Chesa. He shoved away the man sucking at his nipple, sending him sprawling. The drenched man's chest bled from a bite wound. "You venomous shit! Be careful!"

The herd of scholars around the spectacle roared with laughter. Chesa stole the moment to scurry away with her soaked robes. The next minute, she found herself in the privy again, sucking the narcotic from her robes with alacrity. It seemed the gods intended for this Saturnalia to reward her more than usual. Her head swam, and she stumbled sideways. She felt herself strike the stone wall hard, but her mind only elected to focus on the pleasure of the stone against her skin. Her heart throbbed in her ears as her body flushed. The perfect image of the smug ascendant choking to death in her hands flashed before her. She regained her bearings, limp, and crumpled to the privy floor. She struggled to raise a hand, but euphoria subdued any vestigial concern in her.

As she lay stupefied, her head sloshed over the words. "You venomous shit. . ." she slurred. "You venomous shit. . ." Each time she mumbled them, she saw the drenched man gasp and look down as his bleeding chest. Sometimes Chesa wished she harbored venom. She did, in a way, though real venom required life thaumaturgy. If only, like Peony Bianchi, she could touch another thread. Chesa would have liked to envenomate a scholar or two. Scholars amid narcotic euphoria made for such easy targets too. She only needed venom.

"Venomous shit." Chesa laughed as she pressed her head into the cool wall. She scraped her cheek hard across the stone, slurring the words. Then, in a moment of panicked sobriety, she shouted, "Venomous shit?!"

She heaved herself up and stumbled into balance. She needed to find someone. The privy door opened by her hand to reveal a blurring sea of scholars that groped and laughed. Chesa blundered forward into them and prayed she could hold onto her moment of lucidity.

Two throbbing heartbeats later, Chesa found herself stumbling into the main kitchen. Ursielle Hedrigal chatted in a quiet tone with Amus Clutton-Brock only feet from the entrance.

"Ursielle, I need you!" said Chesa. Her voice rang desperate in her ears.

Ursielle's brow furrowed. Amus Clutton-Brock scowled.

"Are you alright?" asked Ursielle. His eyes softened.

Chesa couldn't imagine how she appeared. She had never consumed so much saprolite wine at once. She tried to steady her voice. "The venom!" she said, but the words came out slurred. "I think they intend to put the venom into the fountains. It makes perfect sense. They've been storing it up for Saturnalia!"

Ursielle's reply registered as distant echoes. "You're sure? How do you know?"

Chesa shook her head. "I've got a feeling."

Primara Clifton-Brock guided Ursielle away and scorned, "We have business, you and I. Her rantings about venom can wait for another day. She's drunk. Matters of the Primara Council take precedence."

Ursielle looked pained as he glanced between Clutton-Brock and Chesa. He approached Chesa and lowered his voice. "Let me attend to this, and I'll see what I can do. Keep yourself inconspicuous, and inform Ms. Ash."

Chesa nodded.

As Ursielle withdrew, his mind brushed and hummed against hers. She closed her eyes and listened to its melody. When she opened them, she observed the labyrinth of mind threads swirling in a luminescent umbra around Ursielle. She tried to suppress her thaumaturgical sight,

208

but failed. His mind called to hers, begging to be subjugated. She closed her eyes and focused on her breathing, willing the surging saprolite in her mind to recede.

But Ursielle's were not the only mental threads in her field of view. Dozens of faint coronas extended from the brains of servants as they bustled about the kitchens. Each shimmered in a contrasting hue.

Clutton-Brock cleared his throat and shot Chesa a disapproving glare. She looked upon him and gasped. The tendrils of someone's mind under normal conditions flicked and wound around themselves. They danced to a chaotic cadence, like the minds of the people who bore them. Yet when Chesa peered into the mind of the Architect Primara, she saw a series of knots and rigid braids. His mind suffered the unmistakable scars of a Delver's detailed work—and a powerful one too. Revoking aspects of a subject's will subdued the very essence of the subject's personhood. Such knotting required a thaumaturge to catch the threads of a person's mind, wrench them, contort them, and lash them together. Braids entangled almost every inch of the Architect Primara's mind.

Chesa stood there with her mouth open. Primara Clutton-Brock should be little more than an automaton. Yet there he stood, scowling. How could she not have noticed the workings before?

Her jaw worked to find a way to alert Ursielle to the danger before him. She reexamined all she had conveyed about the venom too. Clutton-Brock had heard her, and he was somehow a Delver's pawn.

Ursielle glanced between her and Clutton-Brock with a calculating expression. "Be about it, Chesa!" he ordered. "Ms. Ash will attend to your needs. Leave the Primara and me to discuss our business." He winked at her, and the muscles in his jaw tightened.

Chesa genuflected and fled.

In the main hall, a short, plump scholar with scant hair donned the golden horns of the King of Mischief. He slid the shaft of his golden scepter into the bare under-crevice of a scholar on the stage. The crowd roared as the receiving scholar mewled.

"He minges like an ascendant!" shouted the King of Mischief.

The crowd went wild.

Chesa found Ms. Ash perched near a serving table.

"Lydia!" called Chesa. "The Delvers! I think they plan to poison the fountains with their mau venom!"

"What?" growled Ms. Ash. "Why?"

Doubt pierced Chesa's euphoria-fueled certainty. "It just makes sense," she stammered. "They've been saving up the venom leading up to tonight. The scholars will be drunk and stumbling anyhow. No one will notice."

Ms. Ash shook her head.

"Wait! There's something else!" Chesa wracked her muddled brain. "The Primara Clutton-Brock has been manipulated by a Delver some-how!"

"What?!" snapped Ms. Ash.

"It's the most complex coercion of a subject I've ever seen," said Chesa. "I'm shocked he's even able to hold a conversation. Whatever they've done to him, I bet they'll do to everyone else tonight."

Suspicion eroded away the skepticism on Ms. Ash's features. "If the Delvers are apt for a coup, then we'll stop them. Scan Primara Okondo for manipulations. If she's alright, I'll get her to help us. She hasn't touched a drop of saprolite wine herself. Go check the other Primaras too. Then. . ." Ms. Ash's voice cut off. "Then get the Bianchi girl and her friends out of here."

Across the room, the King of Mischief sentenced several scholars to strip bare on stage. He removed his scepter from the first scholar to another thunder of applause. A servant handed the king a frayed whip, and he lashed at the backsides of his new victims. Then he cackled and poured saprolite wine over their wounds.

"There!" Ms. Ash pointed at the Weaver Primara, nestled in the crowd across the room.

Scanning thaumaturgical energies at a distance required considerable energy. Chesa drew upon the enhancements provided by her saprolite wine to witness the Primara's mind. Even though she was aided by saprolite, the wispy threads orbiting Okondo's brain flickered in and out of perception. Then a cry escaped Chesa. Braids of Okondo's mind sat arranged like a bird's nest tucked into otherwise normal tendrils. The nest even seemed cozy in a way.

"She's been manipulated too, though not so bad," Chesa whispered.

Ms. Ash's lips compressed. "Very well. I'll ask the servants to guard the fountains and keep their eyes peeled for Delvers skulking about. I'll do the same."

"I'll see to the other Primara," said Chesa. She turned to flee, but the old servant woman grasped her arm.

"And Chesa. . ." Ms. Ash paused. "Stay alive. I, for one, like you that way."

Chesa flashed Ms. Ash a wicked grin and darted away.

The Sounder Primara lurked in the next hall. A retinue of archivists surrounded Aurora Kakoff, who appeared to be taking notes on the other attendees. Chesa took a vantage point hidden behind an amorphous ensemble of copulating scholars. She peered into the Primara's mind and sighed with relief. Kakoff's mind remained unaltered. Her threads danced unknotted. At least that meant the Delvers' influence bore limits among the administration.

Scholars began thinning from the halls, rendering Chesa's search easier. They stumbled away in pairs, triads, or larger groups. They discarded their robes like snakeskins on the floor. Chesa found the Evader Primara, Tafos Anaktisi, dreary-eyed, with a young-looking man beneath one arm and a plump woman Chesa recognized as an ascendant beneath his other. They lumbered toward an exit. With an effort of will, Chesa scanned the Evader Primara's mind. She glanced into the minds of the two younger individuals as well. None of them showed signs of manipulation, though their mental networks caressed the coronas of the others nearby. Chesa's muscles sagged with relief.

Someone bellowed nearby, and Chesa turned, expecting to find another pair of scholars amid sodomy, but she discovered Ms. Ash advancing on her instead.

"I found Kakoff and Anaktisi," said Chesa. "They're clean. That means only two Primaras are compromised."

"That we know of," countered Ms. Ash. "Seems Klepsydra left early."

"Then I'll get the ascendants," said Chesa.

Ms. Ash flashed Chesa a smile. "Good girl. I'll see that the fountains are watched. We should be in the clear soon enough, thanks to you."

Chesa let that small compliment fill her, and she departed.

Packed against the food tables in the main hall, Peony Bianchi, Roland Ward, and Tara Langcraw stood with the most conservative students in attendance. They gawked at the waning spectacles of flesh and clung to each other like prudish rats at sea.

Tara starred daggers at a dark-haired girl writhing against one of the low-ranking Delvers at the room's center. Delver Garland Roger, one of Nash's toadies, draped a pair of well-veined arms about Lavinia Thalsem. She returned his gropes and then some. Neither gave any indication that they noticed their audience.

For good measure, Chesa drew upon what little strength remained in her reserves to scan the minds of Peony, Roland, and Tara.

The corona of threads that undulated around Roland Ward moved with a greater sense of purpose than any Chesa had ever seen. They glided like tectonic plates. The swirling energies that emanated from the Langcraw heiress stood motionless. Then, as though they were releasing bound-up energy, they shot out in various directions and reorganized into a new geometry. They remained placid for but a second before they skittered back to their original conformation. The loop repeated, revisiting the two states. Chesa wondered what that could mean. On the other hand, Peony Bianchi's threads moved with such celerity that it dizzied Chesa. Yet nestled in her tendrils eeled a small cluster of knots—subtle, but unmistakable.

Chesa approached the ascendants with more authority than she dared on any other occasion. She hoped her bravado might make them compliant.

"Ms. Ash has requested that I escort the three of you back to the ascendants' quarters now. There are concerns about your safety," said Chesa. Though she genuflected, she kept her eyes fixed on the three youths.

They exchanged side-eyed looks before Tara withdrew into haughty stillness. Peony kept her dark eyes on Chesa, her expression unreadable.

"We do not take orders from servants, be it Ms. Ash or anyone else!" snapped Tara.

"I apologize for my—" Chesa began, but Tara cut her off.

She shook her head side to side. "No, Chesa. An apology will not do for your insolence. I do not know your motives, but I do not trust my safety in your hands."

"Ms. Ash really sent you?" Peony asked.

Chesa nodded.

Tara opened her mouth, but this time Peony interrupted her. "I trust Ms. Ash, Tara, and I believe Chesa."

Tara gaped at Peony.

"I trust her too. I d-don't know Ms. Ash much, but I trust who Peony trusts," added Roland. "And Chesa has never done anything but help me."

Tara scoffed at their mutiny. "I suppose I am outnumbered then, am I?"

"Not at all," said Peony, her tone relaxed. "You can stay here. Roland and I can go with Chesa." A smile touched her mouth.

"And leave me alone with these degenerates?" cried Tara. "I could be assaulted!"

"Pick your p-poison," Roland answered. "I'd rather you come with us, but I won't force you."

Tara's mouth fell open. "Well. . ." she sputtered. "I will not allow myself to be imperiled so. And, well, since you have requested my company . . . I . . . I . . . I will grant you. . ."

"Tara," Peony sighed, "let's get going. We'd be honored by your company."

Tara's jaws clapped shut.

"And I'm honored to escort you," needled Chesa.

"We'll go," agreed Peony. "But only under the condition that you never refer to me or any of us as a 'liege' or 'master' again. Save all that for someone who wants it."

Chesa's eyebrows shot up before she could help it. "If you so request."

"We do," said Peony, placing an emphasis on the word "we."

Chesa decided at that moment to set aside the puzzle that the ascendants presented for another day.

Within the hour, all three ascendants resided behind their doors. Chesa thanked the gods that none of them had offered any further resistance. When she returned to the main hall, the dimmed room appeared almost empty.

Servants saw to the drunken stragglers that remained. The helpless, wine-engorged scholars lay about like capsized turtles. They pawed at the floor and wiggled their fleshy bodies as they moaned and drooled, perhaps responding to imagined lovers.

Chesa found Ms. Ash and several other servants as they hoisted up Weaver Ankathi. A slick of saprolite wine cascaded down the front of her pale yellow robes. Chesa glided to Ms. Ash's side and took Ankathi's other arm in an iron grip. The Weaver lumbered to her feet with a whine.

Like Weaver Ankathi, all the remaining scholars were among the oldest, unhealthiest, and least appealing of the menhir's population. They represented the ones left out of the trysts that served as the final ritual of Saturnalia for most. The incapacitated but beautiful scholars had disappeared with the crowds, whisked off by their more opportunistic colleagues.

"I was beautiful once," Weaver Ankathi slurred. "Not long. . ." The woman fell limp, though her eyes remained open.

Chesa studied them. Seeing no comprehension there, she took the chance to speak.

"Did anyone see anything?" she whispered.

Ms. Ash shot her an annoyed look as they dragged Ankathi. "Nothing. I grazed several Delvers and felt no vials. I searched discarded clothing too. No vials." Ms. Ash's voice came out hoarse. "Had the fountains been poisoned, there would be more scholars lying around here. Instead, it's just the usual lot on the floor again this year."

Chesa frowned. Perhaps she was wrong after all.

They moved the groaning Weaver for a long while in silence.

"There is the other matter," said Chesa.

Ms. Ash studied Ankathi a moment before she replied, "Yes?"

Chesa lowered her voice. "The knots on Clutton-Brock were extensive. I observed smaller entanglements on Primara Okondo and Ms.

215

Bianchi. Someone's been manipulating all three. Maybe the same Delver, but maybe not."

The old servant woman's body stiffened at the mention of Peony.

"I didn't see Primara Nash tonight, did you?" asked Ms. Ash.

"No," replied Chesa, realizing she'd overlooked the Delver Primara's absence.

"Then he is the natural suspect," concluded Ms. Ash. "He has the means to work the thaumaturgy, and he's had ample access to both Okondo and Clutton-Brock. There are few times I am not with Primara Okondo, and she is followed by a larger and larger set of allies these days. Council meetings and private rendezvous with other Primaras are the only times she goes unguarded."

"What about Peony?" asked Chesa. "I haven't seen Nash interact with her."

"Good point," murmured Ms. Ash. "Though you said he took an interest in her. Couldn't he have used your notes to intercept her?"

Chesa considered the point. She had delivered a schedule of common activities and routines for more than a handful of ascendants to the Delver Primara. It all stood to reason.

"Is Peony meant to be some pawn or lever to pull?" asked Chesa. "What good could she be to Nash, even as a pawn?" She shook her head.

Ms. Ash offered no answers.

The pair quieted as they neared the Weavers' quarters. There they handed off Ankathi to another pair of servants, who escorted her off to her treetop chambers.

"Be sure to lay her on her side!" ordered Ms. Ash as they carried Ankathi away. "She's likely to vomit again."

After they disappeared, Ms. Ash turned to Chesa. Lines gathered between her brows. "Perhaps Peony is a string tied to the Weaver Primara," she said. "We don't know who was manipulated first, I'll grant you, but it seems to me Peony could have helped Primara Nash gain access to Okondo. Then again. . ." Ms. Ash's voice quieted. "It might have something to do with the anomaly pens. The Weavers have a stake down there. Maybe the Delvers have their eyes on those saprolite wine resources. With Primara Okondo's help and Peony's access, the Delvers could have the means to pipe those new resources their way."

"How shall we proceed?" asked Chesa.

"The Evader Primara's mind was clear?" asked Ms. Ash.

Chesa confirmed.

"Then we need to see if Evader McCray has been manipulated," suggested Ms. Ash. "We need to keep an eye out for unexpected shipments of saprolite wine to the Delvers too. That would provide an indication of their plans. But that still leaves the mystery of all that mau venom."

"There are always plots within plots with the Delvers," offered Chesa. "The venom could pertain to a different operation."

"The Delvers spin the most intricate webs," agreed Ms. Ash. "Perhaps the bridge between the Delvers was not meant to be with the Weavers after all. Perhaps the bridge we're meant to destroy is with the Evaders. The shadow's vision was never concrete."

"Perhaps," admitted Chesa.

"The Disciples will need to meet soon. But for now, I should be going," sighed Ms. Ash. "A good many Weavers will need ginger treatment to aid in their recoveries tomorrow. I've got to start preparing. Take care of yourself, girl."

Chesa watched Ms. Ash's back as the old servant stalked back into the Weavers' quarters. Though her mind swam with possibilities, fatigue needled at the edges of Chesa's senses. So, she determined that the bulk of her concerns could wait for another day.

When she woke in her chambers later, sweat-soaked robes clung to Chesa's body. One shoe still tottered from her foot. The standing lamp in her room burned low. She turned her head from side to side, taking care to nurse the beginnings of a terrible headache. A sudden burst of knocks at her door had her brain singeing with pain.

"Please go away," grumbled Chesa.

"Chesa! We need you!" yelled a familiar voice.

Tricia Higman stood outside.

Chesa groaned low and quiet.

"It's an emergency!" shouted Tricia.

Chesa lumbered to her door, bleary-eyed and fumbling. When she opened it, Tricia's bloodshot eyes stared into her own.

"What. . . ?" Chesa began, but the frantic woman cut her off.

"It's the Delvers, Chesa. Something's wrong!" Tricia shrieked.

Chesa flinched at the sound as pain radiated through her head like a needle driving through an eye.

"What about the Delvers?" she asked.

"Lysander Sze intends to question you," exclaimed Tricia. "He thinks you've been involved in some plot against the Delvers!"

Chesa's heart stopped as every hint of lingering high retreated from her senses. Sze needed to speak with her, about. . . ? Had Primara Clutton-Brock relayed a message of some kind?

"You have to come with me, Chesa, or I'll be in trouble too," cried Tricia. "There's something wrong."

"Has someone bothered to tell Primara Nash about all this?" asked Chesa.

The color drained from Tricia's cow-eyed face.

"What is it?" said Chesa.

Tricia's face trembled.

"Out with it!" snapped Chesa. She drew close to the woman.

"Nash is dead!"

CHAPTER 17

Across an Ocean

TARA COMBED HER HAIR for the tenth time. After a night like Saturnalia, her mind had determined sleep to be an unwise decision. To have been approached by the Tilter Primara should have felt like an honor. She should have felt euphoric. But the Tilters' opaque warning about her peers and some unintelligible bifurcation eclipsed any hope of joy. Not to mention, Tara doubted that powerful ascendants needed intervention from their Primara to manifest their aptitudes. Hope withered eternal.

The Tilters had failed to specify when Tara should expect them. So, Tara went to the dining hall as soon as it opened, fetched some fruit, and returned to her room. She was back only a few minutes when a careful knock resonated at her door.

"Just a moment," she called. She fastened Larus's green amber snood over her hair. Not typically the superstitious sort, Tara nevertheless hoped it might bring her luck. She opened the door and slid into a deep bow of deference.

"Well, I guess I'm getting the royal treatment this morning, huh?" said Lavinia. She beamed at Tara. "Did I interrupt? I thought you might have someone here. . ."

"What?" Tara began. "I would not cheapen myself so . . . though a lesser might." She let an edge of cruelty touch the last.

Lavinia's dark eyes twinkled beneath mussed hair. Tara wondered if she'd ever seen Lavinia grin before.

"Suit yourself!" Lavinia chirped. "What have you got planned for your day off?"

Tara stepped away to let Lavinia pass. She still wore the maroon robes of the Architects of Forces from the evening prior. When Tara had last seen her, the garments lay at the feet of Lavinia's writhing alabaster form. The reclothed version of Lavinia plopped herself down on the edge of Tara's bed and fell back laughing.

"You appear to have had a splendid time," snapped Tara.

Lavinia giggled. "It was amazing, wasn't it? The music, the wine, the scholars. . ."

Tara fought the urge to shout at Lavinia, to tell her to get off her bed before she transferred something vile onto the linens . . . though that impulse risked the Tilters arriving amid a rant.

"Who was your companion last night?" asked Tara. "You two danced with notable, er . . . enthusiasm."

Lavinia rolled onto her side and placed her head on her hand, shooting Tara a devilish smile. "Oh, did we? I'm glad we provided you with some entertainment."

Tara looked away. Lavinia lacked any semblance of shame.

"The pair of you were obstructing our way, and. . ." Tara fumbled.

Lavinia interrupted with a dismissive roll of her eyes and a sigh. "Well, maybe you could have tried enjoying yourself too. Maybe you could have let go a bit and joined us. Would that have been so bad?"

For a moment, the urge to shout overtook Tara again. Lavinia had to be teasing her, right? The thought was preposterous.

Instead of giving the girl more fodder than she deserved, Tara responded in a cool tone, "Such a generous offer, but no thank you."

Lavinia wiggled her way to the head of Tara's bed and smelled her pillows with a sigh. Tara cringed.

"Excuse me, Lavinia," she exclaimed, "but is there an especially good reason you are huffing my pillows?"

Lavinia paused a moment. Then she huffed the pillows again and faced Tara with a fiendish grin. "I just wanted to know what it would have smelled like . . . had you been there. I think you would have enjoyed yourself. Perhaps I can show you sometime."

Tara only managed, "No, that will not do, thank you."

Lavinia rolled from Tara's bed and threw herself atop her own. She tunneled beneath her blankets and groaned with satisfaction. Tara was not sure she could handle this jubilant version of Lavinia for any extended length of time. She found herself longing for the venomous, sharp-tongued Lavinia of old.

A second series of knocks at the door sent a wave of relief through Tara. She approached the door with cold grandeur, avoiding Lavinia's girlish bedroom eyes. As before, she swung the door open with a fluid gesture and bowed. "Tilters, I am honored to make your acquaint-ances."

"Tilters?! What're you t-talking about?" cried Roland Ward, looking stunned and stupefied as ever. "I d-didn't see you at breakfast?"

"What are you doing here?" howled Tara.

Roland tripped over his words. "I, uh, d-didn't mean to disturb you. Aren't we supposed to be at the archive this morning?"

Tara sighed. She hadn't told him. The debauchery of the evening before had distracted her. Now Lavinia distracted her.

"Roland. . ." she began. "I'm not working at the Central Archive with you anymore. The Tilter Primara has arranged for special tutoring for me. They've petitioned the chancellor to remove me from classes too."

"All of them?" asked Roland.

Tara confirmed.

"W-we'll hardly see you!" said Roland.

A pang of concern tugged at Tara. She'd grown fond of spending time with her friends.

A purr that became a growl called from behind Tara, and she turned. Lavinia slunk over her bed, mimicking a cat, arching her back and whimpering.

"If either of you are lonely," Lavinia cooed, "you know I've got plenty of free time today. Maybe I can provide some company, hmm?"

Roland's mouth dropped open. "W-what's wrong with her?" he whispered.

"That is an excellent question," Tara replied with no little disgust. "She has been like this all morning. She appears to have had a very special evening with a gentleman scholar." Tara cleared her throat. "Lavinia, I'm going to wait for the Tilters outside with Roland. It was nice seeing you." She gathered her belongings and fled.

"You're going to do great at your lessons today, Tara. I just know it!" cheered Lavinia.

As the chamber door closed behind her, Tara dropped her voice to a whisper. "You know, I disliked Lavinia before—very much so. Now I am beginning to realize that the old Lavinia was more tolerable than I ever gave her credit for. She's been suggestive all morning. If you value your virginity, Roland, I endorse you staying clear."

Something like sheepishness flashed across Roland's face, and his cheeks darkened. "W-whatever you say," he replied.

"Although. . ." Tara continued. "There is the off chance she's had a stroke or something. Perhaps you can keep an eye on her, from a distance. If you see or hear anything strange, perhaps reach out to the Evaders to have her assessed."

Roland nodded his agreement.

A pair of tall women, one with long black hair with skin the hue of tree nuts and a second with cropped red hair, approached together. Each wore the billowing, midnight-kissed amethyst robes of the Tilters.

They glided without a sound, their feet concealed beneath rippling fabric.

Every muscle in Tara tightened. Roland followed Tara's gaze and stumbled back from the approaching Tilters. Tara dropped into her lowest bow. Roland tripped into a genuflection. The pair of Tilters paused several paces away.

"Tara Langcraw," the dark-haired Tilter chimed.

"Yes," said Tara.

The red-haired Tilter gave Roland a considering look before speaking. "Primara Klepsydra has requested your attendance. We will collect you here each day until your progress becomes satisfactory."

It burned Tara to be reminded of her floundering.

The dark-haired Tilter settled Roland with a passive long look. "You are not permitted to have guests during your lessons."

The paler Tilter fixed her eyes on something distant and unseen. "Roland Ward will have to wait here."

A muscle in Roland's back spasmed hard enough to be visible through his robes.

Tara turned to Roland. "Perhaps I will see you at dinner?"

The pale, red-haired Tilter added, "You will be returned to your chambers for isolated study this afternoon. We will have other matters to attend to."

"We should be going," said the dark-hair Tilter. Her tone rung with a quiet finality.

With that, the two Tilters turned as a pair in a slow circle, like great boats turning at sea, and glided back in the direction from which they had come. They did not turn to see who followed.

Tara touched Roland's shoulder. "I'll see you soon!" she whispered. Then she ran to join the retreating Tilters.

"I'll c-come back here after the Central Archive?" Roland called, but his voice trailed off into the distance.

The Tilters guided Tara into an obscure outcrop of the menhir. They rounded corridor after unassuming corridor, with only dusty laboratories or servants' rooms extending from them. No one traveled here by accident.

The way Tara saw it, the Tilters navigated around factions more numerous and more powerful than themselves. Their lives existed as a dance among the feet of giants—giants who no doubt considered the Tilters a contemptable nuisance to their scheming. It struck Tara as a precarious way to live.

The corridor runner transitioned to dark purple, and Tara's heartbeat quickened. Two sets of amber eyes emerged from pooled darkness in the distance. As Tara approached, two hypertrophied felids resolved around them, their delicate tails tucked around the base of their feet. The ruddy brown of their short coats and wide triangular faces with delicate chins made their breed unmistakable. The guardian Tilter mau in the Central Archive avoided archivists and clerks alike.

"Pardon the mau," said the red-haired Tilter in a breathy tone. "They were separated from us yesterday. They can be codependent at times, though always on their terms. They hardly ever leave the Tilter's den. Remember, Tara Langcraw, the less the other factions know of our companions, the better."

A series of billowing drapes, like the weighted curtains of some tremendous stage, extended from the ceiling to the floor at the end of the corridor. Six bright standing lamps sat to either side, drenching the space in white light. The purple fabric drank the light in and extinguished it, not so unlike the Tilters' robes.

The two Tilters turned to Tara and spoke in unison. "This way!"

They placed their hands into evaginations of the fabric and slid their forms through an unseen seam in the furls. Tara followed. Parting the fabric presented no trivial matter. The heavy curtains bore considerable weight, and the bottoms appeared anchored down by bags of small stones. One layer of fabric gave way to another, and then another, and so on. Each weighted drape stood layered in tight succession, with less than a few inches between one layer of recurving drapery and the next.

Tara felt as though she swam through ocean waves. No light reached the inner layers, and the fabric billowed and slid all around her. She turned, enveloped in so much material that she lost her orientation. She reached out for a wall, but found herself wound up in drapes too voluminous to right herself. She could detect nothing of the Tilters who'd led her here. The seams of each layer staggered with no pattern from side to side, which forced her to move laterally in search of the path forward. For every seam Tara succeeded in finding, she was thrice tricked by dead ends, forcing her to feel her way back in search of another way. Her chest grew tight. She crouched down, hoping she might slide beneath the curtains. But the bottoms of the inner layers seemed to pass beyond the floor of the corridor, their ends unreachable.

The air went stagnant, and Tara's breathing accelerated as she called out, "I fear I am lost! Can someone please help me?"

No reply came. Layer after layer of material, denser than water, deadened the sound of her calls. There seemed no chance that someone could hear her cries. She tried to continue onward, but only became further entangled. Every choice she made resulted in another dead end more labyrinthine than the last.

She tried to retreat back to the entrance—or to where she thought it must be—but quickly realized that rediscovering the seams behind her imposed an equivalent challenge. Anxiety and doubt overtook her. Her throat tightened with each breath. Finally, she sagged to the floor, defeated. She placed her head between her knees, unable to see her own fingers, and caged her eyes. She dug her fingernails into her scalp to feel something distinguishable amid the fabric ocean.

After several minutes, Tara detected movement from the darkness somewhere behind her. At first, the motion was so faint that she thought she imagined it. But it grew.

"I'm here. I . . . I don't know where 'here' is any longer. I'm trapped!" she called. She tried to steady herself.

No one answered, but the sensation of movement drew closer. Then, jolting her with surprise, something seized each of her shoulders. With a wrench of ironlike strength, they lifted her, setting her on her feet. She felt the form of someone taller than her, a woman, pressed tight against her back. Tara resisted the urge to cry her thanks. The firmness of the hands, their brutal puissance, quieted her emotions.

One step at a time, the woman behind her guided Tara forward, through layer after layer of the drowning fabric. Still heated and flustered, Tara lost her sense of time, but then, faster than her entry began, a sliver of illumination pierced a seam just beyond where she and her guide stood. They moved together into that light, and it showered over them, blinding Tara. The hands released her, and Tara collapsed to the floor, blind and disoriented, like some cave organism exhumed from its home. A pair of voices pityingly clucked their tongues as she lay on the floor, immobilized by blindness.

"Perhaps we should have warned you. That barrier has kept more than a few malevolent scholars from reaching our home," said a voice Tara recognized as the red-haired Tilter.

The dark-haired Tilter echoed, "We'd hoped you'd fare better than that in the Azurite Ocean. We didn't even manipulate any potentialities to thwart you. You will need to grow much, Tara Langcraw."

"Was that some kind of test?" asked Tara.

The red-haired Tilter replied, "Only in the sense that any challenge reveals the caliber of a scholar, Tara Langcraw. But there must come a day when you can cross such spaces even as one of us acts to prevent you. You must come to wield your own destiny in the face of others who would take it from you—and there will be many who try."

Tara blinked.

The outlines of her two Tilter guides, each with smaller brown blurs of mau perched at their feet, resolved into view. Two rows of lamps on each wall flooded the corridor around her in light. They must have blinded anyone who passed through the Azurite Ocean. As her eyes focused, Tara turned to examine the face of the woman who had saved her. Tilter Avevaios stood over her crumpled form.

"Welcome, Tara Langcraw," said Avevaios. "We've been waiting for you a long time."

Tara blinked again, and the world sharpened. Her two guides and Tilter Avevaios stood over her. A few paces beyond them, the corridor opened on a stonework cave. Unlike the usual pale yellows and subdued earthen tones used elsewhere in the menhir, gleaming stone veined with lapis lazuli, amethyst, and onyx enshrined the Tilters' den.

A small gasp escaped her.

"You find it impressive?" asked the dark-haired Tilter.

Tara gave a slow nod.

The dark-haired Tilter turned away, her mau falling in behind her. Then she cast a look over one shoulder. "If you are lucky, you may one day call this your home." She paused. "But that will never happen if you just sit there gawking."

The red-haired Tilter turned to follow the first. Their expressions remained still as glass. Tara hauled herself up and straightened her robes before following.

The room beyond appeared carved in relief from one giant slab of marble or smooth aggregate. A few tables dotted the domed space, each cut from the same colorful stone as the rest of the chamber. The irregular coloration blended the furnishings with the walls and ceiling.

They tricked Tara's eyes, making it difficult to discern where a table or bench began and ended until she almost blundered upon it.

Several Tilters, each in pairs and in billowing robes, sat at the tables. Two pairs were engaged in chess matches. The others read from dusty tomes or simply stared off into nothing. One Tilter sat murmuring to herself. As Tara passed, her breath caught. Only skin-toned pits resided where the murmuring Tilter's eyes belonged. All the Tilters sat or stood so erect that they seemed inhuman. Several glanced up from their tasks or swiveled their eyes as Tara entered.

Primara Klepsydra stood alone at a table. Upon it sat a huge hourglass. Several inches of open air resided between its two halves. In that space, silver sand descended in lazy spirals, bifurcating and unifying again and again, before gliding back together into the bottom half of the hourglass. The Primara plucked a shimmering granule from its path between the two halves and studied it. She replaced it with a grimace.

"It is good to have you here, Tara Langcraw," said Klepsydra, her tone somber. "Your life will bring much change to the world."

Tara swallowed. Could she really be a subject of prophecy?

"I. . ." Tara whispered. ". . . suspect it must be a great burden to see the future."

The Primara's frown deepened.

"I did not mean to offend," Tara added.

"No Tilter can observe the distant future with any reliability," Klepsydra confessed. "I would fear for the safety of any sister who could. No, Tara Langcraw, a future disturbance must be very great for us to detect it, and not so distant, at that."

A long silence passed. The falling grains of the hourglass slowed. Primara Klepsydra flicked her magnificent eyes to Tara. "Do you know why our quarters are referred to as a 'den'?" she riddled.

Tara thought it might have something to do with the mau. Perhaps the Tilter mau harbored greater gregariousness than the other breeds.

"Incorrect," said the Primara. "Try again."

Tara reminded herself that unspoken exchanges could be the norm with some Tilters. Perhaps the den's name had something to do with its architecture? Though Tara feared to ask.

"No, Tara Langcraw, architecture is not the inspiration for its name either," answered Klepsydra. "And there are no humiliating questions here. We will treat you with the respect of any sister."

"'Sisters'?" echoed Tara. "You make it sound as though you are all related."

The Primara's eyes sparkled. "In more ways than one," she replied. She angled her head back and forth as she spoke. "I believe that each of us shares a single origin, in the most literal sense, a single matriline. But the line before us is too long and stuttered to confirm anything of that view, even for us."

"So, we are a single noble bloodline?" asked Tara.

She studied the women present. Though their coloring differed, the Tilters shared many of their unusual features. They all bore triangular faces and large-set eyes. None exhibited curvaceous or petite physiques. But the regional differences between the sisters gave Tara pause.

"Your skepticism is appreciated," said Klepsydra. "We are family because we share in each other's gifts and weaknesses and value each other's lives as our own." The Tilter Primara's eyes met Tara's. "When one of us dies, we all feel the loss of power. Preserving each of our sisters makes the collective, and the individual units comprising it, greater. We do not infight as other scholars do. We are not individuals. We are aspects of a whole."

The sentiment struck Tara harder than the first time she'd heard it with Tilter Avevaios. Since she'd come to the Amber Menhir, Tara had so often observed the way the scholars vied with one another. Yet the Tilters of the Hourglass relied on each other for their thaumaturgical strength, which cast their interests in a very different light.

"You see what this means," agreed the Primara. "Though our numbers are few—only eleven—our power exceeds any other faction's by its philosophy."

Tara nodded. "Is that why it's called a 'den'? Is it meant to reference the Tilters' collective nature? If so, then why not a 'nest' or a 'hive'?"

The Tilter Primara's face twisted with distaste. "We are not so numerous as a hive. Moreover, a hive serves a queen. The Tilters are egalitarian. Had not the menhir forced us to select a Primara, we would not have one. The term is meaningless when we pass through the Azurite Ocean. It washes away inequality. As for nests, those are places to deposit young. They are but fertility shrines, nurseries of tragic responsibility. Our den is neither." The Primara inclined her chin. "Most Tilters are barren."

Tara thought of her mother.

The Primara waved her hand at the hourglass, and one of the floating paths of sand bifurcated into two. "In time, you must learn to wield three powers, Tara Langcraw," the Primara explained as she walked in a slow circle around her. "The weakest and least predictable of our gifts is that of foretelling. While on occasion some of us have witnessed a prophecy, such occurrences are rare. Visions beyond a few moments hence occur only when we are at our full number."

The Primara flicked out two fingers. "Our second purview is that of time manipulation. The zone of impact for this gift is greatly limited—though it is what provides us with enviably long lives."

A vision of the Endless One—the ancient Tilter that headed the Pearl Menhir—provided a morbid reminder of how severe a Tilter's longevity could become. Tara's mother feared the Endless One more than any other force in existence, though she never articulated why.

The Primara paused her meandering to fix Tara with a drowning gaze. "The final aspect of our gifts is that of temporal auditing. Though it at first seems trivial, we leverage it to great effect." The Primara smiled, her facial muscles moving as though they scarcely knew their way. "Her auditing allows a Tilter to view the recent history of objects and events. A single Tilter working in isolation may be able to revisit the previous few seconds." The Primara cocked a sly eyebrow at Tara and resumed the slow tilting of her head from side to side. "At our full number, we can scan back hours, or longer at times, provided that enough saprolite wine or other objects of power are present." Primara Klepsydra nodded toward her hourglass. "This is why we are so often called to investigate odd occurrences within the menhir."

Tara's chest tightened. "What sort of odd occurrences?"

"Most often?" the Primara frowned. "Deaths."

"Deaths?" echoed Tara with trepidation. She possessed no interest in becoming some kind of forensic investigator.

Klepsydra laughed. "Child, the acrimony among the scholars is no facade. Orchestrating a tragic slip for one's rival is too tempting a morsel for most. We catch many a scholar, provided we are alerted soon enough for our powers to be useful. If too much time elapses, then our audits can deliver no insights."

"What happens when they're caught?" Tara asked.

"They are subdued for admission into the anomaly pens. Waste not, want not," intoned the Primara with coolness.

"If there are just the three powers, and foretelling is so flawed, then how do you read my mind so reliably?" asked Tara.

"Ah, but a tool can be used in a great many ways," the Primara said, resuming her pacing around Tara. "I cannot read your mind. Not even a Delver can. But I can allow an event to pass and then study it."

"I don't understand," said Tara. "How does that do anything to help you read thoughts?"

The Primara clucked her tongue exaggeratedly. "Auditing the immediate past allows me to observe the possible outcomes of that moment. Sometimes we can observe potentialities that were unlikely to have occurred, but could have. Tilters can observe the potentialities, and in some cases, select an alternative over the one they first experienced."

Tara's head swam with the implications. "Then we have control over the world around us?"

"No, child," the Primara sighed. "In many instances, the path we first experience is the only probable outcome. In others, the outcomes we would favor are present in the distribution, but are so slight that they escape our grasp." Sadness laced the Primara's voice. "Still, even knowing that certain potentialities existed can give us insights. Imagine knowing that an ally risked betraying you."

Tara tried to work out how the gift allowed the Primara to read her thoughts. Perhaps a different variant of herself, in a different potentiality, spoke the thought aloud. If so, then the Primara might have sensed those possible outcomes and answered the question Tara had only thought in this reality.

"Early on in the initiation of our faction, someone proposed naming us the Lionesses of the Hourglass," the Primara mused. "Of course, that highlights the puissance of our abilities, which would not do."

The red-haired Tilter beside Tara spoke in distant tones. "To be forewarned is to be forearmed, Tara Langcraw. We have few advantages over the other noble factions. Our moat of secrecy must be wider and deeper than the rest."

Tara shook her head. "You mentioned a warning, at threat of some kind. A bifurcation? What did you mean?"

Primara Klepsydra's eyes went lax. "We have detected fractured probabilities on the near horizon for the menhirs. We do not know its precise nature, but we have learned that you, as wells as Peony Bianchi and perhaps Roland Ward, have all attracted an unhealthy amount of attention. Strings are beginning to draw taut all around you. We need you to be ready for whatever may come. Before you leave this place. . ."

The Primara produced a pearl from her robes. She rolled it between two fingers and smirked.

One side of a split within the floating sand before Klepsydra grew heavier than the other.

"The greatest weapon against our foes is collaboration," she reiterated with a smile. "Most scholars cannot imagine relying on one of their peers, or gods, or a servant. It is the Tilters' way to ask for and accept help when it is needed, and to give aid in turn. Let not yourself become an island, Tara Langcraw, and remember that an unexpected ally is always the most powerful."

Tara's face twisted in confusion.

"Your first martial lesson will be to play chess with me, Tara Langcraw," announced the red-haired Tilter. "Are you ready?"

"For a game?" Tara blurted out. "I have a million questions."

"A game that will prepare you to face adversity on a great many fields, if you learn your lessons well," Primara Klepsydra corrected.

"But—" Tara uttered with a start.

"Tilter Clythia Borgia will be your first opponent," continued the Primara.

The red-haired Tilter who'd guided Tara before bowed her head in acknowledgment.

Primara Klepsydra retreated to the entrance of the Tilters' den. Tara's dark-haired guide departed with her, leaving Tilter Borgia and Tara alone before the great swirling hourglass. Tilter Borgia gestured to an unoccupied chessboard.

Tara knew the game, though the Tilter pieces were spindlier and more delicate than those at her estates. They seemed worked from polished stone. Her mother deemed it essential that members of the noble bloodlines receive training in games of strategy. Perhaps her mother had learned the game at the menhir? Golden-hued rock with flecks of white composed the pale army, while crystals of midnight-azure, black, and indigo rendered the darker pieces.

"Which shall I. . .?"

"I will play black," asserted Tilter Borgia. She seated herself on the stone bench behind the black army. The Tilter took care to ensure that her billowing robes cascaded over the bench just so. "Tilters play the black army. Though the other noble factions may exalt the supposed benefits of tempo and the advantages of priority, the Tilters know the greater advantage resides in observation of the opponent."

Tara spent the remainder of her morning suffering a series of the most withering defeats imaginable. She executed one imbecilic mistake after another, always when she should have known better. Each time Tilter Borgia engaged her queen, Tara's lingering prospects of survival wasted away like parchment in a flame. As soon as one game ended, Tilter Borgia gestured for Tara to reset the board and begin again. Borgia displayed no emotion, no regret, no enjoyment. She exhibited nothing but icy indifference from one game to the next.

After what seemed like an eternity, Tilter Borgia rose from the board, announcing, "We are done for the day, Tara Langcraw. You do not play well." Tara opened her mouth to speak, but the Tilter barreled over her. "Each time you approached an intelligent choice, a different Tara reconsidered it. You. . ." She pointed a finger at Tara's chest. ". . . are the product of their failures. You possess too much uncertainty about how to act under pressure." She sniffed. "A lethal trait. You will need to expunge it. Worser yet, you are a miser, and you cower in the face of risk." Tilter Borgia flicked the top of the white queen. It toppled and rolled onto the floor to clatter at Tara's feet. "At times, one must risk one's greatest assets to see an opponent undone."

"But I. . ." Tara started.

Borgia lifted a pacifying hand, and Tara quieted. "And remember, if the situation does not appear to be in one's favor, then change it," she warned. "Add a little disturbance. That is your only option when you cannot properly take control of the board, Tara Langcraw."

The woman's words stung at Tara worse than any wasp.

Then her opponent added in an imperious tone, "Scholar Avevaios and I will escort you back. The remainder of the Tilters have been called to the Delvers' quarters. An accident, apparently." Tilter Borgia cleared her throat. "We will see you back to your room, but then we are needed elsewhere." Tilter Borgia walked away from the board, expecting Tara to follow.

When they reached the ascendants' quarters, commotion tainted the air. The ascendants moved like a hoard of anxious ants. Tara felt eyes on her as she and the two Tilters passed. Several of the ascendants gestured in Tara's direction, and her stomach twisted into knots.

The Tilters moved to pass a raucous group of ascendants, who fell silent and parted to let them by. Avevaios paused and gestured to a man Tara recognized as a promising force thaumaturge.

"What is going on here?" Avevaios demanded.

The man looked around at the other ascendants, seeming uncertain about whether to speak.

Avevaios's blue eyes narrowed. "Out with it!"

"There's been some kind of attack," he grumbled. "We don't know who all is involved. All we know is that some people got hurt. The Evaders of Death are here. No one is allowed to enter or leave. There's to be an investigation."

"What kind of investigation?" Tara blurted out. She looked around for signs of Roland or Peony.

"Into the murder, of course." The ascendant sneered at Tara, fixing her with a malevolent smile. "They say Roland Ward might be involved." He twisted Roland's name like a dagger. "People are saying he'll go to the anomaly pens for this."

The Tilters of the Hourglass traded neutral looks.

"They think Roland Ward killed someone?" Tara gasped. "He's harmless! Where's Peony?" Despite her words, her breathing turned frantic.

A hand grasped her shoulder.

"Do not worry, Tara Langcraw," said Avevaios with a voice like granite. "We will get to the bottom of this."

CHAPTER 18

Accusations

"**S**HE'S ATTEMPTING TO MISLEAD us again," sneered a woman's whining voice.

Chesa had time enough to observe something flicker from the corner of her eye. The next thing she knew, she blinked her watering eyes open again. Her vision tunnelled, and her mouth filled with the acrid saltiness of blood. She ran her tongue along the inside of her mouth, where the blow had landed. A pair of her top teeth wobbled. She twisted her hands, but the ropes binding her arms remained firm. She supposed it did not matter. Escaping her interrogation chair could not free her from her current circumstances.

"Chesa," sang the voice of Lysander Sze, "how many times must we go through this?"

Chesa ejected a bolus of phlegm and blood from her mouth in reply.

Delver Sze advanced on her. They locked eyes as he drew himself close, one side of his mouth quirked up.

"Let us start at the beginning, hmm?" He hummed the last word. Despite everything, he still bore an acidic cuteness to his every gesture. "When you were Primara Nash's concubine, at what point did you start plotting against him?!" Bits of his spittle misted Chesa's face.

A slow smile spread across Chesa's ruined mouth as she replied, "Disliking someone does not mean I murdered them, my liege."

She had said the same before. Perhaps her interrogators hoped exhaustion might overwhelm her. Perhaps they were right. Perhaps after she shattered, she would confess to Nash's murder and everything else. Whether or not it any of it was true would not matter. At that point, they could do anything they liked to her.

"But you meant him harm, Chesa. We know this is true. We have read it from your mind," chided Sze as he backed away from her. "Do you expect us to believe that his treacherous whore played no part in his sudden demise on Saturnalia, the very night made for heedless acts?"

Chesa scoffed.

The Delver ambassador laughed. "It is too much for credulity. We already have enough evidence now to execute you. What does this last bit of honesty matter? Why withhold it so?"

Chesa's head thrust back, not of her own volition, and her nose angled upward. A cascade of hot water slid down her sinuses, behind her eyes, and burned her ears. She gurgled and spat the water out, but it kept coming. She tried to snap her head to one side to obtain relief. She tried to close her throat, but failed. She opened her mouth to gasp for air, to gasp for help, for anything. But the water kept coming, and she inhaled it. She wrenched her hands against her bindings. She jolted her body to try and topple her chair. But all her attempts remained futile. She knew then that she would die here.

"Enough of that!" snapped Delver Sze. "She can't confess if she's drowning, you idiot!"

The water vanished.

Chesa sat dazed. Her eyes no longer burned. The phantasmal sensation ceased with such abruptness that it could not be real.

An ugly bit of laughter touched the woman's voice behind Chesa. "We've been doing it your way all night, Lysander. It pains me to inform you, but you haven't made much progress, my dear. We must be getting about it now."

Monica Ravel enjoyed a more reclusive life than almost any Delver of the Mind. Her studies on phantom sensations were revered by her peers. An insane grin split Chesa's face as she wheezed out a laugh. Who could have known that such esoteric studies on amputees from the anomaly pens would have spawned such vicious advances in the Delvers' interrogation tactics? Certainly not Chesa.

"Quiet!" snapped Sze. Beads of sweat collected on his brow as he rubbed his clammy hands on his robes. "Who helped you to slay the others?" he howled with a vindictive kick at Chesa's shin.

A stab of pain shot up Chesa's leg, but the sensation faded away into the backdrop of other aches. Chesa's mouth, slurred with her own blood, only managed a suicidal chuckle. "I have no idea who slayed any Delvers last night, my liege." If the scholars were going to kill her, and perhaps she deserved it, then she saw no harm in poking a little fun on her way out.

Sze looked back at Ravel for confirmation.

"She's being honest, on the whole, but everything she utters contains an evasive element," said Ravel. "I venture she knows something pertinent."

Sze let out an exasperated sigh. Then he kneeled before Chesa, like he was speaking to a child. "Chesa, Chesa, Chesa. . ." he crooned in descending tones. "It won't be long until the whole menhir hears about the events of last night. I won't be the only one asking questions either. Dozens of brain-dead Delvers of the Mind. . . Well, that's the sort of thing that garners attention in the Amber. Are you suggesting that something like that could have happened without betrayal of the deepest kind?" He sighed. "I know you know something. Delver Ravel has confirmed as much. We know you meant the Primara harm."

Chesa rolled a dismissive shoulder.

He clucked at her theatrically. "If you confess to your crime now and tell me everything, there could be a path forward for your life. I could work toward that goal with your help, but you would need to cooperate and confess."

Chesa let out a wheezing gurgle. "If the evidence is so firm, why am I being questioned? What is it you need from the mouth of a servant, Sze?"

At that, he stood and backhanded her. Her ruined mouth flicked to one side with the blow.

Delver Ravel chuckled from somewhere behind Chesa. "She was being honest there, for her. Chesa, dear, you're far more impertinent than your little genuflecting would ever suggest!" Ravel appeared in Chesa's periphery. A smug grin plastered her snubbed features as she sidled up. She touched Sze's arm and smirked. "She makes me wonder how many of the other servants are the same."

The pair stood before Primara Nash's bed. It was still draped with the red linens that suited Nash's predecessor. In fact, Chesa recognized little difference in the chambers since Primara Kensington's reign. Her history here had her grinning.

"Oh, Lysander, do you think she's losing it at last?" Ravel whined with false concern. "Do you think she'd enjoy another little nasal irrigation?" She pouted her swinish lips as she learned into Chesa. "Would you like that? Hmm? No?"

Lysander Sze studied the bedchamber. He avoided looking at the twitching mass behind him.

Chesa's swollen eyes only just allowed her to make out the remains. There, atop Primara Kensington's crimson sheets, squirmed the incontinent husk of his successor. Primara Nash had suffered a notably short tenure. Though he still survived, in the broadest sense, his recovery seemed dubious at best. His vacant eyes searched around his bedchamber. He grinned and licked at his lips with swirling motions. From time to time, he whimpered.

Chesa had chanced inspecting the state of Nash's mind hours prior. On Nash, the swirling, luminescent vines of the mind she knew from living beings, like the tentacles of some brilliant sea creature, flapped in impotent hemispheres, separated by a severed region. It appeared to Chesa like some thaumaturgical creature had burst from him. The ruins of Nash that lingered moved in anemic spurts between long bouts of quiescence. Two empty vials sat on the nightstand by his bed.

Lysander Sze walked over to Nash's dresser. Upon it sat the small chest that had once held more than a hundred vials of Delver mau venom. Sze picked up one of the vials and tilted it back and forth. "Do you recall what this is, Chesa?"

Chesa stifled another smile. "Anything worth doing is worth overdoing, my liege."

"What's that supposed to mean?" Sze snapped.

"It means, as I have already conveyed, Primara Nash was hoarding mau venom," Chesa confessed. "I knew that this was the case. He threatened me with it."

Delver Sze's voice rose and became more clipped. "Is that why you killed him? He threatened to poison you, so you killed him first?"

"My liege, I did not poison Primara Nash. I did not participate in his death, and I do not know who did. I only knew of the venom," Chesa conveyed. "I assumed the Primara was collecting a large volume of the liquid for an assault on another noble faction. It appears it was used against him instead."

Delver Ravel interrupted. "Not only him, dear. Someone administered the poison to many others too. That level of coordination without drawing the notice of other Delvers would require the cooperation of servants. If you want us to believe that you were not involved in this catastrophe, then surely you know suspects among the other servants? Tell us their names."

Chesa shrugged. Whoever they were, they worked horrendous mental damage on their victims. Mau venom alone produced no such effects. If a mau bite could do that, well, Chesa doubted the scholars would permit the beasts the freedom they enjoyed at present.

"Perhaps if I knew what the mau venom did in detail, I might be of more assistance to you, Masters," Chesa offered. She was curious how the venom might have been used. If she could survive the day, perhaps the information could prove useful.

Sze peered at Chesa. He gave Delver Ravel a questioning look, who threw up her hands.

"Seems harmless. . ." Sze's voice trailed off. "It isn't as though the mau are going to let you milk them. Though it might be fun to have you try. . . Delver mau venom is a sedative, akin to dreamflower. It makes the subject's mind more malleable to thaumaturgy. We don't use it often. Mining it is laborious, for obvious reasons."

Chesa cleared her croaking throat. "Then why was Primara Nash storing it? What large thaumaturgical working did he have planned?"

Delver Sze squinted at Chesa. Ravel adjusted her robes.

"There are glimmers of wisdom from you, Chesa," replied Sze with a hint of respect. "I suspect Primara Nash had a great many schemes I was not privy to. Unfortunately, his closest allies are all gone now."

Chesa thought she saw a path for escape, if Lysander would take her bait. If she could stall her interrogators for long enough, other noble factions would eventually hear of the murders. Most factions possessed ears in the others. That meant the Tilters would arrive soon. Gods knew, the Delvers hated the Tilters more than anyone. With a suitable delay, Sze and Ravel might fear slaying her outright. Killing Chesa might suggest their own culpability.

"Primara Nash never shared a close relationship with me," Chesa murmured. It was true. "Nor did I know of the venom's potential. It seems to me that fellow Delvers of the Mind are the most likely culprits. Perhaps his political rivals?"

Sze's smirk faltered for a moment. He exchanged another look with Ravel, who gnawed her lower lip. Everyone knew Nash hated them both. If Chesa was right, they both feared being questioned themselves, especially in the absence of a more obvious suspect. Perhaps that was why she luxuriated in her present circumstances. Luxuriated. . .

"Perhaps there is still a thaumaturgical signature of the event that killed Nash?" Chesa suggested. "Perhaps a more powerful Delver could use it to discern what happened?"

The two grimaced at her words. No doubt they had each scanned his mind several times in the prior hours.

"Was he injured mentally?" Chesa added. "If so, that would provide further evidence that a Delver of the Mind, perhaps a coalition, was involved. No servant could do that. . ."

Ravel licked her bleeding lips.

Chesa baited the hook. "I know there was friction between you both and the Primara. But I do not think you would have harmed him so," she caressed the morbid lie. "You have both made it clear you are committed to finding his killer." That was partially true. "I can help you. I have seen much, and I can move about the menhir without notice. Perhaps I can help you find the perpetrators. You would no doubt be rewarded for discovering them. One of you would be made Primara, and I would be in your debt."

Chesa watched the scholars and held her breath.

Something behind their eyes twinkled. They exchanged new and enterprising expressions beneath calculating brows. Chesa suppressed a smirk. There could only be one Delver Primara.

"We will return," said Sze.

The two Delvers retreated to the bathing chamber. Delver Ravel sat

243

on the edge of the marble tub while Sze remained standing. Though she could not make out the words, Chesa noted their gestures, which grew in intensity. When they returned, dangerous smiles slicked both their faces. Chesa's plan, it seemed, may have worked.

"You have proposed an interesting model, Chesa—one that Delver Ravel and I think is worth exploring," said Sze. The corners of his sneer curled. "We will allow you to assist us, under the condition that you tell no one of your allegiance to us. You will tell no one what you observed this day. You will not betray any aspect of our investigation. Is that clear?"

Chesa glanced back at her long-lost pearl. It sat haphazard among Primara Nash's former finery. She stared at it and reminded herself of her strength. She had escaped worse before. She turned back to Sze and nodded.

"Say it aloud!" spat Ravel. "Slave!"

Chesa swallowed. "I agree."

Before she finished the words, Ravel crossed the distance to Chesa and gripped her by her swollen face. Chesa struggled, but the scholar pressed hard on her cheeks. Ravel dug her fingers into the joint between Chesa's upper and lower jaw. Chesa twisted her head as Ravel pried her mouth open. Soon Chesa found herself biting into bits of her own cheek. Ravel pulled a vial of liquid from her robes and removed the stopper with her teeth. Chesa tried to turn away, but the scholar poured the fluid into Chesa's mouth and laughed.

"Stop acting like a child, dear," she oozed. "We must have our assurances. We cannot simply take your word for it. We need a binding contract, and we're not permitted troth stones anymore." She clucked her tongue. "Trust, dear, but verify."

Chesa coughed and tongued some of the venom out, just as more sloshed between her ruined lips.

A moment later, a high-pitched ringing started in Chesa's ears. It seemed distant at first, but grew louder. As it did, it drowned out every other sound. Delver Ravel's lips worked, but no sound came. The edges of Chesa's vision turned gauzy. The haziness at her periphery grew until streaks of white reached the center of her vision. All of Chesa's pains retreated. The last thing she saw were Ravel's pig snout and greedy brown eyes. Then it all went white.

Chesa jolted awake. Icy sweat slicked her body as she examined her surroundings. She resided in her room. Sze and Ravel appeared nowhere to be seen. She reached up to touch her lips. Though a subtle crease resided where the split had been, her lips seemed healed. She touched the sides of her face and tried her legs. They worked.

"Easy now, girl," said Ms. Ash.

Chesa jolted again.

Chesa's fellow Disciple sat on a chair against the wall. Ms. Ash placed a firm hand on her shoulder.

"I don't know what time the Delvers took you last night, but they tore into you," warned Ms. Ash. "You're lucky the Bianchi girl noticed them depositing you in your room. She told the Ward boy, who sent for an Evader. Seems one of the Evaders owed the boy a favor."

"The Bianchi girl helped me? Why?" Chesa croaked through her leathery throat.

"Fool girl," chuckled Ms. Ash. "Bianchi's taken a shine to you since you provided her those linens. Though, I was near enough when the Bianchi girl found you. Primara Okondo has me following her—calls Bianchi her 'investment.'"

"Investment?" echoed Chesa.

"Hush, now," said Ms. Ash. "I sent for broth when I noticed you stirring. You need strength, and your throat sounds like a toad's."

"Lydia," Chesa barreled on, "are you quite sure Bianchi is our Blurred Keystone? It just seems to me that anyone with two brain cells could apply that moniker to anyone. For all we know, this prophecy could refer to the Langcraw heiress, or Roland Ward!"

Ms. Ash's smile vanished. "People with greater gifts than you or I possess have indicated as much. Change is on the horizon. As for Bianchi, I feel it must be her. I feel it in my bones."

Chesa opened her mouth to ask if Ms. Ash had seen Ravel or Sze, but as she did, the very sounds that produced their names slipped out from under her attention. She thought of their faces, but then their features jumbled and anonymized into an inky, incomprehensible blur. Chesa tried to articulate what had happened with the mau venom next. Again, the words and images drifted apart in her grasp.

"Something's wrong," warned Chesa. She tried to detail the deaths in the Delvers' ranks with Nash, and someone. . . The facts slithered apart.

"I'm feeling better now. I had a lot of bruises and cuts earlier," Chesa recited in hollow tones. Well, that sentence worked.

She willed herself to mention the slap she had received from Delver Sze, but mental fog descended on her. She couldn't remember why she'd opened her mouth. Something about a mean scholar. . .

Ms. Ash clenched her jaw. "I understand," said the old woman. "I don't know what those Delvers did to you, but I can see they've covered their tracks. . ."

Chesa stood and fetched a fragment of parchment from beneath her bed. Perhaps the Delvers had overlooked something. After all, most servants remained illiterate their entire lives. Yet as soon as Chesa put quill to paper, the spelling of the words disarticulated and floated away.

A knock came at the door.

Chesa and Ms. Ash both gave a start. Ms. Ash rose and bustled to answer it, but paused to grant Chesa a tentative expression.

"Go ahead," choked Chesa. "Open it."

Ms. Ash jerked the door open. There stood Lavinia Thalsem.

"Ms. Thalsem!" shouted Ms. Ash. She swept into a bow. "I did not expect you. How may I be of service?"

Lavinia peered around the servant's quarters before a warm smile spread across her face. "I heard a rumor that Chesa was summoned to the Delvers of the Mind late last night, and was hurt. Someone called an Evader. I wanted to make sure Chesa was alright," said Lavinia. Concern lines blossomed at the edges of her eyes.

Ms. Ash paused before answering, "Word travels quick down here. . ."

Too quick and coincidental for Chesa's liking. Despite her fatigue, Chesa fueled a kernel of her energy into her thaumaturgical senses and peered at Lavinia.

A nimbus of threads danced about Lavinia's mind, as with any healthy thaumaturge, though the network about Lavinia surged as strongly as any scholar's. Chesa began to let her scan subside when she noticed a small tangle of threads, almost invisible, nestled at the base of Lavinia's brain. There, just to one side, curled a circlet of knotted braids.

One of Chesa's eyebrows lifted.

"Is everything alright?" asked Lavinia.

Ms. Ash dropped her center of mass an inch.

"Everything's fine. . ." said Chesa. She tried to sound as exhausted and innocuous as she could, which was not difficult. "The Delvers were forceful with me this morning. I made some foolish mistakes in my service."

"Is there something wrong with the Delvers?" Lavinia asked sweetly.

Ms. Ash met Chesa's gaze and inclined her head. Chesa fought against the sudden tension rising throughout her body.

"Not that I can remember," said Chesa. Not untrue. After all, the mental block prevented her from revisiting the particulars.

Lavinia squinted at the pair of servants.

Ms. Ash granted Lavinia a motherly smile. "If you will allow me, Ms. Thalsem, I'd like to make some fresh tea for Chesa and see that she gets rested up. Perhaps I can make a pot for you? Will you be in your room?"

"No," barked Lavinia. "I'm spending the day with the Architects. I'll come check on Chesa later."

Ms. Ash bowed to Lavinia. "As you say, my liege. I'll be sure she's all healed up for you. Good luck with your studies! Though, the whole menhir knows how well you're doing!"

"Yes, that's nice," Lavinia sniffed. "Until then, Chesa." She winked at Ms. Ash with a glimmer in her eye and departed.

Ms. Ash closed the door.

Chesa's body wilted.

"A nasty thing, if there ever was one," grumbled Ms. Ash. "Why do you suppose she gives a fig about the Delvers?"

"Ms. Ash. . ." Chesa whispered. "Someone's altered her mind. Another pacifying knotwork, and whoever did it rendered it almost invisible. I only thought to examine Lavinia because she obviously knew more than she let on."

"There's been quite a lot of that," murmured Ms. Ash. "Peony and Lavinia both now. Would you say the knots are similar?"

Chesa rolled an indecisive shoulder. "Maybe. They were both delicate workings."

"But the Ward boy and the Langcraw girl remain untouched?" asked Ms. Ash.

"Last I checked," Chesa replied.

Ms. Ash began pacing. "We should scan them again," she said. She liked to use "we" in a liberal sense. "Perhaps we should warn Ms. Bianchi that she's being manipulated, if you believe she still has her free will intact. I'll see to fetching her and Mr. Ward. You, see if the Langcraw girl is back from the Tilters. Since Lavinia Thalsem is gone, perhaps I can bring Peony and Roland to Ms. Langcraw's chambers. Easier to move them than Ms. Langcraw. . ."

"Fine, though I note I'm charged with fetching the difficult one . . . again. . ." muttered Chesa. "Aren't I the sick one?"

Ms. Ash smirked before retorting, "Your complaint is noted."

Chesa donned her robes with a groan.

"Ready?" said Ms Ash.

Chesa nodded.

"Quick as you can, girl," said Ms. Ash. "We move against an enemy who appears to be gaining ground."

"Agreed," Chesa murmured. "I won't dally."

Ms. Ash opened the door and departed. It seemed the time for tenderness with the little ascendants was over.

Chesa navigated her way to the ascendants using the least populated and most obscure corridors she knew. Few scholars resided in the halls, and even fewer ascendants, which was good. She found the halls about the ascendants' quarters the greatest ghost town of them all. She turned the corner nearest Tara's room and paused before her door. Footsteps sounded from within. Tara was home. Chesa gave the door a firm knock and readied herself to manage the frosty ascendant.

Several moments passed in silence.

Chesa knocked again, this time harder.

Nothing.

She sighed. Ms. Ash had given Chesa a job to do. So, she knocked a third time, this time so hard that she felt her teeth rattling.

The door snapped open. But in lieu of the fair-haired Langcraw heiress, Chesa locked eyes with Lavinia Thalsem. Chesa glanced over the girl's shoulder. No one else resided in the modest chamber. A storage chest that Chesa thought to be Lavinia's sat slung open. There, nestled among her effects, sat a white orb partly covered by a garment. It almost glowed in the room's lamplight.

"Here for your questioning, Chesa? You've properly recovered, have you?" Lavinia sneered.

Chesa stepped back.

"No, no, Chesa," Lavinia chided. "Were you not looking for me?"

Chesa opened her mouth to answer, but Lavinia interrupted her.

"In!" she spat, as if Chesa were a dog.

Chesa obeyed . . . for now.

Lavinia closed the door and gestured for Chesa to seat herself on Tara's bed. Chesa complied while Lavinia perched upon the room's only stool.

"Not so ill as you first suggested, hmm?" snapped Lavinia. "Perhaps the Delvers did not punish you as they ought to have, if a single Evader of Death could mend you so well."

Chesa dropped her eyes and wrapped herself in practiced deference. She'd weathered worse circumstances. This wasn't even the most worrisome interaction of the day.

"As you say, my liege," murmured Chesa.

"What of the Delvers today? You were questioned?" asked Lavinia.

Keeping her eyes down, Chesa mumbled a few confirmatory noises.

The cold-faced ascendant studied Chesa in silence for a long moment. "Have they prevented you from talking about it?"

Chesa didn't answer.

Lavinia sighed. "I can tell they have."

Chesa nodded and forced herself to shake like an animal before its master. But how did Lavinia know that Chesa had been stifled by the Delvers?

Lavinia clucked her tongue. "You won't be much use, then. You can go. I just don't have time to fuss with you now."

Chesa lifted herself and slumped toward the door. Something failed to add up here. Why would a budding Architect of Forces be so concerned with the Delvers? The two factions enjoyed a tenuous truce. Though, even if that were not the case, neither faction would disclose their politics to an ascendant. Chesa decided to take a chance.

"Master?" Chesa asked, pitiful and puling. "May I inquire how you came by that?" She pointed to the white sphere among Lavinia's belongings, meeting Lavinia's eyes.

Lavinia scowled.

Chesa drew upon the fumes of whatever saprolite wine remained in her, if anything.

"It's a thought paddock, idiot, and it's none of your concern," Lavinia hissed.

"Did you obtain it from the Central Archive?" asked Chesa. She knew, outside of those clerking in the archive, that ascendants never saw its interior.

Lavinia sniffed. "I did not obtain it from the Central Archive," she confessed.

"Then how did you come by it?" probed Chesa.

Lavinia's coolness snapped. "As though it's any of your business! It's Tara's. She's been receiving special instruction from the Tilters, and they gave it to her for study. She's shown great progress with her aptitudes."

The tension between them grew so thick that Chesa could have swum through it. She opened herself up to her thaumaturgical gifts, allowing herself to gaze upon Lavinia's mental nimbus. Energies swiveled around the ascendant's brain in ensembles, like a mass of serpents ready to strike. Chesa leered at Lavinia, preparing a very special strike of her own.

"Lavinia," said Chesa in a flat tone, "that can't be true. You see, Tara doesn't have any thaumaturgical abilities at all. I'm afraid you'll have to try again. . ."

CHAPTER 19

An Arising Situation

CHESA LET THE LINGERING vestiges of the saprolite wine flood into her mind. She flicked her hands through a series of cowing thaumaturgical expressions. But as familiar to her as it was, the clumsiness from Chesa's lack of formal education betrayed her.

Lavinia's dark eyebrows shot up. "An anomaly?" she breathed, her tone disbelieving. "Help!" she screamed.

Lavinia rose and kicked her stool out from under her in a fluid motion. The sinewing tendrils of her mind lashed forward in a rush. Chesa knew strikes like this one. A quick jab of energies like Lavinia's dazed many an unwary target. Such a daze risked providing Lavinia with more than enough time to bash Chesa's temple open with the stool.

Chesa abandoned her sedation work and slung herself to one side, narrowly missing Lavinia's attack.

"Mind thaumaturgy?!" Chesa cursed.

The ascendant before Chesa laughed, her tone a mixture of contemptuous defiance and lingering shock. "Not going to make this easy, are you?" She cackled. "Two Primaras, both too stupid to see the hooded serpent in their laps!" she scoffed. "What a laugh they'll all have when they learn that Nash's little concubine bears such gifts!"

If Chesa had not intended to kill Lavinia Thalsem before, she had no choice now. Better death than the anomaly pens. She lifted herself and opened her senses to the storm of energies swirling from Lavinia's mind.

A lightning storm of thaumaturgy sizzled and cracked around Lavinia. Bits of energy skittered through the air, almost colliding with the tendrils emanating from Chesa. One of Lavinia's slenderest bolts arched toward Chesa, this one more modest than the first, but surgical in its precision. Chesa twisted on her back heel to avoid the strike. This time, however, Chesa maintained a slow crescendo of her own working. Her opponent, whoever it was, was no mere student of mind thaumaturgy, wunderkind or not.

Chesa kept her eyes on the serpentine lances that flicked around Lavinia. But with her attention so transfixed, she overlooked the obvious. Lavinia lifted the discarded stool by a leg and threw it one-armed. Chesa dodged it with a short dash, but she tripped over the corner of Tara's bed mid-evasion. She rolled with the fall and landed in the space between the bed and the wall.

A moment later, Lavinia stood above Chesa, with several cords of her mind ready to strike down.

"No force strikes?" hissed Chesa, desperate to stall her demise. "Who are you?"

"Goodbye, Chesa," Lavinia cooed. The nimbus of energies surrounding her mind grew vast and cyclonic. Her readied bolts flickered toward Chesa in synchronicity, too many to evade. The strikes pummeled her pitiful psychic resistance. As each landed, her head rung with white, tinny blindness. After the third strike, her vision relaxed, and her world became a watery blur.

Chesa tried her extremities, but none of them answered. An object—Lavinia, no doubt—loomed toward her. Chesa smelled hints of the ascendant's lilac perfume. She struggled to kick Lavinia, to organize a mental attack of her own, but her body ignored her pleas. She just lay there, helpless. A twinge of pity for Liam Kensington touched Chesa's thoughts, but only just. She focused on her breathing, closed her useless eyes, and prepared herself for death's kiss.

A cool piece of glass or perhaps a knife pressed hard against the side of Chesa's neck.

"I admit, I would rather have had you first," Lavinia whispered. "Though it wouldn't be the same without my equipment, I'd love for Nash to have known I had his pet one last time before seeing her off. . ."

Whatever resided in Lavinia released a predatory chuckle.

A knock at the door cut Lavinia's gloating short. She went still before pressing the blade into Chesa's neck a hair farther.

A louder series of knocks rang at the door.

Lavinia sighed. "It doesn't matter if they find me with you. There won't be anyone left to contest my word."

The blade bit into Chesa's skin slowly as Lavinia pressed into her neck.

The air rippled with energy, followed by a sonorous crack, like thunder.

"What—?!"

A bestial bellow cut Lavinia's query short. She leapt from Chesa and retreated in a spidery blur.

"Tara?" panted Roland.

He must have broken down the door. Chesa thanked the gods that fabled farm strength was more than mere legend. She tried to scream, but her voice would not come.

"Oh, Roland! Thank goodness you're here!" Lavinia sobbed, her voice weak and desperate. "A servant attacked me! I was only just able to subdue her!"

Wood crunched underfoot somewhere near Chesa.

"Wh-who attacked you?" breathed Roland.

"A servant?" yowled a familiar voice from farther off. "That can't be!" barked Ms. Ash.

Chesa blinked. The blurred edges of the room resumed some semblance of shape.

Lavinia's hazy form climbed over the top of Tara's bed toward the entry. "Chesa broke in and attacked me!" Lavinia whimpered. "It took everything I had to defend myself!"

"She's dead?" asked Ms. Ash in a flat and noncommittal tone.

The sharpness of Chesa's vision returned in earnest. She tried to speak, to call out, to explain the danger, but nothing came. She tried to thrash, to make any sort of commotion, but only managed to produce the most anemic wiggle of one foot and a groan.

"Not yet," Lavinia whimpered.

"Then we should recruit the Tilters to resolve this matter," declared Ms. Ash. "I'm glad you're safe, Ms. Thalsem."

"Ms. Ash? Roland? Is everything alright?" called Peony.

Lavinia's sobbing abated. "You don't believe me?" she asked in a girlish mewl.

With another bout of effort, Chesa thrashed her limp body, leveraging the wall beside her to flip herself from her back to her stomach. One of her arms flopped beneath her.

"She's coming to!" cried Lavinia. "We have to kill her now before she attacks again!"

"Kill her?" said Roland. "We can restrain her until the Tilters arrive. They can f-figure out why she attacked you."

"She's dangerous!" Lavinia explained, her voice ever so tender. "We need to. . ."

"We'll wrap Chesa up in force workings," Peony's voice sounded from somewhere inside the room now. "No one has to endanger themselves."

Chesa rallied her strength. This time she groaned and murmured something disorganized and incomprehensible. She lifted herself using the arm pinned beneath her. Her entire body prickled like a phantom limb. She cocked her head up to face the scene.

Ms. Ash stood near the bed, not far from Chesa.

Chesa maneuvered her shaking legs beneath herself. She wobbled and fell back against the wall behind her. She remained alive, for now. Should she die today, at least she had company nearby. That surprised her.

Peony, in her spindle heels and cinched black robes, stood just inside the splintered doorway. A gash ran down its middle, as though wrought by a huge axe. Chesa doubted even Roland Ward possessed the strength to split it with such precision. That meant force thaumaturgy.

Lavinia and Peony locked eyes just paces apart. Peony loomed at a far greater height, with a skeptical expression. Lavinia, despite her wet eyes, stared back with boldness. Roland squared his shoulders up with Lavinia and placed himself between her and Ms. Ash.

A wheezing laugh escaped Chesa. Had she not known better, she might have concluded he meant to protect them.

"I'm too weak," Lavinia wept. "I don't know if I can hold her."

Peony looked her up and down. "I think Ms. Ash and I can contend with Chesa," said Peony. "Roland, go find someone to get the Tilters. Lavinia, why don't you have a seat, or you can leave, if you need to. You've been through a lot. . ."

With an effort of will, Chesa blurted out, "That's not Lavinia!"

Everyone acted at once. Chesa clawed at her thaumaturgical senses, begging for her sight to open, but her powers slipped from her grasp. Ms. Ash stood up, squared her stance, and palmed a shard of broken washbasin near Chesa's feet. A lick of crimson blood adorned a part of its white mortar. Something like panic flashed across Peony's face as Lavinia stepped forward and thrust the meat of her palm up, faster than a serpent's strike, into the center of Peony's painted face. The strike landed with a wet crack. Blood gushed from Peony's nostrils. She stumbled back into a dresser with a crash, sending their Veils and Poisons deck flying through the air.

"Peony!" Roland yelled.

The ebony-skinned ascendant stumbled back on her heels. Roland rushed toward her.

"Time's up, girl," said Ms. Ash with a glance at Chesa. "Can you stand?"

Chesa shook her head. "Run," she slurred.

Ms. Ash rolled her eyes. "The whole point is to save you!"

Roland seized Lavinia by the throat and lifted her like a broken doll. Miniscule scratches and unseen blemishes on Lavinia's skin turned red and streaked across her alabaster form. Styes blossomed along her eyes, and cold sweat slicked her body within seconds. She coughed up green sputum embellished with red. The ascendant's microbiome had turned its back on her.

Chesa failed to stifle a sneer.

In a motion that best belonged to a viper, Lavinia twisted her entire body and launched a kick upward at Roland. The boot of her heel landed square in his throat with a pop. He tumbled back into Peony, sending all three to the ground.

Chesa finally seized her powers and structured them with whatever coherence her mind could manage. The mental forces surrounding Lavinia radiated with malevolence, like discolored skies before a funnel cloud descended. The small coronas around Peony and Roland wavered like candles before an approaching deluge.

Lavinia bounded to her feet. She struck at Roland as he still crouched on all fours. Half a dozen bolts of mental energy hurled from the chaotic aura enveloping Lavinia. Her eyes became hollows at the center of a mental typhoon. As the bolts landed, his back arched like a longbow, with a series of cracks. He collapsed convulsing to the floor.

Ms. Thalsem did not spare his form a glance. She stepped over his shuddering mass and grasped Peony by her throat. Lavinia's hand pulled back with an accompanying hiss as her lip curled.

"Oh, Peony, no wonder you're such a brute of a thing. Don't worry, darling. . ." She twisted the last words in mockery. "I won't tell a soul. . ."

Chesa fluttered through thaumaturgical notes as fast as her hand had ever managed.

Lavinia thrust her hand with viperine speed at Peony, but this time, she appeared prepared for the attack. Peony swept an arm up in defense. Her strike connected with Lavinia's at the full height of its extension and landed with a visceral pop. Lavinia's arm bent upward and away at a stomach-churning angle. She recoiled from Peony with a hiss, clutching at her wilted arm.

Peony stepped forward and over Roland. She positioned herself between him and Lavinia.

Lavinia crawled backward over the bed, cowering from Peony's approach like a worm retreating into its hole. The energies around Lavinia surged without warning, like a storm's resurgence following its eye.

Chesa gasped.

A bolt of mental energy shot toward Peony. It connected, but only just. She tottered backward. Frantic, Chesa hurled her lariat of loose swirling energies toward Lavinia. The lazy series of thaumaturgical loops descended around her.

Chesa wrenched at the working. The loose swirls snapped tight around Lavinia's maniacal storm and constricted. A second and third bold of energy hurled out from Lavinia, but the energy recoiled in on itself, landing back within the nexus from which it had come. Chesa heaved at her mental constriction, stealing precious inches from around Lavinia.

"Difficult to manage so many opponents," sneered Chesa, "isn't it?"

"Amateur. . ." said Lavinia.

To Chesa's astonishment, the girl tapped into a root of energy not in evidence before, perhaps from saprolite wine consumed the night prior. The monstrous storm about Lavinia redoubled and frayed at Chesa's constriction. Their time drew short.

Lavinia turned toward Chesa, slow and patient, as her storm finished eroding the last bits of Chesa's efforts. "Thought you could ambush me, did you?" She chuckled. "It takes more than the likes of you to subdue a full scholar of the Amber Menhir!" She scoffed down at Ms. Ash, who clasped her makeshift blade, refusing to leave Chesa's side.

Behind Lavinia, something glimmered with a metallic sheen.

Peony rose and swiveled with a water jug in hand. In a fluid motion that sent spray into the air, she snapped the pitcher into the side of Lavinia's head. Her pale neck twisted with the blow. Peony's motion followed through with Lavinia as her head cracked a second time, wet and soft, into the wall.

Peony pulled back at once.

Lavinia crumpled. A damp sponging of blood on the wall beside her evidenced where her head had connected. Peony gaped down at Lavinia's twitching body.

"What did I do?" she whispered. "What're we going to do?!"

Ms. Ash stood from beside Chesa and straightened her robes. "Do as I say, girl. I've got a plan."

CHAPTER 20
Alliances Most Unorthodox

MS. ASH RELEASED A long breath through her nostrils and took stock of the room.

Peony knelt beside Roland. She ran a finger down the side of his face. Though the girl's tenderness touched Ms. Ash, their present circumstances required her practiced execution.

"Chesa, attend to Roland. We need to know if he's alright," she ordered. "Ms. Bianchi, you and I need to talk. Chesa can help him better than you can."

Peony's brow furrowed. She granted Chesa an uneasy glance.

"None of that. We haven't the time," Ms. Ash chided. She approached and placed a hand on Peony's shoulder. "We all need to know what Ms. Thalsem did to Roland. I'm afraid you won't be much use for that. Come."

Peony hesitated, but followed. Ms. Ash shot a quick glance at Lavinia's remains to reassure herself that they hadn't stirred. There had been enough surprises for one day.

"Have a seat," said Ms. Ash. She gestured to Tara's bed.

Peony sat so that the pair were eye to eye.

"Ms. Bianchi," asked Ms. Ash, "can you tell me what you saw here today?" Her voice carried the coolness of a practiced interrogator.

Peony examined Roland's slumped form. Chesa knelt to one side of the boy, peering at his head. Peony bit her lip.

Ms. Ash cleared her throat and let some tenderness dissipate. "What did you see here today?"

"Something was wrong with Lavinia," Peony answered in a low voice. "She claimed she was attacked by Chesa, but then, she didn't want to keep Chesa alive for questioning either."

Ms. Ash nodded. "I also thought that seemed odd. What else?"

"Then, Chesa said Lavinia wasn't Lavinia—and Lavinia attacked," Peony muttered. "She used some working I couldn't see. Something was off with her."

"What do you mean?" Ms. Ash kept her voice devoid of emotion.

Peony seemed blithe to the danger before her. Her words came out airy and distant. "Lavinia wasn't using force thaumaturgy. I opened my senses to see her threads, so I could respond. She didn't touch a single strand. I would have seen if she used life tendrils too." Peony faced Ms. Ash.

"Just a stunning working," announced Chesa in a hushed voice. "He was struck harder than me, but he'll be alright."

Ms. Ash examined Peony for some inkling of a response. Peony faced Roland and made to rise, but Ms. Ash placed a firm hand on her knee, and Peony stilled.

"I know that wasn't Lavinia," Peony added flatly. Her eyes remained on Roland. "She couldn't hide anything that made her superior to anyone else. A second thaumaturgy? She would have flaunted it."

Ms. Ash kept her tone neutral. "If that's so, and someone other than Lavinia was controlling her somehow, then we could all be in danger."

"I saw that Chesa helped us too," Peony went on. "Even though I couldn't really see it. Just like she's helping now."

Chesa went rigid over Roland's stirring form. He groaned some-thing incomprehensible.

"Oh? What do you mean?" asked Ms. Ash. Her hand slid to the shard of washbasin tucked in her robes.

"None of it is my business," Peony added. "Not anyone else's either—apart from the fact that I owe Chesa."

Ms. Ash raised an eyebrow and pulled her hand away from the pocket containing the shard. She liked the Bianchi girl, her garish attire and manner of speaking. Few traits displayed greater rarity in the Amber Menhir. But the girl would soon be a scholar. Scholars were fickle. Ascendants changed when they ascended. Every servant knew it.

"How do you suppose you can repay her?" asked Ms. Ash.

"I've seen what the menhir does to people like Chesa," Peony scoffed. "I'd hide too."

"Peony?" Roland moaned. He blinked toward Chesa and flinched. "Ch-Chesa! It's . . . it's you!" he stammered. "What're you doing?"

Chesa glided away from him with graceful flicks of instinctual cer-tainty, donning a mask of coolness. She looked toward Ms. Ash. "What do you think?"

"Roland!" Peony cried. She rose and brushed past Chesa, who scowled at her back. She knelt and planted a flurry of hysterical kisses across his face and brow.

Ms. Ash couldn't prevent a smile. "A difficult situation," she sighed at the lovers. "Under normal conditions, I'd suggest cleaning up loose ends and delaying the Tilters. Make like none of us were ever here."

At the mention of lingering evidence, Chesa's eyes darted to the distracted ascendants. The muscles in her neck tightened. The sudden sparkle in her eyes made Ms. Ash a bit uneasy.

"But! The evidence will be difficult to clean up, for a variety of reasons," Ms. Ash continued. "We could claim that Lavinia simply disappeared after leaving with a scholar during Saturnalia. But then there's the issue of the door."

Chesa glanced at the ruined entry and groaned, "No kidding."

"How did the confrontation begin?" inquired Ms. Ash.

Chesa slid over to Lavinia's storage chest. She lifted a gleaming white sphere and brought it to Ms. Ash. "I questioned her over this," she explained. "Lavinia claimed the thought paddock was Ms. Langcraw's, that Tara was studying its contents. I knew that was false and said so. Then Lavinia attacked."

"Do you have any idea of its contents?" said Ms. Ash.

"I cannot open it, and I wouldn't be able to read its contents besides," replied Chesa with a frown.

"Maybe I can help!" said Roland. He lifted himself from the floor with some difficulty. "Can I hold it?"

Chesa shot the lumbering ascendant a skeptical glance. She met Ms. Ash's eyes.

"Why not?" said Ms. Ash.

Roland took the thought paddock and slid a finger along its equator. His eyes went wide. "It's one of the missing ones!" he exclaimed. "LaTorre's! They've all been missing for months! But none of the Delvers had them . . . or so they said."

"LaTorre?" Chesa sneered. "You mean the slobbering Delver in the basement?"

Roland nodded.

"Hmm," growled Ms. Ash. "Boy, how does the Central Archive track its visitors?"

Roland shrugged. "It reads the thaumaturgical aptitudes in our blood."

"Chesa, collect some of Lavinia's blood," barked Ms. Ash. "Boy, see if the Central Archive reads her blood as an Architect's or something else. Can you do that?"

Roland grimaced. "The s-system won't accept anything other than a fresh droplet from a living person."

"I see," said Ms. Ash. "We have business to attend to, Chesa. As for you two. . ." She shot both ascendants a glare. "I might need you both to meet with some associates of mine in confidence. But we'll need their approval first. In the meantime, we need to undo the knot we've created for ourselves here." She gestured to Lavinia. "Fast."

"How can we help?" asked Peony. "We can say it was an accident. We don't even have to lie. I can say Lavinia attacked me. That's true too! We fought, and there was an accident. . ." Peony's voice trailed off. "Do . . . do you think they'll punish me for that?"

Chesa grimaced.

"I'm not sure," Ms. Ash admitted. "Lavinia showed extraordinary promise. The Architects will work hard to see her killer punished."

Roland's eyes brightened. "But Peony's an Architect too! They'll believe her! R-right?"

"Maybe," warned Ms. Ash. "But Peony's spent more time with the Weavers than with any Architect. That won't play well. The Weavers have signaled to all that Peony is theirs."

Roland frowned just as Peony raised a tentative hand. "What about Primara Okondo?" she asked. "Maybe she could help us. If she knew what happened, she would explain it to the Architects. Right?"

Chesa rolled an indecisive shoulder.

"You have a point," said Ms. Ash. "The Weavers hold a significant political advantage these days too. It might work. . ."

"Th-then it's settled?" asked Roland.

"Now hold your horses, boy!" barked Ms. Ash. "We've got serious things to discuss. It may not even work. Even if Okondo takes Peony's side, the Architects won't take this lying down! They've got strings everywhere, and deposed or not, some of their contacts will respond to their call."

Roland and Peony exchanged looks.

"But I've got strings of my own," Ms. Ash added, letting a bit of pride enter her voice. "Roland, you and Peony get your story straight. You heard something strange from inside Lavinia's room. You knocked, and she didn't respond. So, you opened the door by force. Then she attacked you. Don't be too specific. Keep everything vague and loosely true. Be sure to emphasize how stressed and traumatized you were and are. It's all still a blur. Ask to speak with the Weaver Primara."

"If the Delvers scan you for deceit," Chesa added, "a healthy dose of truth in your lies can throw them off."

Peony and Roland exchanged frowns.

"Good, keep those worried expressions! Sob a bit, if you can work yourself up to it," Ms. Ash continued. "With luck, Primara Okondo will intercede, and there won't be a trial. Do you think you can do all that?"

"I'm not good at lying," Peony confessed. "But if you think that's the only way. . ."

"Good gracious, child, you're living in the menhir now!" scolded Ms. Ash. "You should be used to being lied to, and you should perfect the skill yourself."

"Alright," Peony replied. She did not sound certain.

"Good," said Ms. Ash. "Now, if you will excuse me, Chesa and I must be going. We've got to get to work on our parts, and we can't do that here!"

"But what do we do with Lavinia?" added Roland. "You won't be here to help us?"

Ms. Ash's voice came out an octave higher. "Help you? Use your head, boy! If we're anywhere near this situation, they'll take our heads just for the fun of it! We've got to be as far from here as possible without drawing suspicion. We can't be any help to you two if we're dead.

And good gracious, if you see any Tilters, for the love of the gods, stall them!"

"But. . ." Roland started, but Ms. Ash interrupted him.

"Now, boy. I mean it," she ordered. "Take Lavinia's body to someone. Call for healing. Confess. Cry. We'll see to the next steps."

"What should we do with this thought paddock?" asked Roland. He lifted the sphere in his giant hand.

"Hide it!" ordered Ms. Ash with a roll of her eyes. "Chesa, come."

Chesa darted to Ms. Ash's side without a sound. Ms. Ash paused at the destroyed door. She dared a quick glance down the corridor to either side. Seeing no one, she gestured for Chesa to follow.

"Good luck!" Chesa giggled.

Ms. Ash guided Chesa to a branch of servant workrooms not far from the ascendants' quarters. They slipped into a kitchen, where a thick layer of dust slathered every surface. The only light came in from beneath the door to the hall. When Ms. Ash was sure they were alone, she turned to Chesa, but Chesa spoke first.

"Lydia!" she yowled. "Whatever fondness you have for the Bianchi girl is misplaced. It isn't just your hide on the line here!"

Ms. Ash laughed in reply. "Chesa, if the Bianchi girl is prepared to out you as an anomaly, then what makes you think she'll preserve my flabby backside?" Her laughter retreated some. "We play with both of our skins at stake. But the winnings are greater than you think."

"What?" hissed Chesa. Though she glared, Ms. Ash thought she heard panic in Chesa's tone.

"Chesa," Ms. Ash soothed, "if those two feel they can trust us, if we share this secret together, then perhaps we can form an alliance."

"An alliance?!" cried Chesa. "You think we can trust a scholar with our safety? You're out of your mind!"

Ms. Ash interjected, "I think those ascendants are different. I wouldn't venture any optimism on the Langcraw girl, I confess, but those two have a tenderness to them. And they seem to be in love or something."

"What does that matter?" Chesa whined.

"It makes all the difference," Ms. Ash explained with cool serenity. "If they are in love, neither will do anything that risks hurting the other. We're not the only ones who stand to lose something by the truth coming out about today."

Chesa gazed at Ms. Ash with her mouth open.

"Chesa, believe me. Love often hijacks decision-making in the most absurd manner, but here, I'm sure it could work to our advantage," Ms. Ash continued. "And the fact that you've saved them may win them over in earnest as well. Don't forget, they saved you when the Thalsem girl insisted on killing you outright."

"They were just there for Langcraw. They wouldn't have done anything of the sort if it were only about me," Chesa complained.

"I don't believe that," Ms. Ash rebuffed. "Much is at stake for them too. The entire menhir could be in danger. If the Delvers have discovered a way to hijack another's will completely, it could undo everything."

"Trusting these ascendants is a mistake," Chesa scoffed. "What were you thinking, referencing the Disciples right in front of them?!"

After a long pause, Ms. Ash replied in a hushed tone, "Perhaps you're right. We'll consult with the other Disciples, at least. In the meantime, we need to see if the Bianchi girl's request for an audience with Okondo is taken up. I'll do my best to ensure that the Weavers act to defend her. The Ward boy too."

"Fine," Chesa snapped. "Just remember, I was against this entire plan."

Chesa did not wait for confirmation from Ms. Ash. She flung open the door to the hall and stormed away.

Ms. Ash remained in the forgotten kitchen. After a long moment, she opened a cabinet matted over with cobwebs. There, sitting at the back of an otherwise empty shelf, save for pest excrement, sat several bottles of saprolite wine. Ms. Ash concluded that it was time for Okondo to enjoy a very special vintage.

A week later, Ms. Ash held a serving tray, as usual, and watched the Weavers as they held another celebration over the misfortunes of the other factions. Okondo lounged in her sunken throne, flanked by Weavers who had, only a few weeks prior, been some of her most problematic adversaries. Ms. Ash suspected that they all detected the shifting tides and had moored their ships in the harbor of the Primara's growing clout.

Primara Okondo wore sheer harem pants cut from her favorite pale green fabric. Her feet were bare, save for her toes. Rings of braided rose gold adorned each. She tossed her tight bob of blonde curls about as she gestured with a heavy glass of saprolite wine. It was all Ms. Ash could do to prevent herself from grinning each time one of the scholars gulped their libations.

"Tell me again! I want to hear it!" Okondo pleaded, pouting with her eyes. She sipped another bit of luminescent wine. "Start from the beginning."

A subtle dose of dreamflower with saprolite wine never failed to loosen lips.

Delmar Cutner, once Primara Okondo's only reliable contact within the Evaders of Death, sat with three others. Each had donned their champagne-colored robes and showered the Primara and her vassals with complimentary platitudes. The grim-faced Delver Cutner leaned forward and said, "It would be my pleasure, Primara Okondo. Nearly thirty of the Delvers of the Mind were found dead or brain-dead the morning after Saturnalia. A dozen Evaders were called to revive them."

"Which they could not," sang the Primara, swishing her glass.

"Which they could not," Cutner agreed with a strained smile. "The life energies of half of them had been snuffed out completely by the time we arrived. Post-mortem evaluations conveyed that they all experienced brain trauma. No doubt an inside job. The half that died suffered embolisms or bled out from injuries to the neck. The latter were the most gruesome parties."

"Tell me again what happened when those incompetent Tilters arrived," Okondo squealed, kicking her beringed feet back and forth in the air.

"Useless," Cutner agreed. "They arrived too late and in too few a number to be effective. They did, however, recover evidence that the Delvers had stalled their arrival to the scenes. The Delvers no doubt wanted to conduct their own investigation. Or perhaps the Delvers needed time to cover up whatever scheme they'd orchestrated."

"And the brain-dead Delvers? The ones not slain outright? What became of them?" the Primara prodded.

"To the anomaly pens. All of them," intoned Cutner, his voice somber. "Too late to participate in the saprolite band study. Though, with the chancellor's recent approval to administer saprolite bands on large swaths of the anomalies henceforth, the lives of the incapacitated Delvers will not be wasted."

"Yes, well, let us not forget how integral the Weavers' support was to ensuring that Evader McCray's petition was approved," said Okondo with an edge of warning behind her mischievousness. "It would not be wise for the Evaders to betray the generosity of the Weavers."

"Just so," agreed Cutner. He lifted his glass of saprolite wine in acknowledgment. "The spoils of our venture will be split with the Weavers, no matter how much Evader McCray continues to pester the chancellor on the matter."

"You would think McCray could grasp the futility of his objections by now," Okondo pouted. "Does he really think that his little petition actually saw its way to Amber Chancellor, and was approved, by his endorsement alone? Impossible. All the Primara had learned of his little plan and angled to see it killed. I alone saved it."

"McCray is better kept in the dark," Cutner warned.

Primara Okondo's face drooped as her eyes rolled back. Her head tottered a moment before she snapped to attention once more. Several Evaders repositioned themselves in their sunken thrones and fussed with their robes.

"The poor thing," dismissed Okondo. "Well, the board is being swept clean. The Architects are bridled. The Delvers that remain sentient are too disordered to accomplish anything. I'd wager half of them will be implicated in the mass murder and sent to the anomaly pens before long. The most formidable politicians among their ranks are gone now anyhow. The Tilters and the Sounders remain as irrelevant as ever. Who is left to contest our rule?"

The Evaders' faces flashed with agitation that they might have hidden, had not they imbibed enough saprolite wine to kill a mau. The Weavers in attendance exchanged weasely smiles. One or two of them snickered.

Ms. Ash made her rounds in the shadows behind the sunken chairs, scanning for empty glasses. She listened for any sign of new information. Not an eye in the lot of scholars remained alert in earnest.

"What of my request to meet with Anaktisi?" inquired Okondo.

"Ah, I almost forgot," Evader Cutner whined. "I've informed the Evader Primara of your interest in brokering some meetings with yourself, Anaktisi, and interim Primara Sze."

"And?" snapped Okondo. She pulled herself up and leaned forward in her seat. "What did Anaktisi say?"

Cutner exhaled, avoiding Okondo's gaze. "Tafos is a coward. The deaths of two Delver Primara and the cowing of the Architect Primara have rendered him uneasy. He's afraid to meet with you. Anaktisi's also concerned with the data we're receiving from the new saprolite band study. Seems things aren't as promising as they once appeared. His political capital dwindles."

"The worm!" Okondo spat. "Tell Anaktisi he can bring an ally. Tell him you'll come!"

Cutner winced. "I'm not confident that he trusts me."

Okondo smiled. "Then convince him. Arrange the meeting. I don't want to hear any more excuses. Just get it done."

"I'll do my best," mumbled Cutner.

A long silence followed.

"Time for some more good news!" Okondo interjected.

"Oh?" said Cutner.

"Peony Bianchi, my favorite pet, appears to have fallen right into my lap." Okondo giggled. "Of all the creatures to have inspired my plans, it was little Ms. Ash who fastened the bridle on my little investment."

Ms. Ash froze as she poured saprolite wine into the goblet of an Evader.

"It appears Bianchi's beloved, Roland Ward, got caught up in an altercation with Lavinia Thalsem," slurred Okondo.

Several Weavers in attendance shifted in their thrones. The Evaders eyed them.

"Roland Ward?" asked Evader Cutner. "Is he significant?"

The Weaver Primara snorted. "No. His line's just another collection of farmers. His consequence stems from his involvement with my Peony. Seems the two are in love, or so claims Ms. Ash." Okondo gulped down the rest of her glass and licked her chops. One of her eyelids drooped as she gave the Evaders a serpentine smile. "Isn't that right, Lydia?"

Ms. Ash genuflected. "Very much so, I think."

"As I was saying. . ." Okondo swirled her empty glass. "Roland invaded the quarters of another ascendant. He claims he heard screams. When he forced himself in, Lavinia attacked. Says he killed her by acci-dent. A claim that cannot be substantiated, despite two Tilters arriving on the scene quite soon after his confession. . ."

"Where is he now?" asked Cutner.

The Primara smirked. "He's confined to his bedchamber and guarded by Architects."

"Ah," Cutner hummed. "I'm sorry. What does this have to do with Peony?"

"Well," Okondo cooed, "she claims she witnessed part of the exchange and can corroborate his story. Ms. Ash alerted me to my little Peony's plight. I've agreed to meet with Peony about the matter."

Weaver Ankathi, the ascendants' instructor, huffed, "You don't intend to help her, do you? For all we know, Peony was his accomplice! I've never seen an ascendant who better fit the description of a subver-sive Blurred Keystone."

Cutner scoffed, "You can't really be that superstitious. . ."

"It's possible Peony helped Ward," Okondo conceded. "I honestly don't care. I intend to ensure she remains loyal. Prophesized Keystone or not, she will be ours. If she somehow brings about the collapse of the menhirs, then whatever rises in their wake will be of our own design."

Weaver Ankathi crossed her arms with a scowl.

"Perhaps I'll question this Roland Ward too. He may relinquish more details to us, with a little . . . encouragement?" Okondo smirked at the other Weavers. "Which means I'll need you there, Delmar, for each meeting. I'll ask Delver Sze to be present too. I will tolerate no lies from these ascendants. Besides, Sze's in need of allies more now than ever. The whole menhir suspects his involvement in Primara Nash's demise."

Evader Cutner leaned back in his throne and pulled a long sip from his glass. He cleared his throat. "When would you like me ready?"

"Let them sweat it another week or so. . . That should poise Peony to accept whatever deal I propose. It might help ensure the compliance of the Ward boy too," Okondo added. "He may yet be useful to me."

"Very well," agreed Cutner. He set his wine glass on the armrest of his throne and stood to leave. The other Evaders rose too.

"Leaving so soon?" inquired Okondo. One of her eyebrows lifted.

"We need to make arrangements. Besides, we should not be gone any longer than is necessary. Primara Anaktisi distrusts us enough already. I fear if we linger that no amount of reassurance will convince him of our loyalty," Cutner droned. "And I would be of far less use to you then. . ."

Okondo batted her eyes. "I'll see you soon enough. But don't forget, I want to hear good news about my forthcoming meeting with Anaktisi soon. I know you won't disappoint me."

The Evaders fled. One or two even stumbled on roots in their rush. Not one of them dared a glance back at the Weavers in their flight.

"Ms. Ash!" Okondo slurred. She collapsed back in her seat. "Just one more glass!"

CHAPTER 21

Setting the Stage

OLLOWING THE DELVER MASSACRE, Chesa spent her days attending to Delver Sze's every whim. He donned the mantle of interim
Primara now, which only embellished his penchant for sadism.
Chesa had never quite grown fond of living with the ascendants. Too
hot down there. Besides, Sze's personality aside, the post-massacre Delvers' quarters offered her several unexpected pleasantries. Fewer Delvers,
for instance, meant fewer mouths to levy demands. It also meant fewer
meddlesome eyes, a prize Chesa deemed as priceless as any.

Chesa finished her morning grooming in her room and reached for
her robes, but froze. A protrusion stood out in a pocket that did not
belong. She threw up her thaumaturgical senses at once. She was in no
mood for further surprises. But no sign of mental workings resonated
forth, though that relieved her little. She licked her lips and reached
into her robes with two timid fingers.

Something brittle brushed her fingertips. She blew out a sigh as she
removed a curved shaving of wax. A series of letters were etched upon
it. Their arrangement would have meant nothing to most, but not her.
In moments, the wax melted into a slick of something like mud from
the warmth of her hand.

"It has to happen sometime," she sighed.

Chesa hated the idea of contesting Ms. Ash's proposal to the other

Disciples. After all, Ms. Ash had played no small part in Chesa's own induction. But the old woman's faith in Bianchi was not substantiated by anything Chesa had seen, and the Disciples' mission remained too vital to be derailed by some romantic fancy. So, Chesa donned what remained of her pearls beneath her cowl and left her rooms, ready for battle.

The abandoned workroom near the Tilters' den echoed far too much for Chesa's liking. It resided too close to active labs as well. Ursielle assured them that the shadow watched over their affair—whatever that meant. Wooden furniture crowded the room, as with similar spaces, as though designed to forever keep servants downtrodden and self-anonymized.

"Have you two lost your senses completely?" pleaded Chesa. "We're Disciples! They're of the noble blood!" She scoffed. "Our very mission is to undermine their power, to bring about a Blurred Keystone, not play into their hands!" She stared daggers at Ms. Ash and Ursielle Hedrigal.

"No decisions will be made without the lesser consensus, Chesa," Ursielle Hedrigal assured her. "Though I do appreciate you providing your unfiltered opinion on the matter. . ." He gestured to Ms. Ash. "Please continue."

Ms. Ash nodded before carrying on, "Ward and the Bianchi girl helped rescue Chesa, and in the process, learned of her aptitudes. Ms. Bianchi did not articulate whether she knew what kind of thaumaturgy Chesa used, or Lavinia during the altercation. Though it is wise to suppose Bianchi will sort it out."

Mortimer Palmer leaned forward with a smirk on his narrow face. "The situation places you both in danger. If either ascendant informs a scholar that Chesa is an anomaly, then they'll discover Ms. Ash has been hiding that fact. If Ms. Ash is compromised, then the rest of us will follow."

Chesa found herself nodding her agreement. The bird-faced anomaly pen specialist and she had never resided on the same side of an argument. She held back a gag.

"We could be facing the complete undoing of the Disciples," Mortimer concluded. "Our only weapon against the workings of the Amber Menhir, frail as it is, could be ruined! Whatever the benefits of a possible alliance, it cannot be worth it. A possible alliance!" he seethed.

A long silence followed.

"Gamaliel, I'd like your take," said Ursielle.

The freckled Architect specialist's jaw clenched. "The Architects have incurred a great slight with the death of the Thalsem girl. She was a prodigy. Though Ms. Bianchi has shown herself to be a competent force thaumaturge, I suspect they will always resent her. I doubt she will be a powerful ally," said Gamaliel. "There will be eyes on her for years. Can we bear such added scrutiny? We are made to scurry like vermin as it is!"

Ms. Ash cleared her throat. "But Peony Bianchi did not confess to the crime, in the end. The Ward boy conveyed it was he who slayed Ms. Thalsem. If he survives, then it is he who will bear the scrutiny."

Gamaliel and Ursielle gave cautious nods.

"But the Ward boy and the Bianchi girl are practically one and the same!" Chesa retorted. "They are together, always. If we attempt to recruit her and leave him, then she will betray anything we say in confidence back to him."

"They might not be together for forever. . ." Ms. Ash sighed. "Young love is fickle. Though I see your point." She adjusted the neckline of her robes. "It is not a difficult thing, forcing a spike between lovers. We could sever them, though I'm not convinced it's necessary. . ."

"We've already been told of the worst-case scenario," Rachel Bourke, the Evaders of Death expert, chimed in. "What of the best case? What could be gleaned by allying ourselves with mere ascendants?"

"For starters," Gamaliel replied, "we'd have agents who can move in places when and where servants cannot. If either of the ascendants rises to a position of influence, then we'd have levers from both top-down and bottom-up vantages."

"We could obtain access to saprolite wine," added Rachel Bourke.

Chesa felt her heart lurch forward. Her breath caught, and a part of her brain just behind her eyes released a pang of unanticipated plea-sure. "I had not considered that point," she whispered.

"What about thought paddocks?" said Mortimer Palmer. "Perhaps they could obtain access to those?"

"Thought paddocks can only be released from the Central Archive by trained thaumaturges," Chesa muttered. "But back to the saprolite wine. How much do you think we could obtain, and where would we store it?"

Ursielle adjusted his titanic form on his stool. Chesa thought he too might be fond of obtaining more of the narcotic drink. He seemed to avoid meeting her eyes. Prude.

"But," interrupted Ms. Ash, "Roland Ward is already working in the Central Archive as a clerk, is he not?"

"What of it?" snapped Chesa.

"Well," Ms. Ash replied, drawing out the word, "he could take pos-session of thought paddocks as they're returned. With saprolite wine and someone to infiltrate the Central Archive . . . imagine how many doors could be opened. Thought paddocks do go missing. . ."

The point bore a significant punch, even for Chesa. Much of the power scholars possessed over anomalies came from their superior training. With access to the vast discoveries of the menhirs, and the energy to fuel them, Chesa reasoned she could become as powerful as any Delver. She gulped several times unconsciously, garnering worried looks from other Disciples.

Rachel Bourke broke the silence. "Could we, in theory, begin to construct an archive of our own? Perhaps anomalies outside could come here to study?"

Chesa scoffed, "I don't imagine many anomalies will come running for the possibility of reading a few thought paddocks! Toads don't form lines to throw themselves into the jaws of snakes."

"Thought paddocks are encrypted in a language inaccessible to servants too," Ms. Ash added.

"For now," Gamaliel retorted. "But Ms. Bianchi may be able to learn the languages of one, perhaps two noble factions. In theory, she could help our members learn those forbidden codes, or configure their contents into something more accessible, but in ciphered tomes of our own."

"Speculation!" Chesa snarled. "If the noble factions learned we were educating lay society about their coded languages, they would kill us all and destroy our records."

"They would do that if they knew anything about us anyhow," countered Mortimer.

An awkward pause followed.

"How would we go about approaching the ascendants?" asked Ursielle.

"We intercept them," offered Ms. Ash. "Guide them to a meeting point of our choosing. Tell them of our cause, and convey what their help could mean for it."

"'Tell them of our cause. . .'" recited Chesa. "Really? Tell them we're a bunch of servants working to undermine the menhirs? Tell them we think the menhirs are evil and long ago abandoned their mission, if they ever really had one? Idiotic!"

Ms. Ash's mouth twisted with agitation. "Yes, Chesa. I think Peony has had front row seats to the menhir's atrocities, and Roland Ward has experienced them vicariously. I think the pair of them would be—are—sympathetic."

"And they're still young," added Gamaliel. "Ascendants make the ideal candidates. They haven't yet accepted the entirety of the menhir on its terms."

"Young outsiders. . ." Rachel Bourke whispered as she stroked her jawline.

"Plus," said Ms. Ash, "they've already shown a measure of friendship and loyalty to me, and to you too."

The dusty kitchen buzzed with renewed excitement.

"I am prepared to call a vote on the matter," called Ursielle.

Chesa's mouth dropped open.

"Those who stand opposed to our approaching the Bianchi girl and the Ward boy to join our cause, please indicate."

Chesa's hand shot up so fast that she startled herself. She gazed about their group in horror. Only she and Mortimer Palmer had raised their hands. He glowered at the outcome too.

"Those in favor?" Ursielle continued.

All the others raised their hands.

"Then it is decided."

"What?!" Chesa cried. "What if they attack us or report on us when we offer them an alliance? Think of the dangers!"

"I'll select a venue where we can dispose of them, if things go south. . ." Ursielle noted. "Naturally, we shan't tell them of our full resources until we are convinced of their allegiance." He cleared his throat. "As for their allegiance, I believe the shadow may be able to provide an object of influence to lock them into a bargain, provided they enter it willingly."

"You mean a tro—" Chesa began, but Ursielle cut her off with a wave of his hand.

"I'll see what the shadow can provide," said Ursielle. "That is my role."

"When should we intercept them?" asked Ms. Ash.

"Let them meet with Primara Okondo," said Ursielle. "With the Ward boy freed and grateful for your efforts, I believe he and Peony will be ready to swear themselves to our cause."

Ms. Ash stood and brushed off the front of her grey robes. She studied the room. "It seems we have our plan. I'll send missives with the details soon."

"And I will inform the shadow," intoned Ursielle.

"I've got datasets that need some tweaking," added Mortimer with a wink.

"And if this fails?" Chesa whined. "What if we destroy everything we've ever set in motion?"

"Well then, we'd best be ready, Chesa. Everyone must do their part to prepare for the worst," Ursielle replied with a smile.

Chesa sighed. She had given them every warning she could.

"So. . ." Ursielle said with two claps of his hands. "Places, everyone!"

CHAPTER 22

To Have and to Hold

TARA SAT ERECT WITH a grim expression fixed on her supper. Her bowl of lentils, pork shoulder, and wilted greens sat untouched. The spoon in her hand served more as a rearranging tool than a vessel of transference. Peony enjoyed no appetite herself. It had been days since she'd requested an audience with Primara Okondo, and she had still received no reply. Then there was the forthcoming meeting with Ms. Ash's mystery associates. That too frayed Peony's nerves.

Tara studied the letter she had received in the evening mail. The scrawl at the bottom announced it as another from Larus. As much as Tara seemed to enjoy receiving mail, something about Larus's letters always rendered her melancholy. She mumbled to Larus sometimes when she thought no one could hear. Peony wanted to ask how she could help her friend, but Tara shared her feelings only under the rarest of terms.

"How're the lessons with the Tilters going?" asked Peony.

"Fine," Tara replied. She scanned the neighboring dining tables.

None of the other ascendants sat near them anymore. Their peers viewed Peony as a freak because of her ambiguous thaumaturgical identity. They viewed Tara as the most prepossessing and high-flying failure in a century. And Roland, perhaps most forgivable, remained an ugly, stammering giant. At the thought of Roland, Peony fought wetness from collecting in her eyes.

"Has there been progress?" Peony inquired gently.

"Not really," Tara said with a frown. "I've learned a fair bit about the Tilters: how they defend themselves, how they see themselves in the context of the other noble factions, and the like. That's all been interesting. They are kind enough to conceal whatever disappointment they feel about me." The corners of Tara's mouth lifted in a sad smile. She resumed her study of Larus's letter.

"Tara . . . I have a favor to ask of you," said Peony. "Of a . . . sensitive nature."

"Yes?" Tara did not lift her eyes from her letter.

"Following our interaction with Lavinia, I . . . I hid the thought paddock she had," whispered Peony.

Tara stiffened, but kept her gaze down. "Where?"

Peony hesitated. "Well, it's still in your room."

"My room?!" Tara gaped. "That's the first place they will look!"

"Not so fast," said Peony. "You're not linked to the that day with Lavinia." She lowered her voice. "No one would suspect you'd be in possession of the thought paddock. Plus, we didn't have a whole lot of time after Lavinia's . . . accident. . . to hide it. Plus, you've got access to the Central Archive. That seems the safest place to learn about its contents and protect it from falling into the wrong hands again. And even if Roland is freed, people will be watching him."

"But it's all okay for me to ferry around this poison, hmm?" snapped Tara. "I have my homework from the Tilters. I don't have time to be wandering to the Central Archive anymore."

"Please, Tara," Peony pleaded. "You're our only hope, and it's important. Maybe the archivists can determine who's been using it and how. You trust them, and that means something. Please?"

Tara let out a pained sigh and rolled her eyes. "Fine. I'll see about visiting the archive this evening. I don't want it around me any longer than necessary, especially if someone dangerous is after it. I wish you'd warned me sooner."

"Thank you!" Peony beamed. "And I'm sorry."

"I wasn't hungry anyhow." Tara sniffed. "Perhaps I should see to it now. I can't have something like this looming over me."

"Thank you!" whispered Peony.

Tara rose and departed.

Peony scanned the other ascendants, curious to see if someone watched Tara leave. No one seemed to have taken notice of their exchange. No one so much as glanced up from their meals during Tara's departure. So, Peony disposed of her tray and headed back to her room.

She opened her door to find Ms. Ash and Weaver Ankathi standing over her bed. Weaver Ankathi bore her deepest glower. She had donned her emerald Weaver robes, which Peony took to mean she meant business. A bun atop Ankathi's head pulled her skin back tight enough to smooth out many of her most prominent wrinkles. Ms. Ash bore a serious look, though a glimmer of kindness touched her eyes.

"Primara Okondo will grant an audience with you tonight, girl," said Ms. Ash.

"What about Roland?" Peony asked.

"Him too," added Ms. Ash.

"I will see about collecting him," snapped Ankathi. Though the woman stood several paces away, something pungent and vinegary wafted from her that made Peony a bit faint. "Ms. Ash will escort you via another route. We won't have you two colluding!"

Ms. Ash shot the scholar a tiny scowl. "Weaver Ankathi is correct. We want to preserve as much unbiased evidence as possible. I hope you'll understand."

Peony nodded. "Of course."

"Good," said Ms. Ash. "Don your ascendant's robes and ready yourself. We need to leave immediately."

"I may see you there," Ankathi announced. The scholar inclined her head to each of them and left.

"I'll be outside. Get a move on," said Ms. Ash. "Oh! If I were you, girl, I might double up on my robes, hmm? The climate in the Weavers' quarters can be fickle at times."

Peony arched an eyebrow. She considered inquiring further, but Ms. Ash escaped before she could organize the thought.

Deciding to take the servant's advice, Peony doubled up on robes. She grimaced at her bulbous reflection in her standing mirror. She selected a pair of boots with a slight heel. Peony thought their leafy hue might appeal to the Weaver Primara. She hurried to ready herself and was quickly out the door.

Ms. Ash shot Peony an appraising look as the bedchamber door closed behind her. "Follow me, Ms. Bianchi, and don't dally."

Peony glanced over her shoulder as they departed. Weaver Ankathi spoke in hushed tones with the two Architects guarding Roland's room. The three of them paused to study Peony. She wished more than anything to see Roland. Though, knowing he remained well enough to attend a meeting with Okondo provided Peony a small measure of comfort.

"Coming?" called Ms. Ash from the end of the corridor.

With a huff, Peony gave up any hope of seeing Roland and rushed to Ms. Ash's heels.

Though Ms. Ash never favored needless chatter, tonight the woman said nothing. Peony wanted to ask how best to intercede on Roland's behalf, but something about Ms. Ash's pace and bleak expression hinted that she could bear no discussions.

The clear-topped corridor leading to the Weavers' quarters revealed a sky packed with clouds. Only the tiniest clusters of stars peeked through their gaps. The breeze that issued from the Weavers' quarters chilled Peony more than usual. It harbored nothing of its familiar earthiness. Something about that made her uneasy. The perimeter of the forest seemed darker than usual too, causing the towering trees to loom.

"Where are the insects?" asked Peony.

"Dormant," replied Ms. Ash. "They won't be producing any light for us, so mind your step, girl."

"They weren't dormant last time," noted Peony. "Is winter just now manifesting in the Weavers' quarters?"

"Winters can manifest here any time," Ms. Ash explained. "Winter is a mood in these glades. Winter is feral, brutal, decisive, and fair. When that mood fits the Weavers, the climate of their quarters reflects that temperament. All the scholars' quarters have a means of expressing their dispositions."

A shiver ran up Peony's spine, and she doubted it was from the cold.

Despite the wintry frigidity, the huge trees looked as alive and well as ever as the two navigated their way. Frozen earth kept Peony's boots from sinking into the loam. The moss, still green, crackled like crisp bread beneath their feet. Frozen dew speckled the canopy like crystals that caught and cast glimmers of starlight.

Peony followed Ms. Ash down their familiar path to the Primara's meeting chamber. This time, no wind whatsoever touched their path. No fauna unseen called from the canopy overhead. The forest harbored only stillness, as though it anticipated the approach of an apex predator. Again, a chill passed over Peony. She clutched her robes tighter around her.

As they approached the fork in the path that split off to the Primara's chambers, Ms. Ash turned away. Instead, she walked down a path leading to somewhere Peony failed to recognize. Peony paused.

Ms. Ash stopped in her tracks and turned. "This way, girl. The Primara has requested to meet with you at Black Lake."

Something about the venue's name suggested to Peony that the meeting might be a serious one. Still, she bore no protest and followed.

The path to Black Lake wound through a portion of forest commanded by stands of slender trees with white bark. The warm hues of autumn drenched their vaulting canopies. The path finally ducked into a short corridor like the one leading to the chamber where they had held their prior meetings. Ms. Ash paused at the very edge of the corridor, gesturing inward. "Here it is."

They stood together before a frozen lake like a great sheet of glass. A biting breeze sent snow whipping across it. Peony dared a glance up through the transparent ceiling. The swaths of stars that had comforted her before had retreated. Inky blackness above and icy darkness below made the chamber's size impossible to estimate. Only the occasional swirling of snowflakes atop the ice provided her a sense of orientation.

"She's in there?" Peony quavered.

"I suspect," replied Ms. Ash.

A gust of wind sent a cyclone of snow aloft. A low crackling from somewhere deep in the ice moaned below.

"You're not coming?" asked Peony. "How can I convince her to help us?"

Ms. Ash shook her head and took a step closer to Peony. "Swear your allegiance to the Weavers. Offer to pass on any information you glean from the Architects to help fuel the Weavers' ascent. You have something Okondo wants, Peony. Use it!"

Peony swallowed. She placed her foot on the ice and slid her toe back and forth, testing it. Though the surface was slick, it was not so smooth as it first seemed. Sharp little troughs and ridges provided traction. She shunted some of her weight atop one foot. Then she lurched another leg forward. She took care to keep her weight even. One frightened step at a time, Peony stilted her way across the Black Lake towards what seemed its center.

After a few moments, she twisted. "Hey, I'm doing alright, aren't I?"

But Ms. Ash had vanished. Peony couldn't even find the corridor from which she'd come. The undifferentiated blackness behind her and seismic groans of the glacier beneath seemed to amplify.

Peony shivered and continued, slow but steady. Just when she had gained a semblance of confidence in her footing, her back foot slipped out from beneath her, and she crashed to the ice. She hit with a grunt. As she struggled to her hands and knees, something pale beneath the ice loomed into view. She gasped and slipped to her stomach. As she did, the form glided back into the darkness and vanished. Tears formed in her eyes.

"You look lost, my dear," called an inviting voice from behind her.

Trying to right herself, Peony turned to see Primara Okondo approaching surefootedly across the ice.

"I'm alright," Peony lied, just as her knee slid out from beneath her and she fell again. This time the impact knocked the wind out of her. She lay prostrate as Okondo came within a few paces.

"You're brave to have come out here all alone," said Okondo. She crouched to study Peony. "A good number of Weavers won't venture beyond the shores of the Black Lake, especially during unfavorable conditions. . ."

Peony hissed out a small laugh. "They're smart."

"Maybe so," the Weaver Primara agreed. "But they're cowards nonetheless." Okondo stepped forward. "Let me help you up?"

Peony wanted to decline. She hated appearing weak in front of her Primara when so much stood at stake, but she doubted she could stand on her own again.

"That would be nice," she admitted. "Just when I thought I had a knack for walking here, I slipped. Now I can't even seem to stand."

"A metaphor for life, if I've ever heard one," Okondo said with a laugh.

With the Primara's grip like cold-forged iron, Peony found herself hoisted to her feet by the back of her robes. Her feet slid back and forth as they searched for traction, yet somehow, the Primara's grip held until Peony found her footing. Then Okondo laced her bare arm, pale but reddened with windburn, around one of Peony's. Though the Primara only reached Peony's shoulder, her footing somehow rooted her to the ice. Soon Peony walked with ease by Okondo's side.

"There we are," she cooed. Despite only wearing her corset top and billowing pants, she radiated heat like an oven. "You're better at this than you first appeared, my dear. Are you sure you weren't just trying to fool me with feigned victimhood?"

"Hardly. . ." scoffed Peony. "Wait—how're you so warm?"

"Ah. . ." Okondo grinned. "A little trick I learned from a swordfish, sweetling."

Peony squinted.

"Swordfish have a means for keeping their vital bits warm in a sea of cold. I've thaumaturgically co-opted their innovation for myself," Okondo explained. "I'll show you when we leave."

They walked together on the groaning lake, licked by the icy wind, but the Primara's presence warmed Peony. It all seemed right for a time. Then Peony gave her complacent head a shake.

"I should explain why I'm here," said Peony.

Okondo turned to Peony and blinked her green eyes. "It's for the Ward boy, my dear. Everyone knows that."

Peony stiffened. "Everyone?"

Okondo's peal of laughter chimed like sleigh bells. "Of course! You see something special in this Roland Ward, and you'd like my help in saving him."

"You can help?" Peony asked.

"Sweetling, that's what I do!" Okondo chuckled. "I serve my fellow Weavers, as any leader must. And you, Peony, will be one of the most notable Weavers ever to grace the Amber Menhir, mark my words."

"Really?" said Peony. She paused. "You think so?"

"Why, yes!" exclaimed Okondo. She turned Peony to face her. They stood a pace apart, grasping each other's hands. "Believe me, Peony, so many people would give anything to be you. Remember that, please, and protect yourself, for me." She squeezed Peony's hands.

"I don't see it that way," admitted Peony. She turned her head away. "The other ascendants don't even look at me anymore. My instructors all seem to hate me, distrust me, or both."

"But I can see where you're headed, Peony. In time, you will too," Okondo assured her. "Now, explain to me why it is that the Weavers should help your little Roland."

Okondo braided her bare arm back around Peony's, and they resumed their walk.

"I was there, Primara Okondo. I saw it all," Peony began.

"Oh?" Okondo cocked her head.

"Roland only meant to help Tara," Peony went on, "and when we forced our way into Tara's room, Lavinia attacked us!"

"You invaded Lavinia's private quarters, and you were surprised when she defended herself?" queried Okondo.

"It wasn't like that," Peony insisted. "She didn't attack us just as we got in. She was acting strange when we spoke to her. We suggested having the Tilters come to help us, and Lavinia went crazy!"

"Crazy? How?" asked the Primara.

"She lashed out at us with some kind of thaumaturgy that I couldn't see!" Peony exclaimed.

Okondo paused. "How do you mean?"

"I opened my senses to Lavinia after she attacked me. I wanted to fend her off, but she wasn't using force thaumaturgy."

"Oh?" asked Okondo. "What do you suppose she used?"

"Well, whatever she used, she sent Roland tumbling fast." Peony heard the uncertainty in her own voice. She hesitated, and the Primara's arm hardened against her own. "Mind thaumaturgy, maybe?"

"A Delver!" cried Okondo. "Lavinia's a prodigy Architect—everyone knows that. She's shown no other aptitudes. Pluripotency is extremely rare. You must be mistaken."

"I don't know," Peony admitted. "But I know she wasn't using force or life threads, and then, Roland and Tara both said she'd been acting strange all morning."

"Then what do you suppose happened?" inquired Okondo.

A long moment of silence passed before Peony spoke again. "I think it has to involve the Delvers of the Mind."

Okondo paused their stroll and faced Peony. A gust of frigid air sent the layers of Peony's robes snapping around her. "The Delvers. . ." said Okondo, sounding skeptical.

"Yes, I think they'd been messing with her brain," Peony continued. "I guess they've always done stuff like that, but now they've figured out a way to give others access to mind thaumaturgy or something too."

"We can look into it," suggested Okondo. Her eyes seemed locked in thought.

"Thank you!" said Peony. "Roland was really just trying to protect me. None of us ever meant to hurt Lavinia."

"I know you didn't," Okondo reassured her. "We'll make sure the Ward boy is taken care of."

"Oh, thank the gods!" Peony cried out.

"Now to compensation," Okondo continued.

"Compensation?"

"Yes, dear," scoffed Okondo. "This is the menhir. You can't have something for nothing here. Saving Roland Ward will cost me political capital. My time and efforts are valuable, sweetling."

"I do have something I can give you." Peony held her voice cool. "Something no one else can."

Okondo cocked her head, and a sly smile touched her face. "Go on, pigeon. What do you have that I would want?"

"I'll swear my allegiance to you," asserted Peony. The time had come for her to press her advantage. "To the Weavers. This night. I will commit myself."

"My dear." The Primara laughed. "The Architects already think you're mine. Everyone does."

"We could change that!" Peony interrupted. "You and I could work out a plan to have the Architects recruit me. I could gather information about them and report back to you."

"Oh, my, my, my, Peony." Okondo chuckled. "You really do have the instincts of a scholar after all. . ."

"So, we have a deal?" asked Peony.

"No." Okondo's tone echoed in the absolute. "I need more."

"What more can I give?"

Okondo's smile widened. "I need your absolute loyalty, and I need more information from you."

"But I. . ."

"You're completely loyal, you say?" Okondo interjected. She pursed her lips and blinking her mossy eyes. "You've never attempted to mislead me? You're not withholding any information from me? Information that I could use to save Roland?"

Peony swallowed hard. "I've told you everything important."

"Everything you think to be important," concluded the Primara. Her pupils seemed to grow within her sparkling eyes.

Peony thought she detected a knowing tone in the Primara's voice. On instinct, Peony found herself glancing around the bleak lake, like prey searching for an escape. Two forms appeared on the horizon. Okondo had been guiding Peony toward the pair all the while. Peony froze in place.

"Peony, do you know what this is?" Okondo asked with a voice like dehydrated honey. She plucked a white spherical object from beneath the brim of her corset.

The muscles in Peony's neck and shoulders clenched. "Yes," she replied. Her voice went thin. "That's a thought paddock."

"Indeed," replied Okondo, drawing out the word. "Why do you suppose I have one of these on my person now?"

Peony's heart raced. It couldn't be the same thought paddock she'd hidden earlier. There had been no time for anyone to fetch it.

"I don't know," Peony croaked.

"Peony. . ." sang the Weaver Primara. "I know that you've been keeping something from me. . ."

Peony's chest pounded. Desperate, she caved, hoping honesty might buy them all lenience. "I was the one who killed Lavinia, but it was an accident! Roland is innocent. He only meant to protect me. Honestly!"

"That matters not to me, my dear," sighed Okondo. "The question is why the pair of you thought to conceal this object after you slayed the Thalsem girl." Okondo studied Peony with calculating eyes.

"Lavinia had it, and she seemed to be protecting it," said Peony. "Ascendants aren't supposed to have thought paddocks. We were just trying to return it to the Central Archive."

Primara Okondo tucked the thought paddock back into her corset. A wry smile crossed her lips. "I suspect it was important, Peony, but we cannot have this clue going back to the Central Archive. We'll handle this matter internally now. The archivists botched their roles in this matter."

"I've been honest with you now," Peony pleaded. "At least let Roland go now!"

293

Okondo clucked her tongue and braided her arm back around Peony's. "Come," she ordered.

Peony did.

The Weaver Primara guided them, surefooted and slow, to the two forms in the distance.

"I want to believe you, sweetling. Really, I do," cooed the Weaver Primara. "But the truth is that I don't know what to believe anymore."

"But" Peony interjected, but the Primara spoke over her.

"I need assurances," she went on. "I don't believe you withheld information to harm the Weavers. If I thought that, then. . . Well, let us be glad that is not the case."

Just then, something deep and sonic, like an ethereal groan of some titan, resonated from somewhere deep beneath their feet. It sent bits of snow jittering across the ice's surface. Peony's breath caught, and she looked down. She thought she saw something grey and huge pass beneath them.

"The Weavers who avoid Black Lake have a good reason for doing so, my dear," the Primara continued. "The lake is vast beneath us, and life teems under its surface, not all of it kind, pigeon. I am relieved to say I don't think you need concern yourself with life beneath the lake today. Just know that it is there. We hold great power at our disposal, now more than ever."

Peony swallowed hard.

"Lysander!" Okondo called out. "Lysander! Delmar! Sorry to leave you waiting. Peony and I were just enjoying a little chat between girls. Forgive us?"

"It's no matter at all!" replied the sweet-faced Lysander Sze. He clutched his pale grey robes about him.

"Speak for yourself, Lysander," murmured the tall, wedge-faced man beside him, presumably Delmar.

"Peony, my dear, this is Lysander Sze of the Delvers and Delmar

Cutner of the Evaders. They've met you before, but you mightn't remember them," said Okondo.

Each of the men nodded. Their reddened features and grim expressions conveyed that they did not endure the blistering cold air with the same fortitude as the Weaver Primara.

"Now, where were we? Ah, compensation!" chimed Okondo.

"I promise I'll be honest with you, Primara Okondo. I didn't think I was keeping anything important from you," Peony rambled. Her eyes darted between the three scholars.

"Of course not, child, but it is the details that we deem unimportant in a story's telling that are so often the most vital," lectured Okondo.

"Right," agreed Peony.

"Delmar, the scarab, please!" called the Primara.

Cloaked in pale yellow robes, Delmar Cutner did not seem pleased to expose his hands to the freezing air. He rustled and plucked from his robes a crimson silk handkerchief. He handed the folded silk to Primara Okondo.

She unfolded the silk, not taking her eyes from it as she did. As Okondo undid the last of the folds, Peony spotted what seemed like a carving of a beetle worked from a milky grey stone. Some kind of shimmering sediment sat suspended within its otherwise clear body. Okondo took care not to touch the stone as she lifted it.

"Have you any idea what this is?" she asked.

"No," Peony admitted.

"No? Well, have you ever heard of a troth stone?" Okondo continued.

Peony's throat tightened. Both the Delver and the Evader flinched at hearing the stone's name.

"Your eyes say it all, sweetling," said the Primara. "This is the real thing. I am hopeful you will don the stone for me."

Peony took a step back and slipped. She dropped to the ice with thud. "No!" she shouted. "I won't!"

Okondo laughed. "Well, look at that, gentlemen!" She fixed Delmar and Lysander with a playful smile. "At the last, my sweetling revolts! She comes to me for help, and now, when I ask for honesty, she denies me my simple request?!"

"I promise you I'll be yours!" Peony exclaimed.

"Pointless," the Primara sang. "Your words are pointless. You will forever be tempted to hide the secrets of your friends, your lovers, and your fellow Weavers. I won't have it."

"I'm not going to swear on a troth stone for you or anyone!" Peony replied.

"Very well," Okondo replied with a tendril of reluctance. "Then Roland Ward will be sentenced to death. I'll see it done promptly. He will not suffer for your insolence. It wouldn't be right." The Primara turned as though to leave. "Come, boys. She's useless if she cannot be trusted."

She took each of their arms in hers and strolled away. Peony tried to lift herself, but her hand slipped. This time her palm crossed over a sharp spot of ice as it slid. Pain shot up her hand, and she hissed. A gash extended across the meat of her thumb. She sucked in wintry air as she pressed her bloody hand against her robes.

Surrounded by blackness and bombarded by cold, she thought of Roland. She wondered where he was at this moment. She wondered if Primara Okondo had offered him the troth stone too. Peony thought of Tara and wondered if she'd been harmed over the thought paddock, or if she was still back in her room now, searching for an object that was no longer there. A murk of powerlessness descended around Peony, like a wet, smothering blanket.

"Wait!" Peony bellowed. "Don't go!"

Okondo and her escorts turned with wolfish smiles. "Yes?" they asked.

"I'll do it!" Peony whimpered.

Okondo took her time walking back to stand over Peony. Delver Sze and Evader Cutner stayed back. Rather than putting out a hand for Peony to grasp, Okondo exposed and extended the scarab upon its crimson silk.

"Take it," Okondo commanded. "It's the only way."

Peony reached out for the small figurine. Up close, she observed copious ridges carved into its plated wings and spines along its legs.

"You must take the troth stone of your own accord, Peony. I cannot force you," the Primara instructed. "Details. . ."

Peony closed her eyes and grasped the stone. Nothing happened. She found it neither heavy nor light. The gem bore a coolness, but not cold. Holding it caused her no pain. She blinked.

"There," said Okondo. "Not so bad is it, sweetling?"

"No," Peony admitted.

"Now for the promise," Okondo instructed. "The wording for such things is important. This bit of troth stone won't give us more than a single vow. You see, pigeon, it is not slavery I ask of you. Just honesty."

Peony nodded as Okondo leaned in close.

"All I ask is for you to tell me everything pertaining to the day you murdered Lavinia Thalsem." Okondo smiled. "That's all."

Peony felt unsure. What more was there to convey? None of the other particulars seemed dangerous as she reviewed them in haste. She might be compelled to tell Okondo about Ms. Ash being there, but Ms. Ash was the Primara's servant. It was probably Ms. Ash who had told Okondo about the thought paddock.

"I'm afraid we don't have all night, sweetling. I'm a busy person," Okondo sighed. "Quid pro quo."

Peony took in a deep breath of resignation. She told herself that she could do it for Roland, for freedom from her home, and maybe a little bit for Tara too. Peony opened her mouth and spoke the words, "I promise to tell you everything pertaining to the day I murdered Lavinia Thalsem."

The gem warmed, as though some chemical reaction had occurred on her palm. The grey cloudiness within it lessened faster and faster. Bit by bit, the murkiness inside the troth stone receded into nothing, leaving only a perfectly transparent scarab in Peony's palm. She couldn't even make out its edges as she studied it in stunned silence.

"That is the way of the truth, my dear." Okondo clucked her tongue. "It matters not the shape of the circumstances. Once the truth is laid bare, the eye can see through all things."

The Primara stretched out an alabaster hand in friendship. Peony clasped it and hoisted herself to her feet. Okondo wrapped one arm around Peony's.

"Now, poppet, tell me everything."

CHAPTER 23

A Lucky Hand

"**W**ELL, WHAT DID YOU tell her?"

"I told her everything," Peony shrugged. "I decided to trust her."

Tara stared at Peony with her mouth agape, scandalized by the entire affair. "She bullies you by dragging you across some frozen lake, and now you sit there saying you've told her everything, and you trust her? Please tell me I'm missing something."

Peony stared back at Tara over her cards and gave her an apathetic shrug.

"You know, you're really beginning to resemble Roland with all of those shrugs," spat Tara.

Roland stirred from his position atop Peony's rainbow-dyed carpet on the floor. "I h-heard that." He yawned.

"The point is, Primara Okondo kept her word," said Peony. "She saw to Roland's release. I've seen Ms. Ash and Chesa since the meeting. They're both safe. Have a little faith!"

"It was a gamble, Peony, and not one I would have taken," sniffed Tara. She rearranged the cards in her hand and studied them with a smirk. All the bluffing and resource management in Veils and Poisons reminded Tara of rulership. "Three royal serpents," she said as she placed her hand on Peony's bedspread.

Peony frowned down at the serpent triad.

"You're lucky. I'll give you that," Peony said with a weak smile. "It's a shame you won't consider playing for money. You'd make a fortune."

Tara winced. "A Langcraw is no petty gambler or street urchin. As for luck," she mused, "I'd say you used all of yours up by getting off that lake with your hide intact. Practice makes perfect, Peony, and I've a greater taste for work than most, even in cards."

"Not so loud," hushed Peony with a glance toward her door. "Primara Okondo asked that I keep our arrangement secret."

"My mouth is sealed!" called Roland from the floor. He propped his head on his palm.

"It's a wonder she didn't have another troth stone to swear your secrecy," Tara added. "What have you got?"

"A serpent, a badger, two magpies, and a garnet." Peony sighed. Somehow poor Peony only ever managed to assembled hodgepodge hands.

Tara tried to subdue a smile from touching her features, but failed. Peony wore failure with more grace than most. Though, Tara noted Peony's reluctance to accept that winning hand after hand indicated skill, not luck.

"I remember a version of Tara Langcraw that refused to play cards," Peony grumbled. "I sort of miss her. This card-slinging murderess version is difficult to be friends with sometimes."

Tara smirked. "Another hand?"

Peony sighed and avoided Tara's gaze. "What's the point?"

"Maybe Roland will play too. Hmm?" offered Tara. She nudged the sprawling farmer with a foot. "What do you say, Roland?"

Roland groaned in reply.

"Sounds like a no to me," concluded Peony.

"How will you two get any better if you don't practice?" Tara chided.

"One more hand," relinquished Peony. "Maybe I can end on a high note."

"Maybe so," said Tara.

Tara flicked their unspent cards through a series of arcs and splits that still delighted her. She sorted out a hand of five cards for each player. She set several more cards face down between them. Peony stole glances as Roland all the while. The discarded portion of the deck hadn't been reshuffled, which awarded Peony a small advantage. She better understood how to account for the cards played in rounds prior.

"Do you intend to tell Ms. Ash or Chesa about the troth stone?" asked Tara.

"I don't think so," murmured Peony.

Roland grazed a finger down Peony's shin.

She brushed a toe against his leg. "It would only worry them," quipped Peony. "Okondo knows what she knows." She exchanged several cards for those face down between them. Hope sprung in her eyes with each new card.

"I wouldn't be so sure," counseled Tara.

"I think Ms. Ash would respond okay," said Peony in a distracted tone.

"I've said it before: there's just something about that Chesa that isn't right," growled Tara.

"She has her reasons for behaving like a mau in a room full of rocking chairs," replied Peony.

Something about that reply bothered Tara. She squinted over her cards at Peony. "What does that mean?"

Peony grimaced and exchanged looks with Roland.

Tara studied them. "Out with it!" she snapped. "What're you two hiding?"

"We can't say," announced Peony. "It wouldn't be right."

"But you told the Weaver Primara, didn't you?" Tara pressed.

Peony sighed. "I had to. But that doesn't mean I have to tell you. Some things are worth keeping secret for people."

Tara kept them pinned with a scowl. "She murdered Lavinia, didn't she?"

"No," said Peony.

"Well then, she's pregnant," Tara concluded. "Typical."

"Hardly." Peony laughed.

"She's a lesbian? No, that would just be trite," Tara mused. "At least give me a hint."

"No," Roland replied flatly. "S-stop making guesses. We can't tell you."

"It's fine," Tara replied. She shook her head in frenetic little gestures of declination. "It doesn't really interest me anyhow." She could feel a blush climbing up her neck. "So, what have you got?"

Peony quirked a victorious smile. "Two royal serpents, two badgers!"

Tara grinned as she planted her hand on the bed. "Four crowns," she sang.

"Of course you have four crowns," sighed Peony. "It's been wonderful losing to you, but I think Roland and I are off to bed."

Tara looked down at her hand. She wished she could play all night. She rose to leave when she noticed a mischievous smile on Roland's maw. She looked away to find Peony bearing something fiendish in her eyes too.

Tara fussed with her robe's neckline. "Yes, well, it has been a pleasure, but I must be going."

She collected their Veils and Poisons deck and strode to the door, just as a slow triplet of knocks rang out. Tara stepped back. Peony and Roland clambered to their feet with a bit too much haste for Tara's liking.

"See you later, T-Tara!" Roland fumbled.

"Wait a minute. . ." Tara breathed. "Are you two expecting a third?"

"It's nothing like that!" said Peony, but a stench of horror dripped from the words.

Tara let an edge of judgment enter her voice. "Well, we'll just see about that, won't we?" She jerked the door open.

"No, Tara, wait!" Peony shouted, but it was too late.

Two servants clad in cowled robes lurked a pace from Tara. Neither Chesa nor Ms. Ash so much as lifted an eyebrow at her blustering.

"Ms. Langcraw," said Ms. Ash. She dropped into a genuflection. "I did not expect to see you here so late."

Chesa also genuflected, though her gaze did not drop in any sign of deference.

"I should say the same of you," scoffed Tara. "What's going on here?"

"It's nothing," said Peony with just a little too much urgency. "Ms. Ash and Chesa just said they would come meet with us sometime this week."

"Meet with you?!" Tara cried. "Haven't you four gotten into enough trouble already?"

"It's kind of you to be so concerned, Ms. Langcraw, but I can assure you, there will be no mischief tonight," soothed Ms. Ash. "We'd like to meet with Peony and Roland in private though, if you'd be so kind."

Tara went rigid and sniffed.

"Please, Tara," Peony interjected. "We'll see you tomorrow?"

"Fine," Tara lied. "I expect to hear all about it at breakfast."

She soared between Ms. Ash and Chesa, who bowed as she passed. Tara refused to deign them with further acknowledgment. She held her head high and her face still. She suppressed the urge to look back, no matter her curiosity.

When she arrived at her chambers, Tara took the room's only stool and paused before her reflection. Her features donned the Langcraw pane of glass, immutable, respectable, and ancient. She could not allow the silliness of the menhir's antics to imperil her better judgment. After all, most everyone's time at the menhirs turned out to be little more than a fleeting political pageantry. Only the vain or stupid, or both, thought otherwise. Who really thought they were going to be the one to solve Calamity? Not Tara. No, in time, her friendships with Peony and Roland would atrophy to no more than a collection of warnings to her own daughter. Delaying the bitter elixir of reality benefited no one.

Tara fussed with Larus's snood on her dressing table. She tried to think of what Larus would say at a time like this. Really, the more Tara thought of it, the clearer it seemed. Roland Ward was a country bumpkin Weaver with a heart of gold, but a brain of likable mush. Peony Bianchi displayed the kindhearted recklessness of a girl who hurt those close to her and orchestrated her own early demise. Tonight, they made their own choices. It just happened to be that those choices included loitering with two servants implicated in the murder of her former roommate.

Tara glanced at Lavinia's empty bed. The room seemed to grow a little colder. Members of the noble blood must be free, but they must also bear the consequences of their choices. Tara knew that. Peony and Roland were no different.

Larus's snood slipped from Tara's hand with a little clatter. She looked down to find her knee vibrating like a child's. She stilled it and sniffed. If Peony or Roland got hurt, they had only themselves to blame. They were adults . . . somewhat. Tara's knee launched back into motion. How long had it been? She opened her mouth to ask Lavinia, but paused as she realized her stupidity.

Tara reminded herself that she could enjoy a clear conscience regardless of the night's outcome. As she considered that, the image of Lavinia's form, wrapped in bed linens, still and discarded at the feet of the Evaders flashed across Tara's mind. She wondered how many bedsheets it would take to envelop Peony. Such a gangly thing, Peony, and much too tall for any proper lady of the noble blood. And they did not make bedsheets large enough to shroud Roland. Tara shook her head, trying to still her mind. But the images of Lavinia, who became Peony, who became Roland, wedged themselves behind her eyelids. She sighed at her own tediousness.

Tara fixed her reflection with a glare. "Leaders who know better than their subjects have a duty to help protect them." She sounded like her mother. "Peony and Roland are not your subjects," she reminded herself. "But should that matter?" She scoffed. "All the training in the world, and no one told me that part."

Well, if her thoughts would not leave her be, Tara concluded that she owed it to herself to act. Peony and Roland might resent her for interceding in their little plans, but being a good friend required making friends angry at times. Tara rose from her self-interrogation and hid the Veils and Poisons deck under Lavinia's mattress. After all, Tara could not let the world think her tawdry if she somehow met harm while executing her duty. She donned Larus's snood, hoping for once that it might bring her luck.

A minute later, Tara knocked on Peony's door and straightened her robes. She took in a deep breath and steeled herself for a confrontation. After a long moment of stillness, she knocked again.

"Peony!" Tara called. "We must speak."

No one answered, so she knocked a third time.

Nothing—not even Roland's mouth breathing.

Tara peered about the corridor for evidence of where they might have absconded to. Apart from an inebriated ascendant stumbling back to their bedchamber, the hall seemed empty.

"Why am I here again?" Tara growled to herself. "I'm doing what I'm supposed to here, gods be good, how about some help?"

Just then, out of the corner of her eye, a shadow flickered at the end of the corridor leading to their classes. Tara looked up. "I suppose that will suffice."

She followed the movement to the junction at end of the hall and listened. Muffled voices murmured in the distance. Tara dared a glance around the corner. At the far end of the adjoining corridor, Ms. Ash led the four around another junction of halls toward the Weaver and Evader classrooms.

Tara waited several breaths and followed to the next crossway. Again, she paused to listen. A door creaked only a little away. She dared another look around the corner to find Peony, Roland, Ms. Ash, and Chesa slithering into their Weaver classroom. Tara pulled back and sagged against the wall behind her.

"What am I doing here?" she whispered. "This is none of my concern."

The door to the Weaver classroom closed with a click. Despite her words, Tara glided to the space just outside their class and waited.

"What kind of cretin am I turning into?" she murmured. Tara knew she stalked her friends for only virtuous reasons: to help. "But if that's so," she whispered with a smirk, "then why am I whispering?"

A breeze passed over Tara's slippered foot, and she reeled back against the wall with a hiss. A modest wind flowed through a gap beneath the doorway.

"You are wound so tight, Tara Langcraw, because you're not meant to be here," she whined beneath her breath.

She could just hear Larus's would-be reply: "Sensible young ladies don't go wandering around abandoned hallways in the middle of the night, drumming up trouble for themselves."

"Yes, but maybe. . ." Tara murmured. "I cannot count myself among the ranks of sensible young ladies any longer. . ."

Her eyes descended upon the crack beneath the door, and she smiled. A moment later, Tara bellied forward like a thieving serpent, angling her ear so that she could listen.

"We should wait for Mortimer to arrive before we begin," said a young man's voice.

"I agree," said an older man in an authoritative tone.

"Mortimer was supposed to be here an hour ago," sneered a voice Tara recognized. It was Chesa's.

"Patience," pleaded the authoritative man. "There is no reason for alarm. Enjoy the menagerie—though be careful not to disturb it."

Nocturnal birds nattered to one another in the long pause that followed.

"I don't like being around so many animals," mewled Chesa. "Too many eyes on you at once is never good."

"It won't be long now," said Ms. Ash. "Peony, Roland, sit tight over there."

"Sure," called Peony. "Let us know when you're ready."

"Mortimer said he would be administering end point protocols for the saprolite band study," said a breathy young woman.

"We can spare a moment," said the older man. "If he doesn't arrive soon, then we'll proceed without him."

"I've said this was a bad idea since the beginning," sneered Chesa. "We've been forced to meet in an exposed location, and now Mortimer is late. We should abandon this endeavor now. We can meet another night."

Green light flickered from behind Tara. She stumbled to her feet and turned. For a moment, she saw nothing but a hallway leading back to the ascendants' quarters. She crouched to resume her eavesdropping, just as a shadow loomed into view at the far end of the hall.

"Oh, please, no. . ." she whined. Tara rushed to one of the two other doors nearby and tried it. It rattled, but did not budge.

"Please. . ." Tara pleaded.

She rushed to the second door, the one that led to their Evaders' classroom, and tried it. The handle screeched in protest as she jerked at it again and again, but it too abandoned her.

"To the flames with this!" she snapped.

A pair of luminescent eyes appeared at the end of the hall near the ascendants' quarters that could only belong to one creature. A Weaver mau stared at Tara with greedy emerald eyes. It issued a hiss like a giant serpent.

"This cannot be happening!" cried Tara. She yanked at the door again and again.

The mau tucked its body low, accentuating its shoulder blades as it darted toward her in spurts.

"Where is your scholar?!" Tara called.

More shadows flickered at the distant junction. Then two more pairs of green eyes with slitted pupils bolted into view. As though egged on by the new mau's arrival, all three animals sprinted toward Tara with their fang-like teeth exposed.

"Shit!" Tara spat.

The mau left only one option for her. Tara tore to the Weaver classroom and tried her last chance of escape. It opened.

"Help me!" she cried.

The mau streaked toward the door, almost too quick to be seen. She leaped through the door and slammed it behind her. Though the mouths of several servants moved all around Tara, all she could hear was the throbbing of her own heart in her ears.

"Tara?" Peony's voice registered as a distant echo.

"Ms. Langcraw?" barked Ms. Ash. "What is the meaning of this? You're not welcome here."

Tara's entire body tingled as she sagged against the door.

"The mau," she gibbered. "There's mau, a lot of mau. You must help me!"

"Mau?" bellowed the authoritative man Tara had heard earlier.

Tara burbled something indistinct in reply.

"What sort of mau?" asked Chesa. She spoke as though she were discussing her preferred laundry practices.

"Green eyes," murmured Tara.

"Weaver mau. . ." said Chesa.

"What're they doing here?" said Ms. Ash. "Were they following you, girl?" She gave Tara a glare that could wither a flower.

Tara lacked the energy and coherence to respond to the servants' insolence. "I . . . I. . ." she stammered. "I don't know."

"Well!" said Ms. Ash. "It looks like they have, girl. Mau mean trouble. . ."

Then pain lanced up Tara's backside as though red-hot nails had sunk into her rear and ripped sideways. She screamed and shimmied away as a chunk of her robes ripped free of her and out underneath the doorway to the hall.

"Wh-what. . . What?!" Tara whimpered.

For a second, nothing happened. Then a paw with extended claws shot out from beneath the door. First one claw, then several. The mau issued disdainful hisses as their claws scarred the weathered stone.

Chesa hauled Tara up by her wrist. A moment later, Peony and Roland appeared beside her. Peony leaned down to inspect Tara's rear.

"You're lucky," said Peony. "The mau tore out a chunk of your robes and underdress, but it barely broke the skin." She reached out and touched the wound.

Tara winced and pulled away.

"It's bleeding more than it ought to," said Peony. She pulled a container from her robes and opened it. A pile of makeup powder resided within it. "Hold still," said Peony. She dabbed heaps of the powder through the gaping hole in Tara's robe.

She recoiled. "Ouch! Peony, do you mind?"

"Hold still and stop acting like a baby," scoffed Peony. "It's already working."

Tara pulled her tattered robes to one side to expose a bare portion of her bottom. True to her word, Peony's powder congealed with Tara's blood to form scabs over several puncture wounds.

"What are we going to do?" asked Tara.

"They can't open the door," said Roland.

As he said this, the door before them shuddered with the impact of what had to be the full weight of a mau. Then came another thud, followed by another.

"Perhaps," counseled Chesa, "but mau don't generally wander about the menhir on their own either."

Tara swallowed hard. "What do you mean?"

"She means," said Ms. Ash, "we're likely to have Weavers here soon."

"That's okay, right?" asked Peony.

"I wouldn't bet on it," said Chesa. "We should barricade the door and find another way out."

"What do you mean?" cried Tara. "There's only one way in and out of here, and that's through that door, and those things are out there!"

Chesa approached the windowed walls and looked down intently. Peony joined her.

"Oh, no, no, no," said Tara. "You're not—"

A louder pair of booms at the door cut her off. The impact sent cages of birds squawking in desperate chorus. The birds' cacophony triggered cages of rodents to wake and add to the raucous fervor.

"We can just wait here for the scholars to arrive, right?" moaned Tara. "Right?"

"I'm afraid the scholars are the problem, Ms. Langcraw—as is usually the case, you'll find," instructed Ms. Ash.

Ms. Ash joined Chesa and Peony. All three of them walked up and down the glass panels of the room's exterior wall. Another pair of shuddering strikes landed on the door.

Tara faced the titanic male servant who appeared to be in charge. "There is no way the mau can break through that door, right?" she asked. Her eyes turned misty.

"I'm not sure," he admitted. "Ursielle Hedrigal. Nice to meet you, Ms. Langcraw."

A crash of shattering glass caused Tara to whip around. Spidering cracks sinewed across the entirety of one of the room's peripheral panels. A giant wooden bench lay on its side just before the panel, covered in a film of powdered glass.

"Again?" suggested Ms. Ash.

Chesa nodded, and the two women grunted as they lifted the bench. They walked several paces back from the injured panel with the bench borne between them.

"Ready?" asked Ms. Ash.

"I've been waiting my whole life. . ." cooed Chesa.

The pair ran at the panel. As they drew within a few paces, they hauled the bench up and let it loose. As Tara watched, horror stricken, out of the corner of her eye, she saw Peony gazing at the bench with one of her palms outstretched. The bench did not sail so much as shoot through the air before Tara's eyes, as though jettisoned by some enormous catapult. It struck the center of the panel, causing the glass to warp around the projectile as it shattered outward. The bench soared down into the night.

Several moments passed before it struck some surface below. Bits of glass continued to flick off from the broken frame until only a clean, square hole into the inky night remained. Peony dropped her arm and dabbed at her brow. Chesa and Ms. Ash exchanged proud smiles.

"Nice job," panted Peony.

The three of them approached the ruined window and peered down.

Peony called back, "It's maybe a fifty-foot drop to the next ledge, but I don't know what rooms those are."

"The ascendants' dormitories," replied Chesa in a matter-of-fact tone.

311

Peony looked wide-eyed at the servant.

Chesa smiled. "Not my first time scaling the menhir, Ms. Bianchi."

Peony burst into a nervous laugh. "Well, it's a good thing too!"

Amidst the calling animals in their cages, Tara abruptly realized the door had gone silent.

"Do you think they gave up?" she asked Ursielle.

"I would bet not," replied the boyish man beside Ursielle. "Name's Gamaliel Stork." Despite the man's short and stocky frame, something in his brown eyes encouraged Tara.

"They'll be back soon enough," warned Ursielle, "if they've left at all. Mau do not so easily give up on cornered prey."

Tara approached the door and reached out for its lever. "Perhaps, if they've let up, we can take this chance to leave. . ."

"Maybe," agreed Gamaliel.

Ursielle grimaced.

"In here!" called a familiar old woman's voice from just beyond the door. "The mau have them pinned in my classroom. Come quick!"

"Weaver Ankathi?" cheered Tara. "I'm so glad it's you!" She grabbed the handle just as someone gripped her by the waist and hauled her backward.

"Barricade the door!" called Ursielle.

The servants moved with expert proficiency, flipping tables and hauling furniture against the door. In moments, a hulking pile of furniture lay flush against it.

Meanwhile, Tara flailed against her attacker. "Unhand me!" she cried. "That's Weaver Ankathi. She means us no harm!"

Despite his modest size, Gamaliel kept an iron grip around Tara's midsection. "I would not be so certain, Ms. Langcraw," he grunted. "Those were Weaver mau, and they weren't wandering this portion of the menhir by any accident. Best we find a way out of here, quick."

Cold realization descended on Tara, and she ceased her struggling. Gamaliel released her.

The door behind the barricade groaned, and the groan morphed into an alien sigh. Before Tara's eyes, the stout door bloated with water. It warped like unpainted trim work left derelict for decades. It swelled and pressed against the stonework around it, causing its edges to rot and flake. Moss and bracketing fungus of every hue blossomed over its surface.

"What're they doing?!" cried Tara.

"Breaking in, I'd say," said Ursielle. He hoisted himself from a stool and lumbered toward the barricade. "If we don't do something fast, they'll turn the thing to dust in no time." The pear-shaped man turned to the servants and ascendants scattered throughout the room. "For anyone who can wield a useful thaumaturgy, we could use your help. Chesa, Peony, Ms. Ash, see to our escape route."

"We're on it!" called Ms. Ash.

Behind Tara, Peony guided her hands through a series of flowing movements. As she did, a vine beside the broken window surged forward, winding down from its hanging perch. It sent tendrils through the open frame and out. It wrapped coils around furniture and along the metal frames that ribbed the greenhouse. Its tendrils thickened into woody vines, which allowed further tendrils to seek out other footholds. Other tendrils found unspent soil in the pots of other plants, churning their loam grey in seconds.

Roland plodded over to the makeshift barricade.

"Anything you can do would be helpful," said Ursielle. "I'll see about condensing the air around the entry. It should at least slow their progress."

Roland stretched his hands toward the barricade and took several slow breaths. Ursielle murmured something quiet and incomprehensible as he fixed an unblinking stare on the doorway. The advance of the fungal brackets slowed at once, though the door continued to fall apart beneath its own watery weight. The tight grey bun of Weaver Ankathi's hair showed through the growing gaps. Several mau released desperate hisses. Two other scholars flanked Weaver Ankathi, neither of whom Tara recognized. They both wore emerald robes and grim expressions. Tara put Gamaliel Stork between herself and the shredding barrier.

He twisted his head. "Don't you have something useful you can do?"

"Like what?" Tara replied.

"I don't know," snapped Gamaliel. "Use whatever kind of thaumaturgy you've got."

Tara was too terrified to feel sullen. "I'm fruitless," she mumbled.

He clenched his jaw. "Well, find a place to hide."

Tara wanted to do more, but she knew better. Someone like her could only be a liability in this exchange, so she fled. She first considered trying to stuff herself into one of the animal enclosures, but quickly thought better of it. An armored rodent with distended udders stared up at her as she passed its home. A cluster of its offspring, nearly as large as their mother, darted back and forth, desperate for an escape. Beside them sat the enclosure of the narcoleptic bog lizard, which had once so fascinated the ascendants. That was before they all realized it never moved. Tara went to brush by its enclosure, but paused as something caught her eye. Behind the lizard cage lay a gap between the glass and the wall, just large enough for someone shapely—like herself—to hide. She sucked in a breath and hoisted her arms above her head as she wormed back. Meanwhile, the madonna rat and children watched her with skeptical tilts of their heads.

"Deemed dubiously idiotic by rats. . ." Tara wheezed to herself. "Gods, let it not end this way. . ."

She sucked in air as she reached the sizable space behind the lizard's enclosure. She crouched there behind the reptile and watched. The lizard did not so much as open its eyes.

Bits of faltering barricade nearest the door sprouted fouling fungus and mosses, but as soon as they blossomed, they turned black and sloughed off. Their decay surged and ebbed in time with Roland's thaumaturgical gestures.

Across the room, the others assessed the progress of the vine, now thicker than Tara's thigh, that snaked across the class, out through the ruined window, and below. Though its gnarled anatomy appeared as if it could provide ample grip, Tara deemed remaining behind the lizard to be her safer option.

A woman with pale features and flaxen hair crawled through the window and down the vine with little display of effort. Only a little away, Peony sagged like a ragdoll on a bench, no doubt fatigued by her efforts in growing the colossal plant. Chesa placed a hand on Peony's shoulder, but faced the entryway. Her other hand glided through a series of gestures.

"She's an anomaly. . ." Tara gasped. "Good gods, I'm surrounded by them!" Her head swam with realizations that only abject fear could have kept at bay. "That's what Peony and Roland have been hiding! We could all be put to death!"

Despite Roland's and Ursielle's efforts, the three Weavers proved the more potent force. Bits of furniture crumbled, slow and steady, as mau ripped their claws through the gaps, opening them wider. Their green, glinting eyes darted as they worked, desperate and wild.

Roland turned toward the vine team. "They're c-coming!"

Chesa's hand motions accelerated.

Gamaliel joined Ms. Ash before the vine. "You should go next!" he said.

Ms. Ash rolled her eyes. "Now is not the time for chivalry, boy. I've seen many more days than you have. Get going!"

Gamaliel looked for a moment like he might protest, but then he started out the window and down. As he did, the first of the mau scrambled through the fortifications. It shot across the room, too quick to track. It leaped from tabletops to benches to bird cages like a psychotic tumbler.

"They're in!" called Ursielle.

As he did, a mau sailed from a hanging cage to land atop his back. It sank its fore-claws into the meat of his shoulders. He screamed as the creature latched its fangs into the base of his neck and thrashed. Ursielle stumbled to the ground as it kicked its hind limbs in paired jerks. It sliced wet, meaty fillets from the man's back as he screamed. In moments, the beast had turned most of Ursielle's midsection into a stomach-churning slurry.

"Ursielle!" cried Ms. Ash. She lurched toward him, but paused as a second mau joined the first. It latched its fangs into the rear of his neck and wrenched with spastic jerks.

A Weaver crawled over the wreckage that had once been their barricade and lifted his hands in an odd geometry. In reply, Chesa hurled something unseen like a lasso toward him. He groaned and toppled to the floor, twitching. Chesa bounded toward him, producing a stubby knife from her robes as she went. She descended on the fallen, and with one practiced motion, jammed the oyster shucker into his neck. Her pupils flared as she lifted herself up from the dispensed Weaver.

"An anomaly attacked Roderick!" called a second Weaver as he slid over the pile of debris.

"Fetch Bianchi and dispose of the rest! The Primara will understand!" spat Weaver Ankathi as she followed in the wake of the second Weaver.

Chesa scuttled back like a rat, darting beneath tables and bounding over enclosures with the grace of a cat burglar. Despite her elegance, she did not spot the third mau that bounded at her flank.

"Ch-Chesa!" Roland warned. "Your right!"

She rolled sideways and tumbled to the floor just as the mau sailed over her and crashed into a huge aquarium of riverine fishes. The glass crunched, cracked, and shattered. Thousands of gallons of seed-eating fish, freshwater seagrasses, and flowering lilies cascaded onto the livid, hissing mau. It slid on the sudden wave of river debris and screamed. When it rose again a second later, it limped. Chesa lay only a little away from it, balled up and motionless.

"Enough!" spat Ankathi. She aimed an outstretched palm at Roland.

He made to dart out of the way, but a moment later, he stumbled back. His eyes rolled back into his head, and he collapsed.

Ankathi pivoted to Peony, who was still slumped on the bench, too exhausted to look up.

"Stupid children!" Ankathi chuckled. She lanced an arm at Peony, who fell with a thud.

Ms. Ash darted between Peony and the advancing Weavers and squared her shoulders.

"I never trusted you!" sneered Ankathi as she eyed Ms. Ash.

The servant clasped a shard of aquarium glass in one hand as her only means of defense.

Ankathi laughed at the anemic display. "I've always known you were a toddling little tumor. It always feels so good to set things right!"

Ms. Ash advanced with surprising speed. She almost closed the distance between her and the scholars in moments, but Ankathi produced a flourish of hand gestures with the speed to match. Ms. Ash stumbled sideways and fell on the ground, murmuring.

Ankathi gestured to the Weaver left standing. "Grab Bianchi. I'll collect Ms. Ash myself. But first, I need to attend to another small matter. . ." She strolled to the engorged vine with a sneer. She placed one hand on the coil nearest to the window. "I'm still not very good at weaving threads of life yet, but this should be simple enough." As her hand contacted the vine, its flesh singed back, charring as though burned by an invisible flame. The vine sizzled and split. There came a pair of screams, and a moment later, soft thuds.

"Best leave beanstalk-climbing to the fairy tales, eh?" jested Ankathi.

The other Weaver dragged Peony by her braids. "This one weighs more than she looks," he carped.

Ankathi grabbed Ms. Ash with one arm, and with a grunt, hoisted her over a shoulder. "Remind me to select a younger one the next time we're permitted to go shopping," Ankathi wheezed.

They made their way together through the debris toward the exit. Tara knew she had to do something, but each time she considered a plan, she recalled Gamaliel's advice. In an exchange like this, what use could a spoiled, barren little princess be?

"What should we do with the others?" asked Ankathi's henchman.

"Let the mau have their fun." Ankathi chuckled. "I could do with a few less of these Weaver beasts around my chambers anyhow. They make me miss our own."

Chesa rose to her feet, clutching a blood-matted wound over one hip. Though her face seemed pale, she kept her eyes on the two mau consuming what was left of Ursielle. They raised their heads to consider her. Chesa sighed.

"Ms. Langcraw!" Chesa called through gritted teeth. "If you could do anything to shift the odds here in our favor, now would be your time!"

Tara contemplated whether she cared enough for Chesa to attempt saving her. After all, sparing an anomaly had to be a crime. Yet something deep in Tara's gut quivered at the thought of seeing a member of her own species, perhaps her tribe, fall victim to something so malevolent as a mau.

Roland produced a weak groan and stirred. One mau turned and began stalking towards him.

"Now, Tara!" screamed Chesa.

Tara whipped about her crawlspace, desperate for a means of interceding. She watched in horror as the mau moved in spurts toward Roland. She thrashed and screamed, trying to distract the mau, but it only spared her a quizzical glance. Chesa glided backward, weaving between toppled tables and animal cages, never taking her eyes off the mau pursuing her. She thrust objects in its path, but they did little to slow the beast.

In a final scream of desperation, Tara kicked at the glass in front of her. She cried out as the tank teetered forward, causing her to fall, backside first, to the ground. The tank righted itself, but only just.

Tara's eyebrows shot up in sudden realization.

"'If the situation does not appear to be in one's favor, then add a little disturbance,'" she recited. She wedged her body between the glass tank and the wall, hoisting herself up. When she reached the top of the tank, she braced her back against the wall and thrust outward on the glass with her legs.

The towering glass enclosure rocked forward in one cataclysmic moment. The mau ambling toward Roland looked back with wide eyes. It gave a distressed hiss and darted for cover. Tara screamed as she plummeted to the floor. The tank before her shattered outward into a million shards. The giant bog lizard within slid on a wave of sediment into the middle of the classroom.

The bog lizard lay motionless for a long moment. Then, ever so slowly, it raised its gnarled head and opened its bright yellow eyes. Its giant forked tongue slipped out the side of its mouth and whirled a pair of tonguelets. The mau pursuing Roland reversed course and darted at the bog lizard's flank with outstretched claws.

The bog lizard was over twenty feet in length. None of the ascendants had ever seen it do anything more than lazily accept a dead rabbit
set beside its face. Evidently, however, the bog lizard had been saving
up all of its energy for the unlikely day that it could be free.

Its eyes flicked to the mau, and just as the mammal drew within
paces, it whipped its crocodilian head in a blur and snatched the mau
by its midsection. The mau yowled bloody murder as the lizard bit
clean through its ribs with a series of bloody pops.

The mau pursuing Chesa swiveled its head to see the source of
its ally's cry. It decided against a reprisal and darted at the exit, where
the third mau still struggled to stand. The bog lizard tracked the darting mau and scampered to intercept it. The marauding lizard's feet
struck the ground with such force that Tara feared the stone floor
might shatter.

Chesa ran to Roland, arcing her path away from the lizard and
toppling enclosures as she went. Their freed inhabitants ran, flew, and
slithered toward the exits. Chesa and Tara reached Roland at the same
time.

"Will he be alright?" asked Tara, splitting her attention between
Roland, Chesa, and the giant lizard, who gripped the second mau in its
jaws and whipped its head around twice, turning the mau into a lifeless
sack of flesh and fur.

Chesa studied Roland, then looked up at Tara. "Just another stunning. He was just glanced by the mind strike."

Roland's eyes fluttered open. "We r-really have to stop making a
habit of this," he said with a weak smile at Chesa.

"But then, what would I do with all my free time, Mr. Ward?" She
chuckled.

The titanic lizard made swift work of the injured third mau. Animals fled the classroom in droves, avoiding the lizard as they did. It
ripped through what remained of the wooden debris in front of the

door as though it were a stack of children's building blocks. Then it went off in pursuit of all the could-be prey it had admired for so many years.

"Where's P-Peony?" asked Roland.

"Gone," said Chesa. "She and Ms. Ash were taken by the Weavers."

"Gone?!" cried Roland. "We have to g-go after them!"

Chesa gave the farm boy a slow, predatory smile, exposing her canines. "We agree on this point, Mr. Ward."

"What about me? What about me?!" cried Tara.

The pair fixed Tara with frowns and spoke in unison. "Go back to your room."

"My room?" she spat. "I can't be any use to you there!"

Roland and Chesa exchanged pained looks.

"It's safer there. You c-can't use thaumaturgy anyhow. You'll just get hurt," said Roland. His tone remained gentle but firm.

"I agree," added Chesa as she helped Roland up. "Oh, and Ms. Langcraw," she said over one shoulder as she ambled to the door. "On your way back, do your best to avoid the giant predator you've just unleashed on the ascendants' quarters, will you?"

Roland gave Chesa a worried look. Then he turned to Tara. "You've d-done great, Tara. You saved my life, but Chesa and I can handle this from here."

Tara's words failed her.

Her allies scanned the corridor beyond, and then they went.

Tara yearned to join them, but she knew they were right, more likely than not. Without any thaumaturgical powers, she would be useless in a fight against the Weavers. She could only be a liability. Not to mention, she was fresh out of emergency predators to unleash on her foes. Besides, she didn't even know how to get to the Weavers' quarters on her own. She sagged to the ground with a sigh.

"There has to be a way to help," she said into the air.

She couldn't place why, but it seemed in that moment that something was there with her, some greater presence. A moment later, a knowing grin spread across her face.

CHAPTER 24

Safekeeping

A MOTHERING VOICE CALLED to her through the haze.

"Peony. . ." the voice pleaded. "Come back to me, darling!" Something soft brushed against Peony's arm. "You're alright now."

Peony's eyes opened a sliver. Fatigue blurred her vision as she found herself in a forest bathed in gentle green light. The trilling melodies of insects serenaded the glade. Peony shook her pounding head. She reached up to massage her temples, but discovered that her arms were unresponsive.

"No, darling, don't struggle," sang the reassuring voice. "If you need something, you need only speak it to me."

Peony closed and opened her eyes again. This time the silhouette of a slight-statured woman appeared in her periphery. A halo of tight blonde curls ringed her face.

"Primara Okondo?" Peony croaked through leathery lungs.

"Yes, sweetling, it's me," said Okondo. She brushed the side of Peony's face. "Are you hurt?"

Peony wasn't sure. Her thoughts came to her muddled, as though she had consumed too much wine and had not slept. "What happened?"

The Primara clucked her tongue. "You got yourself into trouble, sweetling, and I had to intercede. Again."

"How?" said Peony. She blinked past the exhaustion crusting her vision and realized she lay atop an ensemble of exposed roots. Thick woody vines coiled tight around her wrists and forearms. She tried to raise her foot and found it tangled too.

"Why. . ." Peony began. "Why am I tied up?"

The Primara let out a long sigh. "Because, pigeon, you tried to harm yourself."

"What?!" Peony cried.

Okondo walked about Peony's wooden prison in a slow, deliberate circle. Other robed scholars loomed in the forest some distance away, cloaked half in shadow.

"Sweetling, I asked you to take care of yourself. For me," Okondo said sweetly, but an edge of frustration prowled in her tone. "And in so little time, you found your way into consorting with riffraff of the most dangerous kind. You nearly destroyed my Peony." Okondo's voice turned frosty. "I had to pluck you from a classroom that you and your consorts vandalized."

"That can't be true," Peony protested, though inside, she was not so sure.

"Oh, but it is," Okondo assured her. "Several of your friends were gravely injured."

"Roland?" Peony cried out. "Not Roland?!"

Again, Okondo clucked her tongue. "The Ward boy and Ms. Langcraw have not yet been recovered. But don't worry, I have friends out looking for them for us."

"What . . . what about Ms. Ash?" Peony asked.

"Yes," the Primara sighed. "We've collected her."

Peony's aching body sagged with relief. She craned her head to examine the clearing around her. Out of the corner of her eye, she observed a stout figure lashed to an arboreal perch not unlike her own.

"Is that her?!" cried Peony. "Is she okay?"

Okondo turned her attention to the faintly breathing form. "Yes. We need to determine how much she knew and whom she's told. She may yet offer us a useful vantage point."

One of the green-robed figures approached the Primara, revealing herself to be Weaver Ankathi.

"Any word from the ascendants' quarters?" asked Okondo.

"No," Ankathi replied. Her tone seemed hushed. "The menhir administration knows there's been a disturbance. Fortunately, the bog lizard is their primary concern at the moment. We're doing our best to track down the remaining liabilities. We've sent forces to recover them."

Primara Okondo's small smile vanished. "Too many signs point in our direction now. I told you to extract or dispose of the lot of them!"

Ankathi stepped back. "We left a triad of mau. I deemed the odds remote that. . ." she bumbled. "Perhaps the sedations we've been working on them have made them less lethal?"

"You've already explained the rationale for your failure to me," Okondo scoffed. "Get the others. I need to begin the transition now, for my and everyone's safety. Your incompetence has forced our hand!"

Ankathi whimpered. "Is there anything I can do?"

Okondo paused and sneered, "You can try our little experiment over there." She gestured to Ms. Ash's sleeping form. "Help us test the limits of our future options."

Weaver Ankathi followed the Primara's gaze to Ms. Ash, then shrieked, "But she has no thaumaturgical aptitudes whatsoever! What if I become barren? What if I'm trapped?"

A breezy tone entered the Primara's voice. "That is the price you pay for your stupidity. If it is any comfort, my theories indicate that you should retain command of mind thaumaturgy. I wasted generations fretting about the compatibility of different noble factions. 'Twas time wasted. Fortune forever favors the ambitious!"

325

"Very well, Savanna," whispered Ankathi. She returned to the stand of trees with the other Weavers.

"Well, pigeon," said Okondo, fixing Peony with a doll's smile. "It appears you and your friends have put me in quite a predicament."

"Savanna?" asked Peony. Connections fired off in her mind in rapid succession. "LaTorre?"

Okondo's grin faltered, but only for a moment. A Weaver mau trotted up from another stand of trees and seated itself at the Primara's side. It eyed Peony and issued a hiss, its emerald eyes shimmering in the insectile glow of the forest.

"Sedated, indeed." Okondo looked down at the mau beside her and laughed. "An incompetent scholar blames her circumstances." She frowned at Peony. "Some have called me LaTorre, though that custom will perish in time," she cooed. "I have gone by many names. No one alive truly knows me anymore. But I do like the name 'Peony'. I assume your parents were not happy you chose it, hmm?"

"But you're a Weaver? I've seen you use life thaumaturgy," breathed Peony. She reached out for force and then life thaumaturgy, but her head swam as she grasped, finding neither.

"Oh, no, sweetling. I've put a mental block on you. So long as I'm here, you won't be accessing any of your abilities." The Primara laughed. "A little dreamflower does wonders."

Peony wrenched at her bonds, but the vines restraining her did not give way.

"What do you know about my family?" Peony spat. She knew she could find a way out of this, if she could only stall.

"Not much," Okondo admitted. "A rather quiet bunch where you are concerned. I'd hoped to learn more about you before sending my calf to the abattoir." She caressed Peony's face. "I'd like to have shown you some joy before the end. For what it's worth, I will make your family pay for whatever they've done to you, with interest. . ."

326

"Abattoir?!" cried Peony. She wrenched her body this way and that. The vines groaned, but held.

"You are part of my grand experiment, poppet. An experiment that has, I'm afraid to say, claimed more than a few promising thauma-turges. I'd hoped to stay in my present form for several decades, but then you came along and provided an opportunity too tantalizing to ignore."

"You're working with the Delvers?" hissed Peony. "You've been working with them all along!"

Primara Okondo's expression turned sympathetic. "Close, dump-ling, but not quite." She clucked her tongue. "Mind thaumaturgy has always been my forte. But when the chance to add another string to my harp was offered by an unusually trusting Weaver Primara, well, I couldn't refuse."

"So, you stole the body of another scholar to wield two aspects of thaumaturgy? That's what's happened to the missing Delver thought paddocks?" exclaimed Peony. "You're hiding your work!"

"More or less," scoffed Okondo. "I know it all sounds so sinister, but believe me, I've uncovered truths about this place that will shake the world. And you'll help."

"Someone will notice if I've changed. Ms. Ash too!" warned Peony, feverish to stall a moment longer. "Too many people know us."

"Hardly," Okondo sneered. "Primara Nash and I have had eyes on the ascendants for months. We know who is safely isolated and who isn't." She stroked Peony's hair as she breathed, "No one will notice you've changed, Peony. People are only ever looking inward."

Okondo was right, Peony realized. "But why me?" she said. "You must have been targeting me since the beginning!"

"Avarice has always been my weakness," Okondo replied coolly. "To wield two aspects of thaumaturgy proved too tempting to ignore. But the opportunity to manipulate three. . . Well, that supplanted two."

Ankathi returned with a dozen other Weavers. Peony wondered how many might be under the control of the Delvers. A herd of grey Weaver mau trotted among them.

Okondo snapped her fingers. "Someone bring mau venom!"

Several Weavers searched their robes. A gaunt-faced woman with short brown hair produced a vial first and placed it in Okondo's hand.

"She'll be needing a vial too," the Primara sneered as she gestured to Ankathi. "She's offered to break new ground in our studies . . . by being the first to colonize a layperson."

Several Weavers exchanged troubled looks.

"Isn't that right?"

"I have," Ankathi murmured. She stared at the ground before her feet.

Another Weaver handed a second vial to Ankathi. She gazed at the liquid in her palm as one might a viper, coiled and ready to strike. She went and jostled Ms. Ash. The servant woke with a start.

"What're you doing?" Ms. Ash snarled. "Get your hands off me!"

Ankathi grasped the sides of Ms. Ash's plump cheeks and pressed them until her mouth opened. Ms. Ash thrashed, but Ankathi's grip moved with her. The Weaver poured the vial's contents down the servant's throat. Ms. Ash stammered and went limp in moments.

"Ms. Ash!" Peony called. She thrashed. This time, one of the vines loosened, and she lifted a useless leg.

"Don't worry, sweetling," Okondo cooed. "Hers is a life with meaning now. What remains of it will be in service to hosting the next stage of our study."

"What's happening to her?!" cried Peony.

Okondo pursed her lips. "You know, pigeon, I'm not really sure what happens to the other person. I assume they just . . . slip away," she said with a sinuous wave of her hand. "I've heard old Okondo still paints flowers down in the anomaly pens, in my old host. . . Well, assuming she's still alive-ish down there. . ." Okondo released a pleasant sigh. "It will be strange to be a boy again after so long."

The Primara pressed Peony's mouth open. Though Peony beat her body against her bindings, it seemed no use. As the venom cascaded down her gullet, Peony's tongue became a lifeless blob. She tried to scream for help, but her words came out as nothing more than unintelligible slurs. A rivulet of drool escaped her mouth and cascaded down her robes.

"You're doing wonderfully," Okondo assured her, as though speaking to a slow child. "Look up! Look at me!" She guided Peony's flopping head up by her chin until their eyes met. A primal desperation or strain lurked behind Okondo's pupils that Peony had never noticed before.

The periphery of Peony's vision turned hazy and then went black. The darkness closed inward in rings. Bit by bit, Peony's world collapsed, until only the terrified black disks at the center of Okondo's eyes remained. Then everything went dark.

Something crashed, and several mau screamed.

"What's happening?" yelled a voice Peony did not recognize. "Savanna," it continued, "we need you!"

Peony's head slipped sideways, and her world snapped back into view.

"What is the meaning of this, Nash?" Okondo slurred. She sat perched atop Peony's lap.

A skeletal-faced Weaver with brown curls stood beside her. "Someone's here!" the scrawny woman screeched. "One of the sentries hasn't returned. We sent two more mau to investigate, but neither came back."

"What are you talking about?" Okondo barked. "You cannot disturb a transition, Nash! How many times have I told you this? Can I trust you with nothing?"

The scrawny woman gulped. "I apologize, Savanna, but we may be under attack. I feared for your safety. I. . ."

"You idiot!" Okondo growled. "Who would be attacking the Weavers in their own quarters? It's suicide!"

"Roland. . ." Peony slurred.

Okondo's jaw tightened. "Send forces to investigate. Bring mau. We may find some useful targets. If we shuffle ourselves well, it will be harder for anyone to sort out what's happened." The Primara licked her lips. "The gods have blessed us with an opportunity to uncover a nest of saboteurs and to have my Peony on a platter all in one night. We cannot foul this up."

The gaunt Weaver—Primara Nash, or so Peony supposed—retreated into the woods. In no time, the other Weavers vanished deeper into the glades too. Nash returned a minute later.

"We should have the interlopers addressed in no time, Savanna," she assured the Primara.

"How's the transition to the laywoman going?" Okondo sniffed.

Everyone turned their attention to the other prisoner.

Ms. Ash opened and closed her eyes. "Are you alright, girl?" she mumbled.

"For now." Peony chuckled. A drunken veil of relief passed over Peony to hear Ms. Ash's voice again.

Weaver Ankathi lay slumped over Ms. Ash. Her head rested on one of the servant's shoulders. Her tongue flopped loose out of her gaping mouth as her body spasmed.

Nash glanced between Okondo and Ankathi. "I don't think the transition was successful. . ."

Primara Okondo lifted herself from Peony's lap. Then she pivoted toward Nash and backhanded her. "You imbecile!" Okondo shouted. "That could've been me!"

"I didn't mean to. . . But it wasn't!" Nash whimpered.

Peony tried to think of a means of saving herself and Ms. Ash. Perhaps they could use the scholars' tendency to infight somehow, if she were clever?

"You, Nash, will be her replacement!" Okondo spat. She pressed a finger into the skinny Weaver's breast. "After this matter in the forest is done, you'll colonize Ms. Ash. Her potential is too great to be wasted."

Just then, one of the vines that pinned Peony's arms sprung to life. It hurled itself toward Okondo's legs before she could react. It wrapped around her ankles and tightened with a snap. She fell to the ground with a grunt.

"Someone!" she cried. "Get this thing. . ."

But the vine swelled to the size of a python and dragged her into the forest before she could finish the thought.

"We're under attack!" she screamed from somewhere in the dark understory. "Kill them!"

Weavers emerged from all around the forest and assembled in the clearing around Peony and Ms. Ash.

The skeletal Nash shouted orders. "Caspian and MacClery, you subdue that vine working! Protect Savanna! Rogers, Strassman, Therus, help me guard Bianchi!"

Two more of the vines tethering Peony sprung to life and lanced at Nash. Weaver Strassman spotted the assault and moved between Nash and the whipping vines. Strassman swum his arms in arcs, and the vines' assault slowed to a halt with strained pops.

Peony seized the moment. She hauled herself to her feet, and despite one ankle remaining tied, lunged at Strassman. She punched hard at his throat, aiming for the fleshy bulb at its center with the full momentum of her body. A brittle pop echoed through her fist, and Strassman ceased his working. He toppled to the ground, sucking and wheezing as he clasped at his swelling gullet.

"Move!" screamed Nash.

Caspian and MacClery, no doubt Delvers in disguise, ran to where the Primara had disappeared. Mau hisses and screams rang out from all around the understory and canopy alike.

The other Weavers advanced on Peony with celerity. Their arms swirled in emphatic thaumaturgical gestures. Peony went to initiate her own, but before she could try, the vines around her reanimated and lashed her back to her prison.

A bellowing roar came from the treeline. Then Roland Ward, covered in mud, moss, and blood that did not appear to be his own galloped into view. The Weavers nearest Peony swiveled their attention just in time for Roland to barrel through Therus. The little man screamed and crumpled as Roland buried a shoulder in the man's chest and followed him to the ground. Roland stomped a knee into the man's ribs with a crunch. Coronas of rotted flesh speckled Therus's body in moments, churning his flesh into black loam. Life thaumaturgy surged all around Roland's huge form.

"Be careful!" Peony called.

Roland pivoted toward Nash.

"They're all Delvers!" she warned.

Nash danced backward as Roland lumbered to his feet. Then, with two quick flicks of a hand, Nash constructed a working Peony could not detect. Roland darted to the side to avoid the attack, but Nash tracked his evasion. Roland grunted and fell sideways with a crash.

"Rogers, make sure he stays down!" demanded Nash. "Secure him while I see to Bianchi."

Rogers dragged Roland's limp form to a tree, while other Weavers worked to sever the vine that ensnared Primara Okondo. Only now could Peony see the clumsiness of their life thaumaturgy, even by her own standards.

Nash turned to Peony and chuckled from within his scrawny Weaver victim. "Seems your paramour was devoted to the last."

Over Nash's shoulder, a slender form in grey melted out from a pool of shadow beneath a stand of trees.

Nash laughed. "You know, Ms. Bianchi, you caused quite a lot of anxiety." The gaunt shell shrugged. "I'm still not sure what all of the fuss was about. Blurred Keystones and anemic prophesies have never interested me. The menhir will never fall to the likes of you, nor any layperson."

The robed figure in the shadows resolved into Chesa, who bounded up through the clearing.

Peony steadied herself and trained her eyes on the moss-covered ground beside her feet. She did her best to mimic the weakness and deference the scholars so often enjoyed in their servants. She channeled Chesa.

Nash approached and brushed Peony's lips with a bony thumb, sighing, "I would have enjoyed getting to know you better."

Chesa seized him from behind and pressed a stubby dagger to his neck.

"Nice work, Chesa!" Peony cheered. "They're all Delvers! They're just possessing these Weavers! That one's Nash."

"Well, well, well," Chesa purred into the skinsuit's ear. "Who is the predator and who the prey now, Primara Nash?"

"Chesa!" spat Nash. "You greasy eel! I should've dispensed with you when I had the chance!"

The grin that appeared on Chesa's face had Peony's hair standing on end. "Well, Master," Chesa growled, "we all have our regrets. . ."

Then her face abruptly went slack, and her eyes dilated. The dagger fell from her grip.

Nash twisted in her arms and shoved her to the ground. The body-hopping Delver Primara picked up Chesa's fallen blade and fell atop her. With two ugly jerks, Nash opened the servant's neck. Chesa's mouth worked for a few seconds, and then she went still.

"Chesa!" Peony breathed. "No. . ."

Primara Okondo—or Savanna LaTorre, Peony supposed—strolled up with MacClery. Tall and handsome in his new body, the disguised Delver looked nothing like the red-haired bully Peony had known from her trip to the menhir so long ago. The third scholar who'd gone to help the Weaver Primara lay still on the ground at the edge of the clearing.

"Your pesky minx hurled quite a strike against me, Nash. I was lucky Caspian stumbled into its path. Fool," sneered Okondo. "Now, where were we?"

The forest fell quiet, save for the grunts of Ms. Ash, who still strained at her vines. Peony gave the spirited old woman a weak smile. They'd lost.

"Nash." Okondo caressed the face of Nash's elderly skinsuit. "You did well. You may colonize Mr. Ward now."

At the far edge of the clearing, Roland stood lashed by a network of roots to the trunk of a tree.

Okondo cleared her throat. "I'll take Ms. Bianchi. One of you two. . ." She gestured to MacClery and Roger. "Take Ms. Ash."

The two opened their mouths as if to disagree, but Okondo dismissed them with a wave of her hand.

"Work it out, and hurry," she snapped.

Nash searched his robes. "I'm out of venom!" he panted.

"Fetch some from the fallen," scoffed Okondo. "After we've transitioned, we'll need to figure out what to do with these bodies."

In the end, Rogers was the one tasked with saddling Ms. Ash. He replicated the same sequence of gestures and whispering that Peony had observed earlier. Nash performed the same with Roland. Okondo caressed Peony's chin and murmured, "Let's try this one more time, with feeling. . ."

Peony couldn't bring herself to fight. Layer by layer, her world decayed until only the Primara's pupils lingered.

"It's over now," whispered Okondo. "Rest for me. . ."

A mau screamed nearby. Okondo jerked, and Peony's world resumed once more.

"What now?" shouted Okondo. Sweat slicked her curls against her scalp, and her face twisted with fury.

A flock of Weaver maus arrived in grey blurs from all over the forest. They tumbled into the clearing, panting. A moment later, a horde of Weavers joined them.

"Attend to the perimeter!" screamed Okondo. She gestured to the clearing. "Move!"

A young Weaver whom Peony had never seen before stepped forward. He glanced at the bodies dotting the clearing. "There's been an attack. . ." he began.

"Of course there's been an attack!" Okondo raged. "While the lot of you were off chasing Ward and Chesa, they circumvented you and assaulted me—in the midst of a transition!"

Nash fell limp to the ground before Roland. Then Roland blinked, and a knowing grin crossed his mouth. It resembled the same sickening grin that had featured on Nash's skinsuit a moment prior.

"Someone let me down," Nash called in a haughty tone.

Hearing the snide inflection come from Roland's throat sapped every bit of remaining energy from Peony.

"Cowing the boy took longer than I thought," complained Roland's voice. "Cleverer than I suspected."

The Weaver body hosting Rogers collapsed to the ground with a blank, unknowing stare a second later. Ms. Ash's eyes dazzled with something malevolent. She glanced at the limp Weaver body atop her and laughed.

"A hand would be nice. I'd very much like to see if I can weave a bit of mind thaumaturgy. . ." the skinsuit whined. "I didn't sign on for this fiasco to be a fat old woman the rest of my life."

With an absent wave of her hand, Okondo dispatched scholars to aid Ms. Ash's possessor.

Another Weaver stepped forward, looking sheepish. "No, Savanna, it wasn't just Roland Ward and Chesa. There's something else in the forest. A mau tried to attack it, but the thing broke the mau's neck. We tried a thaumaturgical assault, but all our attempts failed! It chased our forces out of every treetop path back to here."

Okondo stood up. "What do you mean?!" she shouted. "What was it?"

The Weavers shot each other uncertain looks. "Some sort of cloud," said one of them.

Something small flickered in the canopy at the perimeter of the clearing. Its ruddy hue contrasted with the sea of yellow foliage of the autumn leaves. The Weaver maus turned almost in unison and produced a sea of hisses at the interloper.

The small blur teleported to the base of the ghostly stand of trees and resolved into the form of a diminutive mau. It displayed a triangular head and huge amber eyes. It studied the mass of Weaver maus with indifference.

"A Tilter mau?" whispered Okondo. "Here?"

Cracks like lightning strikes resounded in rapid succession from all around the forest. Then an inky nimbus of whirling liquid the size of a barrel hurled toward the clearing. By the green light of the Weavers' quarters, its path through the trees proved almost impossible to follow. The thunderous crackings sounded like they came from the nimbus itself.

The maelstrom reached the edge of the clearing and halted. The tangled whisps of ink about it fell limp, and the forest became silent. There, at the edge of the clearing, stood Primara Klepsydra. Billowing robes of purple so dark that they were almost black drenched her form. She studied the mass of Weavers before her with an iron expression. Her huge eyes paused upon Peony, Roland, and then Ms. Ash.

"What is she doing here?!" Okondo hissed. She locked eyes with the Tilter Primara and sniffed. "It does not matter the foe. We possess abilities she cannot fathom. Kill the time witch."

"Watch out!" Peony slurred through flaccid lips. "She's Savanna LaTorre! They've got Roland and Ms. Ash!"

No one moved.

A pathetic screech broke the pregnant silence as Tara Langcraw stumbled out from the forest in mud-stained robes. She panted like she'd been running for hours. Through her drunken haze, Peony smiled. Bit of twigs and burs riddled every inch of Tara's locks.

"Ah, the last of our liabilities has delivered itself to us. What a lucky day," Okondo called, though her voice quavered. "Kill the barren Langcraw, and subdue Klepsydra. I will reward whoever subdues the Tilter with the opportunity to have her husk."

Primara Klepsydra put a slender hand on Tara's shoulder and spoke without taking her eyes off Okondo. "Stand back, Tara Langcraw. We will attend to these thieves."

Rolling thunder pulsed through forest with such seismic furry that it sent leaves and stones dancing. Clap after clap of thunder grew until the end of one strike became indistinguishable from the start of the next. The stormy sea of sound had the hairs on the back of Peony's neck rising, along with her spirit. Her drunkenness retreated as branches and leaves rained down from the canopy. The mau around the Weavers panted and pressed their shaggy bodies against the ground. Several of the Weavers took hesitant steps back and eyed the forest as though searching for an escape.

"Go back to my room, hmm?" puffed Tara. She pulled a fleck of debris from her favorite hairnet. "I think not!"

CHAPTER 25

Prideful Tactics

SONOROUS CRACKS OF POWER echoed all around Tara. No matter what happened, she had done her part.

Weaver mau slunk toward Tara and Primara Klepsydra, bearing needle-like teeth. The felines kept their bodies close to the ground, where their grey fur blended with the undergrowth.

"What's the plan?" Tara whispered.

"For now, Tara Langcraw," Klepsydra murmured, "we play black and punish every mistake."

Tara blinked.

"Stay behind me," said Klepsydra.

Tara stepped back just as one of the Weavers wound their arms through thaumaturgical gestures. A pale tree only a few paces from Tara groaned and snapped midway up its trunk. Its crown toppled down at her, and its branches warped into daggers. Tara hurled herself to one side.

Klepsydra did not flee. She only gazed up at the falling tree.

"Move!" Tara cried.

Klepsydra remained a statue.

A split second before the limbs pinned her like a butterfly in a specimen box, the tree skittered back to its original position. It did not slide back. It did not move in reverse. Simply, one moment it threatened

338

to skewer Klepsydra a dozen times over, and the next, it took a new course, crashing down in the path of the Weaver forces. Tara gaped at the wall of shaking yellow leaves that provided cover now, not a threat.

Tara examined their flanks for surprise assaults and spotted Chesa. She lay still at the edge of the clearing only a little away. A sheet of liquid garnets as dark as any saprolite band covered her neck.

"Chesa. . ." Tara breathed. "No. . ."

A Weaver stumbled around the fallen tree and let out a furious yell as she slung something underhanded and invisible at Klepsydra. Tara went to flee, but the Tilter Primara only cocked her head at the assault. The Weaver jolted back at once. This time, she stumbled on the hem of her robe amid her working and fell with a yelp.

Tara blinked. "You're doing all that?"

A subdued smile touched Klepsydra's icy face. "In battle, Tara Langcraw, chance plays an outsized role. So long as the Weavers remain reckless, we can hold them at bay. Your bog lizard will not stall the menhir administration forever. Time is on our side."

Tara began to smile, but paused. "What happens if they aren't reckless?"

"Then there will come a moment when all probabilities point to our demise," Klepsydra said coolly. "Then a Tilter will impose the greatest casualties possible on her foe."

Two Weaver mau bounded over the yellow leaves. The heavy felines leaped onto branches and trunks. No angle of landing proved impossible for them as they used their tails to grasp and balance.

One of them closed in on Klepsydra. When it drew within paces, the Primara lifted her arms in a protective gesture. Her robes swept into a billowing flutter, like a moth whirling wings on too many axes. The fabric jumped and cracked between different positions until it became an abyssal cloud of fabric around Klepsydra. The mau's outstretched forepaws neared the fabric's perimeter, only to have its legs entwined.

In the same moment, the mau skipped through space to appear on the opposite side of the nimbus, where it hurled through the open air like a screaming shotput. It landed against the side of a tree with a crash.

A second mau went for Tara. She let out a squeal and turned away as it leaped at her. Tara braced herself for death's kiss, when something hit the back of her knees hard, collapsing her in a heap. The woolly mau whizzed over her head and landed in a skid on a patch of moss. It turned toward her and hissed.

"Would you warn me before. . ." Tara began, but halted herself as she went to rise. A little Tilter mau sat atop her chest. It kept its eyes on the Weaver mau and issued guttural chirps. Then it streaked off into the forest in a ruddy blur. The larger Weaver mau screamed and followed. Like its scholars, the Tilter mau skipped and blurred between positions, never seeming to fear the larger force that threatened it.

The Weaver mau gave chase as well as any predator in nature, following the small mau from tree to tree and back. But the Tilter mau always managed to disappear just before the larger mau could make a strike. The Weaver mau grew angrier and less precise with each failure. When it finally paused its assault, the Tilter mau pounced. The Weaver mau lunged to defend itself, but the Tilter mau skipped a few inches to one side, gliding past the larger mau's anterior. Something blurred around the Weaver mau's head, and it screamed. A heartbeat later, streaks of crimson poured from its ruined eyes. It writhed and whirled in a storm of claws. The Tilter mau only tucked its body into the groove of a tree to study its flailing pursuer.

Tara rose just in time for more clouds of fabric to arrive in the understory all around her and Klepsydra. As they slowed, they each resolved into a willowy Tilter layered in the flowing robes that ascendants deemed so absurd. In moments, all eleven Tilters descended into the stand of ghostly trees. The echoing thunder in the forest stilled. The Tilters exchanged still expressions.

"What now?" asked Tara. "They've killed Chesa, and Peony said they've got Roland and Ms. Ash!"

"Compulsion," Tilter Avevaios intoned as she glided to Tara's side. "Their bodies are their own no longer."

Tara felt the color flee her face. "Then we're too late," she whispered. "This was all pointless. I should never have involved any of you."

Avevaois studied Tara with cool eyes. "It is well that you involved us, Tara Langcaw. Our work here is not done."

"If everyone's dead," Tara argued, "what good is endangering all of you?"

Klepsydra scoffed, and something glittered behind her huge eyes. "Remember to pity our adversaries, Tara Langcraw." She nodded to the other Tilters. "For it is a pitiable thing to forever be stuck in time."

"That's nice," Tara went on, "but if everyone's already dead. . ."

"Observe the western route potentiality," said Avevaios. "It was comparatively unguarded. It gets us here sooner, though the line is slick."

The other Tilters exchanged nods, even the eyeless sister.

One by one, the women lifted their chins. Tiny, almost imperceptible smiles tugged at the corners of their mouths. The air grew tense, like fabric with too much static. Anything material beyond their group began to jolt between different positions, until the whole world melted into a noncommittal blur of almost-shapes.

Tara gasped.

She and the Tilters remained the only distinguishable forms. Even the patches of soil beneath their feed blurred into an average of all the textures of the forest floor. Without warning, the forest around them resumed its shape. They stood beneath a different stand of trees, bearing red leaves instead of yellow. Beneath the darker canopy, the Tilters seemed almost invisible in their dark robes, even to Tara.

"Where are we?"

Klepsydra placed a pacifying finger on Tara's lips and whispered, "A different potentiality has been selected for our use. Only we will ever know what could have been. Stay back." The Primara pointed to a clearing ahead.

Ms. Ash and Peony sat lashed to chairs worked from roots and branches. The Weaver Primara sat atop Peony's lap, while Weaver Ankathi straddled Ms. Ash. The second pair locked eye to eye and whispered.

"Ms. Ash!" Peony cried.

She did not answer.

"Do not worry, sweetling," Okondo replied. "Hers is a life with real meaning now. What remains of it will be in service to hosting the next stage of our grand study."

"What's going to happen to her?!" asked Peony.

Okondo pursed her rosebud lips. "You know, pigeon, I'm really not sure what happens to the other person. I assume they just . . . slip away," she said with a wave of her hand.

Klepsydra gestured forward with two fingers. In answer, the strata of fabric around each Tilter whipped into nimbuses of potentialities. The ground and trees shook as the forest exploded with the sound of thunderclaps.

Primara Okondo stood from Peony. "What's going on?!" she spat. "There's something over there. Nash, gather the Weavers!"

But before the Weavers could respond, the nimbuses around Tara moved. Some spun off deeper into the forest. Others darted into the clearing. Okondo enjoyed only a moment before one closed on her. The nimbus blurred, and Okondo's face cracked to one side, sending her blonde curls bouncing. A second crack of almost-fabric sent her sprawling. Roots and vines rocketed up from all around her at once, shielding her in a writhing sarcophagus and separating her from her attacker.

Weavers spat curses and mau screamed as the Tilters harried them. Roots shot up from beneath the soil to ensnare the Tilters, but the temporal lionesses flickered back or aside with breathtaking grace. Any workings of invisible thaumaturgy hurled towards the Tilters always seemed to just miss their mark to strike a Weaver ally instead.

More plant matter shot up around the Weaver Primara's defensive tomb, doming both her and Peony from the broader exchange. Fuzzy leaves that resembled hearts sprouted all along the tendrils.

Tara edged closer to the clearing, taking care to avoid the exchanges. Perhaps she could find a means of saving one of her friends, or Chesa.

Here and there, Weavers hauled up blockades of gnarled roots between themselves and the Tilters. Entire trees sprouted up from nowhere with sinewy pops to swat at the Tilters like unruly insects. But the swirling nimbuses of fabric flicked about the animated forest, frustrating and demoralizing their unprepared opponents.

Someone seized Tara by her hair and dragged her backward.

"What's a pretty little bird like you doing here?" whispered the woman.

Tara thrashed and caught a glimpse of a gaunt-faced Weaver with dark hair behind her. Tara tried to fetch one of the weapons she had taken from the Tilters' den. With luck, she could bludgeon her assailant. But her attacker only gripped her tighter.

"Don't struggle. . . You and I can make a little trade, hmm?" the woman assured her. "You'll be a fine little hiding place until the dust settles. Who knows, perhaps I'll slip from you into Klepsydra, assuming the witch survives."

"Help!" Tara screamed.

Her attacker covered her mouth with a bony hand. Tara bit down, but her captor rewarded her efforts by stuffing a fist down Tara's throat, and she gagged.

The Weaver dragged Tara into a pool of shadow too dark for anyone to see. She twirled Tara around and slammed her against a tree with strength that mismatched the Weaver's elderly visage. The bark of the tree expanded and grew over Tara's chest, pinning her in place. The skinny Weaver locked eyes with Tara and searched for something in her robes. As she lifted a foreboding vial of liquid, something caught Tara's eye in the canopy a little away.

A glimmer of light passed over Tara's face. The Weaver whirled to defend herself. A hooded figure met the Weaver with two swift slices that opened the Weaver's neck in a ruby cascade.

A wet sigh gurgled from her throat as the Weaver sputtered, "Chesa! You. . ."

She fell, pressing on her throat with one hand. With the other, she initiated some kind of thaumaturgy, but Chesa stepped on her wrist until her body twitched.

"Nash? Is that you?" Chesa smirked down at the ruined Weaver. "You were always so fond of those unnecessary flourishes with your mental strikes." She clucked her tongue.

"Chesa. . ." Tara whispered. "Uh, a little less villainizing, and a little more helping, please?" She gestured to her bark prison.

Chesa released an annoyed breath. "Always the killjoy, aren't we, Ms. Langcraw?" A stubby blade appeared in her hand and came to rest against Tara's throat.

Tara's heart stopped.

"Hold still, please," sneered Chesa. "I don't want any blame for marking up your enviable skin. . ."

A minute later, Tara and Chesa bounded into the clearing just as Roland Ward lumbered out from a stand of trees by Ms. Ash. He held the body of a struggling Weaver by their throat. Small cuts and bruises rotted and festered across the Weaver's skin. His flesh decayed into loam and rained from Roland's hand as he lumbered into the clearing.

Tara froze, staring at the grotesque image, and blinked. Chesa went to Ms. Ash.

"Hold still. We're getting out of here," said Chesa. Though she lacked sculpted muscle, Chesa's hands moved with precision. The bonds holding Ms. Ash snapped as Chesa wrenched at them with her blade.

"Mr. Ward!" barked Ms. Ash. "See to Peony!" She indicated the mound of vines and heart-shaped leaves near the clearing's center.

Roland charged like a rhinoceros, sending up chunks of moss and soil in his wake. He struck the dome with an elephantine brutality far too great for his mass alone. Vines tangled his feet and crunched beneath his boot with woody snaps. The hut collapsed into a mound of debris. Roland dragged the remaining vestiges of its structure ten paces farther before he slowed. Vines and leaves rotted into nothing wherever they touched him.

Roland fell to the ground panting as color drained from his face.

"Roland!" Tara cried. She ran to aid him just as Chesa loosed the last of Ms. Ash's bonds.

All three women descended on Roland. Up close, Tara could see that blisters covered his hands and neck wherever the plants had touched him.

Ms. Ash covered a hand with the hem of her robes and pulled one of Roland's fingers up to study it. Chesa sidled to the former dome and examined the wreckage.

"Heart attack hairs," said Ms. Ash. "Hard to see, but easy to feel. Some Weavers can even sprout them on their own bodies."

"He's dying?!" Tara gasped.

"No," assured Ms. Ash. "But he's going to be down for some time, and he won't have much sleep for a while. If he were sickly or a bit older, I'd be concerned."

"I can get rid of the hairs," said Roland. "I just need a minute or two. . ."

"I'm not sure we can spare that," said Ms. Ash.

"Lydia," Chesa interjected, "I believe we have a problem."

Ms. Ash dropped Roland's hand and turned. The lumbering farm boy placed his head between his knees.

Tara put a hand on his back. "Hang in there, Roland," she whispered. "You've done spectacularly."

"You h-have to go help Peony," he whispered. "I'll be okay. Just help Peony."

"About that. . . Okondo is gone," called Chesa. "With Ms. Bianchi."

Tara leaned toward Roland. "I'll be right back. Hold on." She joined the servants at the perimeter of the ruined dome. A tunnel lined with gnarled roots resided at its center.

Chesa crouched before it and smirked. "It leads that way." She pointed off through the forest. "What's over there?"

Ms. Ash let out a long sigh. "Black Lake, and little else."

"Where Okondo assaulted Peony with the troth stone?" asked Tara.

The two servants blinked at her.

"Maybe so," said Ms. Ash. "But that's a story for another day. Black Lake holds a weapon that Okondo, or whoever she is, may think to use as a last resort. She'll also have the luxury of privacy on the lake. . ."

"We need the Tilters!" declared Tara.

All three of them looked around. Mau screams and the thunderous cracking of Tilter robes echoed in the distance, but only incapacitated Weavers and mau remained in the clearing. The corpses closest to Roland sprouted with fuzzy fungus and decayed into mounds of black soil.

"We should wait for the Tilters to return?" Tara corrected.

The two servants exchanged uneasy looks.

"I'm sorry, Ms. Langcraw," Ms. Ash replied. She placed a hand on

Tara's shoulder. "But I'm afraid we don't have time for that. If you want to help Peony, then it will need to be us, and now."

They were unexpected allies, to be sure, but they were all Tara had.

She drew in a deep breath and let it out slow. "What's the plan?"

It required the strength of all three women to guide Roland into a crown of fallen canopy large enough to conceal him. He murmured at his swollen hands, imbuing them with life thaumaturgy that lessened their swelling and eased their purple hue.

"I'm sorry, Roland," said Tara. "This is the best we can do."

Roland looked up at her and offered a brave if half-hearted smile. "I'll manage."

Tara hoped he was right.

"We can provide sentiments another day, provided we all live," ordered Ms. Ash. She gestured in the direction of Black Lake. "For now, time to get a move on."

They followed Ms. Ash to a short corridor not far away. There, the distal end of Okondo's escape tunnel surfaced at the entrance to a great dome. Peony's description captured Black Lake to perfection. Inky water beneath the ice reflected the stars and moon to form a second sky, while powdery snow danced across the ice.

"Keep an eye out beneath us," order Ms. Ash. Already the howling wind reddened her features. "Okondo might try to summon the Denizen to assist her if she's cornered."

"'The Denizen'?" Tara repeated.

"A creature gifted to the Amber Menhir by the Pearl Menhir when its mother split," Ms. Ash explained. "For a time, it resided here without incident. As it grew, however, it attacked land animals and even scholars that drew too near at night. It shuns the light. The Weavers

347

brokered a deal with the Architects to freeze the lake to prevent it from obtaining meals when it shouldn't."

Tara gulped.

One foot at a time, the three of them traversed the ice, guided by Ms. Ash. They moved together. When one stumbled, the others helped her resume her balance. The ice groaned and popped beneath their feet.

"That doesn't sound good," Tara called over the stormy din and whipping snow. "Do you think that's the—"

"Denizen?" said Chesa. "I think we'd hear a great deal more than some pops from that."

The wind surged, catching Tara's robes like sails. She braced herself to prevent another fall. Chesa's cowl slid back and lashed in the wind. She wore her dark hair in waves, like the lake beneath them, and adorned with modest pearls. The wind wrenched one free. It fell to the ice and danced away, guided by the snowy chaos.

"No!" Chesa cried. She shambled toward where the pearl had fallen. It sailed along the ice faster than any person could navigate and vanished. Her shoulders sagged as she stared off into the storm.

"It's no matter, Chesa!" Tara shouted. "I'll get you others. We just need to find Peony and get out of here before we all freeze!"

Chesa only stared off into the storm.

"We can worry about jewelry later," said Ms. Ash. "We've got a bigger fish to—"

"There!" Chesa interrupted. She pointed a finger. "They're just there on the horizon!"

"She's right!" said Tara.

Two indistinct lumps that might have been snowdrifts resided in the distance. One paced.

"Excellent work," said Ms. Ash. "Whatever you've got to defend yourselves, ladies, best ready it."

348

Tara placed a hand on the ensemble of projectiles she'd stolen from the Tilters' den and hoped her athleticism had improved since her time in Sandenvale.

Chesa flicked her hands through a sequence of precise gestures as they advanced on Okondo. For Ms. Ash's part, she fished several fist-sized stones from her robes. Tara prepared to launch her own anemic assault, but prayed the exchange would not call for it.

Primara Okondo paused her pacing and faced Tara and her allies as they drew within a dozen paces. Peony lay huddled in a ball beside Okondo. A bank of accumulated snow concealed half of her shivering body.

"Careful to not hit Peony!" Tara indicated the trembling form.

Chesa prowled to Tara's right and Ms. Ash to the left, flanking the Primara.

"Savanna!" Chesa called. "What is there left for you now? Whatever your plan, rest assured, the Tilters will address it," she feigned with unctuous sympathy. "Ms. Bianchi is no longer a hiding spot."

Okondo stepped back from the oncoming triad. "Maybe so," she spat. She glanced down at Peony and grimaced.

"Hadn't thought of that?" Chesa chuckled.

Ms. Ash darted to the left in a crouch.

"Quiet!" snapped Okondo.

Chesa strutted forward, occupying Okondo's attention. "You should have thought this through." She clucked her tongue.

"Silence!" Okondo shouted. Black veins surfaced across her neck and chest. Her eyes darted between Chesa and Tara. "Maybe you're right about the girl," Okondo sighed as she stepped back from Peony. "But chaos can be fertile ground for new plans!" She crouched, and keeping her eyes on Chesa, placed a palm flat on the ice. Something seismic and ancient pulsed beneath them in answer.

"Now!" snarled Ms. Ash from Okondo's flank. She lobbed a rock overhand at Okondo with more speed than Tara had imagined her capable of.

Okondo fell back onto all fours and scuttled backward like a spider. Her nails and bare feet dug into the ice as though it were mud. Ms. Ash's rock flew past and clattered to the ice.

Tara hoisted a chess piece a little smaller than her forearm from her robes. Hues of purple, gold, and azurite flecked its dark stonework. She hurled the bishop overhand at the skittering Primara. It tumbled end over end, as though counterbalanced for throwing. Okondo twisted her body in a lazy dodge, but the piece skipped through space at the last and found purchase in her ribs with a meaty thud. She grunted and pressed her hand to her side where it had struck. She hauled herself up to her feet and eyed her assailant.

"I. . ." Tara muttered. "I mean. . ."

Okondo produced a series of thaumaturgical notes as she studied Tara. "I really must thank you for that," she sneered.

Chesa tossed something invisible in the Primara's direction. Okondo's eyes widened, and she faced Chesa. But already the servant turned one hand over the other, as though spooling a ship rope. Okondo gasped and jerked forward, succumbing to one unwilling step and then another toward the anomaly. The Primara's arms and shoulders tensed with black veins as she was reeled in like a swordfish.

"Keep it up, Chesa!" Tara called as she readied a marble knight. "It's working!"

Ms. Ash hurled another rock. This one just missed the Primara's head as she twisted with viperine polish. The ice where the rock had landed boomed, sending a cloud of snow into the air.

The chamber went still. A second boom sent the ice underfoot shuddering as sinuous crevices spread across the lake. Tara danced away from a finger-width crack at her feet and hurled the marble knight. Again, Okondo eeled to one side. Yet as she did, the chess piece flickered midway through its arc and hit her temple. She stumbled to the ground.

"You. . ." she hissed. "You're barren!"

From the corner of her eye, Tara saw Ms. Ash angling toward Peony. They needed a distraction.

"Maybe so," Tara admitted. "But evidently someone doesn't need thaumaturgy to get the better of a Primara? Or is that just you?"

"You insolent little—" Okondo snarled.

Ms. Ash darted toward Peony as a third strike beneath the ice sent an explosion of water into the air like a frozen volcano. A gaping hole resided in the ice a second after. Ms. Ash tumbled and slid. She rose to all fours and scrambled to Peony's side. Even Chesa slid backward on the trembling ice, and for a moment, seemed to lose her concentration.

"Idiots!" Okondo eyed Ms. Ash's mawkish display and laughed. "Welcome to round two, darlings." She stretched out her hands like a bird freed from a cage.

A column of water shot up through the hole in the ice. Every eye present turned to witness the field's newest entrant. A towering, segmented creature slithered up to the ceiling and twisted a chittering maw to face Okondo. Its insectile jaws opened one ratchet at a time and latched like a spring-loaded bear trap. Chitinous teeth ringed what Tara guessed was its barnacle-laden head. Tiny bone protrusions like legs jutted out across its entire body, or at least what Tara could see of it. The creature looped one coil of its serpentine body around the base of the hole in the ice, stabilizing it. Everything in Tara's body screamed for her to flee.

"Kill them," Okondo scoffed. She issued an inviting gesture of her hand toward Peony and Ms. Ash.

The beast gave a stridulatory growl, like a hundred ridged organic plates scraping past one another. It descended toward its prey.

"No!" Tara screamed. She sprinted to her friends huddled on the ice. Her lungs burned as she sucked in wintry air. In that moment, the Denizen and her friends were all that existed for her. She thought of Roland. Tara plowed into her huddle of allies with somewhat less grace than she favored. The impact sent all three of them sliding over the ice, like a human raft caught in unseen rapids.

The jaws of the great worm struck the ice a moment too late. Its ballistic mandibles snapped through everything in its path like late spring slush. The frozen lake exploded beneath the attack. Shards of ice hurtled off in every direction. More cracks formed, sending ice rafts rocking and drifting over black water. The worm lifted its head and faced the Primara.

Tara and Ms. Ash tried to hoist Peony to her feet, but stumbled.

"Stupid animal!" Okondo called. The raft of ice beneath her feet listed, sloshing water over her feet. She hopped from one ice float to the next until she reached a stable peninsula where Tara and her friends lay prone together.

"Out of rocks and rooks to pitch at me, hmm?" Okondo laughed as she darted past them to a safer portion of the peninsula. "Well, isn't that just too bad?"

"Peony, if you've got it in you, I could really use your help," Tara whispered.

"There!" Okondo shouted, pointing to where Tara and Ms. Ash cradled Peony before her.

The worm ratcheted back its jaws while Okondo initiated a working, but paused to press her hands under her arms. She resumed in vain, but paused again to rub her palms together. "You've got to be kidding me!" she snarled.

"It's too cold?" Tara realized. "She can't get the gestures right!"

"Whatever you do," Ms. Ash said hurriedly to Tara, "save Peony. She's the Blurred Keystone. Keep her safe."

"She's the what?" said Tara.

"Peony?" Okondo scoffed. "The Blurred Keystone? Can you not see what is so plain before you? I have been both man and woman. I wield two aspects of thaumaturgy and will one day harness six! I am the architect of the siege engine that will reinvent this world! I am the Blurred Keystone!"

"The what?!" Tara blurted out.

Tiny cracks and pops crescendoed from the ice all around the Primara. She gave a start and stepped back. But her foot, wet and glistening, landed atop a tiny opalescent sphere. The Primara cried out in surprise and stumbled. Her other foot landed upon another cluster of the clicking beads, too small to be thought paddocks, and she clattered to the ground. A huff of air escaped her mouth with a half yelp.

There, only a dozen paces away from her prey, stood Chesa. She whipped clusters of pearls from her scalp and slung them across the ice at Okondo.

Something dark passed over the starry sky, and Tara glanced up to see the Denizen falling upon them.

"Go!" she shouted.

Tara and Ms. Ash grabbed each other's hands and hoisted themselves off the ice in unison. Then each took one of Peony's arms and dragged her toward safety.

Okondo's face twisted as she prepared another working aimed at Tara and her allies. "I'm going to enjoy turning you into automatons!"

The Denizen landed on the tip of the ice peninsula with a crash. The impact sent the peninsula adrift as the beast's weight tilted one side of the float into the air and the other down toward its jaws.

Horrified realization spread across the Primara's face as she faced her creature. Only she remained atop the newly formed float. She went to hoist herself up, but slipped atop pearls too modest, too lowly, for anyone's notice. Freezing water flooded over the peninsula, soaking the Primara as she flopped upon the ice again and again.

"No!" she called. "Wait! Langcraw! I can help you live forever!"

Tara ignored her screams.

Okondo slid, slow and tortuous, on the huge fragment of ice toward the worm's mandibles. At last, she sank her talons in the ice and paused her descent. "No, no, no!" she whimpered. "Save me! If you knew what this place has done, you'd save me! You must!"

Tara faced Okondo and considered in that moment what she, or anyone, must and must not do. She recalled her lessons from the Tilters. Then Tara reached into her pocked and caressed the last of her given tools. "I'll decide what I must do," she breathed. Then she darted at the watery seesaw, the black queen clutched in her hand.

Okondo's eyes met Tara's. "Good girl! Help me!"

Tara launched herself into the air, up and over the Primara, who ogled at Tara with bewildered eyes. For an isolated moment, an envelope of luck seemed to hum about Tara and through her. She landed on the ice and slid toward the Denizen, only just dodging its jaws. She latched onto one of the bone protrusions on its side. Tara's added weight sent the precarious seesaw tipping farther into the air, and Okondo's grip failed. She slid, faster than before, toward the Denizen's mouth.

"This can't be!" LaTorre screamed from her stolen body.

As the tendrils that extended from the worm's anterior contacted Okondo's flesh, its jaws clamped down through her. Primara Okondo, or Savanna LaTorre, or whoever she'd been, burst into a mangled ruin of sinew, bone, and blood beneath the ballistic clap. Hot viscera splashed over Tara, and she sighed, too exhausted to question the source of momentary warmth. Icy water surrounded her a moment later.

Tara kicked towards the surface, or to where her numbed mind deemed the surface might reside. But something dragged her down. She felt the black queen in her hand, and with a will effort, let it go. It toppled and sank into the abyss. A bit of stupefied guilt touched Tara's thoughts as it vanished. A few heartbeats later, her head breached the surface. She sucked in air on instinct alone.

A cluster of thought paddocks, white and pristine, bobbed in the wreckage of the Primara's remains. In their midst bobbed a sphere almost like the others, but black. Something about that made her laugh.

"I found the thought paddocks." Tara shivered. "And they float!"

Then everything went black.

CHAPTER 26

The Monolith Shifts

PEONY PACED THE VESTIBULE clad in the most conservative hues of face powders she owned. Tara deemed the subduing measure necessary, given their precarious circumstances. Peony paused before her reflection in one of the room's gilded columns and sighed.

"Did you hear anything new about Roland?" she asked.

Tara regarded her with flat eyes. "Chesa says he's recovering fast. Though we didn't have long to talk."

"Right," said Peony. She resumed her pacing.

The ruddy wooden panels that lined the waiting room bestowed the space with the musty scent of distinguishment, like a stately library. Peony never found such spaces welcoming.

"What kind of wood do you suppose this is?" she asked, unsure why she kept initiating unwelcome conversation.

"Mahogany," Tara answered with a wave of her hand. "A tropical tree. Some people import it from the islands around the Pearl Menhir."

"Ah," said Peony. "That makes sense."

She tapped her foot and tried to ignore the walls. The faces of countless former chancellors loomed down at Tara and Peony. Some of them bore the soft smiles of pleasant grandfathers. Others donned stern expressions, like judges. Women occupied but few of the frames.

Among those, most appeared as though they had worked hard to resemble men, and succeeded. Peony smirked at the irony.

"What do you suppose they'll do with us?" she asked.

Tara blew out a slow, contemplative breath. "I'm not sure. I've never heard of anything like this happening. Nobody knows how many Delvers were involved in LaTorre's schemes, and they're certainly not going to come stepping forward now to announce themselves. That endangers everyone."

Peony studied Tara's regal countenance with a little envy. "Do you think they might reward us?" she asked. She doubted it—though she doubted many things now.

Tara shrugged. "Perhaps you and Roland. I doubt I'll receive anything."

More doubt.

"Why not?" asked Peony.

"You've displayed thaumaturgical aptitudes. I'll soon be gone," Tara sighed.

Peony considered sitting beside Tara. She wished to touch her friend's hand, to provide her comfort—but the Langcraw heiress's frostiness walled her away.

"You helped stop LaTorre too," Peony assured Tara. "She wasn't going to stop with the Weavers. The whole menhir owes you. Primara Klepsydra's been in there advocating for you all morning. That carries weight."

Tara shrugged. "She's been in there all morning summarizing the results of her investigations. She won't waste time advocating for a failed protégé."

Peony opened her mouth to disagree, but closed it.

"Derek Arachvelle was sent away this week," Tara added. She studied the ground at her feet. A faint mist collected in her eyes.

"Lavinia's friend?" Peony asked.

Tara nodded. "If we define 'friend' broadly, then yes. Do you remember? He said he might never develop thaumaturgical aptitudes, and he didn't. I won't be far behind."

Peony took a spot on the waiting bench beside Tara, who turned away.

"At least. . ." Tara's voice cracked. "At least they've placed that moratorium on studies of failed thaumaturges. At least," she whispered, "I'll be spared that embarrassment."

Rumors had spread faster than usual through the Amber Menhir since the exchange on Black Lake. Each tale bestowed the supposed confrontation with a different flavor of inaccuracy. The one thing they all got right was the healing. The morning after LaTorre's demise, every Evader of Death in the Amber had been recruited to the Delvers' quarters, where they attempted to heal those incapacitated on the night of Saturnalia. All such efforts failed. The chancellor suspended all operations in the anomaly pens pending further investigation too.

"Have some hope," said Peony. She placed a hand on the bench not far from Tara's and waited.

Tara did not face Peony, but placed her small hand atop Peony's. Tara's breathing slowed, and some of the tension in her neck subsided.

The wooden door to the Amber Chancellor's office opened, and Primara Klepsydra glided out. Her robes dragged on the floor as she approached. She considered Peony with her huge eyes, but a moment after, she turned to Tara. Tara blotted her face with the sleeve of her robe.

"The chancellor will see you now, Tara Langcraw," intoned the Tilter Primara. "You too, Ms. Bianchi."

"Do you know what's going to happen with us?" asked Peony.

Klepsydra looked Peony up and down. "I have a sense of the likely outcome, but that is for the chancellor to decide," she replied. She cocked her head. "I have given him much to consider."

"What does that mean?" Peony blurted out before she could prevent herself from speaking.

An odd smile wriggled over Klepsydra's lips. "It means, Ms. Bianchi, everyone involved should choose their words and actions with care." She inclined her chin. "Starting this instant."

Peony gulped.

"Tara Langcraw, before I go, I have a favor to ask of you," said the Primara.

"Yes?"

Klepsydra pulled a pouch from her robes and handed it to Tara. It rattled as though filled with stones.

"What's this?" asked Tara.

"Pearls," Klepsydra replied in a sly tone. "I suspect you'll know to whom they belong. Tell her I've grown weary of picking up after her. Tell her I've kept one I borrowed at the beginning of the year for myself. The rest should be there, including one she dropped in a very special bath." With a wink, she glided away, not sparing them another glance. The gentle swishing of robes dissipated down the corridor.

The door to the chancellor's suite groaned as Tara pressed it open. Peony's skin tingled with anxiety. Even more portraits of chancellors come and gone scaled the walls up to the vaulted ceiling. A map of the Spiral hung near the entryway, with such detail that Peony spotted vassal villages from her old estates. They seemed so distant now, almost irrelevant.

Tara and Peony passed through beams of light that emanated from gilded lamps. The room smelled of pipe smoke and old parchment. Peony eyed the boundless bookshelves and wondered if a single person could read so many volumes in their lifetime.

"Tara Langcraw and Peony Bianchi!" called an inviting voice.

Ivan Rustavich, the Amber Chancellor, reclined on a cushioned chair before a low table. He packed a pipe with nico leaves. A letter rested on the ample arm of his chair. He stood and approached them with an outstretched hand. Tara took his hand and genuflected. Peony followed Tara's example.

"I've been so looking forward to meeting with you," he said. "Join me for a drink?"

". . . With us?" Peony asked.

"Of course! You two are heroes. Come, come, come!" He gestured them into studded leather chairs with armrests the size of small tables.

Peony and Tara took their places.

The chancellor approached a set of illuminated shelves, where in lieu of books, crystal decanters sat arrayed in pleasing arcs. Their patterned surfaces sent beams of twinkling light across the room, like so many stars. He placed a single sphere of ice in each of three glasses.

"Which do you prefer, brandy or whiskey?" he asked.

Peony considered admitting she didn't much like either, but thought better of it.

"Whiskey," Tara mouthed at her. "More distinguished."

"Whiskey, please!" said Peony. Brandy reminded her too much of home anyhow.

"For me as well, please!" Tara replied. She adjusted herself in her seat.

"So easy to please!" the chancellor noted with a wink. He poured their drinks and set a glass before each of them before taking his seat. "An invaluable quality in all people." He held up his glass and smiled. "Cheers! To new friends!"

Both Tara and Peony exchanged dubious glances between themselves and their drinks.

"Relax!" said the chancellor. "You two are among friends now. Please!"

The three of them clinked their glasses and sipped. The chancellor lit his pipe and puffed.

"I haven't seen many scholars smoke," noted Peony. "It's nice to smell nico again. Reminds me of home."

The chancellor's grin widened. "I suspect it should, Peony. This cultivar comes from your very estates."

"It does?" said Peony. She hesitated to say that she herself despised her family business.

"Well, yes!" the chancellor exclaimed. "The Bianchi family produces some of the finest strains on the continent. By far the most economical source too, from a standpoint of logistics." He puffed merrily on his pipe. "I've been working with the bursar to ensure that all the menhir's nico comes from your estates henceforth."

"My family would be honored," replied Peony.

"No one will enjoy it more than I!" The chancellor beamed.

"Chancellor," Tara began, "I was hoping we might speak about some delicate matters."

Peony shifted in her seat.

The chancellor frowned, but then lifted his eyebrows. "Of course! Tara, we can discuss anything you like. Why, I've just notified your mother of the great contributions that you and your friends have made here!"

"My mother?!" Tara yelped.

"Indeed," chimed the chancellor with another draw on his pipe. "Why, I've got her reply just here."

"You received mail from my mother?" Tara asked beneath furrowed brows.

He lifted the letter beside his chair and opened it toward her.

Tara's mouth dropped open in a very unladylike manner.

"For all her doubts about the menhirs. . ." He reached over and touched Tara's forearm. "Eva Langcraw is positively effusive about your performance here. And I feel the same way."

Something about the man's voice made Peony yearn to make him proud.

"I would not call my time here a great success," Tara corrected with a small grimace. "After all, I've no thaumaturgical aptitudes. What's to be proud of?"

"No aptitudes?" the chancellor gasped. "Why, that's not what I've heard at all!"

Tara squinted. "What have you heard?"

"I have it on good account that the Tilters' range of influence was heightened the night of the Okondo debacle, because of you. Without you, the Weavers might have won! Although, I suppose it is more correct to say that those were Delvers you assaulted." The chancellor chuckled. He puffed his pipe and regarded Tara. "Primara Klepsydra said it herself. Without your assistance, Ms. Ash and Ms. Bianchi would be no more."

Tara's face solidified into something unreadable. "I saw no threads of time. I have created no thaumaturgical working. By all accounts, I'm barren."

"That is materially false, Ms. Langcraw," corrected the chancellor. "There are many accounts of you aiding the Tilters. I trust their word on this matter."

Tara opened and closed her mouth several times before sipping her drink.

"Does this mean Tara can stay?" asked Peony.

The chancellor stared at the orb of ice spinning in his glass of whiskey. "The truth is, I've never heard of a situation like this, Ms. Bianchi. Menhir doctrine states that ascendants who are unable to see and touch the threads within their first year will remain forever barren. The barren are sent home."

Peony drew in a tight breath.

Tara's face grew paler.

"But you don't intend to do that with Tara?" suggested Peony.

"We will get to that." The chancellor took another sip from his drink and pursed his lips. "The Evaders are still determining whether LaTorre's victims will ever recover. The LaTorre allies we've captured so far say that their victims were transferred to their old, brain-dead bodies."

"Like Okondo," Peony noted. "She was in LaTorre's old body." She recalled the painted flowers that the brain-dead scholar recapitulated over and over on the anomaly pen walls.

The chancellor winced. "We owe those poor scholars every chance of recovery. We've found even more discarded husks these last few days. Regrettably, we've no idea where their former occupants have fled." He cleared his throat. "So, for now, all studies on thaumaturges, even failed ones, have ceased, until we know for certain that the victims won't recover. So, you can rest assured, Ms. Langcraw!" He squeezed Tara's hand and released it.

Tara studied the ground at her feet.

"Does that include the saprolite band study?" Peony asked. "That one seemed so important to everyone."

The chancellor's jaw clenched. "The results of that study suggested an equivocal improvement on prior practices. The study and our plans are chilled, for now." He eyed Peony. "Best not to speak about that, Ms. Bianchi. It remains a testy subject with the Evaders."

"So, I don't have to leave?" Tara managed. "Or I just won't be experimented on?"

The smile lines about the chancellor's eyes faded. "You can see the predicament I'm in, Ms. Langcraw. By menhir law, you should be released. Yet, I have it on good authority that you're a functioning Tilter, capable of amplifying your sisters' strengths as much as any." He lifted his pipe and puffed. "The menhir might benefit from a more capable force of Tilters."

Some of the color in Tara's face returned.

"It is all unprecedented. Some might call Tara. . ." The chancellor eyed the two ascendants. ". . . anomalous."

Tara drew in a quick breath.

Peony's body tensed. "What's that supposed to mean?"

"It means. . ." The Amber Chancellor drew out each word. "Tara exhibits an unorthodox pattern of thaumaturgical expression. Many scholars would be anxious to study that sort of thing."

"But that won't happen?" Peony added.

The chancellor clucked his tongue. "The Tilters are satisfied with Ms. Langcraw's aptitudes, meager as they are, and advocate for her retention." The chancellor sucked on his teeth. "But I suspect that other factions would advocate for expelling her on the very same evidence. They'll give all sorts of preposterous reasons, but mostly, they favor that their various deeds remain secret. Another Tilter, even a meager one, is an unwelcome nuisance to most."

"So?" said Peony.

"Do I stay or go?" Tara whispered.

"The way I see it. . ." The chancellor sipped his drink. "The only thaumaturges who could detect Ms. Langcraw's true aptitudes are her sisters. They have every incentive to keep her nature secret." The chancellor smirked at Peony. "And I would be happy to safeguard that secret as well."

Doubt roiled like a nest of worms in Peony's gut.

"I'm staying?" said Tara. She sounded on the verge of bursting. "If so, I promise I'll do everything in my power to foster my aptitudes!"

The Amber Chancellor leaned over to cup Tara's hands in his own. "I'm happy to be your ally."

"I get to stay?" Tara repeated. Hope flooded into her.

The chancellor smiled. "I'm permitting you to stay, dear girl. Your secret is safe with me."

Some of the tension in the room retreated.

"Chancellor," said Peony, "what about the remaining LaTorre allies? Can't they just jump into body after body? What's to stop them?"

The chancellor set his pipe and drink aside. His lips firmed. "I share those concerns. LaTorre's scheming touched every faction, and the Primara Council itself!" His brow furrowed. "And those are just the impacts we know of. We must track down what's left of her insidious cabal."

"Well, at least there are Delvers loyal to the menhirs to assist you," offered Tara.

The chancellor gave Tara a weak smile. "If only it were so simple. The fact is, we cannot know which of the Delvers remain loyal. LaTorre's protégés have every incentive to hide their allegiance from each other and the other factions."

"True immortality is forever alluring," whispered Tara. "It spawns much jealousy."

"Given the unseemly artifacts we've discovered in LaTorre's possession, I don't think mere immortality drove that loathsome creature," said the chancellor. "But we have hope!"

"Thank the gods!" Peony chuckled. "I could use some of that right now!"

The chancellor smiled. "Well, for starters, though not all of La Torre's thought paddocks have been recovered, I predict that we've detained enough to prevent more scholars from sorting out her body-snatching ways. That's thanks to you two!"

"How can you be sure someone else won't just pilfer the thought paddocks from the Central Archive again?" asked Tara.

"Ah!" replied the chancellor. "We're moving those particular thought paddocks to an auxiliary archive. Very wet there."

Tara and Peony exchanged looks.

"Supposing that works," Peony asked, "how will you find the last of LaTorre's followers without the Delvers to help?"

The Amber Chancellor sighed. "There will be an investigation. The Menhir Conclave has promised to leverage every resource to track these vermin down and expunge them. That means scholars from other menhirs—all of them. Moreover, were I betting man—and I am a betting man—then I'd predict you both will garner ringside seats to that affair."

Peony and Tara exchanged hesitant looks.

"Can the Amber Menhir count on you both?" he asked.

Tara nodded first, then Peony.

"Then none of us here have anything to fear," sighed the chancellor.

"What will happen to Ms. Ash and Chesa?" Peony asked. "They helped rescue me. Without them, LaTorre would have succeeded. Are they safe too?"

The chancellor sipped the watery dregs of his drink. "Klepsydra advocated for the two servants as well." He leaned back in his chair. "My personal assistant was discovered dead in a ransacked classroom the night of the LaTorre debacle." The chancellor cleared his throat. "I do not yet have hard evidence, but I suspect that his death too is linked with the LaTorre situation." The chancellor eyed Tara and then Peony.

"That does seem possible. . ." deflected Tara.

"Seeing as they are your friends," the chancellor drawled, "I think we can do something for them. With Ursielle gone, I do need a new assistant. Ms. Ash has the experience necessary, and the surprise turn-over in the Weaver leadership presents a fine opportunity to change her post. She could work here with me."

"What about Chesa?" Tara interjected. "She can't go back to the Delvers. She'll be a target!"

The chancellor's eyes widened. "Oh? Is that so, Ms. Langcraw? Then what would you have me do with the orphaned servant?"

Peony and Tara exchanged looks.

"She'll need to be posted somewhere safe," said Tara.

"If you insist," said the chancellor. "I could shuffle her elsewhere. I am nothing if not a useful friend to your cause."

"Thank you," said Tara, though the muscles in her cheeks rippled with something akin to nausea.

"Superb!" cheered the chancellor. He stood and fetched himself another glass of whiskey. He set the decanter on the table before them and smiled. "So, I think we have a deal?"

"A deal?" Peony echoed.

"Indeed, we've made a great many agreements this evening," the chancellor pronounced. "I'll abide by my end of our bargains, and I trust you two to do the same."

"Remind me of what our sides are again?" Peony probed.

"She means that with all due respect," added Tara.

The chancellor chuckled at them both. "But of course! You two will assist the Amber Menhir with the investigation into the remaining LaTorre allies. You won't go writing home to start any fuss. You won't accept the bribes of any other menhirs either. I, in turn, will allow Ms. Langcraw to remain at the Amber, and I will ensure that your servant allies remain unmolested for their parts in the demise of several scholars. Does that seem fair to you?"

"I. . ." Peony fumbled.

"I'm afraid I haven't got all evening," admitted the chancellor with a grimace. "Power comes with so many an obligation. . ."

Peony imagined Chesa and Ms. Ash's lives without the chancellor's support, or worse, with his ire.

"I can accept those terms," said Peony.

"Me too," said Tara.

The chancellor swirled his glass. "I thought the pair of you could tell a good deal when you saw one."

They all sat together in painful silence for several heartbeats.

"Chancellor," said Tara, "LaTorre mentioned something about a Blurred Keystone before she died. Does that term mean anything to you?"

The chancellor squinted at Tara. "A myth once popular among Independent Cities. It claimed that a scholar of ambiguous identity would lead a revolution against the Menhir Conclave."

"LaTorre thought she was the Blurred Keystone," Tara explained.

"Many supposed Blurred Keystones have been proposed, and slain," said the chancellor dismissively. "No revolution has ever followed, Ms. Langcraw. It's just a story dreamed up by layfolk. When people don't have anything powerful or intelligent left to say or do, they write a fantasy."

"We've got to stop acting like this!" Peony exclaimed. "It's ruining everything!"

He lifted his chin. "Whatever do you mean?"

"Distrust between scholars. Investigations, implied threats, and all the rest," Peony sighed. "It's a waste of time, and it prevents real progress from being made."

The Amber Chancellor adjusted his glinting honey-hued robes. "Go on," he said.

Peony stole a glance at Tara. Her friend nodded.

Peony took a deep breath. "Can't there be a menhir where scholars work together? Where they don't see each other as rivals to be manipulated?"

"Where the scholars treat servants with some semblance of respect!" Tara added.

"And where anomalies aren't treated like chattel," said Peony.

Something like doubt flickered in the chancellor's eyes. "It is not that I disagree with you," he groaned. "There are many problems within the menhir. I grant you both that. And our relationship with lay society could be improved." He gritted his teeth. "It's just that the menhirs are very old monoliths and not as malleable as one might prefer. Changes require special circumstances."

"Special circumstances!" Tara exclaimed. "Isn't the LaTorre situation a special circumstance?"

The chancellor's lips firmed. "Though I find your enthusiasm inspiring, it is not so easily done."

"But. . ." Peony began.

"Hear me out, Ms. Bianchi!" he interrupted. "I do not disagree with your vision. Still, exacting lasting change requires time and restraint." He paused to eye each of them. "The voice of change must come from respected members of society too. No one will listen to the emphatic pleas of the uninitiated."

Tara frowned at Peony.

"That said," the chancellor added, "I think you two could be just those voices."

Tara's face brightened.

"But," warned the chancellor, "we need time to groom you both, and the menhirs, for such a transition. You'll need someone who has a means of liaising with these people. One menhir cannot make the changes you request in isolation."

"Maybe so," agreed Tara with a shake of her head.

"You see," the chancellor assured them, "the problem is vast and tangled. Yet I think the three of us, by working together, can bring the continent renewed hope."

A painful paused followed.

"So," the chancellor finally added, "what do you say?"

"Say?" repeated Peony.

"Can we work together?" queried the chancellor. "First, we address the LaTorre issue together, and then we use the recovery to create the groundwork for lasting change!"

Peony looked at Tara. She blew out a breath and shrugged.

"Chancellor," Peony said, "I guess you've got yourself a deal."

"Superb! Now, I must see to some other matters." He rose and gave them both a tender gesture to the exit. "I believe there's a present or two waiting for you back in Peony's room. Run along!"

Peony and Tara genuflected and departed with their thanks.

When they arrived at Peony's room, they found the door open. Inside, in lieu of one bed, two crowded the modest space. Tara's travel trunks and other belongings lay at the foot of the new mattress. Roland sat on the edge of Peony's bed. Chesa and Ms. Ash stood beside Tara's. A new deck of painted playing cards sat atop Tara's pillow.

"Roland?!" Peony exclaimed. "You're alright!" She charged him. He had only enough time to lumber to his feet before she thrust her arms around him.

Roland winced as he put his arms around her and chuckled, "Easy, Peony!"

Ms. Ash cleared her throat and eyed the door. "We can't stay long. You'll have plenty of time to embrace each other later."

"After I'm out of earshot too," mewled Chesa.

"Uh, perhaps while I'm out getting tea later," Tara put in. "With brandy."

"What, no more whiskey?" prodded Peony with a grin.

Ms. Ash closed the door and dropped her voice to a whisper. "There's going to be an investigation."

"We know," said Tara. "We're meant to help with it."

"Uh-huh," said Ms. Ash. "And you understand the position this'll place you both in?"

"With the Disciples badly injured. . ." Chesa started, but her voice trailed off. "Maybe broken forever."

Peony released Roland. "You think it could be a trap?"

"No need for a trap!" Chesa laughed. "The circumstances are lethal enough all on their own. The Amber Menhir will not take an investigation lying down. Anyone assisting foreign scholars will be in serious danger."

"More danger," Peony sighed.

"The chancellor has assured us of his assistance moving forward," offered Tara. She lifted the new Veils and Poisons deck from her bed. They bore gilding and more delicate paintings than any Peony had seen. Tara set them down and eyed them like a venomous spider.

Peony turned to Chesa and then Ms. Ash. "Do you think the Amber Chancellor will keep his side of the bargain?"

Tara shook her head. "We can only hope."

"We can plan," Chesa corrected. She winked at Tara, which to Peony's surprise garnered a wink in reply.

"'An unexpected ally is often the most powerful,'" Tara recited. That garnered smiles from both servants.

"In the end, it's the smallest things that run the web of life," Roland added.

"What if he betrays us? What if this is all just another manipulation?" Peony's voice turned thready.

Of all the responses, Tara beamed at Peony. "Sweet Peony, I pity the next scholar who sees us as easy prey. If I've learned anything from the Tilters, it's how unprepared the scholars are to face a force united." She reached out and touched Peony's hand. "Our little pride is not bound to contain scholars alone either. The menhir is not ready for our kind of coalition today. But one day soon, it will have to be. Mark my words."

"It's funny," Ms. Ash mused, "the shadow conveyed something just like that this morning."

"We should be going," said Chesa. She stood and brushed off her robes. "We need to investigate some missing Architect servants. Plus, the Primara are discussing a proposal to confine the surviving Delvers to their quarters until after 'privileged administrative actions' have been executed."

"Ah." Ms. Ash chortled. "I'm sure the Delvers will love that!"

"You have no idea," Chesa added with a roll of her eyes.

"Stay safe, children!" ordered Ms. Ash. She bustled herself and Chesa out the door. "Until another day!"

"Until another day," recited Peony in a low voice. "Let's hope it's a brighter one."

Tara fetched their old Veils and Poisons deck from within her mattress. Apart from a little dust, it seemed no worse for the wear to Peony.

"Well, if we're to be playing intrigues. . ." Tara cooed with a smirk. "How about we practice with some lower stakes?"

Peony scoffed, but winked at Roland.

"Lower stakes." Roland laughed. "We could all use some of those."

Something in Tara's expression curled with fiendishness as she shuffled the cards with expert precision. "Now, would either of you be upset if we put a little money on these hands? After all, we could all use a little practice!"